NEW STORIES
FROM THE SOUTH

The Year's Best, 2000

The editor wishes to thank Kathy Pories,
whose taste, skill, and tact are essential
to this anthology.

Edited by
Shannon Ravenel

with a preface by Ellen Douglas

NEW STORIES
FROM THE SOUTH

The Year's Best, 2000

Algonquin Books of Chapel Hill

Published by
ALGONQUIN BOOKS OF CHAPEL HILL
Post Office Box 2225
Chapel Hill, North Carolina 27515-2225

a division of
WORKMAN PUBLISHING
708 Broadway
New York, New York 10003

ISSN 0897–9073
ISBN 1–56512–295–x

.

CONTENTS

Ellen Douglas

PREFACE: LIKE A VASE OR A DANCE OR A PAINTING

Susanne Langer, the twentieth-century philosopher who seems to me to have written most cogently on the subject of art, at the beginning of her great book *Feeling and Form* defined art as "the creation of forms symbolic of human feeling." Not mirrors to the world, not instruction, not entertainment, not even beauty, but the creation of forms symbolic of human feeling. Langer says that the human animal is preeminently a symbol-making creature. We make forms that help us to feel and understand the significance of the buzzing blooming dying chaos of our experience. A story, like a vase or a dance or a painting, is such an art form. It presents to the human mind and senses an "as if" world, a symbol, new with every writer, that makes the reader say, "Yes, that's how things are. I hadn't thought of it quite that way before, but that's how things are."

Flannery O'Connor wrote that "a story involves, in a dramatic way, the mystery of personality." "I lent some stories to a country lady who lives down the road from me," she wrote, "and when she returned them, she said, 'Well, them stories just gone and shown you how some folks would do.'"

And John Berger, the British critic, poet, and storyteller writes, "often art has judged the judges, pleaded revenge to the innocent and shown to the future what the past has suffered, so that it has never been forgotten." And, "art runs like a rumour and a legend because it makes sense of what life's brutalities cannot."

But don't the first and third of these writers disagree with each other? Isn't Berger saying with the words "judged the judges" that storytelling is didactic, moralistic, and isn't Langer saying that it is not? Why do I feel so strongly that they both speak the truth? Flannery O'Connor's neighbor, I think, answers me. *Them stories just gone and shown me how some folks would do.* The storyteller presents an imagined world, cruel or benevolent, joyous or tragic, but stripped of all irrelevancies and the reader responds with, *Yes! That's how things are.* The reader's life may indeed be changed, not because the writer has lectured him, but because of the power and truth of the story. If the reader judges the judges or pleads revenge to the innocent, it's because she has been moved by the story, the symbol.

We know of no people, no community of humans from as far back as we can go, who did not make stories. Stories with heroes and villains, stories with characters confronting fate, stories that transformed experience into symbols that gave meaning to human lives, that made the listeners, the readers weep or laugh aloud — and indeed act, as perhaps no moralist might have made them act.

One of the mysteries of the human world is that there have always been communities of artists in every medium, periods when individuals in a particular corner of the world produced the flowering of a particular art. That's been true of storytellers in the South, and off and on we speculate — perhaps spend too much time speculating — about the whys and wherefores of that flowering.

A major role of the South in our history has been to be the anvil on which the nation's metal is beaten into its still evolving shape. Sometimes we've been leaders, sometimes villains, sometimes victims or scapegoats. Whether we're black or white, the fire has been turned up under our lives (and perhaps consequently under our stories) again and again. We have known honor and betrayal, slavery and freedom, brutal poverty and obscene wealth, religious fanaticism and racism, the intimacy and support of still-functioning communities and the loneliness of the outsider. And our artists have been among those who have wielded the hammer, shaped the metal of our destiny. They have striven to make sense of what life's brutalities cannot, have voiced our region's tragedies and dilemmas, have forced the nation to turn and look at these and to see that they are not simply the South's tragedies and dilemmas, but the nation's and indeed the world's.

All of our artists have had a share in this shaping, but particularly music makers and writers.

One sees immediately that blues and jazz and rock, and even rap and hip-hop, clearly run like rumors and legends and make sense of what life's brutalities cannot make sense of. But our stories function in this way, too. One thinks immediately of Faulkner's "Dry September," and Welty's "Where Is the Voice Coming From." And then a spate of titles and writers comes to mind—from Kate Chopin and George Washington Cable to Richard Wright and Zora Neal Hurston to Peter Taylor and Ernest Gaines and Richard Bausch and Anne Tyler.

At this point I seem to hear the voice of another writer who generalizes, as did the three I have quoted, and who, like them, speaks especially to the South. The Irish writer Frank O'Connor, who is one of my favorite storytellers, wrote in *The Lonely Voice*, "always in the short story there is this sense of outlawed figures wandering about the fringes of society." And, "there is in the short story at its most characteristic something we do not often find in the novel—an intense awareness of human loneliness." He goes on to trace the essential loneliness of the short story character from Gogol through Chekhov to Joyce and Katherine Anne Porter.

Story after story in this year's *New Stories from the South* illustrates the writer's abiding concern with making an artwork expressive of human feeling, stripped of the extraneous, the irrelevant. Again and again a story runs like a rumor and a legend, making sense of what life's brutalities cannot. And I find in these writers a deep and sympathetic perception of the tragedy of human loneliness.

Finally, as Flannery O'Connor's neighbor said, "Them stories just gone and shown you how some folks would do."

PUBLISHER'S NOTE

The stories reprinted in *New Stories from the South: The Year's Best, 2000* were selected from American short stories published in magazines issued between January and December 1999. Shannon Ravenel annually consults a list of one hundred nationally distributed American periodicals and makes her choices for this anthology based on criteria that include original publication first-serially in magazine form and publication as short stories. Direct submissions are not considered.

NEW STORIES
FROM THE SOUTH

The Year's Best, 2000

Mary Helen Stefaniak

A NOTE TO BIOGRAPHERS REGARDING FAMOUS AUTHOR FLANNERY O'CONNOR

(from *The Iowa Review*)

M y mother went to school with her, and so did my Aunt
Mimi. That much is bald-faced fact. I personally tape-
recorded their recollections of the future famous author, starting
two years ago, when my mother and I drove down to Macon to
see Aunt Mimi. My relatives don't blink an eye when I come around
with my notebook or my tape recorder. They chalk it up to my
having made a career out of going to school. They used to be right
about that. I used to be working on a Ph.D. thesis about famous
author Flannery O'Connor—until last Thursday, when I burned
it like a heretic, page by marked-up page. Now all I'm trying to do
is set the record straight.

They attended Peabody High School in Milledgeville—my
mother, her sisters, and Flannery O'Connor—on the campus of
what is now Georgia College & State University, home of the
Flannery O'Connor Bulletin and repository of her manuscripts and
memorabilia. In addition to their alma mater, O'Connor and my
mother share their year of birth (1925), their first name (she was

Mary Flannery then, of course; my mother, like me, is Mary Helen), and the loss of their fathers (both named Ed) at an early age. It was not my mother, but her older sister Mildred—my Aunt Mimi— who graduated with O'Connor in 1942, after which the future famous author moved on to the women's college. My mother and Aunt Mimi did not aspire to higher education. They lived outside Milledgeville on a farm their grandfather rented, and in their neck of the woods, finishing high school was a long shot. I'm glad to have a graduation picture of my mother seated on a straight-backed chair, wearing the pale chiffon formal that Mimi had worn the year before, a corsage of carnations on her shoulder. (It was supposed to be roses, but the florist ran out.) Somebody must have a similar photograph of Mary Flannery O'Connor. My mother is very beautiful in hers, slender and hopeful, layers of chiffon draped over her thighs.

Aunt Mimi was seventy-three and hospitalized for heart trouble two years ago when I made the first of what my thesis supervisor later called my "nearly unintelligible recordings of an elderly woman talking about someone who may or may not have been Flannery O'Connor." Aunt Mimi sat up in her hospital bed like a swami, in a pink satin turban and robe, happy to help me out any way she could. She said, "The Catholic girl? I remember that girl." Aunt Mimi knew the usual things about her: Mary Flannery was shy, she could draw pictures of people "like a son of a gun," and she was famous for bringing a live chicken into Home Ec class wearing "little bitty pants and a coat" she'd made for it. Having said that much, Aunt Mimi leaned toward me over her bed table, and added, "I always figured it was because she was Catholic that she was so peculiar, but then you all are Catholic and I bet you never made a suit for a chicken, did you?"

"No, ma'am, I haven't," I said, checking to make sure the tape was rolling in my recorder.

"That girl was smart," Aunt Mimi went on. "Teachers loved her. I reckon they liked getting invited over to the house, too. You all have seen the house they lived in. On the same block with the old Governor's mansion? Big white columns and all?"

My mother and I had driven past the house earlier that week. We'd seen big white columns but also peeling paint, rotting porches, shutters falling off. I told Aunt Mimi that the famous author's home had fallen into disrepair since her mother died.

"Don't take long for a house to rot in Georgia," Aunt Mimi said. That fact struck her as funny. She started to laugh, which turned into wheezing and then a bout of coughing that sent the volume needle on my tape recorder frantically to red. I handed her a plastic cup of water, and when she could talk again, she said hoarsely, "What d'you reckon they'd do with all the rooms in a house that big?"

My mother spoke up from her chair under the TV. Her voice is faint and echoey on the tape because she's too far away from the microphone, her Georgia accent faded by five decades of living in Milwaukee, Wisconsin. "They probably closed part of it off," my mother said, "like Mrs. Sawyer did her place in Hopewell."

Before I could ask about this Mrs. Sawyer, Aunt Mimi said, "They must have had a couple of rooms set aside for *him*."

"Him?" I said. I try to avoid leading questions.

"Her daddy," Aunt Mimi said confidentially. "He was real sick. It was something pretty ugly."

"Lupus," I said. They didn't have the drugs they have now.

Aunt Mimi continued. "That's why they come to Milledgeville in the first place from Atlanta. You can't hardly blame that girl for being glum."

"I believe it was Savannah, Mimi," said my mother. "They came from Savannah."

"Maybe so," Aunt Mimi said. "Anyhow, I know he died not too long afterwards."

"It was a few years," said my mother.

"February '41," I said.

"That sounds about right," said Aunt Mimi.

"Did you go to the funeral?" I asked her.

"Whose?" she said.

"Mr. O'Connor's."

Aunt Mimi gave me a look. "Of course I didn't go to Mr. O'Connor's funeral. They were *Catholics,* honey. He would've got buried out of the Catholic church. St. Joseph's. Little bitty church about the size of this room."

My mother spoke up again. "St. Joseph's is in Macon, Mimi. The Catholic church in Milledgeville is Sacred Heart."

"I call them all St. Joseph's," Aunt Mimi said, and she leaned back against the bed and closed her eyes. Aunt Mimi has my mother's high cheekbones and the kind of fair skin that's flawless until about age fifty but crinkles all at once thereafter, like watered silk. Poor Aunt Mimi was not so much crinkled as puffed up like a pastry the day we visited her. The doctors were surprised she could wiggle her pinky without going into cardiac arrest. She opened her eyes and said, "I'll tell you one more thing I do remember. When she come back to school after her father died, I felt like I ought to say something to her, what with the way our daddy had passed on not long before."

"On Christmas Day, 1936," my mother put in.

"It was hard, though," Mimi said, "because I never could catch that girl's eye, until one day when the home economics teacher put us both fixing something at the same stove. Poor girl had to look at me then, so I quick told her how sorry I was about her daddy." Aunt Mimi coughed and cleared her throat. "I also said, 'At least you still got your mama,' which was more than we had, of course. I reckon now that it wasn't the best thing to say, but it was what I come up with at the time."

"What did she say to that?" I asked. On the tape you can hear my excitement at the prospect of a direct quotation from the famous author.

"Mary Helen, I don't think she said a word." Aunt Mimi paused. The silences between her sentences get longer and longer as the tape rolls on. "I think all she did was look at me." Aunt Mimi turned her head toward the window and added slowly, "She had gray eyes." From across the room my mother made a face at me to say that her sister was too tired to talk anymore. I raised my eyebrows to say I could see that and pushed STOP on the recorder. "Gray eyes," Aunt Mimi said again. "Like that." She was looking out the window. "Like the sky fixing to rain."

My mother didn't remember the gray eyes or the dressed chicken, but she did report having seen Mary Flannery O'Connor with the Catholic priest in a luncheonette downtown. My mother was not a Catholic herself, not yet. That came after she met my father—an Army Air Corps corporal from Milwaukee, who used to stand on the bus from the base into Macon to save the crease in his pants. She married him, and when he shipped out, she moved up north to live with his family, a houseful of Hungarian Catholic immigrants who couldn't understand a word she said. Back in high school, my mother was still a *de facto* Methodist in a family of Baptists—the one kid who refused to dunk her head under the water—but she knew the man she saw with Flannery O'Connor had to be the Catholic priest. What other kind of man could get away with wearing a long black dress in Milledgeville, Georgia, in 1941?

The way I picture it, my mother, Mimi, and their older sister Dottie are in Rosie's Ten-Cent Store after school one day. They're hanging around the cosmetics counter, examining pots of rouge and shaking little round boxes of Pond's Dusting Powder. They're touching blue heart-shaped bottles of *Evening in Paris* that they can't afford to buy, waving the bottles under one another's noses, hoping to catch a whiff through the glass stoppers. A clerk stationed beside the cash register is watching them like a field mouse watching three hawks. My mother and her sisters are tall, sturdy, nice-looking girls: two brunettes and Dottie, a redhead, who is past twenty and married already. At 5'6" my mother is the smallest of the three, the one whose cotton dress (made by Mimi from a pattern in Home Ec) is clean and ironed and smartly belted (another of Mimi's fashion ideas) but still too big for her. They're all three busy figuring prices and deciding what their pooled resources—Dottie's tips and some quarters they've earned picking cotton—might buy, when a girl's voice floats over to them from another part of the store, saying things like "I dunno, Father," and "Do you think so, Father?" It's the "Father" part that catches my mother's ear, and she turns and looks across Rosie's Ten-Cent Store to the luncheonette, where the Catholic girl is sitting in a red booth with Father Whatsisname.

Now my mother knows that, whatever he may be, the priest is not the Catholic girl's father, because the Catholic girl's father is dead. He died last winter of some unsightly disease, or so the girls said at school. My mother's own father has been gone much longer, having succumbed to a massive sinus infection at the Veterans Hospital in Macon when she was twelve. To make matters worse, he was preceded in death by her mother, who had died in childbirth the previous June. My mother's mother had only enough time to name the baby after her favorite sister, Gladys Mae, before the doctor left and the hemorrhaging began. All the while I was growing up, whenever I objected to what I considered my mother's nagging and meddling in my life, I had to hear about how *she* would be only *too glad* if she had *had* a mother to interfere with *her* life. One time I came back with, "You only *think* so because she *died!*" It's hard to have to remember that you're the same person who once said a thing like that to your mother.

My mother has always had less to say about her father—a carpenter who spent weeks and months away from home on construction jobs—but she does have one very clear memory of him sitting on a kitchen chair next to the stove with the new baby in his lap, a tiny head cradled on his knees and little feet kicking at the folds of his trousers. The baby's wearing only a diaper in the heat. Her barrel chest and belly are mottled pink, like marble. The rest of the children are gathered around—my eleven-year-old mother and Mimi and little Eddie, Jr., previously the youngest, and Dottie, the oldest, at sixteen. My mother remembers how the kerosene lamp on the table made all their faces look yellow, and how if you touched the baby's palm she'd grab your finger and hold on. Their father was saying that the best thing they could do for their new little sister was to give her to Uncle Rutherford in Tallahassee, because Uncle Rutherford and his wife didn't have any children and would raise her like their very own. My mother and her sisters tried to talk him out of it. They said three big girls could take care of one little baby, couldn't they? But their father had already made up his mind, knowing, perhaps, as his daughters did not, that no matter how bad things are, they can always take a turn for the worse. Sure enough, right before Christmas that same year, my mother's father went into the Veterans Hospital, where he died, leaving the rest of the orphans to their grandparents, except for Dottie, who took herself off her grandparents' hands by dropping out of high school and quietly getting married.

Something about the way Mary Flannery O'Connor said, "Do you think so, Father?" to the priest in the luncheonette must have made my mother recall that scene in the kitchen. She was going on sixteen herself now, almost five years had passed since her father died, but suddenly she was seized with longing. Maybe all she wanted was to say it herself: *Father. Do you think so, Father? Do we have to, Daddy? Do you reckon Mama'd want us to give her away? Do you? Daddy?* Whatever she was thinking, all of a sudden the bottle of *Evening in Paris* became a blue blur in her hand and she was crying in public, a big girl—almost a woman—crying like a baby right there at the cosmetics counter, in Rosie's Ten-Cent Store.

"What in the world is the matter?" her sister Dottie said when she saw, and then Mimi moved in, putting her arm around my mother, leaning so close that strands of her dark hair clung to my mother's tears, whispering in her ear, "Are you sick, sugar? You got cramps?"

My mother was famous in those days for hair-trigger sensitivity during her time of the month, a condition that her sisters blamed on the harsh way that the Curse had befallen her. Sometime between the summer evening when her mother bled to death and the Christmas day news about her father, my mother had a surprise in the outhouse. She was barely twelve years old and completely unprepared. Either of her sisters might have read the signs and clued her in, but recent events, understandably, had preoccupied them. No one thought to connect the fact that little Mary was shooting up tall as a weed, for example, with what must inevitably follow. When my mother ran to the outhouse one afternoon in November and saw the red stains in her pants, she could only think that her mother's bloody fate had caught up with her, which, of course, it had, but not in the sudden and deadly way my mother must have feared.

Mimi found her out there that evening. Nobody, including my mother, could say for sure how long she'd been sitting over the drafty hole in the wooden bench, with her ruined underpants wrapped around her ankles and her goose-bumpy arms drawn up under her dress for warmth (like somebody had tied her up and left her there, my Aunt Mimi told me, tears in her eyes sixty years later). With a history like that behind her, my mother could hardly be blamed for getting weepy every month, cramps and hormones aside, but when Mimi took the bottle of cologne out of her hand and asked her if the Curse was upon her, she shook her head.

"Then what the heck are you crying for?" Dottie said.

In a voice gummy with tears, my mother could only say, "He ain't her father."

"Who ain't whose father?" said Dottie.

My mother shot a look at the luncheonette.

"The Catholic girl?" Mimi said.

My mother nodded, and they all looked at the red booth where Mary Flannery O'Connor was sitting across from the priest. She was smiling at him now, covering the little gap between her front teeth by tapping her index finger against her lip, as if she were telling him to hush. She was not a particularly attractive girl, although Mimi believed she could have been better looking if she tried. Sitting across the aisle from her in class, my Aunt Mimi had thought more than once that if *she* could afford to live in a house like the one that Mary Flannery O'Connor lived in, she would also shell out a few dollars for a nice permanent wave and clothes that didn't look as if she'd made them herself. (In fact, O'Connor's mother

made them for her.) She was wearing one of her most unfortu-
nate dresses today, a blue velveteen with a gathered neckline and
gold trim that made her look like a bottle in a drawstring bag.
While Mimi and Dottie and my mother watched, Mary Flannery
O'Connor tugged at first one and then the other of her long blue
sleeves. They heard her say something like, "Well, Father, I'll tell
her what you said."

Meanwhile (and to me this is the most amazing part since I can
count on one hand the number of times I've seen my mother cry
in my lifetime), she was still blubbering by the cosmetics counter,
repeating tragically, "He ain't her father."

"Of course he's not," Dottie said. "That's what all Catholics say
to their what-do-you-call-it, their priests. You know that."

"He ain't," my mother said again. She was unable to explain why
this was suddenly a problem for her, but the anguish in her voice
worked on her sister Mimi like a call to arms. Mimi straightened
her shoulders and pressed her lips together, causing Dottie to
exclaim, "Mildred! What are you thinking to do?"

My Aunt Mimi has mellowed with the years, but they tell me
she was a warrior in her day—broad-shouldered, small-waisted,
wide-hipped, slim-ankled, and tall—almost 5'9" in her stockinged
feet before she started to shrink with age, which happens sooner
than you think. Mimi shook off the hand that Dottie had laid on
her arm and strode away from the cosmetics counter. Before my
mother and Dottie could decide if they should run out the door
of Rosie's Ten-Cent Store and into the next county right now,
Mimi was standing next to Mary Flannery O'Connor's table and
looking down at the future famous author. It was to O'Connor's
credit, my mother would say, that she didn't flinch or duck her
head, but looked the formidable Mimi full in the face, while the
priest looked up and down from one to the other like somebody
measuring the distance between two points. Their Aunt Gladys
had taught all the girls (as my mother taught me) that the rudest
thing you could do in the world was to talk about a person while
that person was sitting right there in front of you. ("Like they was

invisible," Aunt Gladys would say, shaking her head.) So the first thing Mimi said was "Excuse me, sir," to the priest, a pale fellow with rounded shoulders. Then Mimi turned to O'Connor and, putting her hands on her hips, she said flat out, "Your daddy is dead and you know it. So how come you're calling this man 'father'? He ain't your father any more than I am."

Until recently, whenever I imagined this moment, I would try to make that priest keep quiet and let the future famous author say something that Aunt Mimi might remember, or my mother overhear, something they could report to me 50-some years later. I know it didn't happen that way. I know the priest said, "See here, young lady!" and proceeded to explain to my Aunt Mimi selected points of Catholic dogma regarding the sacrament of Holy Orders and priests as spiritual fathers and the like, to which Mimi responded, after waiting politely for him to finish, "Beg your pardon, sir, but us Baptists don't put much stock in *spiritual* fathers." She drew herself up straighter and added, "Except, of course, for God Almighty."

Mary Flannery O'Connor's gray eyes must have widened at the audacity of my Aunt Mimi, while the priest's face turned a shade of red significant enough to attract the attention of my mother's Aunt Gladys, who had just stopped on the sidewalk outside the big front windows of the store, having left her husband in Garrison's Grill with his Packard parked out front while she ran down to Rosie's to pick up some thread. My mother's Aunt Gladys was an energetic woman with the same fine skin and cheekbones as her nieces. From the sidewalk, standing in the shade of a faded awning, Gladys had looked inside the store and immediately spotted Dottie and Mary at the cosmetics counter, turning their pockets out for a pair of scowling salesclerks. Then, as if that weren't bad enough, the scene in the luncheonette caught her eye. From Mimi's stance and the red face and Roman collar on the man in the booth, Gladys couldn't help but conclude that her niece was having an argument with the Catholic priest. Knowing Mimi, Gladys thought, they were arguing religion.

Aunt Gladys usually tried to make allowances for her dead sister's daughters, ignoring their oddities as much as possible, but this looked like a situation that required the intervention of her own special talents. Her husband used to say that if she hadn't been born female, Gladys would have made a first-rate salesman or a powerful preacher. "Six to one, half-a-dozen to the other," Gladys would say. In addition to her quick wit, she had a mesmerizing blue gaze and a way with words that could talk anybody into or out of anything. Within minutes of her entry into Rosie's Ten-Cent Store, Aunt Gladys had rescued Mary and Dot from the irate sales staff. Liberated, the girls fled to a corner in the rear of the store, by the hanging rolls of oilcloth, where they had a clear view of their aunt bearing down on her next objective: the red booth in the luncheonette.

Now we're getting to the part of the story that disturbed my thesis supervisor even more than my incendiary tendencies. Although no one could have known it at the time, I believe that my mother and her sisters were about to witness an important moment in the life of Flannery O'Connor. It was the kind of moment the famous author liked to inflict in her stories on the characters she loved best, which is to say, on the ones most likely to be shot, gored, drowned, or abandoned. (Never let your mother read these stories to your aunt who has a heart condition, by the way. They'll find the one with the grandmother and hold you personally responsible when somebody shoots her dead.) But you know the kind of moment I mean. Remember the story with the black lady who gets on the bus and sits down right across from Julian and his mother, wearing the same damn purple hat that Julian's mother is wearing? And remember how Julian—unaware that he's the main character in a Flannery O'Connor story—thinks smug thoughts about the lesson his aging Southern belle of a mother must be learning from her hat-shaped slice of humble pie? Little does he know, as he watches his mother's face go gray, that he's looking in the wrong direction, attending to the wrong detail, that he—not she—is the author's target. Of course, in real life, your mother doesn't have a brain-addling stroke just to prove that you're a bigger bigot than she is. In real life, the moments of grace are never so clear cut, the gestures never so totally right as all that.

Still, I did burn my Ph.D. thesis in a seldom-used women's restroom on the third floor of the Graham P. McGranaham Humanities Building last Thursday. It took me seventeen minutes to reduce the first 166 pages to flakes and ashes in a foot-operated flip-top waste receptacle—the white heavy-duty kind intended for discreet disposals. I proceeded methodically, keeping the tip of my foot on the pedal and cradling the stack in the crook of my arm, dealing pages off the top like cards, dedicating them alternately to Aunt Mimi and to Mom. ("She loves me, she loves me not," I said at first, until I realized I had an even number of pages.) Can you picture it? Toe down, top up, *whoosh*. Talk about discreet. I didn't even set off the fire alarm. My little gesture might, in fact, have gone undetected, if a toilet hadn't overflowed on the second floor, sending the Director of Composition one floor up to relieve herself. She opened the restroom door just as the top flipped up for page 167 with a little belch of smoke and a leaping tongue of flame.

They called me into the dean's office on Monday morning and made me stand on the Persian carpet in front of his mahogany desk while my thesis supervisor told the dean that he had found my thesis —no small task, since it had been buried on his desk for most of a semester—to be two-thirds unbridled fantasy. He didn't discuss the other third. Instead, he attacked my sources and said that if I wanted to write my family history, or a tribute to my mother, I should go ahead and write it, and not try to give it some kind of literary *significance* by dragging one of this century's finest writers —"the Chekhov of the South," he called her—into it. He said my psychologizing of O'Connor's vision was unscholarly and banal, which is one of their favorite words. When my thesis supervisor's mustache stopped twitching at the end of his nose like a whisk broom and it was my turn to speak, I drew myself up the way I imagined my Aunt Mimi would do, and I told him and the dean, borrowing my figure of speech from the Chekhov of the

South, that there's every kind of blindness in the world, and each of us suffers from our own variety.

Things do happen that change people forever.

From the rear of Rosie's Ten-Cent Store, my mother and her sister Dottie watched the little drama in the luncheonette up front unfold like a silent movie. They saw Mimi stepping back from the red booth to make room for Aunt Gladys. They saw Aunt Gladys fast-talking Father Whatsisname, who was on his feet by now, trying to look taller than the women. Gladys strung him along for a few minutes, the fingers of her left hand splayed on her breastbone to indicate how deeply mortified she was by her niece's behavior. Then she offered her hand for a shake. From the back of the store, the girls saw the priest reach for Gladys's hand. They saw him stop for an awkward moment with his right arm stuck out in front of him like a pump handle, and then he recovered, taking their aunt's left hand—the one she'd offered in the first place—in both of his and giving it a priestly squeeze. Most important, from the biographer's point of view, they saw Mary Flannery O'Connor, still seated in the red booth, her glass of Green River untouched in front of her, and her gray eyes on a level with the end of Gladys's right arm.

Now the fact is that Aunt Gladys's right arm ends about an inch below the elbow in a little knob of flesh that peeks out of her three-quarter-length sleeve from time to time, when she forgets to keep her apron tossed over it. She was born that way, with a regular left arm and a short right one, a deprivation that didn't keep her from finding herself a Packard-owning husband (long before the county got overrun with horny enlisted boys, she liked to point out) or from giving birth to a two-armed son. My Great-Aunt Gladys will be 89 this year.

If I have so far neglected to mention her arm, my intention was *not* to manipulate my dear reader—as I was accused in the margins of the thesis that went up in smoke. It was only to make you see my Great-Aunt Gladys as other people saw her, as you would have seen her yourself if you had met her back then. The first thing people noticed about Aunt Gladys was her eyes, sky-blue, wide open, welcoming as a pair of outstretched arms. Even now, with cataracts clouding them, her eyes take you right in, they make an insider out of you before she opens her mouth to speak, which is the second thing people noticed about Aunt Gladys—her voice. It's high-pitched and wavery now, but it used to be rich and relentless. (Aunt Mimi tells me, by the way, that if I could have taped *that* voice, my thesis supervisor would be singing a different tune.) The story goes that Great-Uncle Elmo fell in love with Gladys at first sight and sound, helpless to resist the double whammy of her voice and eyes across the counter of the baked goods booth at a church bazaar. He didn't even *see* the short arm until he called on her days later. ("My goodness, Gladys!" he exclaimed at the door. "Whatever did you do to your arm?") The point is, *nobody* sees Aunt Gladys's arm; not even the priest noticed it until he reached for a hand to shake.

O'Connor was looking in the wrong place, that's all—she was attending to the wrong detail. Maybe, having watched her father scab up and die, she was already on the lookout for proof that the flesh was weak, wrong, fatally flawed, and finally useless. Maybe that's what kept her gaze fixed like a dissecting pin on that stub of an arm. I wish I could have been there. I wish I could have put my finger under Mary Flannery's pouting, pointy chin and tilted it up, up to Aunt Gladys's face, which was kindness itself, up to her eyes, which were steady like O'Connor's but without the clouds, without the storm approaching, not gray but blue—I have to say it— blue as the vault of heaven.

But I wasn't there, and as Aunt Gladys stood talking beside the red booth, her short right arm kept peeking out at Mary Flannery O'Connor, who had forgotten by now about the priest across the table from her and the strange confrontation with a girl she hardly knew from school. Mary Flannery was paying no attention to Mimi now, nor did she see my mother and Dottie leaning forward, shoulder to shoulder, in the back of the store. In fact, if you had told her that Gladys was speaking to the priest in Latin, Mary

Flannery O'Connor couldn't have said that you were wrong. Her whole attention was pinned to the little knob of flesh at the tip of Gladys's arm, which poked in and out of sight like the pink snout of a little animal playing a grotesque game of hide-and-seek in her sleeve. The rest of Great-Aunt Gladys, like my mother and her sisters, shrank in the future famous author's mind to distant points of local color. For Flannery O'Connor, with lupus lurking in her cells and Jesus in her heart, only the tip of Gladys's right arm was a revelation. It was an early encounter with the enemy, it was a blind prophet, it was like one of her own babies, it was like the same damn hat.

Mary Helen Stefaniak earned her MFA at the Iowa Writers' Workshop. Her fiction has appeared in *Epoch, The Antioch Review, The Yale Review, The Iowa Review, Agni,* and other publications. Her collection, *Self Storage and Other Stories,* was published by New Rivers Press and received the 1998 Banta Award from the Wisconsin Library Association. She teaches at Creighton University and is working on a book of three novellas.

ROD STRAMPE

*A*ll the scenes in "A Note" are wholly imagined, but the biographical information—both about O'Connor and about my mother's family—is, to the best of my knowledge, true. Some names have been changed, composite characters created, and a few dates rearranged. My Aunt Sissie does not appear in the story, but I would like to acknowledge here, with gratitude, that she is the one who really said, "I call them all St. Joseph's."

Although I have never authored, much less burned, a dissertation, every story I have ever written is in some sense an argument with Flannery O'Connor, as well as a tribute to her. This story happens to be the only one that mentions her by name.

Thomas H. McNeely

SHEEP

(from *The Atlantic Monthly*)

Before the sheriff came to get him, Lloyd found the sheep out by the pond. He'd counted head that morning and come up one short. He did the count over, because he was still hazy from the night before. And he'd waked with a foul smell in his nose. So he had gone into Mr. Mac's house—it was early morning; the old man would be dead to the world—and filled his canteen with white lightning. He felt shaky and bad, and the spring morning was cold. He shouldn't have gone to town the night before.

The sheep lay on its side in some rushes. A flow of yellowish mucus was coming from its nose, and its eyes were sickly thin slits that made it look afraid. Lloyd thought the sheep honorable—it had gone off to die so that it wouldn't infect the rest of the flock. Lloyd knew that the sheep's sickness was his fault and that he couldn't do anything about it, but he squatted down next to the animal and rubbed its underside. In this hour before sunrise, when the night dew was still wet, the warmth and animal smell felt good. Lloyd moved his hand in circles over the sheep's lightly furred pink skin and lines of blue veins, its hard cage of ribs, its slack, soft belly. Across the pond the sun peeked through the Panhandle dust over a low line of slate-gray clouds. With his free hand Lloyd took his canteen from a pocket in his jacket, clamped it between his knees, opened it, and drank. For a moment the liquor stung the sides of his tongue; then it dissolved in him like warm water. The sheep's lungs lifted up and down; its heart churned blood like a slowly pounding fist. Soon the sun broke free and the pond, rippled by a slight breeze, ignited in countless tiny candle flames. When Lloyd was a child, Mr. Mac used to tell him that at the Last Judgment the pond would become the Lake of Fire, into which all sinners would be cast. Lloyd could still picture them falling in a dark stream, God pouring them out like a bag of nails. The sheep closed its eyes against the light.

When Sheriff Lynch walked up behind him, Lloyd started. He still caressed the sheep, but it was dead and beginning to stiffen. His canteen felt almost empty; it fell from his fingers. By the sun Lloyd saw it was almost noon. Big black vultures wheeled so high above that they looked the size of mockingbirds. Uneasiness creeping on him, Lloyd waited for the sheriff to speak.

Finally the sheriff said, "Son, looks like that sheep's dead."

"Yessir," Lloyd said, and tried to stand, but his legs were stiff and the liquor had taken his balance.

"You look about half dead yourself." The sheriff picked up Lloyd's canteen from the dry grass, sniffed it, and shook his head. "You want to turn out like Mr. Mac? A pervert?"

Lloyd wagged his head no. He thought how he must look: his long blond hair clumped in uncombed cowlicks, the dark reddish-gray circles around his eyes, his father's dirty herding jack hanging off his broad, slumped shoulders. Sheriff Lynch stood there, his figure tall and straight. He wore a star-shaped golden badge hitched to a belt finely tooled with wildflowers. His face was burnt the rust color of Dumas County soil, the lines on it deep, like the sudden ravines into which cattle there sometimes fell. His eyes were an odd steely blue, which seemed not to be that color itself but to reflect it. He studied Lloyd.

"That probably doesn't make much of a difference now," he said, lowering his eyes as if embarrassed.

"What?" Lloyd said, though he'd heard him.

"Nothing. We just need to ask you some questions."

Lloyd wondered if Mr. Mac had found out about the sheep somehow. "But I ain't stole nothin'," he said.

"I'm fairly sure of that," the sheriff said. A grin flickered at one corner of his mouth, but it was sad and not meant to mock Lloyd. "Come on. You know the drill. Hand over your knife and shears and anything else you got."

After Lloyd put his tools in a paper bag, the sheriff squatted next to the sheep and ran his hand over its belly. His hand was large and strong and clean, though etched with red-brown creases.

When they got up to the house, Lloyd saw three or four police cars parked at odd angles, as if they'd stopped in a hurry. Their lights whirled around, and dispatch radios crackled voices that no one answered. Some policemen busied themselves throwing clothes, bottles, and other junk out of Lloyd's shack, which was separated from the house by a tool shed. Others were carrying out cardboard boxes. Lloyd recognized one of the men, name of Gonzales, who'd picked him up for stealing a ten-speed when he was a kid. Lloyd waved at him and called out, but Gonzales just set his dark eyes on him for a moment and then went back to his business. Mr. Mac stood on the dirt patch in front of the house, his big sloppy body looking like it was about to fall over, talking to a man in a suit.

"If you're gonna drag that pond," he said, his eyes slits in the harsh, clear sunlight, "you're gonna have to pay me for the lost fish. I'm a poor old man. I ain't got nothin' to do with thisayre mess."

The man started to say something to him, but Mr. Mac caught sight of Lloyd. His face spread wide with a fear that Lloyd had never seen in him; then his eyes narrowed in disgust. He looked like he did when he saw ewes lamb, or when he punished Lloyd as a child.

"Mr. Mac," Lloyd said, and took a step toward him, but the old man held up his hands as if to shield his face.

"Mr. Mac." Lloyd came closer. "I 'pologize 'bout that 'er sheep. I'll work off the cost to you someway."

Mr. Mac stumbled backward and pointed at Lloyd; his face was wild and frightened again. He shouted to the man in the suit, "Look at 'im! Look at 'im! A seed of pure evil!"

Lloyd could feel his chest move ahead of his body toward Mr. Mac. He wanted to explain about the sheep, but the old man kept carrying on. The sheriff's hand, firm but kind, gripped his arm and guided him toward a police car.

The sheriff sat bolt upright on the passenger side and looked straight ahead as the rust-colored hills passed by outside. A fingerprint-smudged Plexiglas barrier ran across the top of the front seat and separated him from Lloyd. As always, the hair on the nape of the sheriff's neck looked freshly cut. Lloyd had expected them to take his shears and bowie knife, but why were they tearing up his shack? And what was Mr. Mac going on about? Still drunk, probably. He would ask the sheriff when they got to the jail. His thoughts turned to the sheep. He should've put it out of its misery—slit its throat and then cut its belly for the vultures. Not like at slaughter, when he would've had to root around with his knife and bare hands and clean out its innards. What a Godawful stink sheep's insides had! But this would've been easy. It wouldn't have taken a minute.

In the jail two guards Lloyd didn't know sat him down inside a small white room he'd never seen before. The man in a suit who had been talking to Mr. Mac came in, with Sheriff Lynch following. Lloyd hadn't gotten to ask the sheriff what was going on. The man put what looked like a little transistor radio on the table and pressed a button and began to talk.

"Is it okay if we tape-record this interview?" he asked Lloyd.

Lloyd shrugged and smiled a who's-this-guy? smile at the sheriff. The sheriff gave him a stern, behave-yourself look.

"Sure," Lloyd said. "I ain't never been recorded before."

"Okay," the man said. He said all their names, where they were, what date and time it was. Then he opened a file folder. Lloyd didn't like his looks: he had a smile that hid itself, that laughed at you in secret. Mr. Mac could get one of those. And the man talked in one of those citified accents, maybe from Dallas.

"Okay," the man said. "My name is Thomas Blanchard. I am a special agent with the Federal Bureau of Investigation. I work in the serial-homicide division." He shot his eyes up at Lloyd, as if to catch him at something. "Do you understand what that means?"

"Which part?" Lloyd said.

"Serial homicide—serial murder."

"Nope."

"It means to kill more than once—sometimes many people in a row."

"Okay," Lloyd said.

The man gave him another once-over and said, "You are being held as a material witness in seventeen murders that have occurred in and around this area. You have not been charged in any of them. Should you be charged, you will have the right to counsel, but at this time you have no such right per se. However, as a witness, should you wish to retain counsel, that is also your right. Do you wish to do so?"

Lloyd tried to put the man's words together. Blanchard bunched up his shoulders, like a squirrel ready to pounce. The sheriff leaned back his chair and studied the ceiling.

After he had drawn out the silence, Lloyd said, "I don't know. I'm still pretty drunk to think about suchlike. Would I have to pay for him?"

Blanchard's hand snaked out to the tape recorder, but the sheriff looked at Lloyd and said, "Lloyd, you think you're too drunk to know what you're sayin'? I mean, to the point of makin' things up or disrememberin'?"

"Oh, no," Lloyd said. The sheriff asked him if he was sure, and he said yes. Then the sheriff told him that to retain a lawyer he would have to pay for one. In that case, Lloyd said, he didn't want one.

"Sheriff," he said. "What's thisayre all about?"

The sheriff told him he would find out.

But he didn't, not really. Blanchard asked Lloyd about the night before. He'd gone to Genie's Too, where the old Genie's used to be. He'd brought a canteen of Mr. Mac's stuff with him for setups, because they'd lost their license. He saw all the usual people there: Candy, Huff, Wishbone, Firefly. Dwight, Genie's old man, did the colored-baby dance, flopping around this brown rag doll and flashing up its skirt. Everybody seemed to be having a real good time. Big plastic bottles were on nearly every table; people were talking—men arguing, women listening. People leaned on each other like scarecrows, some dancing slow and close, others just close, doing a little bump-and-grind.

Blanchard asked him if he had met anyone, danced with anyone. Lloyd grinned and blushed and sought out the sheriff, who smiled this time. Lloyd said, "I always been shy. I guess it's my rearing, out on that old ranch. And they got their own group there at Genie's, everybody always foolin' with everyone else's."

By the end of his answer the sheriff's smile had gone.

Blanchard asked Lloyd the same thing about ten different ways —had he seen anyone new there? The questions got on his nerves. He said, "Sheriff, now what's this about?"

The sheriff told him to have some patience.

Blanchard asked about places in Amarillo, Lubbock, Muleshoe, Longview, Lamesa, Reno, Abilene—bars Lloyd had sneaked away to when he wanted to be alone. The ones he could remember were all about the same as Genie's, each with its own little crowd. Blanchard mentioned places from so long ago that Lloyd began to feel as if he were asking about a different person. He drifted off into thinking about Mr. Mac.

Mr. Mac, when Lloyd would ask him where they were, used to say that all he needed to know was that they were in the United States of America. He used to tell Lloyd that where they were was just like Scotland, and then he'd start laughing to himself until his laughs trailed off into coughs. The sheriff had never, ever laughed at him like that. He didn't have those kinds of jokes inside him.

Blanchard began asking personal questions: Did he have a girl-friend? Had he ever? No. How long had he been out at the ranch? All his life—about thirty years, according to Mr. Mac. Was he a virgin?

"Now, Sheriff, have I got to answer that?" In truth he didn't know what he was, because, as he often reflected, he didn't know whether what Mr. Mac had done made him not a virgin.

Perhaps sensing this, the sheriff told him no, he didn't have to answer any more questions. In fact, it might be better to quit for the day. "I'm afraid, though, son, we're gonna have to hold you as a suspect."

"Suspect of what?" Lloyd said, a sweat creeping on him like the cold rain when he herded in winter.

Lloyd woke to the stink of his own sweat, and he seemed wholly that sweat and that stench—the stench was him, his soul. The overhead light had been switched on. It was a bare bulb caged by heavy wire. He glanced at the steel place he was in: steel walls, floor, ceiling, toilet, stool, table. Everything was bolted down. The steel door had a small square high window made of meshed security glass, and a slot near its bottom, with a sliding cover, for passing food. Lloyd hid his face in the crook of his arm and shook and wished he could go to Mr. Mac's for some white lightning.

The door clanked open. Lloyd could tell it was the sheriff even though he kept his face hidden and his eyes shut tight. The sheriff put a plastic plate on the table and said, "I was afraid of this." Then he left.

Maybe the food would help. Lloyd stood up, but his legs felt wobbly and his eyes couldn't focus right. He lurched to the stool, planted himself on it, and held the edge of the table. When he picked up the plastic fork, it vibrated in his fingers. His touch sent a jangling electrical charge through his arm and down his back. The harder he gripped, the more he felt as though he were trying to etch stone with a pencil, yet only this concentration made any steadiness possible. Keeping his face close to the plate, he scooped the watery scrambled eggs into his mouth. He fell to his knees and threw up in the toilet. Curled facedown on the floor, Lloyd felt a prickly, nauseous chill seep into his muscles and begin to paralyze him.

Someone not Sheriff Lynch, who seemed by his step to be burly and ill-tempered, grabbed Lloyd's shoulder and twisted his body so that he faced the ceiling. The floor felt cold and hard against the back of his head. The man spread Lloyd's eyelids, opened his shirt, and put a cold metal disc on his chest. Lloyd had not noticed until now, but his heart was racing— much faster than the sheep's. That seemed so long ago. Mr. Mac was angry with him. The man started to yank down Lloyd's pants. Lloyd moved his lips to say no! No! But his limbs and muscles had turned to cement. His mouth gaped open, but he couldn't catch any air. The chill sweat returned. He was a boy again. Mr. Mac's heaviness pressed the air from his lungs, pinned him from behind, faceless, pushing the dull, tearing pain into him; he choked Lloyd's thin gasps with old-man smells of sweat and smoke and liquor and his ragged, grunting breath. The man rubbed something on Lloyd's right buttock and then pricked it with a needle. He left without pulling up Lloyd's pants.

Lloyd's body softened, and the cement dissolved; a cushiony feeling spread through him, as though his limbs were swaddled in plush, warm blankets. He could breathe. He could not smell himself anymore. "Son," he heard the sheriff say. "Put your pants on."

The two of them sat in the little white room, this time without Blanchard.

"Sheriff." Lloyd's words seemed to float out of his mouth. "Sheriff, what's all thisayre 'bout?"

Sheriff Lynch sat across the table. His face changed faintly as animals and unknown faces, and then the spirits of Mr. Mac and Blanchard, passed through it. He popped a peppermint Life Saver, sucked on it hard, and pulled back into focus.

"Let me ask you a question, first, son, and then I'll answer yours." He reached down next to his chair and put two Ziploc bags with Lloyd's shears and bowie knife in them on the table. Both the shears and the knife were tagged, as if they were in hock. The sheriff pressed them a few times with the tips of his long rust-colored fingers, lightly, as though to make sure they were there, or to remind them to stay still. "Now," he said, "I think I already know the answer to this question, but I need to know from you." He pressed them again. "Are these your knife and shears?"

How should he answer? The sheriff leaned back, waiting, with a look on his face that said he didn't want to hear the answer.

"Maybe," Lloyd said.

"Maybe." The sheriff joined his hands behind his head and pointed his eyes up and away, as though he were considering this as a possible truth.

"Maybe," Lloyd said.

"Lloyd Wayne Dogget," the sheriff said, turning his not-blue eyes on him. "How long have I known you? I knew your daddy and your grandpappy when they were alive. I know more about you than you know about you. And you ain't never been able to lie to me and get clear with it. So I'll ask you again—are these your knife and shears?"

Mr. Mac had given Lloyd the shears when he was sixteen. They were long and silvery. At the end of each day of shearing, after cutting the sheep's coarse, billowy hair, Lloyd would sharpen them on a strop and oil them with a can of S'OK to keep off the rust. The merry old man on the green can, a pipe in his mouth, always reminded him of Mr. Mac.

"What if I say yes?" Lloyd said.

Sheriff Lynch sucked on the Life Saver and blew out a breath. He leaned close to Lloyd and put his elbows on the table. "To tell you the truth," he said, "it doesn't make a whit's difference." He pressed the plastic bags again. "There's blood on these tools matches the type of a young lady people saw you leave Genie's with, a young lady who turned up murdered. And I confiscated these two things from you. So it doesn't make a whit's difference what you say, whether you lie or not. I'm just trying to give you a

chance to get right with yourself, to be a man." He sank back and
ran his hands through his stubbly iron-gray hair as he bowed his
head and looked at the bags. He massaged his clean-cut neck.
"Maybe to get right with the Lord, too. I don't know. I don't
believe in that kind of thing, but sometimes it helps people."

To Lloyd, the sheriff seemed embarrassed about something.
Lloyd wanted to help him. But he was also afraid; he could not
remember any young lady, only smiling dark-red lips, the curve of
a bare upper arm, honky-tonk music, Dwight flinging the colored
baby doll around.

"Okay, Sheriff," he said. "Since it don't make any difference, you
know they're mine."

The sheriff escorted him to the showers, where he took Lloyd's
clothes and gave him an inmate's orange jumpsuit and a pair of
regulation flip-flops. After Lloyd had showered and changed, the
sheriff told him he was under arrest for capital murder, read him
his rights, and handcuffed him. They got in his car, Lloyd riding
in the front seat, and drove the two blocks to the courthouse. The
judge asked him if he had any money or expected any help, and he
said no, which was the truth.

Every morning Sheriff Lynch came to Lloyd's cell and walked
with him down to the little white room, where Lloyd talked with
his lawyer. When the sheriff opened the door to the room, Lloyd
watched his lawyer and the sheriff volley looks under their pleas-
antries. He remembered a cartoon he'd seen: Bluto and Popeye
had each grabbed one of Olive Oyl's rubbery arms. They were
stretching her like taffy. He couldn't remember how it ended.

Raoul Schwartz, the lawyer Lloyd had been assigned, said the
judge had granted Lloyd a competency hearing, but not much
money to do it with. He, Schwartz, would have to conduct the
tests himself and then send them to a psychiatrist for evaluation.
In two months the psychiatrist would testify and the judge would
decide whether Lloyd was competent to stand trial. Schwartz said
they had a lot of work to do. Schwartz said he was there to help.

Schwartz was everything the sheriff was not. He had short, pale, womanish fingers that fluttered through papers, fiddled with pencils, took off his wire-rimmed granny glasses and rubbed the bridge of his nose. When he got impatient, which was often, his fingers scratched at a bald spot on the top of his forehead. Lloyd thought he might have rubbed his hair off this way.

Schwartz wouldn't let him wriggle out of questions, sometimes asking the same ones many times, like Blanchard. He asked about Lloyd's whole life. Sometimes the glare of the white room and Schwartz's drone were like being in school again, and Lloyd would lay his head down on the slick-topped table between them and put his cheek to its cool surface. "Come on, Lloyd," Schwartz would say. "We've got work to do."

Also unlike the sheriff, Schwartz cussed, which was something Lloyd could never abide, and the little man's Yankee accent raked the words across Lloyd's nerves even worse than usual. When Lloyd told him that Sheriff Lynch had been out to talk to Mr. Mac after a teacher had spotted cigarette burns on his arms, Schwartz murmured, "Excellent, excellent. Fucking bastard."

"Who's the effing bastard?"

"Mr. Mac." Schwartz's head popped up just as Blanchard's had when he'd wanted to catch Lloyd at something, only this time it was Lloyd who had caught Schwartz in a lie.

Schwartz began giving Lloyd tests. Lloyd was worried that he might fail them, but he didn't say anything; he had already gotten the impression that this man thought he was stupid. But it was the tests that were stupid. First Schwartz asked him about a million yes-or-no questions. Everything from "Do you think your life isn't worth living?" (no) to "Do you ever see things that aren't there?" (sometimes, in the woods). Then came the pictures. One showed a man and a boy standing in opposite corners of a room. At first Lloyd just said what he saw. But this wasn't good enough; Schwartz said he had to interpret it. "Tell me what you think is going to happen next," he said. When Lloyd looked at it closely, he figured the boy had done something wrong and was about to get a good belt-whipping. Schwartz seemed pleased by this. Finally, and strangest of all, Schwartz showed him some blobs of ink and asked him to make something out of them. If Schwartz hadn't been so serious, Lloyd would have thought it was a joke. But when he studied them (Schwartz had used that word—"interpret"—again), Lloyd could see all different kinds of faces and animals, as he had when he'd talked to Sheriff Lynch about his knife and shears.

It took only one little thing to tell him what the sheriff thought about this testing.

One morning the sheriff walked Lloyd down the hallway without a word, and when he unlocked the door to the white room, he stepped back, held it open, and swooped his hand in front of Lloyd like a colored doorman.

"Mr. Dogget," he said, for the first time making fun of Lloyd in some secret way.

The sheriff turned and let the door close without so much as a glance at Schwartz. Lloyd wanted to apologize to the sheriff. He was beginning to understand that it came down to this: the worse the sheriff looked, the better he, Lloyd, looked. He felt he was betraying the sheriff, with the help of this strange, foul-mouthed little man. Schwartz seemed to see everything upside down. When Lloyd had told him about Mr. Mac, even though Schwartz said it must have been awful, Lloyd could tell that in some way he was pleased. When he told Schwartz about times when a lot of hours passed without his knowing it, like when he'd sat with that sheep, or about drinking at least a canteen of Mr. Mac's white lightning every day for the past few years, Schwartz began scribbling and shooting questions at him. Same thing with the pills and reefer and acid and speed he'd done in his twenties. Even the gas huffing when he was just a kid. Lloyd felt dirty remembering all of it. Schwartz wanted details. Lloyd could almost see Schwartz making designs out of what he told him, rearranging things to make him look pitiful.

"I don't want to do no testin' today," Lloyd said as soon as the door had shut. He sat and leaned back in his chair, arms dangling, chest out.

"Okay," Schwartz said. "What do you want to do?"

"I been thinkin'," Lloyd said. "It don't make no difference if I was drunk or not. That don't excuse what I did."

"But you don't know what you did."

"That don't make no difference. They got the proof."

"They have evidence, Lloyd, not proof."

Another bunch of upside-down words. "But if I can't remember it, then ain't what they got better than what I can say?"

"Lloyd," Schwartz said, his head in his hands, massaging his bald spot. "We've been over this about every time we've talked. I know that it doesn't make common sense at first. But our criminal-justice system—that misnomer—is predicated upon the idea of volition. It means you have to commit a crime with at least an inkling of intention. You can't be punished in the same way when you don't have any idea what you're doing."

This kind of talk made Lloyd's head ache. "All I know," he said, "is I don't want to go foolin' around with truth. It's like the sheriff says—I got to get right with myself and be a man."

"The sheriff says this?" Schwartz's head popped up.

Lloyd nodded.

"Do you talk to the sheriff often?"

"I been knowing Sheriff Lynch since forever. He's like my daddy."

"But do you talk to him? How often do you talk to him?"

"Every chance I get." Lloyd felt queasy. He knew he'd said something he shouldn't have. But his pride in his friendship with the sheriff, perhaps because it was imperiled, drove him to exaggerate. "When we come from my cell, mostly. But any time I want, really. I can call on him any time."

"I don't think it's a good idea for you to be talking to him about your case," Schwartz said.

"And why not?"

"Because anything—*anything*—you say to him becomes evidence. As a matter of fact, I don't think it's a good idea for you to talk to him at all."

"So who'm I gonna talk to? Myself? You?"

For the next couple of days the sheriff didn't speak to Lloyd unless Lloyd spoke to him first. Schwartz must have done something. But the sheriff never looked at him hard or seemed angry. He mainly kept his words short and his eyes on the floor, as if he was sad and used to his sadness. Lloyd wanted to tell him how he was trying to get right but it was hard. Eventually Lloyd realized that even if he said this, the sheriff probably wouldn't believe him. If he were trying to get right, then he wouldn't be letting this Schwartz character make him look pitiful. Each morning Lloyd rose early, dressed, and rubbed his palms to dry them as he sat on the edge of his bunk, waiting. When he walked in front of the sheriff down the hallway to the white room, Lloyd could feel the sheriff's eyes taking him in. He tried to stand up straight and walk with manly strides, but the harder he tried, the smaller and more bent over he felt. He was careful not to wrinkle his prison outfit, pressing it at night between his mattress and a piece of plywood the sheriff had given him for his back. He combed his hair as best he could without a mirror.

At night Lloyd lay on his bunk and thought about Schwartz. Of course, Schwartz had tricked him into more tests. Next they were going to take pictures of his brain. Lloyd studied Schwartz's words: "volition," "interpret," "diminished responsibility." They all meant you couldn't be punished for your mistakes. This didn't square with Lloyd; he had been punished for plenty of mistakes. That was what Mr. Mac had punished him for; that was what the sheep died of. When you missed one on a head count and it got lost and fell into a ravine; when you forgot to give one a vaccination and it got sick, like the one that had died before Lloyd was taken away, you were punished. But how could he expect Schwartz, a womanish city boy, to understand this?

On one side were Schwartz and the law, and on the other were the sheep and God and the earth and Sheriff Lynch and Mr. Mac and everything else Lloyd had ever known. Who was he to go against all that—to hide from that terrible, swift sword the Almighty would wield on the Final Day? His fear was weak and mortal; it drove him out of his cell to plot with this fellow sinner to deceive God. Some nights Lloyd moaned in agony at the deceit of his life. For in his pride he had latched onto the notion that since he could not remember his gravest sins (and he believed they were all true, they must be true), he should not have to pay for them in this life. Oh, he would pay for them in eternity, but he flinched at paying here. What upside-down thinking! What cowardice in the face of sins that were probably darker, cloaked as they were in his drunken forgetting, than any he could have committed when he had "volition," as Schwartz called it. Because Lloyd did not know his sins, he could not accept his punishment; but for the same reason they seemed to him unspeakably heinous.

Lloyd lay on his bunk in the darkness and thought about the pictures he had seen of his brain. Two officers he didn't know had driven him to a hospital in Lubbock to get them taken. The hearing was in a week. Schwartz had pointed out patches in the pictures' rainbow colors, scratching his bald spot and pacing. He'd said that although parts of Lloyd's brain were damaged so that alcohol could cause longer and more severe blackouts in him than in normal people, such damage might not be enough for the court to recognize him as incompetent. And the rest of the tests had proved that he had a dissociative condition but not multiple-personality disorder. Lloyd had wanted to ask if Schwartz thought he was incompetent, but he figured he wouldn't get a straight answer.

In the darkness of the steel room Lloyd touched his head, trying to feel the colored patches of heat and coolness that the pictures showed in his brain. He imagined he could sense some here and there. He had come a long way—not many people knew what their brains looked like. But the thought that he might be incompetent frightened him. What if some day one of those big machines they put over his head was put over his chest and a picture was taken of his soul? What would it look like? He saw a dark-winged creature with tearing claws, cloaked in a gray mist.

The knock came to Lloyd in a half dream, and at first he thought he had imagined the sheriff's voice. The whole jail was quiet; all the inmates were covered in the same darkness.

"Lloyd? Lloyd? You awake, son?" The voice didn't sound exactly like the sheriff's, but Lloyd knew that's who it was. He rose and went to the door, too sleepy to be nervous. He peered out the square window. The glare of the hallway made him squint. The sheriff stood in silhouette, but his steely eyes glinted. Looking at him through the crosshatches of wire in the security glass, Lloyd thought that he, too, looked caged.

"I'm awake, Sheriff."

The door opened, and the sheriff said, "Come on." Lloyd could smell whiskey. He followed the sheriff out past the booking area. Everything was still and deserted in the bare fluorescent light. Gonzales dozed in a chair at the front desk with a porno magazine in his lap. The sheriff opened the door to his office, making the same mocking gesture as before, though this time he seemed to be trying to share his joke with Lloyd. He snapped the door's lock and sat down behind his desk. A single shaded lamp glowed in a corner, casting shadows from the piles of paper on the desk and reflecting golden patches from plaques on the walls.

The sheriff pointed at a low-backed leather chair and told Lloyd to have a seat. "Excuse me gettin' you out of bed, son. I figured this was the only time we could talk."

"It's no trouble."

"You can prob'ly tell I been drinkin'," the sheriff said. "I don't do it as a habit, but I apologize for that, too. I been doin' it more lately. I do it when I'm sick at heart. At least that's my excuse to myself, which is a Goddamned poor one, unbefitting a man, if you ask me. But I am. Sick at heart."

He took a long pull from a coffee mug. Lloyd followed it with his eyes, and the sheriff caught him.

"And no," he said, "you can't have any. One of us got to stay sober, and I want you to remember what I'm gonna tell you." He leaned across the desk. "You know what a vacuum is, son? I mean in a pure sense, not the one you clean with."

Lloyd shook his head.

"Well. A vacuum is a place where there ain't anything, not even air. Every light bulb"—the sheriff nodded at the lamp behind him—"is a vacuum. Space is mostly a vacuum. Vacuum tubes used to be in radios. And so on. A place where there ain't nothin'. Is that signifyin' for you?"

Lloyd nodded.

"Good. So we, because we're on this earth with air to breathe, we are in a place that's not a vacuum that's in the middle of a vacuum, which is space. Think of a bubble floating out in the air." The sheriff made a big circle above the desk with his fingertips. "That's what the earth is like, floating in space. Are you followin' me?"

"I think so."

"Well, are you or aren't you?" the sheriff said with sudden violence. Not waiting for an answer, he yanked open his desk drawer and took out a large folding map of the world. He tumbled it down the front of his desk, weighted its top corners with a tape dispenser and a stapler, and came around the desk to stand next to Lloyd. He told Lloyd what it was and said, "I study this all the time. Do you know where we are right now?"

To Lloyd, the shapes on the map looked like those inkblots. By reading, he found the United States and then Texas, and then he gave up. He shrugged his shoulders. "I don't know, Sheriff."

"That's okay," the sheriff said gently. He pointed to a dot in the Panhandle which someone had drawn with a ballpoint pen. Cursive letters next to it said "Dumas." "This is where we are. Two specks within that dot, on the dark side of the earth, floating in space. Over here"—he pointed to Hong Kong—"it's lunchtime. Japs eatin' their noodles or whatever. Here"—he pointed to London—"people just risin', eatin' their sausages and egg sandwiches."

He stepped back, behind Lloyd, and put his hands on the chair. The heat of his body and the smell of his breath washed over Lloyd.

"But look, son," the sheriff said, "how many places there are. It's some time everywhere, and everybody is doin' something."

The sheriff stood there for a few moments. Lloyd felt as he had when he was a child watching TV—he couldn't imagine how all those people got inside that little box. Now he couldn't fathom people inside the little dots. The world was vast and stranger than he had ever imagined.

"We are all here doin' things," the sheriff said, "inside this bubble that is not a vacuum. We all breathe the same air, and everything we do nudges everything else." He stepped over and propped himself on the edge of his desk, next to the map, and crossed his legs. The lamp's soft light cast him in half shadow.

"And this is why I'm sick at heart. Because I thought I knew you. Separation is the most terrible thing there is, especially for a man like me." The sheriff gestured to take in the whole room. "This is what I got. It ain't much. You and I aren't that far apart, son. Both of us solitary. But what you done, son, and I do believe you did all that, that separates a man from the whole world. And that's why I said you need to get right with yourself."

Lloyd bowed his head.

"You don't need to tell me you ain't done that." The sheriff's voice rose and quickened, began to quiver. "You and I both know you ain't. But that itself—a negativity, a vacuum—ain't nothin' to breathe in. Things die without air. So what I'm askin' you is, I want to do my own competency exam, for my own self. This is between Lloyd Wayne Dogget and Archibald Alexander Lynch. I need to know what's inside you to know what's inside myself. So you tell that lawyer of yours I'll stipulate to whatever he wants. Remember that word—'stipulate.' Now get out a' here." He turned from Lloyd and began folding the map with shaking hands. The corner weighted by the tape dispenser tore. Lloyd could not move.

"Shit," the sheriff muttered. He wheeled unsteadily on Lloyd, his eyes wide with panic and surprise at what he'd said. Lloyd could tell he was afraid, but not of him, as Mr. Mac had been. The sheriff was afraid that he might show his own soul to Lloyd and so break out of the bubble in which he lived. "Git!" he yelled. "Go tell Gonzales to take you back! Get outta here before I say somethin' foolish!"

He wants you to do *what*?" Schwartz paced in the little white room, looking at the floor.

Lloyd was sitting at the table, turning his head to follow Schwartz. Was Schwartz right with himself? He repeated what the sheriff had told him.

"What does that son of a bitch want?" Schwartz said to himself.

"I wish you'd stop cussing around me."

Schwartz made a distracted noise.

"I mean it," Lloyd said. "It's offensive."

Schwartz made another noise. He had gathered his lips together into a pucker with his fingers, and he looked at the floor as he paced.

"Especially cussing on the sheriff." When Schwartz didn't answer, Lloyd said, "Are you hearing me? Don't cuss on the sheriff."

"I don't know what kind of game he's trying to play." Schwartz did not stop or raise his eyes from the floor. "But I would guess he's trying to trick some kind of confession out of you."

"Sheriff don't play no games with me," Lloyd said. "He don't have no tricks. You're the one with all the tricks."

"I'll take that as a compliment."

"Sheriff's the one tryin' to help me get right."

"Sheriff's the one tryin' to help you get dead," Schwartz said, mimicking Lloyd.

"Okay, man." Lloyd stood up and pushed his chair away. It squealed on the floor, and Schwartz stopped. Lloyd saw that his own fists were clenched. He hesitated.

"What are you gonna do, Lloyd? Beat me up? Go ahead. I've been expecting this."

"You think I'm stupid," Lloyd said. "And all them tests is to make me look pitiful and incompetent. What do you think that's done to my trying to get right?"

"What do you think that means, Lloyd—'getting right'?" Schwartz moved close to him. He stared straight at Lloyd as he spoke. "It means giving up."

That night, and for the days and nights to come, Lloyd turned over in his mind all he had seen and heard. What he had known before was like some foreign language that now he couldn't understand. The worlds of Schwartz and the sheriff, of man and God, of what was in the law and what was in the fields, began to blur, and yet between them grew a chasm in which he hung suspended. He tried to remember what had happened in the places Blanchard had said he'd been, but he couldn't. He could not make them connect the way the sheriff had said all the people in all those dots on the map did. An indifference grew around him, a thin glass glazing that separated him from the rest of humankind.

The sheriff led him down the hallway to the white room without a word or a look, and left him with Schwartz. The hearing was the next day. Lloyd felt as though he were about to take another test. He had fought with Schwartz tooth and nail over the sheriff's proposal, and in the end had gotten his way by threatening to fire him. After Lloyd sat down across the table from him, Schwartz explained that he and the sheriff had struck a deal: the sheriff had agreed that he would not testify about his "competency exam," as he called it, on the condition that he not have to reveal to Schwartz beforehand what it was going to be about.

"I don't like this," Schwartz said, pacing, clicking the top of a ballpoint pen so that it made a *tick-tick* sound, like a clock. He sat down again, his elbows on the table and his hands joined as though in prayer, and brought his face close to Lloyd's.

"I want to tell you the truest thing I've ever seen, Lloyd. I've seen a man executed. When you are executed in Texas, you are taken to a powder-blue room. This is the death chamber, where the warden, a physician, and a minister will stand around the gurney. Since executions can take place in Texas only between midnight and dawn, it will have that eerie feeling of a room brightly lit in the middle of the night. Before this, in an anteroom, a guard will tell you to drop your pants. Then he will insert one rubber stopper in your penis and another in your anus, to prevent you from urinating and defecating when your muscles relax after you have died. When you are lying on the gurney, the guard will secure your arms, legs, and chest to it with leather straps. The guard will insert a needle, which is attached to an IV bag, into your left arm. Above you will be fluorescent lighting, and a microphone will hang suspended from the ceiling. The warden—I think it's still Warden Pearson—will ask whether you have any last words. When you're finished, three chemicals will be released into your blood: sodium thiopental, a sedative that is supposed to render you unconscious; pancuronium bromide, a muscle relaxant, to collapse your diaphragm and lungs; potassium chloride, a poison that will stop your heart.

"I could tell that my client could feel the poison entering his veins. I had known him for the last three of his fifteen years on death row; he was old enough to be my father. At his execution I was separated from him by a piece of meshed security glass. There was nothing I could do when he began writhing and gasping for breath. The poison—later I found out it was the potassium chloride, to stop his heart—had been injected before the thiopental. Imagine a dream in which your body has turned to lead, in which you can't move and are sinking in water. You have the sensations given you by your nerves and understood in your brain, but you can't do anything about them. You struggle against your own body. But really, it is unimaginable—what it is like to try to rouse your own heart.

"What if everything goes as planned? A nice, sleepy feeling—the sedative tricking your nerves—will dissolve your fear. The question is, will you want it taken away, fear being the only thing that binds you to life? Will you want to hold on to that, like the survivor of a shipwreck clinging to a barnacled plank? Will you struggle, in the end, to be afraid?"

Schwartz slumped back in his chair and began again to *tick-tick* the top of his pen so that it made a sound like a clock. The whiteness and silence of the room seemed to annihilate time, as though the two men could sit there waiting forever. They fell on Lloyd like a thin silting of powdered glass.

"You spend a lot of time thinkin' about that, don't you?" Lloyd said.

"Yes."

"You told me that to scare me, didn't you?"

"Yes."

Lloyd thought that Schwartz might have gotten right with himself, in his own way, by seeing what he had seen and thinking on it. But something still didn't add up.

"How do you know I'd be afraid?" Lloyd said. "How do you know that would be the last thing I'd feel?"

"I don't know that." Schwartz *tick-tick*ed the pen. "You can never know. That's what's terrible about death."

"Lots of things you don't know when you're alive. So what's the difference?"

Schwartz's fingers stopped, and he stared at Lloyd as though he had seen him purely and for the first time. A knock at the door broke the brief, still moment, and Sheriff Lynch entered. He carried under his arm a stack of manila folders, which he put down on the table. Schwartz rose, studying Lloyd. He shook the sheriff's hand when it was offered. His eyes, though, were fixed on Lloyd. The sheriff caught this, but smiled pleasantly and told Schwartz it was good to see him again.

"Lloyd," he said, and nodded at him. He lifted a chair from the corner, put it at the head of the table, and sat.

"I think I need a little more time to consult with my client," Schwartz said.

The sheriff pressed his fingers a few times on top of the folders. "Okay. How much time do you think you'll need?"

"We don't need no more time," Lloyd said, rocking back and forth in his chair. "I'm ready."

"I'd like to look at what you've got there first."

"But that wasn't the agreement, Mr. Schwartz."

"Come on," Lloyd said. "I'm ready."

"Why don't you listen to your client?"

Looking from Lloyd to the sheriff, Schwartz paled. He seemed pinned in place for a moment; then he took off his glasses and rubbed them on his shirt. He put them on again. Sheriff Lynch stared at the stack of folders, his fingertips resting on them like a pianist's, his expression one of patient indulgence toward a child who was finishing a noisy tantrum. Lloyd clenched his hands between his thighs, wondering what would be revealed to him.

"Do you mind if I stand?" Schwartz said.

"Go right ahead." Sheriff Lynch pressed his fingers again to the top folder, as if for luck or in valediction, took it from the stack, and opened it in front of Lloyd. Lloyd did not see at first what was there, because Schwartz had made a sudden movement toward the table, but Sheriff Lynch, with the slightest warning lift of his hand, checked him. He faced Schwartz a moment and then turned to Lloyd.

"Go ahead, son," he said. "Tell me what you see."

When Lloyd looked down, he was disappointed. It was another one of those crazy tests. He saw shapes of red and pink and green and black. It was the inkblot test, only in color. He studied more closely to try and make sense of it. He realized it was a picture of something. He realized what it was.

"I think I got it," he said to the sheriff. The sheriff nodded to help him along. "It's a sheep," Lloyd said.

"Look at it a little more closely, son." Lloyd saw Schwartz again move and the sheriff again check him while keeping his neutral blue eyes on Lloyd. Lloyd went back to the picture. He had missed some details.

"It's a sheep gutted after slaughter," he said.

"Turn the picture over, son," the sheriff said. This time Schwartz did not move and the sheriff did not hold up his hand. Paper-clipped to the back of the picture Lloyd found a smaller photo of a young woman. She had straight brown hair, wore blue jeans and a red-and-white checkered blouse, and sat in a lawn chair, smiling to please the person who held the camera.

"Now turn the picture over again," the sheriff said, in his calm, steady voice. "What do you see?"

Lloyd tried to puzzle it out, but he couldn't. There must be something he wasn't seeing. He studied the picture. As he followed the shapes and colors of the sheep's emptied body, a trickle of pity formed in him for all three of them—the woman, the sheep, and himself—and dropped somewhere inside him. The glaze over him tightened. He could only tell the sheriff that he saw a sheep.

After the sheriff left, gathering the folders under his arm, the room went back to its silence.

"If I'd known," Schwartz said, "I would've had him testify."

"What?" Lloyd said. "If you'd known what?"

"Never mind." Shielding his face with his pale fingers, Schwartz laid his other hand on Lloyd's shoulder. "Never mind, Lloyd. You're perfect the way you are."

They had sat there a long time, the sheriff opening a folder in front of him, asking him the same questions, and then putting it aside. And in each folder Lloyd had seen the same things: a gutted sheep and a pretty young woman. He knew that the sheriff was trying to do something to help him get right, but as the glaze thickened, that chance seemed ever more remote. Before he left, the sheriff had nodded to Lloyd, to acknowledge that he had found his answer, but his gesture was as distant as that of a receding figure waving a ship out to sea. With each drop of pity Lloyd felt himself borne away yet drowning, so that he knew the heart of the man in the execution chamber, suffocating and unable to move, and he wondered how he would survive in this new and airless world.

———

A native of Houston, Texas, Thomas H. McNeely has recently received fellowships from the MacDowell Colony and the J. Frank Dobie Memorial Project at the University of Texas at Austin. "Sheep" is his first published work of fiction. He teaches at the Grub Street Writers' Workshop and Emerson College in Boston, where he is currently at work on a collection of linked stories.

TIM MULAVEY

The idea for "Sheep" came to me while I was working for a nonprofit law firm in Texas that defended death row cases. At the time, I spent many hours looking at crime scene photos, and many hours with the men who committed those crimes. I was struck by my inability to connect what I saw in those pictures with the men I came to know. That moment, and the comparisons it suggested about the criminal justice system's inability to consider how the men they sought to execute came to be who they were, formed the kernel of the story.

All of my models for Lloyd, unfortunately, are dead. The story is a tribute to their courage, and the courage of the people who defended them.

D. *Winston Brown*

IN THE DOORWAY OF RHEE'S JAZZ JOINT

(from *Yemassee*)

I

In walked Russell.

A man in the doorway of a bar—in the doorway of Rhee's Jazz Joint—is no longer a man, he is a piece of an atmosphere and its history, engulfed within a tiny, tight, brass and whiskey and wood world of played and unplayed notes, existing both behind and ahead of time.

That's what Russell Claypool liked most about Rhee's. It was comfortable.

Letohatchee Davenport took down a glass from behind the bar. She dropped in a couple of ice cubes, poured in some scotch, and set the drink on the counter.

"L.C. been in?" Russell picked up the Johnny Walker Red sitting on the counter.

"I haven't seen him," she said.

"What about Dillard or Lester?"

"No, Russell." Letohatchee waved her hand. "Look around. There's only two people here. And no, none of them are here, not Dillard Cleckler, not sorry-ass Lester Sheets, not L.C. Scooba, and not Maxine Kirk."

They stared at each other. Russell watched the face he had seen for most of his fifty-six years. Letohatchee and Russell had fought with each other all their lives, from the time that Letohatchee had moved to Birmingham with her grandparents when she was six. Russell still wore a scar in his left cheekbone where Letohatchee cut him with the top of a can of Pet Milk because he told her that children whose parents die can't have children.

Letohatchee owned Rhee's. Close to twenty years ago she had won it playing poker from a hustler named Reese Alexander, who had hustled it from Lester Sheets shooting craps behind the Dumpster in the alley. When Lester wouldn't take it back because he felt too dumb for losing it, Russell convinced Letohatchee to hire someone to run it for her. For the last two years, since retiring from her day job, Letohatchee ran Rhee's herself with a smile that made it a sin not to order less than three drinks. In that year, there had only been two shootings at Rhee's, one inside—people had stepped over the corpse on their way out—and one outside. Last night.

Russell and his friends had been gathering there most Mondays, Wednesdays, and Saturdays since before Letohatchee owned it.

"You holding back ain't you?" Russell held his glass up between them.

"You'll be here all night," Letohatchee said.

Russell sipped from the glass while he looked around the room. He didn't know the few people in there. His watch read six. They were late, he thought. He and his friends usually got there around five-thirty.

"Lettie, you think they heard?" Russell said, turning back to the bar.

"Of course they heard," she said, kept cutting limes.

"Maybe they didn't," Russell said. "They would have been here, wouldn't have been late, not if they heard."

"They'll be here, Russ." Letohatchee freshened his drink. "What'cha want to hear?" She began scanning the shelf of CD's.

"You know that boy's blood still on the ground?"

"Maybe I'll play one of the young cats," Letohatchee said. "How about some Josh Redman?"

"Children," Russell said, "little children walking right through it, like it's not even there."

"Better yet, I think I'll play some Cannonball."

"And they're stepping right under the police tape like it's a game."

"Or maybe Mingus." Letohatchee had turned to the stereo.

"I bet people don't even know his name. I had to think twice myself, and I've known the boy all my life. It hadn't even been twenty-four hours, and I bet they already forgot his name."

"I got it. We need some blues. That's what we need to hear. Some good ol' slap yo' daddy down-home stanky blues. How about—"

"You remember his name, Lettie? What was his name?"

"Zakie Salem." Letohatchee turned back to Russell, leaned on the bar between them. "Zakie Salem. And it's still his name. He's not dead, Russell. He's not dead, so quit speaking of him in the past tense. You act like only you know the boy. He's been coming in and out of here with those petitions and making speeches and asking for votes for years. Now have a drink and listen to Howlin' Wolf while I finish getting ready for tonight. You know when Arthur Salem plays we get some young people in here."

"I just wanted to know if you remembered what his name was— is." Russell leaned over the bar on his elbows. "Can I have a little more scotch," he said, and then, as if he were a child begging for more, "pleeeease?"

2

In walked L.C.

L.C. Scooba had deadstill eyes set deep in a face controlled by its carved cracks running along his cheeks and splaying outward from the corners of his eyes, the severity of which resembled—in his leathered face—a weathered and crumbling tombstone, full of sharp fissures. He only drank beer. Miller Lite.

"Over here, L.C." Russell had staked out their table. Rhee's was box shaped, and Russell and his friends always sat at a table against the wall nearest the bar, so they could watch people from a distance, and when they came in the door.

L.C. grabbed the chilled glass of Miller Lite, then sat down with Russell, both of them angled where they could see the entire room. Howlin' Wolf seeped down out of the speakers in the ceiling's corners.

"You late," Russell said.

"Last I heard, you ain't give birth to none of my children." L.C. peered over a pair of black half-frames.

"You hear about Zakie Salem?" Russell asked.

"Two bullet wounds. One in the thigh, went straight through, and one in the abdomen. Lost a lot of blood, but he'll be alright."

"I forget your wife's a nurse," Russell said. "I must be losing my mind."

L.C. looked at the door.

So did Russell.

A tall young man and a woman in a red business suit came in. Her skirt was short, halfway up her thigh. "Young people," Russell said to himself. He watched the couple sit next to the spherical stage at the other end of the room.

"When was the last time you saw him?" Russell turned back to L.C.

"Don't know. But he's been calling me at my office for weeks," L.C. answered.

"What did he want?"

"Money, I suppose," L.C. said. "I hear he's trying to run for city council again."

"He's been calling me too," Russell said, "to come talk about Dynamite Hill to those kids he teaches. What he needs to do is teach them how to talk so when they go to college on a sport's scholarship, they won't sound stupid on interviews, embarrassing everybody." Russell removed the stirrer from his drink. "I remember when that boy was still a little boy, around ten or so. Now *he* was bad. One day that little Zakie ran right into my car. I was on my way to work and that boy runs slap into the passenger door on that blue Ford I used to have. I was at that red light by the school's run-down basketball court when I see a bag come flying over the fence and little Zakie right behind. He was still knee-high to a grasshopper. He picks up the bag and runs straight at my car, looking back the whole time to make sure no one's following him. Then *bam*. He thumps right into the door. I know he's cutting class, but I ask where he rushing off to, anyway. He looks square into my eyes, just like Rev. Hazzard does sometimes, looks square at me, and says, 'I'm going home, Mr. Claypool, to turn my roast or it'll burn.' All I could do was laugh. That afternoon—I couldn't turn him in after hearing that story—I told him about Dynamite Hill, about how white folks bombed all those houses around Center Street. You know, I haven't talked about it since."

Russell finished his drink.

"I was there, Russell, just like you," L.C. said. Then, "You talk to his daddy yet?"

3

In walked Dillard.

Dillard Cleckler, III, co-owner of Dillard's Soul Food Emporium, I and II, always seemed to enjoy crowds, even small ones like what was gathering slowly in Rhee's. Talking to people, whether they listened or not. About anything, though his most consistent topic was food. Dillard was a thin man with thin arms usually engaged in some sort of odd gesticulation, as if not having food in front of him to prepare left him in a quandary about what to do with his arms. It seemed he could seldom decide.

"L.C.," Dillard said, approaching the table, "Russell. What are you guys drinking?" He waved his hand at Letohatchee until she came to the table. "Give my friends here another whatever, Lettie." He passed his hand at the glasses on the table. "Give me a Hennessy, please."

"Where's Maxi?" Russell knew Maxine wouldn't be too far from her husband. She managed the Emporium II, and Dillard's drinking. Russell had known Maxine since high school when their parents had set them up on their only date, which amounted to rolling around in an old Plymouth Satellite while drinking three entire fifths of Thunderbird with grape Kool-Aid mixed in. She was the only one who hadn't thrown up that night.

"She's closing up Soul Food Emporium II." With each syllable Dillard swung his arms like an orchestra conductor. He had become prone to do the sweeping movements since going to the symphony last month. His arms would swing like sleeved broomsticks. "Is that Lil' Dime over there? That fool owes me money."

Russell watched Dillard swerve through the tables.

L.C. rose also, going the other way, toward the back of the club where the restrooms were. He couldn't lick an ice cube without having to pee ten minutes later, Russell thought.

People had begun to fill the vacant chairs at the tables nearest the stage, and there were a few more people at the bar. But it was no longer Russell's crowd. His friends were either too busy dying or staying at home praying to keep from dying. The older his friends got, the easier they seemed to find religion. This crowd was young. Rhee's had become a young joint on certain nights, especially when Arthur Salem's quartet played; it would be full of the kind of men, what they used to call *clean* or say were sharp as a mosquito's peter, the type man that Russell could recall being at a previous time in his life; and there would be the kind of women that Russell could remember saying were fine as cat hair, the kind that could get his whole check on payday, the kind he would fall in love with every Friday night.

But it was the absence that moved through him like the slow trickle of ice melting, a drip then another, cooling his lungs, cooling his breath. The absence of that clipboard stacked with petitions for better trash pick-up, better school lunch programs, better policing; Zakie Salem never set foot to ground without his clipboard. "Mr. Claypool," he would say, "I know you ain't down with Islam, but this is for the neighborhood. I'm workin' with those brothers 'cause they doin' somethin' good." And Russell would say, "Boy, ain't nothing I hate more than youthful arrogance. You don't know about this neighborhood's needs. I could tell you stories, boy." Then Zakie would say, "I know, like the one about Dynamite Hill. That's what I want you to tell." Then Russell would say, weary and ready to end it, "Ain't nothing left to say Zakie. It's a different time now." Then Zakie would be at another table, talking to other people, but still glancing back at Russell. Might stop back by before he left.

In walked Maxine,
straight to the bar. A word with Letohatchee. A shot of whiskey. A Vodka Cranberry. She surveyed the people. Maxine Kirk—she had refused to be called Cleckler despite marrying Dillard—had the kind of face that could control her feelings no matter the intensity. She walked with her shoulders high and her chin higher. Her body was fleshy in a way that Russell used to call down-home.

"How you doing, Maxi?" Russell stood when she reached the table.

"Zakie Salem's father was in my place tonight," she said.

"Arthur?" Russell said. "How was he?"

"He was soppin' up mashed potatoes and gravy like he had a tapeworm," she said in an exaggerated tone, then, "How do you think he's doing? The man's son was just shot. Jesus Christ. How is he doing," she repeated. "What kind of question is that? How is the man doing a day after his son gets shot? The man's son stomach splayed out like a bucket of chitlins, he won't set foot in a hospital, and you ask how the man—"

"Cool down, Maxi," Russell said. "Just cool down."

Duke Ellington's big band played low through the stereo. The quiet chatter of conversation had risen, spread throughout the club. Three guys were halfheartedly setting up instruments on the stage.

"I know the man is hurting. I feel for him," Russell said. "I just wondered how he was coping. That's all."

"He asked about you, Russ."

"Me? Why?"

"Don't know," Maxine said.

"You didn't ask?"

"What'd I say, Russ? Jesus Christ." Maxine sipped the cranberry-colored drink. "Just cool down," she said. "Cool down." She said down like dowwwwwwwwwn.

Russell popped a piece of peppermint into his mouth, scanned the people.

"Did you help him out?" Russell asked.

"Help who?"

"Zakie," Russell said. "With any of the thousand projects he's always working on."

"Now, Russell," Maxine said, "you know I don't support those Muslim niggers. If they can't eat my pork ribs, I damn sure ain't eating no damn bean pies. Besides, Dillard and I give money every month to the church."

"You haven't been to church since King was shot," Russell said.

"You only go on communion Sunday to get free wine," Maxine said.

Russell paused, then said, "You know they only serve that sorry grape juice now. I can get Welch's at home. But at least I go, sometimes."

4

In walked Kufere,

barreling straight toward the bar, a hovering shaved head on a thick neck spearing through the people near the door. He was tall. He was taller than Zakie, his older brother. Kurfere Salem's name was the only surviving evidence of his parents' involvement in the sixties Civil Rights struggle and the Black Power Movement. That and a picture of him when he was seven with an afro that could soak up the Atlantic doing his best black-gloved impersonation of Tommy Smith at the '68 Olympics in Mexico City.

Russell could tell he was upset. Even as a kid, Kufere had never been able to keep his emotions below his face. He must be close to twenty-five or thirty, Russell thought. Kufere bent his mass across the bar to talk to Letohatchee, who nodded her head from side to side, shrugged her shoulders, nodded her head again, then turned toward Russell's table. Kufere turned also.

"Isn't that one of those Salem boys?" L.C. said.

Russell hadn't noticed L.C. return. Maxine craned her neck to see behind her.

"That's the youngest one," Maxine said. "Koofoo, or kookoofer, something like that. He comes in the Emporium sometimes. Gets nothing but vegetables."

During the time it took Kufere to walk the thirty or so feet to their table, Russell fought with himself, the way he had when he first heard Kufere's brother had been shot.

Though sitting, Russell was eye to eye, eye to eye with Kufere but he saw Zakie, even though the two only somewhat favored each other. The wide chin, the naked eyes, those were the same. But it was last Thursday, again, and Zakie was speaking. Russell saying yes to make the boy shut up, yes, he'll meet him Friday night even though he won't, and he knows it because he's playing poker with some Masons out in Bessemer. The boy is pushy and Russell doesn't like to be pushed anymore, likes to exist in the simplicity of watching people in Rhee's, their half-smiles and crossed thighs still naturally tight, the smoke blown up and out the corners of dark lips, and the Johnny Walker Red Letohatchee knows to put on the bar when he enters; to listen to Arthur Salem's weekend sax make a young couple sometimes lean in close over their drinks, or cheek to cheek bellyrub a little bit on the dance floor. But not to talk of the distance he came through to enjoy those things, the distance he survived.

Zakie was saying these things now, Russell thinking them, Zakie saying them now the same way he said them then, Thursday, when Russell said yes though he felt, knew, that no was the only answer.

He could hear Zakie saying them as he watched the tight set of Kufere's jaw.

"How's your brother doing?" Maxine asked when Kufere was next to her.

"Ms. Kirk." He said this without looking away from Russell's stare. Then, "Where were you, Mr. Claypool? Were you drunk? Were you trying to fuck some woman half your age?"

"Look here, boy," Russell said. "I was—"

"No. *You* look here. And listen close. I don't like you, and I don't care about all this crap you supposedly went through in the sixties." He leaned onto the table. "All my brother wanted to do was talk to you. He waited outside this damn club until one in the morning. Three hours he waited on you. You're no better than the white folks that screwed up your mind. At least they used to give Zakie donations when he was willing to go over the mountain begging. All you do is sit in this bar and drink. I can't remember a time when I didn't think you were a drunk. That's all I remember about you." His voice was now competing with the music and chatter.

"That was the hospital calling." Letohatchee stood behind Kufere, a hand on his shoulder. "Your sister says you better get back to the hospital. Zakie's condition is worse."

Kufere didn't move, but Russell could see the minute changes in his face. Worry worked between the web of redness into the granite eyes. Russell had nothing to say to the boy. While Kufere had spoken, Russell gathered words for the boy, but now, they were like grains of salt dissolving on his tongue. He watched Kufere straighten. In the moment before Kufere turned to leave, Russell thought he saw in Kufere's face something alongside the anger and worry. Disappointment. Kind of an instinctual disappointment, like when you're upset that something has changed, but you can't remember what life was like before. You don't forget, can't forget, because you really can't remember what the sudden lightness in your stomach, or the quick weakness in your knees is urging you to know.

"I tell you one thing," Dillard plopped down into the empty

seat. "The koofoon boy is right about one thing. White folks. That boy's brother got shot because white folk don't like black folk that don't pray to their God. You know that Koofoofoon, or whatever his name is, don't believe in God. He believes in Allah. What kind of shit is that? Allah."

"That's his brother that hangs with the Muslims," L.C. said. "That was Kufere in here. He's the one that played football at Auburn."

Dillard glanced toward the door as if Kufere were still there.

"I know that boy, too," Dillard said. "He got run away from Auburn for screwing some pink toes. See, it's just like I was saying before. White folk. They'll let a nigger come pull a plow, but when he starts getting too many pieces of white p—"

"Jesus Christ, Dillard. Don't you ever shut up?" Maxine said. She asked Letohatchee for another drink.

"Sure," Letohatchee said, "I'll put it on Russell's tab. And by the way, I made that up about the hospital calling. I didn't want that boy to bust up my bar in the process of cracking open Russell's head."

Dillard looked around for a couple of seconds, then, "You know those Muslims want their own city. They want Africa."

"It's people like you, Dillard," L.C. said, "stupid people like you that call Africa a city that made someone have to create Sesame Street. I think you got your mama's ignorance. Your mama so dumb, she thought a quarterback was a refund."

"Yo' mama so stupid, when it came time to name you she couldn't remember more than two letters at a time, so she just gave you two initials. She couldn't even think of a name for you. Just L.C. Here's a dollar, go buy yourself a vowel so you can turn those initials into a name." Dillard glared at L.C. "Anyway, I know Africa's not a city. I meant they'll name it Africa. Can you imagine living in Africa, South Dakota? White folk would freak." Dillard leaned forward, laughing.

"You know what?" L.C. said, "children these days are crazy. I never would have done anything like Kufere did tonight. Not at twenty, thirty, forty, or fifty, not ever. And you can't say anything to them. They don't listen to anything." He finished his Miller Lite. "I think that's because they don't know anything and think they know everything. Dillard's right about one thing. They spend so much time learning how to kiss white folks' ass they don't learn how to treat grown folk with respect. I could tell them a few things about this world."

Russell knew his friends were trying hard to make him forget about Kufere, but the glacial trickle was still making him shiver inside. His legs stiffened. He needed to stretch them. "I'm going to the bar," he said. "Anybody need anything?" He felt heavy when he stood, like someone large was riding piggyback on him. Dillard placed an order for another Hennessy. Maxine rolled her eyes at her husband. L.C. said bring him another Miller Lite while he went to the bathroom. Then, Maxine started humming along with the Thelonious Monk tune plinking smooth out of the speakers.

As Russell walked to the bar, he recognized the tune but couldn't remember the name. Monk's piano Russell knew anywhere. The notes dropped odd around him, odd dropping odd and between the dropping notes bent time like a minor chord mirage hovering in front of Russell, odd notes like the trinkle tinkle of dropping spoons into metal tins, or rainwater tap tap tapping ploptapping on corrugated tin roofs, bing bang, the trinkle and tinkle and plot and tap dropped odd like odd wasn't odd. Not odd at all.

Like an uglybeauty.

I'm having an epistrophy, Russell said to himself, and smirked.

5

In walked Arthur.

Arthur Henry Salem wore stress on his face which made it look like he was reading intensely at all times, even when there was no book in front of his searching eyes. When he laid his hands on the bar, fingers stretched long and sleek like thin hazelnut-colored skis, but with thick knots at the knuckles. A thin man, Arthur Salem had about as much presence in his clothes as driftwood buried in shallow sand. But Russell knew without looking who was standing next to him.

"What'cha need Art?" Letohatchee said.

"Bourbon and water."

"What kind of bourbon you working on tonight?"

"Basil Hayden," Arthur Salem said, "and forget about the water. Just ice. One cube."

Russell waited until after Arthur Salem sipped his bourbon.

"Arthur, your boy was in here earlier, looking for you," Russell said.

"I know," Arthur Salem said. "He wants me to go to the hospital, but I don't go in them anymore. Haven't been in one since sixty-nine when those crackers strung my brother to that tree out in Leeds and chopped his dick off."

The story was familiar to Russell, and avoidable. At least talking about it was avoidable. It was hard to control what swam through his mind while asleep, the distorted images of corpses and bodies beaten up to, and sometimes beyond recognition. Violence was what he dreamed, what he once lived in the shadow of, but no longer discussed. To talk about it was to make it real, and he refused.

"I don't guess you're playing tonight?" Russell said, even though he had already noticed Arthur Salem's saxophone, which he never let get more than an arm's length away, was not with him.

"My own boy is in the hospital and all I do is call to check on him."

"You know he was supposed to meet me here last night?" Russell said.

"I was here last night," Arthur Salem said, "heard the two shots." He sipped his bourbon, let its warmth settle in his mouth before he swallowed. "I just thought it was another nigger dead. Just another nigger shot and dead. One less nigger to try and steal my horn when I'm leaving a club late."

"I didn't show up here last night," Russell said, "knew I wouldn't."

"He doesn't like being in here when I'm playing. I've tried to teach him about jazz, but he won't listen. Always talking about Islam. Allah." Arthur turned to Russell. "He don't understand, Russell."

The thought had been there. On his tongue. *We* don't understand, three words sitting like three gains of salt on his tongue, the words dissolved into the moistness of his tongue and mouth, unspoken. Russell felt them there while Arthur Salem had talked, and when the feeling left, Arthur Salem had told Russell that Zakie shouldn't have been waiting outside in the first place, that Zakie was the one to blame, that Russell had always been like an uncle to Zakie and Kufere, that Russell had done all that could be expected.

Arthur Salem finished his drink, then drifted out through the chattering people until he reached the doorway. Russell watched him crack the door and stop. Arthur looked back for a second into Rhee's. Through the sliver of an opening, a blade of pale light cut across Arthur Salem's face so that an eye and below was the pale lifeless color of the lamp on the wall outside the door, the other half of his face still in the dim and warm light of the bar. Then he left, and when the door shut, it cut off the outer glow seeping in. Russell thought of a vault door lumbering to closed, but he heard no deep thud of closure, no heavy thud of closure.

The song changed.

Another Monk tune.

In his chest, as he breathed in then out, Russell could still feel the cold trickle crawl slow along his lungs, small icy rivulets that made him shiver under his skin as if he were breathing deeply the frigid air in a closed freezer; the shiver stopped — it just stopped — and he sensed as if he, Russell Claypool, had just walked in.

D. Winston Brown is a writer living and working in Florence, Alabama. He is currently completing work on a novel entitled *Blue Sugar*.

PATRICE TONEY

"*In the Doorway of Rhee's Jazz Joint*" *is rooted in the clash between the savage history of the South and its modern consciousness. The struggle to forget and the inevitability of memory and legacy provide the canvas for this piece. The story is peopled with characters who live as fragments, and by others who have trained themselves to avoid the jagged edges of their own blues.*

Tim Gautreaux

DANCING WITH THE ONE-ARMED GAL

(from *Zoetrope*)

On Saturday, Iry Boudreaux's girlfriend fired him. The young man had just come on shift at the icehouse and was seated in a wooden chair under the big wall-mounted ammonia gauge, reading a cowboy novel. The room was full of whirring, hot machinery, antique compressors run by long flat belts, black-enameled electric motors that turned for months at a time without stopping. His book was a good one, and he was lost in a series of fast-moving chapters involving long-distance rifle duels, cattle massacres, and an elaborate saloon fight that lasted thirty pages. At the edge of his attention Iry heard something like a bird squawk, but he continued to read. He turned a page, trying to ignore an intermittent iron-on-iron binding noise rising above the usual lubricated whir of the engine room. Suddenly the old number two ammonia compressor began to shriek and bang. Before Iry could get to the power box to shut off the motor, a piston rod broke, and the compressor knocked its brains out. In a few seconds Babette, Iry's girlfriend, ran into the engine room from the direction of the office. White smoke was leaking from a compressor's crankshaft compartment, and Iry bent down to open the little cast-iron inspection door.

Babette pointed a red fingernail to the sight glass of the brass lubricator. "You let it run out of oil," she said, putting the heel of her other hand on her forehead. "I can't believe it."

Iry's face flushed as he looked in to see the chewed crankshaft glowing dully in the dark base of the engine. "Son of a bitch," he said, shaking his head.

She bent over his shoulder, and he could smell the mango perfume that he had given her for Christmas. Her dark hair touched his left earlobe for an instant, and then she straightened up. He knew that she was doing the math already, and numbers were her strength: cubic feet of crushed ice, tons of block ice. "Iry, the damned piston rod seized on the crankshaft," she said, her voice rising. "The foundry'll have to cast new parts, and we're looking at six or seven thousand dollars, plus the downtime." Now she was yelling.

He had let both Babette and the machine down. He looked up to say something and saw that she was staring at the cowboy novel he'd left open facedown on his folding chair.

"I don't know, Iry. The owner's gonna have a hard time with this." She folded her arms. "He's gonna want to know what you were doing, and I'm gonna tell him." She gestured toward the book.

"Look, I checked the damned oil level when I came on shift. It wasn't my fault."

She looked at him hard. "Iry, the machine didn't commit suicide." She licked a finger and touched it to the hot iron. "Mr. Lanier has been after me to cut staff, and now this." She closed her eyes for a moment, then opened them and shook her head. "You need to get away from this place."

He pulled a shop rag from the back pocket of his jeans and wiped his hands, feeling something important coming. "What's that mean?"

She looked at him the way a boss looks at an employee. "I'm going to lay you off."

"You're firing me?"

"Last time we had a compressor rebuilt we were down for a long time. Come back, maybe next month, and we'll see."

"Aw, come on. Let's go out tonight and talk about this over a couple of cold ones." He pushed back his baseball cap and gave her a grin, showing his big teeth.

She shook her head. "You need a vacation is what you need. You ought to go somewhere. Get out of town, you know?"

"A vacation."

"Yeah. Get your head out of those books. Go look at some real stuff."

"Who's gonna watch the compressor that's still working?"

Babette took his shop rag from him and wiped a spot of oil from a glossy fingernail. "The new man who watches during your lunch break. Mauvais."

"Mauvais can't operate a roll of toilet paper."

"We'll just be making party ice after this." She looked at him. "At least he's never let the oil get low."

He glanced at her dark hair, trying to remember the last time he'd touched it.

The next morning Iry got up and drove through the rain to early Mass. The church was full of retirees, people who had stayed on the same job all their lives. The priest talked about the dignity of work, and Iry stared at the floor. He felt that his relationship with Babette, such as it was, might be over. He remembered how she had looked at him the last time, trying to figure why a good engineer would let the oil run out. Maybe he wasn't a good engineer—or a good anything. After Mass he stood in the drizzle on the stone steps of the church watching people get into their cars, waved at a few, and suddenly felt inauthentic, as though he no longer owned a real position in his little town of Grand Crapaud. He drove to his rent house and called his mother with instructions to come over and water his tomato patch once a day. Then he packed up his old red Jeep Cherokee and headed west toward Texas.

After a few miles, the two-lane highway broke out of a littered swamp and began to cut through sugarcane fields. The rain clouds burned off, and the new-growth cane flowed to the horizons in deep, apple-green lawns. Iry's spirits rose as he watched herons and cranes slow-stepping through irrigation ditches. He realized that what Babette had said about a vacation was true.

He avoided the main highway and drove the flatland past gray cypress houses and their manicured vegetable gardens. Through sleepy, live oak–covered settlements the old Jeep bobbed along with a steady grinding noise that made Iry feel primitive and adventurous.

On the outskirts of New Iberia he saw something unusual: a one-armed woman, wearing a short-sleeve navy-blue dress, was hitchhiking. She was standing next to a big tan suitcase a hundred yards west of a rusty Grenada parked in the weeds with its hood raised. Iry seldom picked up anyone from the side of the road, but this woman's right arm was missing below the elbow, and she was thumbing with her left hand, which looked awkward as she held it across her breast. He realized that she would only look normal thumbing a ride on the left side of a highway, where no one would stop for her.

When he pulled off, she didn't come to the car at first, but bent down to look through the back window at him. He opened the passenger door and she came to it and ducked her head in, studying him a moment. Iry looked down at his little paunch and resettled his baseball cap.

"You need a ride?"

"Yes." She was pale, late thirties or so, with dark wiry hair spiked straight up in a tall, scary crew cut, and tawny skin. He thought she looked like a woman he'd once seen on TV who was beating a policeman with a sign on a stick. She seemed very nervous. "But I was hoping for a ride from a woman," she said.

"I can't afford no sex-change operation," he told her. "That your car?"

She looked back down the road. "Yes. At least it was. A man just pulled off who made all kinds of mystifying mechanical statements about it, saying it'd take three thousand dollars worth of work to make it worth four hundred. I guess I'll just leave it." She sniffed the air inside the Jeep. "It's awfully hot and I hate to pass up a ride."

He turned and looked at a large dark spray of oil under the engine. "That man say it threw a rod cap through the oil pan?"

She gave him an annoyed look. "All you men speak this same private language."

He nodded, agreeing. "You don't have to be afraid of me, but if you want to wait for a woman, I'll just get going."

"Well, I don't really relate well to most men." She looked at him carefully for a moment, and then announced, "I'm a lesbian."

Iry pretended to look at something in his rearview mirror, wondering what kind of person would say that to a stranger. He figured she must be an intellectual, educated in the north. "That mean you like women?" he asked.

"Yes."

He pursed his lips and saw the day's heat burning her cheeks. "Well, I guess we got something in common."

She frowned at this but wrestled her suitcase into the backseat anyway, got in, and pulled the door shut, adjusting the air-conditioner vents to blow on her face. "My name is Claudine Glover."

"Iry Boudreaux." He turned back onto the highway and said nothing, sensing that she'd begin to speak at any moment, and after a mile or so she did, breathlessly, talking with her hand.

"I've never hitchhiked before. I was on my way from New Orleans where I just lost my job, of all things. My car was a little old, maybe too old, I think, and it started to smoke and bang around Franklin. I just need a ride to the next decent-size town so I can get to an airport and fly home to El Paso where my mother . . ." She went on and on. Every hitchhiker he'd ever picked up had told Iry their life story. Some of them had started with their birth. One man named Cathell began with a relative who made armor in the Middle Ages and summarized his family tree all the way to his own son, who made wrist braces for video-game addicts with carpal tunnel syndrome. Iry guessed people thought they owed you an explanation when you helped them out.

"We got something else in common," he told her.

"What?"

"I just got fired myself." He then told her what he did for a living. She listened but seemed unimpressed.

"Well, I'm sorry for you, all right. But you can probably go anywhere and find another icehouse or whatever to operate, can't you?"

He admitted that this was so.

"I am a professor of women's studies," she said, her voice nipping like a Chihuahua's at the syllables. "It took me a long time to get that position and now, after four years of teaching, I lost it." She raised her hand and covered her face with it.

He rolled the phrase *women's studies* around in his head for a moment, wondering if she was some kind of nurse. "Aw, you'll find some more gals to teach," he said at last. He was afraid she was going to cry. It was forty minutes to Lafayette and its little airport, and he didn't want to experience the woman's emotional meltdown all the way there.

She blinked and sniffed. "You don't know how it is in academics. My Ph.D. is not from the best institution. You've got to find your little niche and hold on, because if you don't get tenure, you're pretty much done for. Oh, I can't believe I'm saying this to a stranger." She gave him a lightning glance. "Does this airport have jets?"

"I don't think so. Those egg-beater planes take off for Baton Rouge and New Orleans."

She did begin to cry then. "I hate propeller aircraft," she sobbed.

He looked to the south across a vast field of rice and noticed a thunderstorm trying to climb out of the Gulf. If he didn't have to stop in Lafayette, he might be able to outrun it. "Hey, c'mon. I'm going all the way through Houston. I can drop you by Hobby. They got planes big as ocean liners."

She wiped her nose with a Kleenex and put it into a shoulder bag. She looked as though she were willing herself to be calm. After a few miles, she looked out at the open land whizzing by, at egrets stabbing for crawfish. She sniffed and wiped her nose again. "Where are you going, anyway?"

"I don't know. Just out west. Maybe go to a couple of cowboy museums. Look at some cactus. See a rodeo." He glanced at her worried face. "What you gonna do when you get home?"

She gave a little mocking laugh. "Cut my throat."

The woman talked and talked. Iry stopped for lunch over the Texas border at a roadside café, figuring a meal would stop her mouth for a while. Their wobbly table was next to a taped-up picture window. He drank a beer with his hamburger, and she told him that she was originally hired because she was a woman and that her gender helped the college administration meet a quota. "Well," he said, wiping mustard off his shirt, "whatever the hell works."

"After I'd been there a year, the English department began considering hiring a black man to replace me."

He picked up his burger and shook it at her. "Yeah, I missed out on a job like that once. The company had to have one black guy at least on this oil rig, so they hired this New Orleans dude instead of me and put him on Magnolia number twenty-two with a bunch of them old plowboys from central Mississippi. He lasted like a fart in a whirlwind."

Claudine raised her head a bit. "When I produced evidence of my own one-sixteenth African American blood, they let me stay on." Iry looked at her skin when she told him this. He'd thought she was from Cuba.

"During my second year, the department brought in other women's studies specialists, and at that point I stopped wearing my prosthesis, to emphasize the fact that I was not only black and a woman, but disabled as well." She waved away a fly. "But they still tried to get rid of me."

"Ain't you no good at teaching studying women?"

"My students liked me. I published articles and went to conferences." Claudine nibbled at the cheese sandwich she'd ordered, brushed crumbs off her dark dress, and put it back on the plate.

She looked at something invisible above Iry's head. It was clear that she did not understand what had happened to her. "They kept trying to let me go."

"That's a bitch."

She frowned and narrowed her eyes at him. "Yes, well, I wouldn't put it exactly in those words. When a search committee member told me they'd received an application from a gay, black, female double-amputee from Ghana, I reminded the committee that part of my childhood was spent in Mexico, and then I played my last card and came out as a lesbian." She picked up the dry sandwich and ate a little of the crust. Iry wondered if she was afraid that eating a juicy hamburger might poison her. "But it did no good. The college found someone more specialized, foreign, and incomplete than I could ever be."

He listened to her through the meal and decided that he'd rather spend eight hours a day with his tongue on a hot pipe than teach in a college.

The two-lane's abandoned filling stations and rickety vegetable stands began to bore him, so he switched over to the interstate. In the middle of a Houston traffic jam, Claudine suddenly asked if he was going all the way to San Antonio.

"Well, yeah, I guess." He felt what was coming and didn't know what to think. She talked of things he'd never known about: university politics, glass ceilings.

"You could save an hour by going straight through instead of detouring for the airport." The statement hung in the air like a temptation.

He shrugged. "Okay." So she kept riding with him west, out into the suburbs and beyond, entering a country that started to open up more as they glided past Katy and Frydek, Alleyton and Glidden. Claudine found a PBS broadcast and listened to a program of harpsichord music, but soon the weakling signal began to fade, succumbing to slide guitars and fiddles. To his surprise, she brought in a strong country station and listened for a while to a barroom ballad.

Claudine grabbed a fistful of her short hair and turned her head away from him to stare out into the brush. "When I hear that music," she began, "I think of my father and his Mexican wranglers sitting out under a tree in the backyard drinking long-necks in the wind. I think of their laughter and of not being able to understand any of it, because I never found one thing to laugh about in that blistered moonscape we lived on."

"You were raised on a ranch?"

"We raised cows and killed them, is what we did. The place was so big, I'd go off on horseback and actually get lost on our own land. One time, I rode out at night, and over a hill from the house there were so many stars and such a black nothing that I thought I'd fall up into the sky. I felt like a speck of dust. The sky was so big I stopped believing in God."

"You had your own horse?"

She looked at him, annoyed. "You are really fixated on the cowboy thing. Let me tell you about my horse." She held up her nub and her voice took on an edge. "He was a stallion who was always trying to run under a tree to rake me off his back. The last time I got on him, I was sixteen and had a date lined up for the prom with a nice boy. When I mounted the horse, he was balky and I could tell he didn't want to work that day. I gave him the spur at the corral gate, and he bolted to a shallow gully full of sharp rocks about the size of anvils. He lay down in them and rolled over like a dog with me in the stirrups. That's how I got this," she said, pointing at him with her stump.

"Ow."

"Now, do you have some ruined or missing part you want to tell me about?"

His mouth fell open for a moment, and he shook his head. Iry didn't say anything for nearly a hundred miles. He imagined that she might be unhappy because of her missing arm, but he'd known several maimed and happy ex–oilfield workers who drank beer with the hand they had left. He guessed at the type of information she taught in her university. Too much of all that weird man-hating stuff is bound to warp a woman, he thought. But from what she told him, he decided she'd been born unhappy, like his cousin Ted who'd won ninety-two thousand dollars in the lottery and yet had to be medicated when he found out about the tax due on his winnings.

The sun went low and red in the face. He drove past Luling and Seguin, where she asked him to stop at a lone roadside table sitting in a circle of walked-down grass. Iry got out and pulled off his cap, pawing at his short dark hair, which in texture resembled a storm-flattened cane field. They walked around the table like arthritic old people until their muscles stretched, and then they sat down on its cement benches. A barbed-wire fence ran fifteen feet from the table, and a Black Angus stepped up and looked at them, pressing its forehead against the top strand of wire. Iry was a town boy, unused to cattle, and examined the animal's slobbery nose, the plastic tag in its ear. Claudine picked up a rock the size of a quarter and threw it overhand, hitting the cow on the flank, causing it to wheel and walk off, mooing.

"I want to drive for a while," she told him.

They stayed in separate rooms in a Motel Six, and the next morning got up early and drove around San Antonio like a tourist couple. She mentioned several times that she wanted to get to El Paso as soon as possible, but he convinced her to stop at the Cowboy Museum, and they wandered from room to room looking at pictures of pioneer cattlemen, displays of branding irons, six-shooters, and leatherwork. Iry stared at the Winchesters, leggings, badges, and high-crown hats as though he were in the Louvre. At the last display case Claudine put her ruined arm on the glass. "This place feels like a tomb," she said. "A graveyard."

He fumbled with the two-page brochure that the woman at the desk had given him. "I don't know. It's pretty interesting. All these people came out here when this place was like some uninhabited planet. They made something out of nothing." He pointed at a gallery of mustachioed *vaqueros*. "What's the difference between one of these guys and Neil Armstrong?"

"Neil Armstrong was 239,000 miles from home."

He looked at the gray in her hair, wondering how much of it was premature. "What you think it was like in 1840 to get on a horse in St. Louis and ride to the Rio Grande, maybe seeing a half-dozen guys in between. I bet the feeling was the same."

"The romance of isolation," she said, heading for the door. "A vestige of obsolete paternalistic culture."

He made a face, as if her language had an odor. "What?"

She pushed open a glass door and walked out, pausing on the bottom stone step. "How many images of women are in this museum?"

"A few," he said. "I bet not too many gals got famous for roping steers and blowin' up Indians."

"It could have been their job. Why not?"

He stepped down past her and turned around to look up into her face. He started to say something, but feared the avalanche of four-syllable words he would trigger down the slope of her anger. Finally, he brought his big, thick-fingered hand up, matching it under her thin white one. "Here's one reason," he told her. "The other's this: women are more family, that is, social-like. They're people people."

She took back her hand. "That's a stereotype."

"Oh yeah? Well, look at us. I'm heading off into the brush to look at stuff, not people, stuff. You're going home to stay with Momma." He expected a scowl, but she looked at him closely, as though he had suddenly revealed another identity to her.

West of San Antonio they took highway 90. The weather became hotter, and the villages squatted at roadside, beaten down by the sun. Some towns like Hondo were brick-and-stucco hold-overs from the last century, while some were just low and poor and could have been in southern Illinois, except for the Mexicans and the drought. The land seemed to be tumbling away from water as he drove the old Jeep west, passing through broad thickets and then open country, a dry, beige world populated by cactus and mesquite, hotter and hotter as they moved toward Uvalde, Brackettville, and Del Rio. She talked over the tinny jar of the Jeep, and he listened and looked. West of Del Rio he stopped and wandered out in the brush to look at the sun-struck plants, and Claudine had to spend twenty minutes pulling needles from his hands.

They stopped at Langtry to see where Judge Roy Bean had presided.

"Now, I've got to concede that here's a real astronaut," she said, standing on a basketball-size rock at the edge of the parking lot. "A wild man comes where there is no law and just says, 'I am the law.'" She motioned with her good arm. "He staked out his territory."

Iry pulled off his cap and scratched his head. He was feeling hot and tired. "Ain't that what professors do? Like what you was telling me in the car?"

She gave him a startled look. "What?"

"I mean, like, you say I'm going to be the Tillie Dogschmidt scholar. She's my territory because I'm the first to read all her poems or whatever and study what all everybody's written about her. That what you called 'carving your niche,' right? Some kind of space you claim, just like the Judge here did?"

She raised her chin. "Don't belittle what I do."

"Hey, I think it's great. You invent yourself a job out of thin air. Wish I could do that." He thought about something a moment, and then pointed at her. "I read a old book called *Tex Goes to Europe*, and in it they talked about castrated opera singers. I bet if you found out some of those singers wrote stories, you know, about what a drag their life was, you could start up a whole department called Castrated Opera Singer Studies."

Her eyes opened a bit. "That's not how it works at all."

"It ain't?"

She stepped off of her rock. "No. Can we please get back on the road."

He pulled open the door to the Jeep and sat down, wincing at the hot vinyl.

She got in on her side. "Am I just not a real person to you?"

He turned up the air conditioner and frowned. "Am I to you?"

On the other side of Sanderson he got a glimpse of the Glass Mountains and sped up, his hands clenching and unclenching the steering wheel. The Jeep began to vibrate.

"They're not going anywhere," she told him.

"I don't get to see mountains too often."

"They're like everything else. You get used to them."

"You got a job lined up when you get to El Paso?"

"Mom knows the head of the English department at a community college in the desert. I just have to show up and sell myself."

"How you gonna do that?"

"Tell them how rare a bird I am. How I'll fill all their quotas in one shot. Aw, geez." She began digging in her bag. "I need a Prozac. I'm sinking down, down."

"Hey. We're heading toward the mountains."

She washed a pill down with a sip of hot Diet Sprite. "You bet."

"I think you ought to forget about all that quota shit. Just tell them you're a good teacher."

She seemed to bite the inside of her cheek. "The world's full of good teachers," she said.

They dawdled over the Glass Mountains and pulled into Alpine at supper. She told him that her credit card had room for one more motel, and they found a low, stucco place on the edge of downtown and got two rooms. The place had a lounge and café, and she met him for supper at eight, ordering a margarita as soon as she sat down at a table. With his burritos he ordered a beer, and the waitress checked his ID. As the girl tried to read the little numerals in the dim light, he looked around at the other customers and the large hats the men wore. Claudine was wearing blue jeans and a white short-sleeve blouse. He looked at her makeup and smelled her perfume, which was still burning off its alcohol, and felt vaguely apprehensive, as though he was having supper with his mother.

"You think it's all right to mix booze with your pills?" he asked.

She made a sweeping motion at him with her fingers. "Let's not worry about that." Her voice was tight.

"You think you got a shot at this teaching job?"

"Oh, they'll need somebody like me," she told him.

"You going to say to them that you're a good teacher? You know, show them those records you were telling me about? Those forms?"

"I'm a crippled black woman and a gay feminist." She put her elbows on the table. "I'm a shoo-in for the job."

He shook his head. "They won't hire you for those things."

"They'll at least need me to teach freshman English." She took a long drink. He wondered if she'd taken another pill in her room.

"Why don't you just tell them you're good with the students?"

"You have to be a certain kind of good," she said, her voice hardening.

"How's that?"

"You can't understand. They don't have people like me in icehouses."

A man in a wheelchair rolled through the front door. He wore a white cowboy hat, and his belt was cinched with a big buckle sporting a gold music note in the center. He coasted into the corner of the room behind a little dance floor and flipped switches on an amplifier. A computerized box came alive with blinking lights. Iry saw the man pick up a microphone and press a button on the box. The little café lounge filled with the sound of guitars and a bass beat, and the shriveled man in the wheelchair began to sing in a tough, accurate voice that was much bigger than he was. Two couples got up and danced. After the song, the food came, and Claudine ordered another margarita.

By the time the meal was over, she was sailing a bit, he could tell. Her eyelids seemed to be sticky, and she was blinking too much. He began to get sleepy and bored, and was wondering what was on the cigarette-branded television in his room, when she leaned over to him.

"Ivy," she began, "it's noisy in here."

"Iry," he said.

"What?"

"My name's Iry."

"Yes. Well. I'm going to get a fresh drink and walk back to my room." She looked at him for a second or two. "If you want to talk, come with me."

"No, I believe I'll check out what's on the tube," he told her.

"You'd rather watch TV than have a conversation with someone?" Her face twisted slightly, and he looked away.

"No, I mean, it might not look right, me going in your room." He felt silly as soon as he'd said it. Who, in Alpine, Texas, would give a damn what tourists from a thousand miles away did with their free time?

Claudine's face fell, and she sat back in her chair, staring toward the door. The music machine began playing "When a Tear Becomes a Rose," the beat a little faster than usual. When the old man sang, he closed his eyes as though the music hurt. Iry stood up and cupped a hand under Claudine's right elbow, right where things stopped.

"What are you doing?" She looked up at him, her eyelids popping.

"Asking you to dance," he said, taking off his cap and putting it on the table.

She looked around quickly. "Don't be absurd."

"Come on, I bet you used to do the Texas two-step in high school."

"That was another life," she said, rising out of the chair as if overcoming a greater force of gravity than most people have to deal with.

For a few seconds she bobbled the step and they bumped shoe tips and looked down as though their feet were separate animals from themselves, but on a turn at the end of the floor, she found the rhythm and moved into the dance. "Hey," he said.

"Gosh." She settled the end of her arm into his palm as though the rest of her was there. The little man did a good job with the song, stretching it out for the six or seven couples on the floor. Claudine wore a sad smile on her face, and halfway into the song her eyes became wet.

Iry leaned close to her ear. "You all right?"

"Sure," she said, biting her lip. "It's just that right now I'm not being a very good lesbian." She tried to laugh and reached up to touch her crew cut.

"You ain't one right now."

"How can you tell?"

"You dance backwards too good."

"That's stupid."

He turned her, and she came around like his shadow. "Maybe it is, and maybe it ain't." About a minute later, toward the end of the song, he told her, "I've danced with lots of black girls, and you don't move like they do."

"You're making generalities that won't stand up," she said. Then the tone of her voice grew defensive. "Besides, I'm only one-sixteenth African American."

"On whose side?"

"My mother's."

He walked her to their table, his hand riding in the small of her back. He noticed how well she let it fit there, his fingertips in the hollow of her backbone. He pursed his lips and sat down, pointing to her navy-blue purse. "You got any pictures of your family?"

She gave him a look. "Why?"

"Just curious. Come on, I'll show you Babette and my momma. They're in my wallet." He pulled out his billfold and showed her the images in the glow of the candle. "Now you."

She reached down and retrieved her wallet, pulling from it a faded, professionally done portrait of her parents. The father was blond and sun-wrinkled, and the mother lovely and tawny-skinned, with a noble nose and curly hair.

"Nice-looking people," he said. "Your momma, she's Italian."

Her lips parted a little. "How would you know?"

"Hey, Grand Crapaud has more Italians than Palermo. I went to Catholic school with a hundred of them. This lady looks like a Cefalù."

"She's part African American."

"When I bring you home tomorrow, can I ask her?"

She leaned close and hissed, "Don't you dare."

"Ah-ha." He said this very loudly. Several people in the little room turned and looked in his direction, so he lowered his voice to say, "Now I know why you really got your butt fired."

"What?"

"You lied to those people at the college. And they knew it. I mean, if I can figure you out in a couple days, don't you think they could after a few years?"

She stood up and swept the photos into her purse. He tossed some money on the table and followed her outside, where the air was still hot and alien, too dry, like furnace heat. "Hey," he called. He watched her go to her room and disappear inside. He was alone in the asphalt lot, and he stuck his hands into his jeans and looked up at the sky, which was graveled with stars. He looked a long time, as though the sky was a painting he had paid money to see, and then he went into his room and called her.

"What do you want?"

"I didn't want to make you mad."

"The word is angry. You didn't want to make me angry."

"I was trying to help."

There was a sigh on the line. "You don't understand the academic world. Decent jobs are so scarce. I have to do whatever it takes."

"Well, you know what I think."

"Yes, I know what you think," she told him.

"You're a straight white woman who's a good teacher because she loves what she's doing."

"You're racist."

"How many black people have *you* danced with?"

She began to cry into the phone, "I'm a gay African American woman who was crippled by a horse."

Iry shook his head and told her, as respectfully as he could, "You're crippled, all right, but the horse didn't have nothin' to do with it." He hung up and stared at the phone. After a minute, he put his hand on the receiver, and then he took it away again.

The next morning he didn't see her in the motel café, but when he put his little suitcase in the back of the Jeep, she walked up wearing a limp green sundress and got into the passenger seat. Five hours later he had gone through El Paso and was on U.S. 180 heading for Carlsbad when she pointed through the windshield at a ranch gate rolling up through the heat. "Home," was what she said, looking at him ruefully. It was the only unnecessary word she'd spoken since they'd left Alpine. "First time in five years."

He pulled off to the right and drove down a dusty lane that ran between scrub oaks for a half-mile. At the end was a lawn of sorts and a stone, ranch-style house, a real ranch house, the pattern for subdivision ranch houses all over America. Out back rose the rusty peak of a horse barn. Iry parked near a low porch, and as soon as he stepped out, Claudine's round mother came through the front door and headed for her daughter, arms wide, voice sailing. Claudine briefly introduced him and explained why he was there. The mother shook his hand and asked if they'd eaten yet. Claudine nodded, but Iry shook his head vigorously and said, "Your daughter told me you make some great pasta sauce." He glanced at Claudine who returned a savage scowl.

The mother's face became serious, and she patted his hand. "I have a container in the fridge that I can have hot in ten minutes, and the spaghetti won't take any time to boil."

Iry grinned at Claudine and said, "Prepariamo la tavola."

"Ah, si," the mother said, turning to go into the house.

Claudine followed, but turned and said over her shoulder, "You are what is wrong with this country."

"Scusi."

"Will you shut up?"

• • •

After the lunch of pasta and salad, he asked to see the barn. The mother had leased the range, but she maintained three horses for Claudine's brother and his children, who lived in Albuquerque. Two of the animals were in the pasture, but one, a big reddish horse, came into a gated stall as they entered. Iry inspected the barn's dirt floor, sniffed the air, and walked up to the horse. "Hey," he said. "You think we could go for a little ride?"

She came up behind him, looking around her carefully, a bad memory in her eyes. "I'm not exactly into horse riding anymore." Her voice was thin and dry, like the air.

"Aw, come on."

"Look, I'm thankful that you brought me here, and I don't want to seem rude, but don't you want to get back on the road so you can see cowboys and Indians or whatever it is you came out here for?"

He pushed his cap back an inch and mimicked her. "If you don't want to seem rude, then why are you that way? I mean, this ain't the horse that hurt you, is it?"

She looked back through the door. At the edge of the yard was the gate to the open range. "No. I just don't trust horses anymore." She turned to face him and her eyes were frightening in the barn's dark. "I don't think I ever liked them."

"Well, here," he said, opening the wooden gate wide and stepping next to the horse, putting his hand on its shoulder. "Come tell this big fella you don't like him because of something his millionth cousin did. Tell him how you're an animal racist." The bay took two steps out into the open area of the barn toward where she was standing, but before he took the third step, she made a small sound, something, Iry thought, a field mouse would make the moment it saw a hawk spread its talons. Claudine shook like a very old woman, she looked down, her eyes blind with fright, and she crossed what was left of her arms before her. Iry stepped in and pushed the horse easily back through the gate. The animal swung around and looked at them, shook its head like a dog shedding water and stamped once. Claudine put her hand over her eyes. Iry slid his arm around her shoulder and walked her out of the barn.

"Hey, I'm sorry I let him out."

"You think I don't know who I am," she said. "You think the world's a happy cowboy movie." She stopped walking, turned against him, and Iry felt her tears soak through his shirt. He tried and tried to think of what to do, but could only turn her loose to her mother at the door and then stand out in the heat and listen to the weeping noises inside.

Two days later, he was in the desert at a stucco gas station, standing out in the sun at a baked and sandblasted pay telephone. On the other end of the line Claudine picked up, and he said hello.

"What do you want?"

"You get that job?" He winced as a semi roared by on the two-lane.

"No," she said flatly.

"Did you do what I asked you to?"

"No. I explained all the reasons why his English department needed me." There was an awkward pause in which he felt he was falling through a big crack in the earth. Finally, she said, "He didn't hire me because there weren't any vacancies at the moment."

"Well, okay." And then there was another silence, and he knew that there were not only states between them, but also planets, and gulfs of time over which their thoughts would never connect, like rays of light cast in opposite directions. A full minute passed, and then she said, as if she were throwing her breath away, "Thanks for the dance, at least," and hung up.

He looked out across the highway at a hundred square miles of dusty red rock sculpted by the wind into ruined steeples, crumpled hats, and half-eaten birthday cakes. Then he dialed the icehouse's number back in Grand Crapaud and asked for Babette.

"Hello?"

"Hey. It's me."

"Where in God's name are you?"

"Out with the Indians in Utah, I think."

"Well, I've got some news for you. The compressor, it wasn't your fault. Mauvais had put mineral spirits instead of oil in the lubricator."

"Did the shop pick up the parts for machining?"

"No. The owner is buying all new equipment. Can you believe it?"

"Well."

"When are you coming home?"

"You want me to come back?"

"I guess you'd better. I fired Mauvais."

He looked west across the road. "I think I want to see a little more of this country first. I can't figure it out yet."

"What do you mean?"

"I met this one-armed gal and she hates it out here."

"Oh, Lord."

"It ain't like that." He looked across toward a blood-red mountain. "It's pretty out here, and she don't want nothing to do with it."

"Where's she want to be, then."

He made a face. "New Orleans."

Babette snorted. "Baby, you're liable to stop at a rest area out there and find somebody from Death Valley traveling to Louisiana to see stuff. Even around here you can't swing a dead nutria by the tail without hitting a tourist."

An Indian wearing a baseball cap rode up bareback on an Appaloosa and waited to use the phone, staring just to the left of Iry. After a minute, he told Babette goodbye and hung up. The Indian nodded and got down in a puff of red dust. Iry eavesdropped, pretending to count a handful of change. He didn't know what the Indian would say, if he would speak in Navaho or inquire about his sheep herd in guttural tones. After a while, someone on the other end of the line answered, and the Indian said, "Gwen? Did you want two percent or skim milk?"

That afternoon at sundown, he was standing on a marker that covered the exact spot in the desert where four states met. Behind him were booths where Indian women sold jewelry made of aqua rocks and silver. In one booth he asked a little copper-skinned girl if the items were really made by Indians, and she nodded quickly, but did not smile at him. He chose a large necklace for Babette and went back to his Jeep, starting up and driving to the parking lot exit, trying to decide whether to turn right or left. No one was behind him, so he reached over for the road map, and when he did, he noticed a paper label flying from the necklace like a tiny flag. It said, "Made in India."

He looked around at the waterless land and licked his lips, thinking of Babette, and the Indians, and the one-armed gal. The West wasn't what he thought, and he wanted to go home. He glanced down at the necklace and picked it up. Holding it made him feel like his old self again, authentic beyond belief.

Tim Gautreaux has published a novel, *The Next Step in the Dance*, and two collections of short stories, *Same Place, Same Things* and *Welding with Children*. The novel was chosen best novel of 1999 by the Southeastern Booksellers Association, and *Welding with Children* was selected as a notable book of the year by *The New York Times Book Review*. His short stories have appeared in *Atlantic, Harper's, GQ, Best American Short Stories, New Stories from the South,* and *Prize Stories: The O. Henry Awards*. He is a native of southern Louisiana, has a PhD in English, and is Writer-in-Residence at Southeastern Louisiana University.

WINBORNE GAUTREAUX

I've taught in universities for thirty years and haven't been drawn much to write about the experience. It's hard to make an academic story lively and fresh. In "Dancing with the One-Armed Gal," I decided to filter a few of the academic cliches through the consciousness of an undereducated, blue-collar kid in order to warp the already warped academic world. And Iry learns a great deal from professor Claudine, in particular that "he'd rather spend eight hours a day with his tongue stuck on a hot pipe than teach in a college."

A. Manette Ansay

BOX

(from *The Nebraska Review*)

for janet cricksen

E ven before Mitchell Johnson pulled into the driveway and
walked up the concrete steps and into the kitchen, he regretted doing what he'd done, but what difference could that make
now? He took three aspirins with a tall glass of water and then sat
at the table, smoking Daisy's cigarettes, Camels, which she'd tried
like the devil to give up. By then it was getting light. The birds
were going crazy in the bushes outside the window. The first few
employees were arriving at the Hardee's across the street, flipping
on lights, raising shades. At some point after he'd left, Daisy must
have come back down and made herself a sandwich—here was the
white plate with its signature crusts, a crescent smear of catsup.
Like blood at the scene of the crime, he thought, and then he thought,
*What crime? She just made herself a sandwich. You think too damn
much, that's your problem.* He picked up a crust and nibbled, putting
his lips where hers had been. She wasn't going to forgive him for
this. You didn't need a Ph.D. to figure that one out. It was very
possibly his last morning in this kitchen, in this chair, tapping ashes
into this ashtray, which she'd made way back in grade school, long
before she'd ever imagined him, Mitchell James Johnson, groan-
ing under her, cupping the warm swing of her breasts and saying

BOX   79

Baby, if you'd leave me, I don't know what I'd do. That was the thing he said sometimes: *Don't leave, don't leave, don't.* He didn't know why he said it. It was a stupid thing to have said, until now. They'd always been perfectly happy together, mostly perfectly happy.

Daisy was upstairs in their double bed, lying on her side, one pillow between her knees and the other under her belly, the way her cousin Jill had shown her. The sheets smelled of Vicks and sweat and fabric softener, and it was not an unpleasant smell. She was ten days overdue. She had another appointment tomorrow; if nothing was happening, they were going to induce. Maybe it would go quickly. Maybe it wouldn't be so bad. Last week, she'd watched the yellow cat have kittens in a cardboard box tucked between the living room couch and chair: six multicolored sacks, six mewling mouths. It was over in an hour, and the yellow cat didn't seem to mind all that much. "Christ Almighty," Mitchell said when he came home from work. He got a beer and sat down in the other chair. Daisy shrugged. What she wouldn't have given for a beer, but she'd already sneaked one earlier. She dangled her hand into the box, tracing the kittens' tiny skulls with her index finger, as the yellow cat purred and purred. Whenever *he* came near the cat, she'd hiss and the hair along her back rose up. But Daisy could hold the cat's head between her palms, tilting her face this way and that, until her eyes glazed over and her body grew limp and her yellow toes splayed with pleasure.

By the following morning, one kitten had died. Daisy nudged it into a plastic bag and gave it to Mitchell to bury it in the yard. She kept an eye on him from the window to make sure he didn't just walk it over to the Hardee's Dumpster like he did with their trash. Later, she made a wooden cross with sticks and a rubber band even though she did not believe that animals—or people for that matter—had souls. Once you were dead, you were dead.

Mitchell said that was ridiculous. He believed in heaven, though he wasn't sure about hell. He thought maybe hell was a kind of reincarnation, so that if you lived a bad life you had to come back

and do things right. He believed there was a purpose to everything, and when Daisy shrugged and said he should prove it, he
told her that God wouldn't have made the world for no reason,
and when Daisy said, then prove God made the world, he said, "If
you found a watch lying on the sidewalk, would you think it just
made itself, or that somebody made it?"

"I'd think somebody dropped it," Daisy said. She could see the
watch—gold, with a man's leather band, slightly worn—and it
delighted her. "I'd pick it up and keep it."

"You're not listening to me," Mitchell said angrily. "I'm trying
to make a point here if you'd just for once in your life pay attention while I'm talking."

It bothered him that the yellow cat hadn't even seemed to realize one of her kittens was gone. "That cat is so stupid," he said.
"Numb as a pounded thumb."

"Maybe it's just she's busy with the other kittens," Daisy said.
"Maybe it's just she knows there's nothing she can do about it now."

Whenever Mitchell criticized the cat, Daisy felt he was criticizing
her, because she'd been the one to take the cat in. She'd been sitting
at the kitchen table late one night, eating bologna and catsup sandwiches on white bread, one after the other. She quartered them to
make each one last longer, to make each seem like more than it was
the way, as a child, she'd broken her crayons so she would have twice
as many. Who could say how long the yellow cat had been watching
from the window ledge before Daisy glanced up and saw her small,
beautiful face pressed against the glass? Daisy often wondered what
had drawn the yellow cat to her house, to her window—was it the
light? Was it merely chance? Or was it—and this was what Daisy
liked to think—that the cat sensed a kindred spirit, another restless
body with a belly full of young? When Daisy opened the door and
called, the yellow cat didn't run away. She marched right into the
house. She hopped into Daisy's lap and began to purr, a loud rough
chortle like the voice of an old woman, perhaps a great-grandmother,
who has raised many children.

The bedroom was just above the kitchen ceiling, and Mitchell

BOX   81

could hear Daisy getting up. The light fixture trembled when she crossed between the dresser and the bed. He lit another Camel. He kept thinking he saw the yellow cat curled up in the other kitchen chair. Several times, he thought he saw it cross the room out of the corner of his eye. Christ Almighty. He imagined the box by the highway, the twine he'd wrapped around and around it and tied with an extravagant, flopping bow, the multicolored paws that reached from the holes he'd dug with his keys—without thinking, a reflex—for air. There had been no other cars. It was still dark, the snowy shoulders of the highway lit by a sharp quarter moon. He got back into the car and punched up the heat and finished his beer before driving away, feeling like he'd accomplished something, like he'd made a statement so loud and clear he could live by its echo for the rest of his life. But then, as he came back into town, he began to sober up. He began to try and piece together what it was, exactly, that they'd been fighting about. Something about Mitchell being too controlling? Something about Daisy not being responsible? The thing was, he couldn't remember how the yellow cat got mixed up in it. It had been well after midnight when Daisy came downstairs for a cigarette and he'd tried, yet again, to reason with her. "You want me to quit smoking, you quit," she said, which was what she always said, but that was ridiculous, he wasn't the one who was pregnant, he wasn't the one putting an innocent baby at risk. He told her if he were the one who was pregnant, he'd take care of himself, for the baby, yes, but also for her, because the baby belonged to both of them. He told her he would have exercised and made regular appointments before there was a problem, and she was just being irresponsible, and if she were so irresponsible now, how could she ever take care of a child?

"It's a little late to think of that now," she said, and she shrugged in her infuriating way. "You're drunk, I've had enough of this."

"I'll tell you when it's enough," he'd said, but she went back up the stairs as if she hadn't heard him, the cigarette burning in her hand. There was this distance around her, and he couldn't pass through it, no matter how hard he tried. But last night had been different. Last night, he'd gotten through. She'd looked back at him once, her eyes glassy with tears, after he'd hollered, "Even that stupid cat makes a better mother than you."

Daisy appeared at the top of the stairs as if his thoughts had summoned her. He snuffed out the last Camel, watched her slippered feet as they lowered the rest of her body into view—the globe of her belly, the tired slope of her shoulders. She had on the same maternity sweater and leggings she'd worn every day for the past week. Her slippers were shaped like dinosaurs, complete with stuffed, spiny tails, and he worried she might trip on them and fall down the stairs and be killed, both her and the baby. He wanted to jump up and help her, but he knew she'd just pull away, the way she did whenever he asked if there was anything he could do. *Nothing,* she'd say. *Nothing, all right?* And all he'd wanted to do was help.

"Morning," he said quietly. She looked at the white plate, the catsup and crusts, but she didn't look at him, not exactly. She cast a longing look at the empty pack of cigarettes. Then she went into the living room, the way she always did, calling, "Kitty, kitty, kitty?" and Mitchell fought the urge to jump up and block her way. He ran his hands through his hair, and then Daisy was standing in the doorway.

"Where are they?" she said.

"What do you mean?"

"What did you do?"

"Nothing."

"Nothing," she repeated. "Like hell."

He fingered the empty cigarette pack.

"Did you leave them off at the pound?" She was looking at him now, she was looking full at him. He made a small sound in his throat. "Which pound?" she said. "In town? Over at the county?"

When he didn't answer, she went to the hall closet, got her coat and purse, and walked out of the house. From the window, he watched her cross the street, still wearing her dinosaur slippers. He made sure that she was safely inside the Hardee's before he began

BOX   83

straightening up the kitchen: the newspapers and empties, the cigarette butts and loose change. He did the dishes, dried them and put them all away. He scrubbed the worst of the burned-on crap from the top of the stove, and he would have swept the floor, too, but he was afraid she'd slip out of the restaurant while he wasn't looking. Perhaps she'd go to live with her cousin Jill, who hated him, and he'd never see her again, and he'd never get to see the baby at all. For the first time in all of these months, the baby seemed real to him, a person he wanted to know. *Don't leave, don't.* He felt the yellow cat brush the backs of his legs. He heard the kittens scratching in their box in the living room, their faint mews, their mother's booming purrs.

In the restaurant, Daisy ordered a cup of coffee and took it to a booth. The windows were painted with candy canes and snowmen and Christmas trees even though it was barely December, and this made Daisy sad. She thought of the yellow cat and her kittens in a small metal cage at the pound, how the yellow cat would be shaking all over from the sound of the barking dogs, how — at first — she wouldn't recognize even Daisy. Daisy wondered if the yellow cat and her kittens could be damaged psychologically by the experience. They couldn't know, as Daisy did, that Mitchell hadn't meant to hurt them, that as soon as he'd had some time to himself to think things over, he'd take Daisy over to fetch them and pay the fee. He was not a bad person, but he sometimes did bad things. He'd slept with two other women during the third year of their marriage. He got in fights and, once, had been arrested for disorderly. But she'd known him since they were both eighteen and now, eight years later, she saw him less as another person than a living part of her own self. She'd tried to explain that to Jill, but Jill just didn't understand. "A cancer is part of your own self, too," she'd said. "But you don't try to love it. You cut it out before it kills you."

Through the window, Daisy saw the door to their house open up. Mitchell came out slowly, looking around as if he did not mean to cross the street and go into the restaurant where Daisy was waiting for him. She stared down at her paper coffee cup, and decided she would not look up until she heard him slide into the booth, across from her. And even then, she didn't.

"You should eat something," he said. "An egg sandwich. Juice."

She tilted the paper cup toward her, watched the slosh of muddy liquid inside. Last night, when he'd said that to her about the cat, he'd been absolutely right. She would be a terrible mother. She was too irresponsible to raise a child. He'd seen into her secret heart and plucked out her very worst fear. After all this time, he still knew her well enough, loved her well enough, to do so.

"I'll get us both something," he said, and he came back with hot-cakes and eggs and juice. She surprised him by eating hungrily and when she finished, she put one swollen hand on his and said, "Where are they, Mitchell?" and he said, "I'll take you to them."

She'd assumed they were going to the county shelter; they had a twenty-four-hour drop box. But Mitchell got on the highway. Surprised, she watched the endless, snowy ditches, the black bones of the trees. Everywhere, there was garbage—colorful bags, bright cups, scraps of paper—and it looked no less festive than the decorations back at the restaurant. A faded billboard advertised—what? There was a handsome man, a smiling woman, but Daisy couldn't make out which product they held between them. Mitchell slowed, pulled over onto the shoulder, continued at a crawl.

"What are you doing?" Daisy asked. For the first time, she was starting to be afraid.

"Watch for the box," he said. "It's here somewhere."

"You left them *here*?"

"I left them in the box."

"They'll be dead, Mitchell," Daisy said quietly. "It's twenty degrees outside."

Mitchell braked, put the car in park. "Here," he said, and then he got out. It took a few tries, but Daisy got out too, and without any help from Mitchell. Her feet were numb in the ridiculous slippers. There was nothing on the shoulder but a piece of twine. "This is it," Mitchell said. "This is the spot." He picked up the twine. It had been cut; the knot was still intact.

BOX 85

Daisy looked up and down the highway. A truck passed, slowing to see if they were in trouble, if they needed help. A woman peered out from behind the driver's window. Daisy waved her on: *Go.* Mitchell was crying. He was off the shoulder now, walking around in the weeds as if the box might somehow be there, camouflaged by abandoned tires, fast food wrappers, dead brush. "Right here," he was saying, "I left them right here, I swear it." Daisy realized he did not yet understand that the yellow cat and her kittens were gone. Another car slowed; this time it was an older couple, their faces furrowed with concern. Daisy took a few steps toward them, but when the man started rolling down his window, she changed her mind. "I'm fine," she called. "Everything's fine." She waved to them as they drove away, and then she walked into the weeds, toward Mitchell, his wet mouth shining with snot and tears. She kissed him, wiped his face with her bare hands as he sobbed, "I'm sorry, I'm sorry."

"It's OK," Daisy told him. And it had to be. There was no other answer to be given. Tomorrow they would induce labor, and then there'd be a baby, and then other things would happen after that. *Someday we'll look back on this,* Daisy promised herself, *and we'll—* but she could not imagine what they might do or think or say, and so she couldn't complete the thought. Instead, as she and Mitchell walked back to the car, Daisy played the wishing game she sometimes played inside her head. She wished that she and Mitchell would both quit smoking and that they'd keep the house cleaner. She wished that Mitchell and her mother would get along. She wished that, when the baby arrived, it would be the thing that was missing from their lives. The thing that, like whatever the couple on the billboard held between them, had faded so much that no one could even tell what it was anymore.

But mostly, she wished she had never visited Jill so soon after her baby had been born. The blood vessels in Jill's eyes had ruptured during delivery, and her pupils were nearly lost in a flaming red sea. She sat miserably on a round, rubber doughnut; she showed Daisy the awful rash between her breasts even though

Daisy didn't want to see it. Whenever Daisy tried to remember the baby—now four years old, a giggling, happy-go-lucky girl—she saw only Jill's eyes, glowing like a demon's, like something out of the hell in which Mitchell wasn't sure he believed.

A. Manette Ansay is the author of a collection of stories, *Read This and Tell Me What It Says,* and four novels, most recently *Midnight Champage,* a nominee for the National Book Critics Circle Award. Her awards include a Pushcart Prize, the Nelson Algren Prize, the AWP Short Fiction Series Prize, and a National Endowment for the Arts grant. Her work has been reprinted in Italy, Germany, Japan, France, Australia/New Zealand, and Great Britain.

STEVE WILLIAMS

*M*y *mother-in-law was driving to work one morning when she saw a box by the side of the highway. Something made her stop and back up for a closer look. When she cut the twine that held the box closed, she found a live litter of well-fed kittens. Within a matter of hours, she'd found homes for all of them. That same afternoon, my father-in-law—who knew nothing about the kittens—was driving along the same section of highway when he saw a couple in a pickup truck. They were driving very slowly along the edge of the road, as if they were looking for something. My father-in-law pulled up beside them to see if they needed help, but the man—who'd clearly been crying—waved him on. That night, he and my mother-in-law put two and two together.*

Years passed. The story stayed with me. I was living in Nashville when a dear friend of mine there went into labor with her first child. She'd taken excellent care of herself throughout the pregnancy, but I'd had a bad feeling all along, and as the hours passed—ten hours, twenty hours—I was beside myself. I couldn't reach her husband or her parents. The hospital wouldn't give out information. Because I could do nothing else, I sat down to write a story. Thirty hours later, her son was delivered by C-section, and I had completed "Box."

Chris Offutt

THE BEST FRIEND

(from *Shenandoah*)

O n the hill above a narrow hollow, a dog sat in the woods
with its head propped over a log. A blue jay called from
a shagbark. The dog twitched an ear, causing fleas to rise and
circle its head before settling back to the black fur. The jay
moved on. From an arched weed stem, a tick slipped onto the
dog's hind shank.

Below the dog at the foot of the hill, a yellow bus stopped
beside the grade school. The driver spat a brown arc of tobacco
against a limestone shelf that jutted from the hillside. Lines of
heat shimmered above the blacktop, the edge of which was soft
enough to hold a footprint. The driver squinted into the murky
shadows, seeking the dog. It was there every day to meet a girl.
The dog was part coonhound and part something the driver had
never been able to name—husky or Lab, maybe wolf. He wanted
to ask the kid, but she walked to school and the driver never left
the bus.

The black dog stood and stretched like a cat. It scratched itself
and the tick fell from the strand of hair it was crawling along and
landed on a fern. The dog followed a game path to the rain gully.
Rocks skittered down the hill beneath its footpads. The dog left
the cool shade of the woods. The sudden sunlight was swift and
harsh as an ax cut, but the dog continued without breaking stride,

accepting heat as easily as the girl had accepted the dog's presence outside the schoolhouse every afternoon for seven years.

A child left the school. The driver spat. More children began spewing from the building. All were bald, shaved by the State to stave off a plague of lice. At the bottom of the hill, the dog stopped, its nostrils opening wide. From the combined scents of sweat, urine and food that marked the human presence in the hollow, the dog smelled the girl. The fur along its neck rose. The dog became very still. Twined with the smell of bus exhaust was the scent of a gray and yellow shepherd that was nearing the girl. The dog charged across the road in a galloping fury.

The driver lost sight of the black dog when it passed by the bus, and looked for it on the other side. It leaped with jaws wide and struck the shepherd in the throat. The shepherd reared on its hind legs. It batted the attacker into the stone wall and clamped its teeth to the black dog, tearing away part of its ear spindled on an incisor. The dogs rolled across the clay dirt and into the throng of children. Older kids dragged siblings away. Within seconds of combat the animals were slinging blood, saliva and clods of dirt into the air.

The principal ran from the school with a coal shovel and hit the black dog on the head. It turned briefly to consider the fresh attack and ruled the man out. The shepherd used this diversion to clamp its jaws over the black dog's head, pulling the left eye partly out and tearing the skin from lid to nose. The principal kicked the black dog. He drew his leg back to kick again. Something struck him in the side and he pivoted quickly, expecting another dog but found a scrawny girl hitting him with a tree limb. Her face was grim. Even her eyebrows were shaved. The principal grabbed the branch and wrenched it, and the other end caught the girl in the mouth. She yelled and the black dog leaped on the principal, claws seeking purchase as it bit into the flesh below the man's ribs. The shepherd lunged for the black dog's throat. The girl began kicking the shepherd, and from the crowd of children came another bald kid who rammed his shoulder into the thin girl. Both children fell to the yellow clay dirt.

From the bus door, the driver bellowed a primal roar that drew the dogs' wary attention to a new and potential threat. They broke from each other and circled, their fur glossy with blood. Strings of spit slid to the ground over their torn jaws. The girl crawled to the black dog and wrapped her arms around him as the dust slowly dissipated. Dislodged fleas hovered about the children, hunting the safety of hair.

The driver stepped from the bus, both arms clasped across his belly, his face white, eyes glazed. A sudden sweat leaked from his hairline. He bent from the waist and began to retch. Children made a circle around him. They dodged the splash of vomit and delivered into the air a laughter that drifted like a fragrance. A blue fly left a spot of blood to land beside the driver's vomit.

When the driver finished, he wiped his face.

"Swallered a chew big as a baby's fist," he said. "You'uns go on and get on the bus now."

There was a cut on the girl's head. She had the makings of a shiner, and bite marks in her arm. Both she and the dog were bleeding freely, but the dog's eye was worse. The girls looked up the gully to the woods, decided against the shortcut and began walking the road. She favored one leg. Through a rip in his shirt, the principal prodded his torn flesh.

Around the bend and hidden from the school, the girl crouched beside the shaded creek that trickled off the slope. Tatters of garbage hung in the trees from spring rains. She and the black dog drank from the ferrous water, and the girl washed the dog's wounds. There were deep gashes about its neck. Most of an ear was gone. The dog bore up to its cleaning without a sound, even when the creek water ran into the open flesh surrounding its eye.

The girl cupped water in her hands and poured it over the cut on her head. Pink water streamed down her face. Her eye throbbed. She realized that she had no choice but to leave one day, and that she still had many years of living before she could go. She leaned against the dog and hugged him hard. They panted together in the cool quiet of the woods. A squirrel watched them from an oak. A hawk veered in the sky, watching the squirrel.

————————

Chris Offutt is the author of *Kentucky Straight, Out of the Woods, The Good Brother,* and *The Same River Twice.* His work is widely anthologized and has been translated into several languages. He has received many honors, including a Guggenheim Fellowship and Writing Writers award. He currently teaches in the Iowa Writers' Workshop.

In 1992, I began writing a coming-of-age novel set in the hills of eastern Kentucky where I grew up, a community of two hundred people surrounded by the Daniel Boone National Forest. My first friend was my dog. His name was Pompey and he escorted me through the woods to school and back every day. He was a great dog and I have never had another.

I knew the book would be hard to write. I didn't know that I would get no further than the prologue before turning away. Eight years and many drafts later, that prologue evolved into "The Best Friend." It is part of a cycle of stories about a woman from the hills. Her name is Lily.

Robert Olen Butler

HEAVY METAL

(from *Louisiana Literature*)

People look at me and my boyfriend, Jared, people from my daddy's generation, and all they can see is my black lipstick and the way I do my hair into spikes and the bits of metal that pierce our noses, our lips, our ears, and they look away again, they think they know us enough to judge us. And they don't know jack shit. They don't know how I dream about the nails in Jesus's hands and feet.

Not that it's the way my daddy would have me dream. My daddy is a man of God. My daddy would take his Bible and it was bound in beautiful calf-skin leather and the paper was so thin and crinkly and yet so strong that not a page of it was torn no matter how many times somebody had rushed through looking for the Word, the Holy Word, but he would take his Bible and hold it up when my brother and me and my mama was sitting around the living room with him and we were all doing our prayers and our studying, he'd hold it up high. And that Bible, full of God's Holy Word, would droop in his hand, it would just go limp over his fingers, the thick shaft of pages, the two page-marker ribbons dangling down. It was so supple. So supple and skin-smooth. And I would have these thoughts. And they would seem to come straight from the mouth of God, straight from His Word. This Bible being held up like that felt like a real private thing. I mean a private thing about a man's body. You know the thing I mean. I don't know why, when I'm talking about how I grew up and all, that I start feeling the taboos again about these words—I mean, of course, a man's cock. I knew—part of me knew—that it was a terrible thing I was thinking. But another part of me thought it was all right. And it wasn't like the part that felt it was all right was the future me, the me that my father would be expecting to go straight to hell. It was the me still believing in the Holy Word. Because every word was true in that book. Every one. True like cosmic true. True in your soul and in the marrow of your bones and true by every hair on your head, which are all numbered by God—you can read that in Matthew chapter ten verse thirty. And, of course, every other hair is numbered, too. How could anything escape the notice of God? He put hair on your head and he also put it around your cock, if you're a guy, or your pussy, of course, if you're a girl, and they've got to all be numbered, too, those hairs. So the fact that the Bible in my daddy's hand made me think of a guy's cock, it seemed right to me, by the Book.

Just consider King David. How beloved he was by God. How great he was in God's eyes. How God loved him to go out and deal with the bodies of Israel's enemies. Because in the Word, which is true for all eternity—my own father taught that as the cornerstone of everything else—in the first book of Samuel in the Bible David fell in love with the daughter of Saul, who was beloved, as well, being made the first king of Israel by God as prophesied by Samuel, and David loved Saul's daughter and what did he bring as a dowry for her? He brought the foreskins off the cocks of two hundred Philistines. He did. You can look it up in First Samuel chapter eighteen. I dreamed about that for a long while, too, even while I was awake. When I daydreamed of my own wedding, blessed by its true Bible-based holiness, and my daddy giving me away to a godly Christian boy, I dreamed of a dowry like this marriage that God had brought to his beloved David. I saw a great black case of fine, supple, calf-skin leather, and

it would be opened, and there they would be, laid out on blue velvet inside, those wonderful intimate pieces of flesh off the cocks of
two hundred boys. Mostly the boys at Sam Houston High School
in Waco, Texas, where I was a sophomore when I first started having this dream.

Of course, my daddy couldn't deal with the literal truth of that
God-approved dowry of foreskins. He believed the things it was
convenient for him to believe. Like the earth is six thousand years
old. That was real important to him for some reason. But ask him
why if a man is wounded in his testicles he's cast out of the church,
which is true forever and ever amen from the book of Deuteron-
omy chapter twenty-three, and you won't get real clear answers
from him, even though, as the father in the family, he's God's
direct representative with divine inspiration—that's in the Bible,
too, somewhere, and he wouldn't let us forget it, but a guy who
gets in an accident and his balls get hurt, why he has to be cast out
of God's house is something my daddy refuses to address. He even
took my Bible away from me for asking. But my daddy put his
own balls in a wringer over that. He wanted me to study the Bible
so that I'd be a worthy daughter of a godly man like him, which
everybody in Waco knew about him. But how could I do that if he
had my Bible? So he had to give it back to me and then he put me
under threat of hell not to read certain parts of the One and Only
Holy Book of the Creator of the Universe, literally true in every
word. But then there was the guy that God got real pissed at and
smote dead just because he touched the ark of the covenant when
he was only trying to keep it from falling on the ground when the
oxen that was pulling the cart it was on stumbled. Course my
daddy would say that God could get killingly angry at anybody He
chose to and nobody could question that, because He's God. And
the same goes for God's direct representative in every family on
earth. Him, for example, my daddy.

And then I read in the Bible that if a son—and you can imagine
that they wouldn't go any easier on a daughter, harder if anything—if a son doesn't obey his parents, even just to eat too much

and drink too much, then the parents are supposed to take him to the elders and have the son stoned to death. This is what God wants, according to His Holy Word. I sure wasn't going to ask my daddy about that one. I'm sure he'd checked that out already and was irritated at Big Government for making that kind of holy justice pretty hard to get away with these days. These days being the corrupt End Times, of course. A disobedient child would be even worse than those kids who went up in smoke, and daddy didn't shed any tears for them, knowing how True and Beautiful was the judgment of God.

We went out to Overlook Hill next to the intersection of State 340 and Farm 2491 so we could watch that Branch Davidian cult in their compound after they'd barricaded themselves up and were holding off the FBI and all. Not really watch. It took binoculars to see anything from there and we just brought our Bibles and our "Forwarding Address: Hell" tracts. There was probably some closer place to go, but this was close enough for daddy, and for a bunch of others, too, because there was all types on the hill. The place was crammed full of those making their righteousness clear to the world as a testament and those acting in sin from their unrighteousness, supporting this cult and its Satan-controlled leader. And there was a bunch of others in between, press people and picnickers and people selling T-shirts and gimme caps and hot dogs and stuff. I wandered away in between prayers and used my own little bit of money when I got hungry and had a Koresh burger, which was cooked over charcoal by a guy wearing a "waco—We Ain't Coming Out" T-shirt, and it maybe was the best-tasting hamburger I've ever had in my life and I was loving it till my father saw me and he came and grabbed this meal conceived in unrighteousness out of my hand and gave me a stoning-by-the-elders look and he threw the Koresh burger down on the ground and crushed it under his heel. There's nothing in the Bible about littering, as far as I know, so this wasn't either here or there in terms of his witnessing to the world, from my daddy's point of view. But he was ready to do me in, as a true witness to God's word, right there and then, if only this was the sort of times when that was possible, but lucky for me it's the wicked End Times instead. So he grabbed me hard by the arm and dragged me back and put me on my knees next to my always-faithful brother and my daddy started to pray for the Triumph of Jesus over the wickedness of the world as was clearly represented by those people hiding and sinning in that cult compound right here in Waco. My daddy may even have started talking in tongues or something because I stopped hearing any sense in his words at all. He was saying things like *hunga marunga adenoid hallelujah*. Everyone we know at church, and at a lot of churches in Waco, would say these were inspired words my daddy was saying, he was filled with the Holy Spirit. But as far as I was concerned he was just fading farther and farther away from me, at that time.

And then it was the next Monday about noon and I was eating maybe the worst-tasting hamburger I've ever had in my life, in our school cafeteria, and thinking about that hamburger on Overlook Hill, when there was a big stir and we all went out to the parking lot and off in the distance, out to the northeast of town in the direction of the Branch Davidians, there was a pillar of smoke as dark as the worst grime you've ever seen, like the color of those people's souls, I thought, and as soon as I did, I knew that thought came from my daddy, how he saw the world.

And that night at the dinner table my daddy prayed to God in praise of how He'd shown us all in this family the true path and saved us from hell where every last one of those folks who'd burned up today was going to feel the fiery wrath of God for all eternity.

And I said, What about the children?

And he said, They have been brought to perdition by their parents. Don't you think there was children in Sodom when the fires came down from heaven and no one was saved except Lot and his two daughters and even his wife was turned into a pillar of salt?

And will you pass me some? I said. Salt, that is.

And my daddy did and I put it on my hamburger which my

mama had made and which tasted pretty bad, it needed more salt than I could give it, but I shook the salt out and I thought of the body of Lot's wife making things taste good long after she was dead.

And I was wondering: If the fires ever were to come down in Waco, on everybody, not just the Branch Davidians, would God first send His angels to the house of this true and faithful servant of the Lord, my daddy, and say, Go, take your wife and your son and your daughter and go from this Waco, for it is full of iniquity and will be destroyed, even the women and the children? And I looked at my daddy then and if the answer was no, God wouldn't do that for this man, then my daddy was full of shit all along about what was right and holy and what wasn't. And if the answer was yes, if God was such that he'd pull the four of us out of here and burn up all the rest and send them to hell for eternity, then that wasn't a God I should give a good fuck about. That's what I realized right there and then.

So I went off. I made my plan and daddy never knew about it till I was gone, but the night before I was hitting the road, he came to my room and knocked real soft and I said, Come in, and he sat on the side of my bed and he said, Honey, I know we have our differences. I know I seem real hard on you sometimes. But I just want you to know that it's because I love you. I care about your happiness, not just today and tomorrow but forever.

My daddy says this real soft and he pats my hand and he goes out without trying to wring any promises or anything from me.

But these were just words, really. Just words. Since then, I've thought about the words that weren't there in what he said and could never be there.

Like: I guess the children are OK, the ones that got burnt up.

Or: Certain things just don't make sense to me either about who God is or what He really wants.

And I've thought about the words that weren't there in what he said but you could hear them lurking outside my door in the hall ready to jump back in his mouth as soon as he left.

Like: I may seem hard but this is the way the God of the Universe wants me to be, so too bad.

Or: We may have our differences but I'm always right.

Or: I love you, but I'd be ready in a second to offer your life up—or in these wimpy times at least just cast you out of the family—if I figure you're lost to God's Word as I see it.

My daddy still had all that in him and on that night he didn't say anything to contradict it, but in spite of my knowing all the shit things he simply wasn't saying aloud, I lay there in the dark after he'd gone and I started weeping and quaking and wishing he meant those other things that could never be. I guess it was the pat on the hand or just the tone of his voice or something, and I knew those things were as empty as his words, they were gestures intended for himself, testifying to what a gentle and understanding father he was when in fact he wasn't anything like that. But still I trembled and wept and then I got angry at myself about it because I knew the truth. I trembled like the tail of our tabby cat when he's taking a shit, but I couldn't quite get Daddy out of my system. Not till the next morning. That's when I went out the door and only I knew what I was going to do and as soon as I hit the end of the driveway, I was fine and I've never looked back.

And I started dreaming about Jesus, about the nails in His hands and His feet and how I felt about that, how close I felt to Him over those nails, even though part of me was ready to throw the baby Jesus out with my daddy's bath water. And I felt a man's body-thing about Jesus at that, as terrible as that sounds. It's like something I've learned later, in the places I've lived in and from the people I've been with. You put metal through your flesh and it's a real intimate thing, is what I've learned. And it really feels like that to me. You say, My body will give way for this hard, sharp thing, you can push a metal thing right through me and there it sits, touching me inside my flesh all the time. You can look at it and you can touch it and you can think about it and you're looking at and touching and thinking about the inside of my body, where I'm really living and where usually it's impossible for any other person to get into. But with these rings and these studs and these nails and spikes, somebody else can flow right on inside me, he can be in here with me. And when I found my boyfriend, Jared, and he found me we just knew that these were things that we had to do with our bodies together. And I knew it was about Jesus, too, from my dreams, though I've never said that to Jared. Not my daddy's Jesus. My own personal Jesus.

Robert Olen Butler is the author of eleven works of fiction, one of which, *A Good Scent from a Strange Mountain,* won the Pulitzer Prize for Fiction in 1993. His latest book is *Mr. Spaceman.* His stories have appeared in such places as *The New Yorker, Esquire, GQ, Harper's, The Paris Review, The Virginia Quarterly Review,* and *The Sewanee Review.* This is his seventh appearance in *New Stories from the South.* He has also made four appearances in *Best American Short Stories.* He lives with his wife, the novelist and playwright Elizabeth Dewberry, in Lake Charles, Louisiana.

EARL PERRY/DAVID RICHMOND

F or several years now my attention has turned more and more to the ways of our popular culture and to the events of our times that capture the public attention. "Heavy Metal" emerged from two striking instances of these concerns—body piercing and the Branch Davidian debacle in Waco— and, in addition, from my long-standing interest in the religious impulse. Once Citrus's voice began to whisper to me from the place of her yearning— for faith and for a father and for a self—the writing itself felt essentially like channeling.

William Gay

MY HAND IS JUST FINE WHERE IT IS

(from *The Oxford American*)

What does a man do when he's at the end of the line and the news is as bad as it gets?

Worrel was sitting on the stone steps drinking his third cup of morning coffee when he saw the Blazer turn off into his driveway. The softwood trees were beginning to green out in a pale transparent haze but the hardwoods were bare yet and he could see the red Blazer flickering in and out of sight between their trunks, the bright metal of its roof flashing back the sun like a heliograph. He'd seen it come a hundred times before, but its appearance was still as magical as something he'd conjured by sheer will, and he hoped the magic held through even such a day as this one threatened to be.

He rose from the steps when he heard Angie downshift for the hill and drank the last of the coffee and tossed out the dregs. He set the cup on the edge of the porch. When she parked the Blazer in the yard he was standing with his hands in his pockets. It was March and the wind still had a bite to it around the edges and he leaned slightly into it with his shoulders hunched.

She cut the switch and got out and stood by the car. She wore dark glasses and pushed them up with a forefinger as if she'd have a better view of him. She looked at him with a sort of rueful fondness.

I didn't know if you'd be ready to go or not, she said.

Yes you did.

Well I don't know why. I can't see why you want to come with me.

I don't want to even talk about it, he said. Are you ready?

She smiled. Ready as I'll ever be, she said.

She slid back under the steering wheel and he came around to the passenger door and got in. She had the motor going but was waiting for him to kiss her and he took her into his arms and kissed her mouth hard. When he moved his face back from hers, her green eyes were open. She always looked at him as if he were the only one who had the answer to some question she had been thinking of asking.

Well, she said. I won't even ask if you're glad to see me.

She felt thin in his arms. He could feel the delicate bonework of her shoulder through her flesh, through the silk of the blouse she wore. She'd been thin ever since he'd known her and he always tempered the strength with which he held her but now she seemed thinner. If he held her as tightly as he wanted, he felt he'd crush her. Yet the flesh of the face turned toward him looked new and unused, scarcely touched by the abrasions of the world or its ministrations.

Where's Hollis?

He had to work. They didn't want to let him off.

The son of a bitch, Worrel said.

Don't say that. He offered to take off anyway and go with me.

The son of a bitch, Worrel said again.

He doesn't know the whole story anyway, Angie said. He just thinks it's tests. I couldn't say the word *malignant*. You're the only one who knows everything.

She said she loved him and he had no cause to doubt it. They were like a drug in each other's veins. A crazy badnews drug, their hands trembled with the hypo, the needle prodded for an uncollapsed vein. The drug they used was rare and dangerous with unknown and catastrophic side effects—you couldn't buy it, it had to be stolen under cover of darkness when other folks were asleep or their attention had wandered.

If he didn't call or if he made no effort to see her, she came to see about him. She always seemed a little harried, almost distraught, glad to see him still there. It was as if she expected to see the house open to the winds and him gone without a trace or a word of farewell, gone to Africa to search for diamond mines or to South America to save souls. But Worrel had given up on prospecting and had come to feel each soul responsible for its own salvation and he was always there. In bed she'd cling to him and call his name as if she were trying to call him back from the edge of something. Warn him.

There had been a time when she was going to leave Hollis for him but the violence of his own recent divorce had sobered her, given her pause. There were other lives to be considered. Hollis had said in no uncertain terms there would be a custody battle. She was not in a good position for one. Hollis was in an excellent position. He was a good provider and a steady worker, and he was also faithful, or at least discreet. Angie and Worrel had started out careful and discreet but the power of the drug had surprised them and things had gotten out of hand: at some point, like drunken teenagers trashing a house, they had kicked down the doors and smashed the windows and sprayed their names on the walls in ten-foot-tall graffiti.

Everything fled from Worrel in the aftermath. Everything: house and car and vindictive wife. Disaffected and disgusted children fleeing at a dizzying pace like animals scuttling out of the woods from the mother of all forest fires, little scorched and smoking Bambis and Thumpers hellbent for elsewhere, and Worrel himself seized in the soft grasp of her flesh, scarcely noticing.

He studied her profile against the shifting woods of late winter sunlight, a little stunned at the price he had paid for so tenuous and fragile a portion of her life, though he never doubted she was worth it.

• • •

They were driving out of Ackerman's Field and nearing Nashville when she glanced over at him. Did you find a place yet? she asked.

Since the affair had begun Worrel had become an addict of shading and nuance, decoding her speech as if there were always hidden meanings. What she'd asked could have meant, *Have you found a place for me and the kids?* or it could have meant, *Have you found a place we can be without your ex-wife coming in and screaming at us?* But it did not mean either of those things. All it meant was, *Have you found a place?* and he discarded it.

I may move in with you and Hollis, he said.

She glanced from the road to him, half a smile, half a grimace. It's not funny, she said. When are you going to stop treating everything as if it were a joke?

Maybe when everything stops being a goddamned joke, he said.

The last of the traffic lights had fallen away now and she didn't need her right hand for shifting, so she reached and grasped his left, pulling it over to the console between them. Her hand uppermost, her fingers laced with his. She squeezed it hard, then just drove clasping it loosely, her fingers calm and cool against his own. There was something oddly comforting about it, and Angie seemed to feel it as well, for climbing into the hills where perhaps she should have downshifted, she just drove on, the transmission laboring and vibrating until they'd made the grade.

If you need your hand to drive just take it back, he said.

She smiled at him, her face an enigma behind the dark glasses. My hand is just fine where it is, she said.

He turned away and looked at the countryside, aware of the scarcely perceptible weight of her hand, and watched Tennessee roll up—bleak trees, buttercups on the shoulder of the road, the leached funeral silks of winter, the cusp of promised spring the world hung onto.

They had been friends before they had been anything else and they could talk or they could ride in comfortable silence. Mostly they rode in silence, Worrel's mind turning up images of her as

you'd turn up pages in an album of photographs and, in the one
he looked at most, her eyes looked as they did in the moment
before he kissed her the first time. He'd known he was going to
and was glad he'd waited until her eyes looked the way they had.
As if they'd been simultaneously asking and answering a question. They'd stepped together and Worrel felt as if she'd slammed
against his chest, as if they'd stepped onto some narrow ledge of
unreckonable height. Looking down made you dizzy and you
might plummet later in the next second, though not now; now
seemed not only enough but all there was. Later there were other
kisses: in hallways, in the moment before a closed door opened,
in the moment between the wash of headlights on a wall and the
slam of a car door, in the moment when footfalls announced
someone was coming but he wasn't here yet. In these tawdry
moments are worlds, universes.

The night before they went to the motel for the first time she
twisted his mouth down to hers and said against his teeth, I think
you're trying to corrupt me. He didn't deny it.

It was seventy miles to Nashville and today it seemed too short
a distance. After a while they joined the insectlike moil of traffic
and she needed her hand back. She was a good driver, effortless,
unpressured, and she didn't even have to look for street signs to
find the medical center. She'd been there before.

In the thin watery light, the Athens of the South perched atop
its hills like something from a dream. The red Blazer went through
the narrow canyons between the buildings with ten thousand
other red Blazers negotiating the narrow canyons and everything
began to look unreal.

The pale transparent light off the facades of the buildings imbued
them with meaning so that they looked to Worrel like monuments
erected and fled by some prior race finer than the present folk who
milled about like maggots working in flesh.

She parked in front of the medical center and they got out. She looked at her watch. We don't have time for lunch before my appointment, she said. Do you mind waiting until we get through here?

Of course not, he said. I'm not even hungry.

Well, she said, uncertain, looking at the building.

They walked toward it. The marble veneer glittered in the sun. It looked like an enormous mausoleum. The statuary on the lawn looked like relics replevied from a tomb so long hidden from the daylight that the thought of time and its unspooling made Worrel dizzy.

He sat in the waiting area with a roomful of other people. Nothing looked right. Maybe he was coming down with something. The pictures on the wall were wrong. A Dali print, a Bosch. Watches melted, marvelously detailed folk were flayed. The pictures seemed part of some surreal scheme to acclimate him to the horror to come.

The people did not seem right either. Everything about them rang false, even their clothing seemed strange, either years out of style or years ahead of its time. When they spoke some of the voices were pitched too high, others dragged endlessly like audio-tape moving slower and slower. Their emotions were out of sync, their anxiety too hyper, their stoicism simply cold indifference.

She'd left her purse for him to mind and dangling it by the strap he went outside and smoked a cigarette. He seldom left the country and his eyes were drawn almost against his will to the jumbled skyscrapers and high-rise apartments. Everything seemed leaned toward some common center, the hazy pastel buildings collapsing on themselves. In the sepia light the city looked as strange as some fabled ruin on the continent of Lemuria.

He put the cigarette out in an urn half-filled with sand and went back inside the waiting room and took up a copy of *Newsweek*. He tried to read an article on a new survey of sexual habits but the sheer amount of work that had gone into producing the magazine he held in his hands made him tired. Lumberjacks had felled trees

that had been shredded and pulped to make paper. Ink had to
come from somewhere. Other folks ran presses, stacked the glossy
magazines, delivered them; the U.S. Mail shuttled them across
the country. Not to mention the people with cameras and word
processors, people with curiosity and the knowledge to ask the
questions to satisfy it. The magazine grew inordinately heavy; all
these labors had freighted it with excess weight. He could hardly
hold it. All the information was encoded in bits that swarmed like
electronic insects and the words flew off the page like birds. He sat
staring at an advertisement for a red Blazer that he was convinced
was the very truck that had brought him to Nashville.

When she came through the doorway back into the waiting
room, days seemed to have passed. He'd laid the magazine aside
and sat clutching her purse. Reaching it to her he pretended not
to study her but he did all the same. Having learned nuance and
shading he'd become adept as well at interpreting her body language. Her smile was a little bright, her movements a little man-
nered: she'd put on the restraints and maybe screwed them down
a notch too tight.

Ready? she asked.

More than, he said, scanning the room one last time as if he'd
mark it as a place to avoid, remember all these miscast faces should
he ever encounter them in old movies on late-night TV.

They went out. The cars in the parking lot glared under the sun.
He felt hollow and enormous inside.

She was reaching for the door handle of the Blazer when he
stopped her with a hand on her arm.

Wait, he said.

Wait? For what?

He was silent a time. Tell me something, he finally said.

I guess there's not much to tell.

Was it bad?

She had her lower lip caught between her teeth. About as bad
as it gets, she said.

He thought for a moment her eyes looked frightened then he

saw that more than fear they showed confusion. She looked stunned, as if life had blindsided her so hard it left her knees weak and the taste of blood in her mouth. He wanted to cure her, save her, jerk her back from the edge as she'd tried to do for him.

But all he could say was, Do you want me to drive?

I'm fine, she said. I can always drive. I like to drive.

Behind the wheel she searched her purse for the keys. I'm starved, she said. Are you hungry?

Yes, he lied.

Where do you want to eat?

She had the keys, the Blazer caught on the first crank, then sat idling. She studied him intently.

I don't care, he said.

You must care.

I don't care, it's nothing, it's just food. Hell, it's just food. He knew she thought that a barbaric notion but that was just the way he felt.

Where was that little Italian place we went to? You had the veal, they had these great salads there. Terrific salads. What was the name of that place?

I don't know.

You must know. The salads had the little cherry tomatoes?

Goddamn it, he said, suddenly angry. They all have the little cherry tomatoes.

She knew him, she wasn't fooled, she didn't take offense. She smiled. I can find it, she said. We'll just drive around, I'll know it when I see it.

I still don't see what it matters.

It matters to me, she said. It was the first time we ever went out to eat. You know, in a nice place. You bought me a bottle of wine you couldn't afford.

As she drove back into the street, she kept looking at the buildings, cutting down narrow crooked alleys, taking side streets that seemed to go nowhere you'd want to be — as if the place where they had the cherry tomatoes would materialize before her, between the tacky country music souvenir stores with their ceramic Roy Acuffs and price-tagged Minnie Pearl hats and the interminable pawnshops in whose dustmoted windows guitars hung by their necks like arcane beasts taken as trophies.

The day was waning, the light stingy and oblique. The sun flared behind the buildings and lent them a stark undimensioned quality. After a while they were hopelessly lost. The city looked strange even to her. They didn't speak. It began to seem to Worrel that they had sought and found their own level.

They trickled down sunless corridors and burst capillaries until they were in the city's dark heart. A city within the city where the blood slowed and thickened and clotted in viscous smears of alizarin crimson dried to burnt sienna around the edges. The tires of automobiles bore it away in fading hieroglyphic slashes. Neon flared, the air had grown heavy with the drone of flies. BAR BAR BAR, the neon repeated. 20 NAKED GIRLS 20. Brands of beer seemed to have the significance of the names of prophets on graven tablets.

Finally she pulled the Blazer to the curb and cut the switch and stared uncertainly about her. They had parked next to a vacant lot. Dead weeds tilted askew by the winds, the sun caught in broken wine bottles. The husk of an Eldorado sat so stripped and demolished it seemed to suffer obsolescence on an epidemic scale. A brown dog came out of the weeds and stood staring at them as if it had news of their coming. It was starved to the point of emaciation, just something that stood for a dog, a concentration that might possibly reconstitute a dog, a dog decocted in smoking electric chambers by a mad doctor who'd seen a dog once long ago and conjured one up with only the vagaries of memory as a recipe.

Adjacent to the vacant lot was a row of buildings constructed of umber-colored brick. Between two of them a narrow two-story house was wedged so tightly it seemed to have no sides of its own, simply its wooden frame front and tin-roofed porch hung parasitically between the brick walls, the rococo gingerbread trim of the porch paint-lorn and rotting. A swing dangled motionless from rusted chains. The front window had been stoned out and covered with a metal sign that read CLABBER GIRL BAKING POWDER. A cracked sidewalk led to the street through packed earth encysted with bottlecaps. Venus flytraps grew in car-tire planters serrated as if pinked by enormous shears.

The streets were full of drifters who seemed to be looking for something that they had lost. The homeless by choice and by circumstance held in common their disconnectedness and the selfsame look of threat in their faces, danger loosely contained, like lightning in a voltaic jar. They looked listless and numb as sleepwalkers, they moved as if the air itself offered hindrance to their passage. A man with shoulder-length blond hair stood on the high concrete steps of the parasite house and had occasional commerce with these streetfolk. He wore a quilted vest from whose cargo pockets he dealt glass vials of some iridescent liquid, smoky and volatile as nitroglycerin. The drifters paid him with bills that he folded onto a thick sheaf of like bills and he treated the money casually as if it were of no moment in itself but simply some happenstantial by-product of the transference of the vials. Occasionally he'd speak into a cellular telephone while watching Worrel with narrowed blue eyes.

Worrel looked away. He felt the uneasy knowledge that at any moment everything could alter. The air felt heavy and volatile, the way it does before a summer storm.

He turned to look at her. Her head was lain back against the upholstery. Her eyes were closed. Perhaps she slept.

He had no doubt that at some point he'd be confronted; it was a given, a law of nature. If she did not drive away, if he did not get under the wheel and take charge himself. Apparently he was not going to. Apparently he was going to sit here and look blankly back into the eyes that locked momentarily with his then slid away, until someone motioned for him to roll down the glass and he did and someone said, in a spray of spit, a reek of splo whiskey, in white-hot crackhead clarity, *What is it with you, motherf—er? And who the f— do you think you're looking at?*

Until the day waned and the light pooled and drained westward and the streetlamps came on and until the pace of the streets altered and moved in a loose disjointed rhythm and fierce chromatic colors that seared the eye and until the day's possibilities became probabilities and then dead certainties and they were hauled from the Blazer and humiliated, made to plead for their lives, urinating on themselves and soiling their clothing while the last vestiges of human dignity fled. Credit cards gone, money gone, pristine Blazer stripped and burned. Surely they'd slit his throat and rape her fair white body, slit her throat and rape his own fair white body, shoot them full of drugs that would send them at warp-speed past any conception of reality the mind was prepared to deal with, snuff them in a blinding flash of light that was the very essence of ecstasy. Their bodies would be found in garbage-strewn alleys, septic hypodermic needles dangling from their veins like fey ornaments, or their bodies would drift pale and bloated in the currents of the Cumberland River until they turned up stranded on silt bars like worn-out whores their pimps had no further use for.

Bring it on, Worrel told their sullen faces. Let me have it, you sons of bitches. You goddamned amateurs. There's nothing you can do to me half as bad as this.

He thought of the people waiting for Angie, beginning to wonder where she was. The kids at the grandmother's, the husband probably wondering why there was no supper on the table. He suddenly felt weary and omnipotent, like a troubled god: he knew something they did not yet know, something that was waiting for them like a messenger with a finger on the doorbell and a telegram in his hand. They did not know, any of them, that they were living in the end times of bliss. The last belle epoque. Not the kids at Granny's, whining where is Mama, not the husband bitching about the fallow table.

They did not know that they were going to have their world blown away, walls flung outward and doors ripped from shrieking hinges, trees uprooted and riding the sudden hot wind like autumn leaves, the air full of debris like grainy old eight-millimeter footage of Hiroshima. A cataclysm that would leave the floor of their world charred and smoking, inhospitable for some time to come.

Just for a moment, though, he was touched by a feeling he could not control, that he had not sought and instantly tried to shuttle to some dark cobwebbed corner of his mind. He wanted to forget it, at the very least deal with it later.

He had felt for an instant a bitter and unconsoling satisfaction that terrified him. Where she sat eyes closed with her fair head against the seat she seemed to be fading in and out of sight like someone with only a tenuous and uncertain reality, going at times so transparent he could see the leather upholstery through her body, her face in its temporary repose no more than a reflected image, a flicker of light off water.

At these moments, all that was real was the grip of her hand, the intent focused bones he could trace with the ball of his thumb. All that was holding her back were the fingers knotted into his own. She was sliding away, fare-thee-well-I'm-gone, vanishing through a fault in the weave of the world itself, but until this moment ended and whatever was supposed to happen next happened, he was holding on to her. Everybody was hanging on to her, all those grasping hands, but for the first time no other hold was stronger than his own.

William Gay's fiction has appeared in *The Oxford American, Harper's, The Atlantic Monthly,* and other magazines, as well as in *New Stories from the South, 1999.* His novel *The Long Home* was published in 1999, and a second, *Provinces of Night,* is forthcoming this year. He lives in Tennessee, where he is at work on a third novel and a collection of stories.

MAUDE SCHUYLER CLAY

This story came to me all of a piece, and I wrote it very quickly. But in the actual writing it altered and grew a little surreal, as if awareness of death darkens the perception of familiar places and objects.

Wendy Brenner

MR. PUNIVERSE

(from *The Oxford American*)

Yesterday you smelled like detergent, having biked to work through the feeder bands of a tropical storm that was stalled just offshore in the Gulf. You clomped in like a draft horse, keys and change jingling, clean shirt steaming sweet ammonia and dripping all over the linoleum in the Xerox room, arms loaded with souvenirs from your recent vacation in a Midwestern state you refused to name: "A Midwestern state of mind," was all you would say.

The reporters and editors received trial-size jars of specialty barbeque sauce: Mackintosh-smoked, Jack Daniels–spiked, Ginseng Zinger, Grand Marnier Infusion. The custodial staff got a box of chocolates shaped like prairie dogs, proceeds to benefit the Midwestern Prairie Dog Relocation Project. For Mabel, the front-desk receptionist, a postcard of the famous fainting goats. For Kenny and Sonny, the other two photographers besides myself, car air-fresheners in the shape of the anonymous Midwestern state.

Kenny said he'd take Sonny's to him in the hospital. "Oh, yes, that's right," you said, your eyes meeting no one's.

After you had given everything out, you turned to me. My empty hands vibrated in anticipation—something was finally going to pass between us. I thought I might faint, like a goat.

"I'm still working on yours," you said. Your tone was both secretive and ironic, I thought, a little anxious but also triumphant, frustrated but resolute—sincere, yet more than a little recalcitrant.

"Is something wrong?" I asked.

"Ha!" you laughed, throwing back your large wet head, sending out an arc of storm-charged droplets. I watched one hit the bulletin board behind you and blur the word *operations* on a memo. The fluorescents flickered, went out, then blinked back on. "Whoa!" someone in the next room shouted.

"You just look a little anxious," I said. "Or, not anxious—worried. Worried."

Your hand moved across your gray-cratered chin and made an amplified, space-age sound. You said, "Well, it takes a worried man to sing a worried song." And then, backing away as if I had stepped too close, though I hadn't moved or even swallowed: "I'll try to bring yours tomorrow. Yours is special."

A wave of something went through me, tweaked my hyped-up aminos. I saw fish leaping out of the sea before a tsunami, strange fuzzy tendrils pushed out of the ground by the shifting plates of the earth. It didn't matter what the gift was. I could feel everything that was happening everywhere, and it was all for me.

My first photo shoot for the paper was the Mr. Puniverse Pageant, in which the editors had jokingly entered you, their colleague, as a contestant. I hadn't met you yet, but everyone was abuzz about the event, the fact that you were going along with it. "And, Jason, you're the perfect man to cover this," the editors said to me with genuine, mean-spirited excitement. "You'll make these dorks feel even more puny, get some great reactions." They were a giggling, sweaty, vengeful group, these editors. They reminded me to get some good shots of you for the bulletin board. "You'll know him—he'll be the *old* one!" they hooted.

Twenty years their—and your—junior, I had my killer summer tan still and was experimenting with a black-market protein powder that had doubled my muscle mass in a month and was probably veterinary steroids, which was fine with me. Smells and sounds were more intense, people got on my nerves more, but I was buff, I was ripped. I had no idea who you were. "Sure," I told the editors. "Whatever."

You did not win the title of Mr. Puniverse, didn't even place—while comically homely, certainly, you are not particularly skinny. Really, you didn't even make an effort. For your talent segment, you told one joke: *What's a potato's favorite TV show? M*A*S*H.*

The reporters from our paper cheered wildly.

Still, I found it hard to look away from you, to pay attention to the proceedings. You were scuffing around the margins of the stage, absentmindedly stepping in and out of your sandals, keeping your eyes down, occasionally glancing up to grin at someone jeering you from the audience. Your gaze at those moments I found staggering. Clapton was playing on the p.a. system—*I've seen dark skies/Never like this/Walked on some thin ice/Never like this*—and the maddening animal smell of barbeque from the concession stand was rolling over me in waves. When I tried to take your picture, the power suddenly drained from my camera, and the shutter wouldn't budge. Luckily, I'd brought a backup.

The winner, the new Mr. Puniverse, was an albino biologist named Bultinck who stood six-two and weighed one hundred eleven. In the interview we printed, he said, "This is a real honor for me. I breed genetically specific mice, for which there is a pretty steady demand. I'm used to people thinking I'm weird." Energized by your presence, I got an inspired portrait of him, a happy freak naked from the waist up, the cold metal of the trophy he clutched making his nipples pop out. His figure appeared to be outlined in light, or hope, coming from some outside source.

Afterward, I pushed backstage, that song still playing in my head—*I've told you white lies/Never like this/Looked into true eyes/Never like this*—and offered you a ride back to the office in what I hoped was a neutral, businesslike tone. My parking meter, when we reached it, had apparently malfunctioned—in digital letters its screen said JAR. "Jar," you repeated, looking at me. I thought: *My god, your eyes*. Together, elbows knocking, we slid your Schwinn, a ladies' one-speed, into my backseat. I could hear the atoms in the cracks of space between us going crazy, buzzing like angry gnats.

Later, when asked if you were bummed about losing the pageant, you said, "You can't always get what you want," and then gave me a look of nearly hysterical satisfaction. I would learn it was your habit to work popular song lyrics with a kind of feverish desperation into your conversation whenever possible, as if they were being pumped into you via secret radio waves and this was the only way to get them out of your system.

In fact, one question I frequently found myself wanting to ask you, later, was: "Didn't the electroconvulsive shock therapy help with the loose association?" But I would die before I'd remind you of something that hurt you.

Though you yourself never spoke of it, everyone at the paper knew and told several different versions of your troubled youth and unjust incarceration in a state mental institution, your close brush with, and lucky reprieve from, lobotomy. In one version, you had simply been a difficult teenager—for a year you refused to eat anything but Necco wafers, refused to read anything but the *Fantasy Baseball Index,* and in your free time snuck out of the house and climbed electrical towers. What choice did your affluent, dim-witted, voting-for-Eisenhower parents have but to commit you?

In another version, you tried to kill your father with a fencing foil. I found that version hard to believe, not because I couldn't imagine you as murderous, but because, in your own discordant, distracted, disintegrating way, you had too much style, too much real dignity for anything as idiotically self-important as fencing. You would have used your bare hands, I believe, or any simple firearm.

Common to all the versions was the length of your stay in the place—three years—and the reason for it: your parents moved across the country for your father's promotion, so you had to wait until you turned eighteen to sign yourself out. Office consensus was that you had come out crazier than when you went in, and this unusual bit of generosity on the part of your otherwise relentlessly critical colleagues—that they would grant you this—was, I thought, a measure of your personal power, your grace. It made my heart swell, like that of some idiot housewife, to think of it.

Never were they as hushed and reverent as when they spoke of your electroshock, how it made you smell roses even in your sleep and see people as cartoons, how it made your thoughts seem to come from a place like a luggage compartment located in the air ten feet above your head, how it made you forget your own name. I thought it must also have been the reason for your eyes—the layered, flickering darkness, the look, at one instant, of both reaching and refraining from reaching.

I couldn't think about it without the edges of my own body starting to crackle and tingle, not in sympathy but with the urge to hurl itself back through time and take your body's place, get between you and the source of the shocks, let the electricity mess with my simple, unspecial brain, my not-fragile self. I could have withstood it, I was sure, especially now with my new bulk. What good were my youth and strength doing anyone here, now? If only I had been there, I wanted to tell you, believe me, you would have come to no harm. Over my dead body.

That night, after the Mr. Puniverse Pageant, I dreamed I broke your bike. An accident—I was riding it, showing off for you, and the brake levers came off in my hands. The next night I dreamed that, together, you and I broke my TV, simply by standing in a certain proximity to each other and looking at it. In the dream, I understood that the TV was a sacrifice: if I didn't get to touch you, it was I who might die.

Though he was straight and shouldn't have been paying attention, Sonny, the senior photographer, quickly noticed me noticing you, and made sure I noticed. He would catch me in the men's room or the parking lot, pull me aside from nothing in particular, and say, "*By the way,* he's not gay," in an obnoxiously pointed, fake-offhand manner, stroking his pubic-looking goatee with his ratty, precise little hand. Sonny von Cher, I called him to my friends. Straight photographers were, in my experience, a bunch of ass-holes, constantly needing to prove that they discerned hidden aspects of things, making it their life's work to unearth and destroy faith wherever they found it. Sonny was always pointing out examples of "unusual beauty" in a pompous, spiteful manner, as though he alone possessed the special power to recognize it, as though the rest of us, the masses, were too stupid and insensitive to appreciate or even know the real thing when we saw it.

Still, he had made his point. I brought it up on the way to Disney Gay Day with Owen, Kirk, Remy, Heath, Germain, Tab, Fidel, and Eddie in the Aerostar we had all chipped in to rent for the weekend.

"Why does Sonny care if you like this old ugly crazy straight guy?" Eddie said. "Does he want him?"

"No, Sonny's got a girlfriend," I said.

"Though she does look like a boy. Or a praying mantis."

"Wait!" Owen yelled. "This guy you're in love with is old *and* straight *and* ugly? Maybe *you're* the one who's not gay!"

"He's not ugly *per se*," I said.

"He's not ugly, per se," Tab said.

"He's not ugly, he's my brother," Germain said.

"I'm telling you," I said. "I just have this feeling."

"Oh, please. Wake me up when we get to the Magic Kingdom."

As usual, Kirk was the only one who would take me seriously. We were lying in the back with the luggage, watching the string of sulphur-pink streetlights snake by in the sky. "Sometimes," Kirk said, "wanting what you can never have is the perfect spiritual position. Your faith develops, becomes an entity unto itself, takes on nearly physical reality—like the relationship we have with the dead, how the dead can sometimes seem more present than the living. Loving an absent partner is beautiful."

"It's not beautiful, it's pathetic," Remy said, leaning over his seat. "The guy is straight. Listen to what Sonny says. Forget about it."

"Who cares what Soon-Yi says?" Kirk said. "That doesn't mean anything."

"Maybe he is straight," I said, "but there's this look he gives me that just—I can't explain it."

"Communion," Kirk said.

"Spare me the *Touched By An Angel* crap, will you?" Remy said. "Don't you remember what happened last year when Fidel hooked up with that 'bisexual' cardiac nurse guy?"

"Cancer care," Fidel said.

"Whatever. I personally don't have the time right now to sit up all night through Jason's nervous breakdown caused by some old freak who isn't even attractive."

"Okay, we won't call you," Kirk said. "God, Remy, you're, like, Touched By An Asshole. You think you're everything."

"I *am* everything," Remy said. "I'm *it*."

Your image swam down to me from between the lights, flashed into me like a thought. I saw you again on the Mr. Puniverse stage, how you pulsed against my eyes as if you had been drawn in some darker, heavier medium than the other contestants, some radioactive kind of crayon. How you seemed the photographic negative of the boring joke that was being perpetuated there, and most other places, most of the time. How it hit me all at once that you were beautiful thinly disguised as ugly, the truth seeping out around your eyes and the vibrating edges of your person, the direct opposite of everyone else there, of most people I'd ever known, including, probably, myself.

Was I wrong, now, to believe you were taking a special interest in me? I thought of the way you stopped dead whenever we encountered each other in the corridor and held up your hands in a gesture of surrender; the way you spoke just a bit more loudly whenever I was working nearby, as if we were animals who had to track each other by sound; the way you sometimes appeared outside the darkroom, said my name, "Jason. . . ," but then nothing else, just stood there rubbing your chin, your eyes both bright and veiled, as if you were trying to remember the rest of the sentence.

"Besides," Kirk was saying, "Jason isn't having a nervous break-down. Look at him, *hello,* he looks great. What have you been doing, Jason, lifting weights again? Your arms look bigger. Don't his arms look bigger? Look at his arms. Is it just me, or are your arms getting bigger? Jason?"

Everything I touched or even glanced at began to suffer surges and drains. Bulbs blew in every room of my apartment, and the coil on my toaster oven went cold. My water pressure fluctuated violently. New shoelaces snapped between my fingers; ink pens burst, unprovoked, in my pockets and desk drawers. My TV changed channels by itself, and my stereo suddenly picked up stations I'd never heard of, transmitted from cities hundred of miles away. Downtown one day, a transformer I happened to walk by exploded, splattering the sidewalk behind me with hot oil. True, my body was growing so rapidly that I was bumping into things like an adolescent, having to adjust my conception of physical space, but I suspected something else at work, something that had visited me once before.

During one weekend when I was sixteen, the year I was coming out, the compressor in my mother's meat freezer, my Sunbird's alternator, and my Swatch battery all suddenly and mysteriously died. Then, our answering machine, which otherwise worked fine, stopped taking messages from Kim Falvey, the girl I was dating. Clearly, it was trying to help me. Some enormous invisible presence seemed very close to me then, bearing terrifyingly down, ripping out what I pictured as notebook subject-dividers in my brain. It peaked one night, and I made my parents kneel on the floor of my bedroom with me and pray, which they did without asking questions: they were good parents.

Kirk, whose father was a Masonic Perfect Master of the Fifth Degree, was actually hallucinating by the time he came out. On the way to school one morning, he said, he saw a giant hairball driving a truck. To escape his family, finally, he wrote a letter to himself from an imaginary friend, Lance, in Pecos, Texas, inviting himself to come visit for the summer, but his hallucinations had become so convincing by then that he was devastated when he stepped off the Greyhound and Lance wasn't there to meet him.

"There's a proven link between repression and increased electrical activity," Kirk had said while we were waiting in line for Space Mountain. "How do you think a lie detector works? So, the longer you hold it in, the worse it's going to get. Now, on top of that, you say this guy had electroshock. Very likely his altered electromagnetic field is messing up your gay-dar. Add to that your own increased chemical conductivity caused by the, ahem, 'protein supplement' you're taking, and interactive aberration seems inevitable."

"That sounds plausible, Kirk," I said, but with all these environmental variables, how can anyone tell who they're in love with, or who's in love with them?"

"Look," Kirk said, speaking more loudly. "This much I know. This is fact, recorded history. The pendulum clock in the palace of Frederick the Great at Sans Souci stopped when the emperor died. Whatever's causing all this to happen—this force, or whatever it is, this wave, or frequency, this configuration of light and heat and matter, this juxtaposition of events and possibilities, this *thing*, whatever it is—it's trying to help you! You just have to have faith in it!" He had his hands on my shoulders and was yelling into my face. A jet roared right overhead then, so low it lifted my hair, and I stared up at its glaring silver underside, which appeared to be smiling at us. A moment later it was gone. Kirk looked worried. He said, "You saw that too, right?"

I wanted to confess, to tell you everything, but there was never the opportunity; Sonny, it had become clear, was trying to keep us apart. He gave me the most distant, time-consuming assignments—the renegade airport emu, the WHIP 102-FM Chevy Touch-A-Thon, the grand opening of the Hair Shanty two counties away—so I'd be out of the office all day. When I returned, after dark, you were always gone. And then you took your Midwestern vacation. The day after you left, the tropical depression pulled up to the mainland and parked there, a perpetual motion machine churning out line after line of storms, as if the world itself had stalled, as if change were no longer possible. It seemed I might never see you again—an unacceptable ending.

Kenny guffawed one morning when I told him where I was off to. "Let me tell you something, bro," he said. "No one's ever even *seen* that runaway ostrich. It's like a UFO, man."

My faith faltered, I'm sorry to say. I had to do something.

I caught Sonny in his cubicle, using a magnifying glass to scrutinize head shots of his Dilton Doily-looking girlfriend, and told him I needed his help. Rain was lashing the windows in ten-minute bursts, and I'd timed myself to approach his desk between them, during one of the eerie, swollen silences, thinking I'd be more likely to get Sonny to go along with me that way—I'd be in the flow, riding the waves of air pressure like a surfer, coasting in to the inevitable end. In the men's room mirror I'd made my face pleasant, expectant, like Mary Tyler Moore's normal expression. I only hoped that suppressing my intentions wouldn't cause a blackout or explosion before I had the chance to carry them out. "I'm having the damnedest time finding that emu," I said. "I need the benefit of your expertise."

Sonny laughed. "You want me to go out in this storm?"

"I'm going. Besides, I thought you said it came out when planes were grounded," I said. "Unless, you know, there is no emu. . . ."

"Oh, there's an emu," Sonny said. "I'll ride out on the tarmac with you, how's that? Show you where it nests. I've gotta go pick up my new lens anyway. But then you're on your own, bud. You're still the new guy, in case you've forgotten."

"Oh, no, never," I said. "Believe me, I feel fortunate."

In my car, he lit a cigarette and said, "You really need to get over this little crush on our Mr. Puniverse."

Something chanted in the engine. *Easy,* I thought. *Just hang on a little longer.* I said, "Sorry?"

"Come on, Jason, spare me."

"Well, we've become friendly," I said. "If that's what you mean."

"He's an interesting guy," Sonny said, his tone implying that he knew everything about you and that I knew nothing. "His father was editor in chief, years ago. Dead now. So we try to look out for him. Keep him out of trouble."

"And?"

"And so the last thing he needs—or the paper needs—is a gay stalker. Where's your ashtray?" Water slammed the passenger half of the windshield, as though aiming for him. "Hey, slow down," he said, "will you?"

"Sorry," I said. We were on the long, pine-lined entranceway to the terminal, a single supermarket-sized building, and the open sky over the runways was visible, striped with wide dark bands, like the shadows of giant fan blades moving in slow motion. I couldn't get there fast enough.

"Turn here behind the rental cars," Sonny said. "It'll take us right out on the tarmac. I hope you've been paying attention to what I've said. I don't care what you do at home, behind closed doors, but I hope you're listening to me. We had forty-five applicants for your position."

"You want to protect him from me," I said, steering to where he was pointing. "Right? *You* want to protect *him* from *me*." I cut the engine, and it knocked twice, some thunder rumbling along with it. We were at the edge of the gate's concrete skirting, facing out on the empty runways, and beyond them the thick stands of long-leaf pine and palmetto scrub, from which the bird would supposedly emerge. A lone prop jet sat at the gate, unattended. I pulled my camera bag from the backseat, pretended to rummage in it. There was the little gun Owen had lent me—shiny, pretty.

"I'd watch the sarcasm if I were you," Sonny said.

"Watch the birdie, watch the sarcasm," I said. Blood rushed and beat in my ears, building in tempo. Sonny was glaring at me, stroking his scraggly chin, and it occurred to me that he might be sneakily appropriating your gestures, one by one, even as he proclaimed himself your protector.

"Look, it's let up," he said finally. "Let's get out there, okay? I don't have all day."

We marched along single file in the drenched grass, parallel to the tree line, his black-jeaned butt twitching self-righteously in front of me. The words I planned to say hurtled through my head.

"You didn't come this far last time, did you?" he said.

"I could never have come this far without you," I said.

"Okay," he said, stopping and brushing his hands together, as though he'd just finished a dirty job. "I'm out of here. I'll grab a cab, and why don't you just not come back in at all, okay?"

"I'm sorry," I said. "I don't think I understand." Thunder boomed as the next band of dark moved in.

Sonny glanced at the sky, then down at his shirtfront, which was beginning to speckle. "Look, I don't want some kind of show-down," he said. "Why don't you just do the honorable thing, the graceful thing—"

"Graceful!" I said. "This *is* a showdown." It was time. "This is a showdown about beauty," I began, but he had already turned his back and was heading for the terminal, his feet slapping into a jog. "Wait!" I yelled. "You f—ing coward!" The wind had picked up, and I didn't think he'd heard me. *You are the enemy of beauty!* I was going to say. *If beauty is to survive, you must be destroyed!* I broke into a run behind him, not to catch up, as I knew he couldn't match me for speed, but because the storm was suddenly enormous, almost upon us. Funny, I thought, it sounds like a locomotive.

Something huge and black and silver was bearing down, crackling and roaring like a metallic bear, moving faster than both of us. *You!* I thought, returning from your vacation just in time—but the planes weren't flying, and you weren't due back until the next day. Still, I knew it was going to help me, and I tilted my head back to greet it, grateful, relieved—I wouldn't need the gun. There was a pause in the noise, like an intake of breath, and then the lightning smacked down a few yards in front of me, knocking Sonny side-ways. His body seemed to hang in the air for a moment as the charge exited it, and then it folded and fell, almost slowly, like a used-up helium balloon, making no sound when it hit the ground.

"Thank you," I said, out loud.

The light had gone back up in the sky and was pulsing on and off there, a signal meant just for me. Rain sliced down finally. I heard the sirens start back at the terminal—the trucks would reach us in seconds, I knew, so I didn't have to do anything, nothing was required of me. I stood there with my hands dangling, like a beautiful girl, helpless, guiltless, perfect.

Before the authorities could get there, though, a figure crashed out of the trees beside Sonny's body, a shape moving tentatively, then quickly toward me, tall and impossibly skinny and outlined in light, a familiar silhouette. *Bultinck?* I whispered. But it whooshed right past, feathers rustling, the smell of burned flesh and roses fluttering in the air behind it.

Wendy Brenner is the author of *Large Animals in Everyday Life,* **which won the Flannery O'Connor Award, and is currently completing a second story collection,** *Soon It Will Work Everywhere.* **She received a 2000 NEA Literature Fellowship. She teaches creative writing at University of North Carolina at Wilmington, and is a contributing writer for** *The Oxford American.* **This is her fourth appearance in** *New Stories from the South.*

CAROLINE NIKITAS

*T*his is an unrequited love story that started out as a poem, though I *don't write poetry (or not any I'd show anyone). I was in unrequited love when I wrote it, which I believe makes one write better, more desperate fiction. Most of the details are true, but rearranged into a fictional context. In times of high emotion, for example, I've noticed a sudden surge of electromagnetic activity in my house: lightbulbs blow, appliances break down, squirrels fall out of trees in my yard. I know some people will say, "You just don't notice it at other times," but they haven't been to my house. My friend Jamie and I really did see a hairball driving a truck, and no one will ever convince us otherwise. We just looked at each other and said, "Did you see that?"*

Karen Sagstetter

THE THING WITH WILLIE

(from *Glimmer Train*)

O n a fishing trip with her father, Anna faced her first authentic test of faith. It was 1890, near Galveston, and the boat had skimmed over the water, out to sea, and his tanned face rocked toward her and away as he pulled oars forward and back, forward and back, in a hard, sure rhythm. She later recalled sounds of waves slapping the sides of the boat, and his voice, telling her facts about the ocean—for instance, how a flounder lies flat on the bottom, two eyes on the same side of his head like a person, not like a fish.

They dropped lines; right away there was a yank on hers, and he helped her manage a snappy little trout. He'd packed sandwiches and cold tea, and he fed them to his child, talking about everything under the sun. When it got hot, he steered toward home, saying that the coast stretched like a lazy cat all the way to Mexico.

Twenty yards from shore, her father reached over the side of the boat and plunged his hand into the water; his sleeve was dark and wet, soaked to the shoulder. He pulled out, sand dribbling down his arm in rivulets, and unwound his fingers to show her: a craggy, pear-shaped shell. He rinsed it well in the sea water, taking his time, pushing mud from the crevices with his thumb, and with the force of his knife pried it open fast, like a man who knew what to do about things.

Inside the shell was a pecan-sized grey blob. Grinning, he caught it up with his fingers. Sugar, open your mouth! She opened up and a fat oyster swam down her throat, tasting like salt water. It was her first completely fresh morsel of seafood.

But in the 1930s people were fishing not for fun but for their lives. So many jobs had disappeared in Galveston, everywhere in the country. When the thing with Willie happened, Anna remembered her father's oyster. Probably that was the moment when she had first become so extremely particular about her seafood.

Willie, clean me a half-dozen flounder, three or four croakers, and a couple of dozen crabs, will you?

Yes, ma'am.

How's your wife? Okay?

Yes, ma'am.

Your children? Gettin' big, I'll bet.

My little boy Raymond isn't too good.

Oh, sorry to hear that. What's wrong?

He don't walk yet. Doctor don't know what to do.

How old is he?

He's four, ma'am.

That must be a worry. Sometimes they take their time. How about the others?

Oh, they're mostly fine. Taller every day. Eat plenty.

Don't I know it.

Your boy okay, ma'am? Your girl?

Yes, fine, okay. Lucy's fine. All grown up. Louis is a mess sometimes.

She almost said, Can't stay still, but didn't so not to hurt his feelings about his own boy.

Willie was the colored man who worked at John's Seafood. He had a bunch of kids, and his wife Patti Ann kept chickens and a vegetable garden to help out. Because he was a true professional, he and Anna got along, but her husband Howard didn't like him.

What's your problem with Willie?

He's slow.

He's not slow. He's fast when he cleans a crab.

Doesn't answer sometimes. I don't like that. Not polite.

He's busy. Tired.

I couldn't do what he does. I hate fish guts.

I don't mind. I'm thinking of what I'll make later.

It's a good thing you have work to like, isn't it?

Howard had lost his job; his car dealership had folded. He wasn't all that prejudiced, but he disliked the idea of a black man having work when he didn't. It came back to his wife making the money for the family, too. Willie was part of that.

Anna Clinton was a very good cook, and she was a hit with farmers and fishermen, who paid to enjoy her thick sauces with the red pepper and garlic.

Scales and shells didn't bother her at all. She liked to watch Willie clean fish because she was looking forward to the money she'd make cooking those fish for the hospital or church. Willie tended his knives so they were sharp and shiny; a gleam ricocheted off the ceiling while he worked, his fish heads scuttled to the edge of the counter, scales showered upward, and you had a beautiful fillet in thirty seconds. The same with oysters—he shucked to beat the band. Where he paused was right at first—to prod the edges of the shell and find exactly the right spot for the oyster knife to go in. Then he pushed it hard and quick, and the shell opened with the sound of a small belch, like a secret getting out, followed by a scrape of the knife that made her mouth water as the oyster tumbled into a jar.

Still, she could see Willie was exhausted. He was six feet tall, with short-cropped, inky hair and a sweet expression. Bent over, like his shoulders were not carrying just him, but invisible weight, too. Sometimes he'd be moving a chaos of entrails into a heap, and he'd stop to prop himself with the broomstick and yawn. Sometimes he forgot to answer and would only nod, which a black man normally would never do in relation to a white lady. Unless he was swaying at the brink.

• • •

Anna had a big order coming up—the Valentine's benefit at the firehouse was two weeks away. As if she needed trouble, the teacher stopped by to discuss her son Louis. She commented that he had a decent mind. Could read well, so what was the problem with his math?

So Howard talked with him man-to-man on the front porch. The end of that week was bingo night at St. Aloysius, the Catholic church, a new client. Meaning they needed to progress from mounds of okra, crabs, shrimp, onions, celery, tomatoes, and rice—by virtue of elbow grease and correct calculations, never mind inspiration—to gumbo. Anna said, Here's a recipe for twelve, and Howard said, You specify how much okra, how many crabs, how many onions we need to prepare dinner for forty salivating people who have Friday night appetites and want to win the jackpot, and write it down for your mother.

Louis reacted by looking bored and rolling his eyes—a very dangerous thing to do, because that bored look always caused Howard's forehead to turn red, and he wasn't going to put up with it for an instant. *Now!* he shouted.

Louis scrammed, leaping away like a hound, over the ottoman in the living room and around the side table with the recipe squashed inside his pants pocket. While his mother planted twenty caladiums in the front flower bed and ironed four shirts, Louis toiled in his room. When he emerged clutching a large sheet of lined paper, the sass had subsided. He'd been stuck on okra because no one knew how many pods were in a bushel. But he'd written:

Gumbo for Forty
1. Okra: two-thirds of a bushel basket
2. Crabs: 3.2 dozen
3. Oysters: 27
4. Onions: 19-¼ @ four inches in diameter
5. Chopped parsley: sixteen tablespoons

Of course, Anna had never in her life used a precise recipe for stews. For her famous cakes, yes, and she had to be fussy about whether to add one teaspoon of vanilla or one and a half. But gumbo came about after an evening at the kitchen table chopping okra while you were sipping iced tea. The idea of 19-¼ onions was amusing, but in the spirit of the math lesson, Anna followed it faithfully.

At John's Seafood, she and Louis shopped together. Anna told Willie that her son figured she needed 27 oysters and 38.4 crabs.

That right, Mr. Louis?

Yes, Willie, the way I calculate it.

Well, you got it. You watch me.

I'd like for Louis to practice his timekeeping, Anna added.

Yes, ma'am.

You're so fast with the oyster knife, could he practice with the stopwatch right here?

All right, Miz Clinton.

Louis observed that Willie shucked twenty-seven oysters in four minutes and fifteen seconds flat. He made a note of this. Instead of four-tenths of a crab, Willie suggested they take half of a giant blue crab's body.

The rest of the week, Willie wouldn't prepare Anna's fish without asking: Did your boy figure this for you, ma'am? If she said no, he'd say, Well, ma'am, won't he be disappointed if you don't check with him?

Before the '29 crash, Anna had been a professional baker. Now her business wasn't weddings and birthdays, but Easter lunch at the hospital or fried fish for the city plumbers' late shift. She usually prepared extra because in Galveston, like all over, there were people who, if they didn't hook a flounder that day, did not eat— regulars at her back porch who would sweep or rake in exchange for a bowl of soup.

After a long day cooking, she liked to go walking on the beach. Anna had never seen a mountain or even a hill. She'd never seen snow. But she'd been born to the Gulf of Mexico, and when she was young, all she wanted to be was wet. On the island, summer heat was treacherous, and her mother didn't object even back in the nineties when she waded into the surf in an old dress. She liked the mush of sand between her toes—hot sand on the beach, wet sand at the water's edge, cool water inching over her feet to her ankles—and she'd push at the tide as it was grabbing her stomach, her breasts, and rising up and over her back while she moved against the friendly resistance of the ocean, like roughhousing with her uncles, wild and safe at once, deeper and deeper, until the water surmounted her shoulders, swells were nipping her cheeks, and her skirts were billowing to her hips. She walked slowly, savoring, and she didn't mind the fish nibbling her ankles; they made her smile to herself. She'd plunge her face under, shaking her head from side to side and snorting out the salty water like a dog in a bath. Dogfish, her mother called her. And she'd swim and trot along, riding the current back, taking a long time for it. She wanted her hair soaked, dripping, wanted water to sink clear though her scalp, and whatever slab of worry was weighing on her chest, well, it dissolved.

No denying it was a nice break to be getting business from the firehouse—fifty chicken-and-dumplings suppers for the annual Valentine's benefit. Louis studied the situation and constructed the shopping list. This led to Anna's visiting a chicken farm to select thirteen and two-thirds pullets which, since she was purchasing them live, was going to be difficult. (Louis's fractions were the current family joke.) She'd arranged to have them dressed, so she left the birds squawking and scratching at the butcher's, and stopped in at John's. Anna and Johnny chatted about the mild February weather and the price of flounder, and then he mentioned that Willie's wife Patti Ann was pregnant with her seventh baby and that Willie hadn't shown up for work for two days. What's wrong, she thought. He needs the money. And who'll clean my fish for me? That was Wednesday morning.

Thursday was the day before the benefit. In the evening the whole family—Howard, Anna, Louis, and sister Lucy—were hacking chickens into stew-sized pieces and tossing skin, bones, and fat to the center of the kitchen table, when Willie knocked on the back door, a child in his arms.

The child had to be Raymond. He was small. Cocker-spaniel sized. Not malnourished—his skin was a strong coffee color and he wasn't skinny—but he was limp. A bag of limbs. Bones bundled together, but not holding him up. His head rolled around on his neck, and he was drooling.

Evening, Miz Clinton, ma'am. Don't mean to intrude. This here's my boy Raymond.

Why hello, Willie. We're cutting all these chickens up. There's a big mess in here and an awful smell.

Can't be as bad as fish.

I don't mind the fish smell.

Really she didn't. To see trout and redfish laid out fat and glistening on ice, begging her for butter, garlic, and lemon, was a pleasure.

The young son Raymond wasn't just slow or sick. He had something terribly wrong with him. He made a constant noise, whimpering and howling, and Willie couldn't shift him around frequently enough to quiet him. Raymond was four years old and had never uttered a single word. He was wearing a diaper.

How is your wife, Willie?

She's all right. Expecting her seventh. We just found out.

Oh, well, that's nice.

Yeah. I suppose. Listen, Miz Clinton, I was wondering. It's Raymond's fifth birthday on Saturday. Patti Ann ain't feeling so good right now, and I want a cake for my little boy here.

As Ann talked with Willie, she kept turning her ear toward her family. The kids and Howard were still at the chickens in the kitchen; the hammer of the cleaver and their chatter created a comforting stir in the background. She had a queasy feeling, watching the idiot child. Willie's shoulder was soaked, and she produced a towel.

What sort of cake, Willie?

I'd like to buy one of your great cakes I've heard about. Chocolate icing. And I want you to write Raymond's name on it. With icing.

Why sure, Willie. Of course, I'll make it. What color icing?

You decide. You can make it pretty. I've heard.

Howard didn't like the interruption and snapped—how did she think she was going to get everything done? Things were on his nerves.

Getting that cake baked in the midst of the chicken bones and biscuit dough with the fire chief's wife stopping in every hour to check on things—the idea got on Anna's nerves, too. But she determined to do it.

She labored over her broth, intensifying it with more and more bones, extra onions and green peppers, boiling it down, and down again. She and Lucy sautéed the chicken pieces, set them aside in bowls, kneaded biscuit dough for the dumplings, and around eleven they put the house back together. With the big mop, Louis washed the kitchen, living-room, and hall floors, and Lucy swept the back porch, where they'd been throwing chicken skin, onion peel, and celery ends onto spread-out newspapers. That is, when she wasn't leaning on the broom yawning. Anna was going to assemble and simmer the stews Friday morning and afternoon, and the event was at 7 P.M., so the only time for the cake was that very Thursday night, late, after the kids and Howard went to bed. Without exactly lying, she gave Howard the impression that she was contriving a treat for the fire chief.

What's the cake for?

I'll give some to people who help us get our dinners together, or maybe to the fire chief, since he's trusting us with the job.

Not a bad idea.

Since the crash, Anna had been working with chicken guts and fish parts and hadn't made many beautiful desserts. "Weddings by Anna" had become known because of a particular specialty: her four-layer spice cake with buttery almond frosting and, on top, a burst of white-sugar calla lilies with yellow stamens and pistils in a surround of blue asters. But now people who had been wealthy in the twenties were driving old Fords and dispatching their children to the justice of the peace to get married. So her longing for the finest lately was expressed with extra spices and sensational gravies.

In the good solitude of the dim kitchen, Anna sifted her best white cake flour twice, so it would be silky and light. She had always known, as if angels were whispering how, about creaming the butter and sugar thoroughly. About using sweet Ware's Dairy butter in the first place. About superior Mexican vanilla and fresh eggs. She still possessed a few bars of premium Swiss chocolate, which she grated and swirled into the batter for a marble cake effect. She whipped six egg whites and folded them in quickly so the cake would be airy, divine.

At two in the morning, aroma flowering from the oven, she took the risen cake out to cool. The frosting came easy. For that she used regular baker's chocolate, melted in the top of a double boiler, and then mixed into the already-combined confectioner's sugar and butter. She spread the cake with the chocolate icing and divided the reserved, not-chocolate icing into three mounds, adding green coloring to one, pink to one, yellow to the other. With her French cake decorator she dripped pink sugar roses, the size of a baby's puckered mouth, in a circle on top of the chocolate frosting, and in the center she wrote, in looping script, *Raymond*. She crafted perfect green stems and leaves and added yellow centers to the roses. Then she removed her sapphire ring—her birthstone—licked the frosting from it, carefully rinsed and dried it, and put it back onto her right ring finger. She believed that something pretty could usually make you feel better, and she felt inspired by its confident beauty, its perfection. "Clear minded" was what the sapphire stood for, and she always wore it while she worked.

Her fourth apron of the day was splattered with god knows what, and she smelled like ground-up animals and plants. As she ran a dishrag around the drain boards, her arms cramped; she was dead on her feet; her feet were somewhere below, far away from the rest of her body.

Really, she thought, one more rose would make it look better, but she stopped at six because it was the boy's fifth birthday: five and one to grow on. Finally, she arranged the cake in a covered cooler so the roses wouldn't subside. At 3:30 A.M. she fell into bed.

Late Friday afternoon, Anna and Lucy were packing serving utensils for the last run to the firehouse hall when Willie rapped at the back door, crumpling a dollar bill in his fist. He was alone.

But Anna had decided that this cake was not for sale. She told Willie that her husband was very strict about how she disposed of her cakes, and he had given her instructions that because Willie had helped so often when they needed a rush order of shrimp or oysters, the cake was to be a birthday gift to Willie and his family. Well, Willie would have not have it.

No, ma'am. No way. I have the money right here and you have to take it.

But you gave me a chance to show my stuff, Willie. Nobody's asking for pretty cakes these days. You did me a favor.

Your cake is just beautiful. Beautiful. His name and all. I don't know how you do it, but it's just right.

Anna couldn't take cash from such a poor man. But there was no arguing with him. (My feet are planted here till you take it), and she didn't have time for a prolonged discussion. He insisted. Okay, she said, I'll take a nickel, and held out her jar of change. He kept dropping coins in until she retracted the jar, so he must've deposited two or three. For a long time after, the clink of his nickels stayed with her, like a deep shiver.

With the cake in the bakery box, Willie disappeared into the alley, and they got busy with the firehouse supper. Sometime during the evening, Anna told Howard the cake had gone to Willie. She wanted to clear that up; she didn't like unfinished business. Howard was enjoying the cheer in the firehouse hall, so all he said was Why'd you give him the whole thing? — to show he could still question her decisions.

By ten o'clock they must have wiped their hands on their aprons a hundred times, splashed gravy onto the floor fifty times, and said you're welcome two hundred times. But they would surely be hired to supply more benefit dinners; the fire chief's wife all but said so, and with four of them working, tidying the mess wouldn't be that bad.

Very early Saturday morning, while Anna and Howard, Lucy and Louis, were sleeping hard, Willie carried the pretty cake and his little boy Raymond to a jetty. There, tied to a piling, was an old but spacious rowboat, belonging to someone, he didn't know who. The weather was perfect: cool, clear-blue sky blooming with pink and orange clouds.

Willie tied his son's legs to the seat so he wouldn't be tossed over in a swell, and joined him in the center of the boat. He rowed east toward the sunrise, passing shrimp boats, cotton ships, and fuel barges, and on and on they went straddling waves, jumping waves, bouncing, riding all the way with the Gulf. After they were beyond sight of the beaches, he aimed a pistol at Raymond's head, pulled the trigger, and then pointed it at himself.

By late Saturday afternoon the boat had drifted back to shore. The cake was still in the bakery box, secured with ropes in the hold between the two bodies. It was intact—fragrant and colorful— except that it had been neatly cut. Two large slices were missing. All the pink sugar roses, with the perfect green leaves and yellow centers, were gone too.

Soon it grew hot again, and hotter still, March to July, and so on. Anna started going to the beach in the early mornings, walking ankle deep in the small waves. Howard found a job selling typewriters, and he and Louis were the ones who on Sundays delivered Anna's étouffées to Patti Ann. She had a baby girl at the end of the summer.

Karen Sagstetter grew up on the Gulf Coast of
Texas. She is editor in chief at the Freer and
Sackler Galleries, Smithsonian Institution, and
editor of *Asian Art and Culture,* a book series.
She studied in Japan as a Fulbright journalist, has
received grants for poetry and fiction, and is the
author of two nonfiction books for younger readers and two chapbooks of poetry. "The Thing
with Willie" won first prize in a *Glimmer Train*
contest for new fiction writers.

JOHN TSANTES

*A*nna's oyster in the story of Willie is based on a childhood experience.
One day out fishing, my grandfather scooped an oyster from the muddy
bottom of San Leon Bay, near Galveston. "Sugar baby," he said, "open your
mouth and swallow this thing." I did it without an instant's hesitation and
I've loved oysters ever since.

My grandfather had a beautiful gift for storytelling. He was always
interrupting his stories with runs of laughter, and I can still see him taking
off his glasses to wipe away the tears that were streaming down. The
neighborly spirit embodied in Anna is inspired by his accounts of an era
more trusting than ours, when people might share dinner from the family
stove with a hungry stranger. Among his stories of the Depression was one
about an acquaintance who took his mentally handicapped daughter—and
himself—to the woods to save his family from further misery. I was very
young, and he didn't elaborate or explain—it was like a two-line item in a
newspaper—but I never forgot.

Melanie Sumner

GOOD-HEARTED WOMAN

(from *DoubleTake*)

Sometimes Mrs. Peppers said bitterly, "Henry is married to the plant," and Louise would imagine her father entangled in the embrace of an overgrown kudzu weed. When Florida was proud of her husband, she called the plant by its name, Southern Board. "Henry is the general manager of Southern Board," she told strangers in a velvet voice.

Every pen, notepad, and calendar at Owl Aerie bore the name "Southern Board." It was printed on windbreakers, penknives, and clocks. When Roderick was alive, he'd told people that SOUTHERN BOARD was stamped on the behind of each family member. During a confused period in her early childhood, Louise had used Southern Board as her last name. When she turned sixteen, Henry gave her a Southern Board keychain imprinted with the company's logo, "The Best Way Is The Safe Way," dangling the keys to a hand-me-down Pontiac Bonneville. The Bonneville had smelled new for the entire year Henry used it as the company car; after that, when he gave it to Florida, it picked up the odors of lipstick, Kleenex, and acrylic paint. In Louise's hands, it had acquired the aroma of a saloon and was known about Counterpoint, by the teenagers, as Partyville.

During the long summers, she cruised Partyville up and down the streets with all the windows down and slurped Tanqueray through a straw while the B-52's blared from the cheap tape deck. Sometimes she put on a tennis skirt and drove out to the Three Bears Country Club, where she smoked pot in the powder room with Drew St. John. When she was really bored, she got into Florida's Clairol Collection and dyed Puff LeBlanc colors that would embarrass even a toy poodle. Florida thought she should get a job.

"The clothing stores would want you to fix your hair every morning," she said, "and they don't pay anything anyway. I'd let you help me out with my Special Art Class, but you don't like retarded people. They get too personal with you. Henry always meant to put Roderick to work at the factory, during the summers—Southern Board pays good money—but your father wouldn't let you work out there. With all those men." Suddenly it seemed to Louise that if she was not employed for a summer at Southern Board, her life would be ruined.

"A corrugated-board plant is no place for a young lady," Henry said, first looking her in the eye, then bending his head down to his paper to confirm that the discussion was over. She appealed to her mother, but Florida was in menopause that year, and half mad.

"Oh, honey!" she cried. She looked as if Louise had wrecked the Bonneville. "Oh, baby, no. No, no, no! You're too spoiled to work. You'd have to get out of bed in the morning. You know your father won't put you in that dirty factory."

In the end, Drew St. John paved the way for Louise by taking a job at Sweetheart Bakery, owned by her father. Mr. St. John, who owned a good chunk of north Georgia, was a gentleman, and therefore, Mr. Peppers deduced, he must be making a lady out of Drew.

Drew and Louise had been best friends since they were five years old, and they were as different from each other as real sisters. When Louise told Drew that she planned to have an affair with a factory worker at Southern Board, letting the word "affair" trail off her tongue, Drew was shocked. She widened her eyes, then narrowed them, letting her lip curl in disdain. She said, "Gross!"

She had a similar reaction when Louise began listening to country music. Louise tried to keep it a secret, but occasionally Drew overheard her singing quietly to herself, "She's a good-hearted woman, in love with a good-timing man," or "Take this job and shove it." Once, she found a Johnny Paycheck tape in Louise's car.

"I don't believe you," she said, holding the tape away from her as though merely by touching it she might become a redneck. "How could you possibly like this shit?"

That summer, no one wanted to know what Louise was thinking. "You don't listen to me!" she screamed at Florida during one of their fights. "You've never listened to me for ten minutes in my entire life!"

"All right!" Florida yelled. "I'm listening!" She set the oven timer for ten minutes. The kitchen was silent. "Well," she said, "I'm listening. Talk." Louise tried to say the things she had wanted to say, but the seconds were like birds flying in her face, and she threw up her hands, screaming, "Stop it!"

"See," Florida said, when the buzzer rang. "You don't have anything to say."

Louise started a diary. Everything she wrote was stupid, but she forced herself to scratch out the words, without stopping, for ten minutes a day. It was like trying to dig her way out of the ground with a teaspoon.

In June, she entered the plant. On that first day, when Raymond Patch, the foreman, led her on a brief tour of the factory, she was terrified. Ceiling lights shot streaks of yellow through the iron rafters, while the Georgia sun bored through a wall of green windows. The heat itself was green. Gigantic machines slammed metal against metal, penetrating the soft Styrofoam earplugs in Louise's ears with a rhythmic, churning roar. The hot air was thick with paper dust and smelled like a skunk. As she followed Raymond Patch deeper into the plant, the odor became so intense she thought she would vomit.

Raymond didn't seem to notice the smell. He was a skinny man with a pointed face and small green eyes fringed by pale, almost invisible lashes. He wore a baggy polyester suit the color of tobacco and an unfashionably wide tie of similar material in a lighter shade of nicotine. He smoked so much that he had to fight for every breath; the expression of concentrated will had become permanent on his face. Apparently, women unnerved him.

"This here is the corrugator!" he yelled, stopping in front of a long ramp of rolling brown paper. "Stay away from it. Two years ago, fellow fell on that and burnt like a piece of bacon." Staring at Louise's shoes, he asked her if she had read the safety booklet. When she said yes, she knew that he knew she was lying. He rubbed his ear, then pointed to a hunk of metal whirring with blades as big as hub caps. "Slitter!" he shouted.

Louise nodded. On the wall next to the time clock hung a calendar marking the days of continuous safety in the plant. When she came to work, Southern Board had gone 212 days without an accident.

All of the men, except Jeremiah, looked at Louise's boots when Mr. Patch introduced her to them. Mr. Peppers had refused to buy her Doc Martens. "You won't be working in a factory for the rest of your life, I hope," he told her at Payless Shoes. She stared glumly at the rack of cheap boots while he laughed, patting her too hard on the back.

Jeremiah Stokes was a strong, handsome man, smart as a whip, with a great, noble heart, and horse sense to boot. Had he been white, he would have been Henry's closest friend. The best Mr. Peppers could do was promote him every year until he was in charge of all the other black men in the plant and had his own office in the back, next to the bailer. He was the only employee at the factory taller than five foot nine, Henry's height, but like all the other men Mr. Peppers had hired, his hands were huge.

"Jeremiah has his own place back here," said Raymond Patch, leading Louise into a small office paneled with pine board. Raymond leaned against his desk, arms crossed, while Jeremiah towered in the doorway. The office was tidier than the one Mr. Patch shared with the two other foremen.

"Jeremiah is as neat as a pin," Henry liked to say. On Sundays after church, he sometimes drove the family out by Jeremiah's small brick house on Hummingbird Lane. Idling the car in front of the manicured lawn, he would exclaim, "Clean as a whistle!" In the driveway sat a polished white Cadillac, which Jeremiah never drove to work. When the Peppers had a big party, he drove it up Mount Zion. On these nights he wore a coat and tie and parked cars for the guests. "Jeremiah is honest as the day he was born," Henry told people.

Now, as Louise stared at the crisp blue curtain Jeremiah's wife had hung on the wall to make it look like there was a window, she wondered, for the first time since she had set her heart on getting hired at Southern Board, if she could hold a job. She figured that someone would come to his senses shortly and say, "What is this little girl doing here?"

"Ready to go to work?" barked Mr. Patch as he stepped toward the door. Jeremiah stepped aside to let him pass, reaching down to turn the cap backward on Louise's head when she followed.

"Your daddy is a good man," he said. "You know that, don't you?"

Within minutes, she was throwing scrap board into the bailer. She continued to do that, with all her strength, heart, and soul, for another seven hours.

After Louise had worked for several days without any mention of being fired, she began to worry about her popularity. Besides a twenty-four-minute lunch, Southern Board workers had two twelve-minute breaks a shift—the white people spent these free periods in the break room at the front of the plant. It was a crowded, smoky little room, but whatever table Louise chose remained empty except for her. The men crammed chairs around the other tables, where they sat elbow to elbow with their black lunch boxes open before them, blowing smoke in each other's faces. Occasionally, a Frito hit Louise in the back of the neck, but when she turned around, all the men had their heads down.

"Well, you're not there to socialize," Henry said, when she complained to him. He leaned forward in his La-Z-Boy and eyed her sternly over the *Wall Street Journal.* I hope you understand that. Just do your work out there and come straight home."

"Hen-ry!" Florida hollered into the intercom. "Lou-ise! Supper!"

"Dad, they throw things at me."

"Throw things?" He frowned. "What do they throw?"

From the top of the stairs, Florida yelled, "Louise! Tell your father to come and eat!"

"Coming," Louise replied, without moving. "Potato chips. Empty chewing tobacco pouches. Pieces of string."

Henry laughed. "That's just their way of being friendly. They're having fun with you, honey. If they didn't like you, they wouldn't tease you. How's old Drewster doing at her factory job?"

"She hates it. She—"

Florida stomped into the den, announcing that she was throwing supper in the garbage can since no one wanted it. She had recently acquired several new jogging suits in alarming colors and would wear nothing else. In these suits, she could flail her arms at Henry and Louise, kick doors shut behind her, and fling herself onto a bed to sob without pulling seams or popping buttons.

"Women need to express their anger," her artist-friend Mary MacDonald told her. "I've started smashing plates in the garage. I have a special hammer. I've painted the word "kill" on it." Florida knew that Henry would have a conniption fit if she broke a plate on purpose, but she took Mary's ideas seriously because she was a real artist: people drove down from Atlanta to buy her collages. "Try some I-Feel-Angry-At statements," she suggested.

Florida felt angry at her hair for going gray on her. She was angry at Henry for not being romantic and for working all the time and thinking about work when he was at home. She was angry at Roderick for dying, angry at herself for not knowing he was allergic to beestings. She was angry at bees. She was angry at Louise for smarting off to her mother and doing as she pleased and never lifting a finger and for not fixing herself up and going out there and getting a cute boyfriend and for turning her back on Jesus Christ. She was angry at Puff LeBlanc for rolling in manure ten minutes after she had picked him up from his monthly appointment at Styles For Pets, forty-five dollars down the drain. She was angry at her parents, who had died within a week of each other last winter, and she was furious at the white-trash tenant who had tossed a cigarette into the 150-year-old farmhouse, causing it to burn to the ground. All afternoon, she'd been angry at Helen Olfinger, who was her own age and the most talented in her Special Art Class, for drinking the green paint, and now she was livid because Henry and Louise would not come to the table before the food got cold. Standing in the center of the den, she announced, "I am not your slave," and stared them down for a full minute before she took off with a tap, tap, tap of her heels on the new wooden floor.

When she was gone, Henry blinked, as if coming out of a dream. Then he said, "I think your mother has supper ready," and began to fold up his paper.

As soon as everyone was seated at the table, Florida bowed her head, squeezed her eyes shut, and prayed, "Lord, thank you for the food you have bestowed on us tonight and for giving me the time to prepare it for my family, in my busy day. Teach all of us to be more grateful. Be with Roderick in the mansion you have prepared for him. Guide Louise and help her to make mature decisions as she grows into a Christian young lady and maybe starts dating some, if that is in your plan for her. Teach her to listen to those who know better and would help her. Help us all to keep smiling and not get discouraged. Amen."

Embarrassed, Henry sank his teeth into the cold tuna melt. Louise, who was only having barbecued potato chips, carried on a conversation with Puff while Florida, now that she had everyone together, took this opportunity to talk about Jesus Christ.

Mrs. Peppers had always been a pious woman, but in the last year, with the death of her parents, the loss of her old home, and the advent of menopause, she had become fervent. If Henry had let her, she would have gone door to door in Counterpoint, saving people. "Are you ashamed of God?" she asked him when he asked her, with a look, to tone it down.

"I am proud to know the son of God," she would say, on the verge of tears. Then she would choose one of Henry's faults, for instance, his concern with public opinion, and take it to town, with a religious angle. "I don't just go to church because it looks good," she told him. "To keep up with the Joneses. That's not what it's all about. If that's why you worship, to see and be seen, then you are going down the wrong path. You better pray about it."

Besides her regular attendance at Bellamy Street Baptist Church, she was active in the Christian Women's Club, where she met with Shirley Frommlecker, whose husband had run off and left her; Lacy Dalton, who had lost a breast; Agnes Gaines, her hairdresser; and several other Protestant women seeking strength and comfort in the Lord. Weekly fellowship with these women—except for Agnes, who was a pill—gave Florida the courage to go on living.

"Witness," the women said, with their waxed lips, holding cups of herbal tea, making it sound soft and alluring, infinitely feminine.

Whenever they went out of town, and Henry's head was turned, she passed out tracts and New Testaments. "Do you know Jesus Christ?" she would ask, with her back straight, her hair perfect, not smiling. She had a purpose. She had God's love.

Back at home, Louise was turning into an atheist and a hellcat.

"I can see it coming," Florida would tell her, with her lips stretched into a fierce grimace.

"What?" she would ask in a taunting voice. "See what coming?" Then she would laugh with the high whine of a girl brought up in a rusty trailer on the edge of town, a girl no one cared about, with no respect for her mother and father. She no longer sent underwear to the laundry room, which told Florida that she had either stopped wearing it, or was in something too fancy to be seen.

"You have turned your back on Him," Florida said. "You'll be sorry, mark my words." Louise mimicked her until she wept.

"You two stop that fussing and fighting," said Henry one morning, lifting his head from his cereal bowl.

"You two? Who is you two?" cried Florida. "Don't put me on the same level with her! This family has a problem. I know you don't want to hear it, Henry. You think the Peppers are perfect. Shoot! Somebody has to face the truth around here. Your daughter is headed down the wrong path. That's all I'm saying. I give up! I wash my hands of both of you. From now on, you can raise her. Just leave me out of it." She started tucking Bible verses into Louise's lunch bag.

One day, while Louise was sitting at her empty table in the break room at Southern Board, reading, "Whosoever therefore shall be ashamed of me and of my words in this adulterous and sinful generation; of him also shall the Son of man be ashamed, when he cometh in the glory of his Father with the holy angels. St. Mark 9:38," a plastic spoon winged past her ear. She ignored it. Then a man called Polecat, because he was skinny and worked on top of a ladder, wedged his thick hand into the plastic window of a Lance's snack machine, pulled out a package of Choco-fil cookies, and farted with such an explosion that Louise jumped. The men howled.

"'Scuse my language," said Polecat, shuffling back to his seat.

Someone said, "The boss's daughter never heard a fart before."

"What the hell is she doing here anyway," asked Smiley, a scar-faced man who never smiled.

"I reckon Henry and Florida are having hard times. I hear they had to cut back on the champagne and them trips around the world. So Henry put the girl out to work."

"Ain't that a shame."

"Naw. They ain't having hard times. They're still sitting pretty up on that mountain. I'll tell you what happened, though," said Jack.

"Jack's the maid."

"Naw, he's the pool man on the weekends."

Jack rubbed his chin, leaned back in his chair with a wise look. Watching his face, the crow's feet around his aquamarine eyes, and the hardened, bitter twist of his lips, Louise thought, He has *lived*.

He said, "See, Henry, he says to the wife, 'Let's you and me do an experiment. Let's us put that girl in the plant. What about it? We'll put a cap on her, and some brogans, and take a couple of pictures for *National Geographic.*'"

"Hey, Experiment," said T. C. Curtis, winking at her as he shuffled to the snack machine.

"T. C., don't mess with Experiment now. This is a scientific operation."

"Just experimenting," said T. C.

T. C. was the one Louise chose to be her lover, by virtue of the fact that he was under forty and had winked at her. He was only her lover in her imagination, where he entered as a seed and grew wildly under the hot green lights in eight-hour increments.

She had used up all of her regular daydreams. While she was shoving boards into the bailer, turning boxes in the printer, or slamming away at the M-12, she thought about T. C. Curtis. With each stack of boards that went down the conveyer belt, his beer belly became less noticeable. By quitting time each day, when her ankles hurt and her eyes stung from sweat, the man was an inch taller and a year younger. After work, when Louise drove the station wagon up the mountain with the windows down, the radio blaring "Scarlet Fever," T. C. Curtis was intelligent, sincere, and hopelessly in love with her.

On the 245th day of safety, T. C. sidled up behind her at the Coke machine, standing so close she could feel the heat coming off his chest, and whispered loudly in her ear, "Will you marry me?"

She took a firm step back and called out in a high, childish voice, "Never!" Her face and neck turned bright pink, and all around, the men watched, laughing. She looked back at the leering, potbellied man in the John Deere cap, and resented him for not being the man she had taken such pains to create.

Being a Peppers, however, Louise did not give up on T. C. Curtis. As the days wore on, 257 days of safety, 259 days of safety, she continued to conduct their romance in the privacy of her own mind, occasionally taking peeks at the real man as he hummed by in a forklift. When she wasn't counting the money she had made so far that day, Louise was giving T. C. a makeover, and she began to write about him at night, in her diary. She wrote with only one rule: Censor Nothing.

Florida and Henry had become limp, gray, and predictable.

"Drudge, drudge, drudge," said Florida on Monday mornings. Henry said, "Back to the old grindstone."

Every night Louise fell asleep with the determination *I will be different*. Each morning, when she reported to Raymond Patch, she stared into his lashless green eyes, praying for an assignment to work with T. C. Curtis, but this never happened. Most of the time, he sent her to the back of the plant to work with the black men on machines that paid a dollar less an hour, but when he was in a bad mood, he put her to work with Dopey.

Dopey was a miracle of the company's insurance benefits policy. Taking advantage of the full medical coverage, he kept himself stoned on prescription drugs. Several times a year, when he overdosed, he took up residence in a private unit at the hospital while his wife cashed in his checks. If he did show up at work, he acted as though he might die at any moment.

When Raymond Patch assigned Louise to the railroad with Dopey, her obsession with T. C. Curtis was the only thing that kept her from quitting. Henry was as much of a neatnik at the plant as he was at home, where he irritated Florida by picking lint up off the carpets, and of all the jobs at Southern Board, tidying up the railroad according to Mr. Peppers's specifications was the most deplored.

"I can't bend my knees!" Dopey hollered to Louise as she climbed down the short ladder to the depressed tracks. "So I'll sweep the trash over the wall, and you pick it up!" Gripping the rails of the ladder with his emaciated, blue-veined arms, and staring at Louise through a pair of foggy glasses whose clear plastic frames had been wrapped with yards of Scotch tape, he screamed over the roar of machines, "And I ain't picking up after no niggers. We only go halfway down. I ain't picking up no watermelon rind." He put one hand across his bony chest, as if the thought of touching a black man's trash was giving him a heart attack, before removing a pill from the vial in his chest pocket. Then he patted a sticky strand of white hair across his skull and settled himself against his broom handle to watch Louise work.

She put on her gloves. Raymond Patch had given her a broom, but it was useless, so she began to creep along the tracks with her back bent, dropping wads of chewing tobacco into her pail. Occasionally she found a scrap of cardboard or an empty coffee cup, but for the most part, since it was the men's custom to stand at the edge of the concrete and spit, she was in a field of chewed tobacco.

Dopey followed her along the top of the wall with his broom, pointing out trash she had missed, and when someone walked by, he swept dust down on her head. He looked exhausted.

Throughout the afternoon, the men came by to see for themselves that Mr. Peppers's daughter was indeed picking up their spit. Polecat and Jack pushed carts of board along the wall, pretending not to notice Louise until Jack jerked the cart to a stop, shading his eyes with his hand as he looked down. "Polecat! What's that crawling down there on the tracks?"

Polecat looked. "Why, that's a rat," he said.

"Naw, not the rat. That other thing. The little fellow. The funny-looking one with the gloves."

"Why, that's Experiment! Experiment, did you fall down there?"

T. C. came by with a big wad of tobacco in his cheek and pretended to spit. Smiley stood beside him and frowned.

When Louise had worked her way halfway down the tracks and had nearly reached the invisible line that divided the front and back of the plant, Dopey emerged from hiding. Standing with his legs spread, as though a great gust of wind might blow him over, he shouted, "All right! We can stop here. I ain't picking up after no niggers."

Louise continued to stomp along with her pail, even though there wasn't anything to pick up, since the black workers didn't throw things into the tracks the way the white workers did. Growing more and more agitated, Dopey followed her along the edge of the wall. "I said all right now! Don't go no further!" He took another pill. "I ain't sweeping up no watermelon rinds, you hear?"

Suddenly, a silence fell over the plant. The corrugator still hissed, the M-12 chugged and banged, and the bailer swallowed, chewed, and spit up scrap board, but the hum of human voice had ceased. The floor, which had been crawling with lines of men engaged in a regular path of social intercourse, cleared out. As if lifted by some magical hand, each employee stood, back bent, head down, over his assigned job. Even Dopey managed to get down the ladder and stroke his broom along the clean tracks.

When Louise raised her head, she was eye-level to her father's black wing tips, polished to a dull sheen, never a shine. He wore a light-gray suit with a navy-blue tie. In the green fluorescent light of the plant, his shirt was whiter than paper. His gold watch and ring hung in the murky air like two distant stars.

"How's my little worker?" he asked, smiling down at her.

"Your daddy is a handsome man," Jeremiah had told Louise once in the same matter-of-fact voice he used when he said, "Your daddy is a good man." She saw this now, and at the same time, understood what Florida meant when she said, "Henry, you're turned off. As soon as you get away from the plant, you turn off like a light." Now, in the plant, he was on.

"Are you doing all right?" he asked.

"Yes, sir." She grinned at him and went back to work. For some time, she was aware of his eyes following her gloved hands as they reached for invisible trash, and she tried to do the job perfectly. When he was gone, she knew it without looking up.

Dopey, having decided it was too much trouble to get back up the ladder, and hoping to stop Louise from cleaning up any more of the wrong trash, parked his broom in front of her and, leaning his wizened body on the handle, adjusted his glasses and began to sing, "Always on My Mind." Louise stared at him, amazed. Dopey could sing.

It was a good summer to sing. Bluebirds, cardinals, and chick-adees woke with the sun and belted out hymns until the heat sent them deep into the woods. On most afternoons, four or five strikes of thunder crashed like cymbals, and the katydids played in stereo all night long. After work, driving up Mount Zion, Louise lip-synched to a country music station with all the windows rolled down in the station wagon, and one night, careening down the mountain to meet Drew for cocktails at a bar on the other side of the river, she sang aloud and off key, "She's a good-hearted woman, in love with a good-timing man." This bar, a tin-roofed shack sitting between the Pruitt Public High School and jail, had never merited a name but was known throughout Bridgewater Academy as the only establishment in Counterpoint that accepted University of Nebraska Swimming Pool Membership cards, veri-fying that the student was eighteen, and therefore of legal age to drink in Georgia.

Drew was waiting for her in the parking lot. She stepped out of her Bronco in a pressed white polo shirt and rumpled khakis, with her hair pulled back into a ponytail. As she walked toward Louise, past a row of Harleys, she snarled.

"Well, there you are," she said in a surly voice. "What a relief." She sighed. "Two rednecks have been doing wheelies around my car. Boy, was I impressed." She drawled, "Hey there, honey! Wanna come out to the lock and dam with us and get fucked up?" Then she did her redneck laugh, a noise that sounded both sinister and retarded, "Huh-huh." Louise was looking around the parking lot for a black Monte Carlo. "Are you coming in, or were you planning to stand out here by the street until you got a date?" demanded Drew, who had been trembling.

They took a small table in the corner, so no one could join them, and ordered a pitcher. The beer was cold, and it made them laugh, showing their twenty-thousand-dollar teeth, bringing pink flushes to their smooth cheeks. So far, the world had marked their faces with nothing more serious than a freckle.

"You won't believe what happened at work today," said Drew, flushing pink to her ears. "There's this huge black guy, Gus, who's always flirting with me? Today I had to work with him. He's horrible. He really is. I mean, he's funny, but he's horrible. We were on the dough line: the dough rolls out of a tube, Gus pushes a button that cuts the dough into slices, and I inspect the slices that come down the assembly. Thus my job title: Inspector. Don't be too impressed. He calls me Inspector Drew. Well, this morning, before I was really awake, I saw this huge roll of dough coming down the assembly line. It kept getting longer and longer; he wasn't slicing it. I looked back at him to see what the hell he was doing, and he goes, "Baby, this is how much I love you!"

When she laughed, she crossed her arms over her chest, pushing her sleeves up over the line that marked her tennis tan. She wore no makeup, no socks, and no jewelry except for a pearl necklace that had belonged to her great-grandmother. She smelled of soap. She was everything that Louise wanted to be.

They were halfway through their third pitcher of beer, arguing about the importance of wang length versus wang circumference, when Louise made a comment about men's balls.

"Stupid!" said Drew, her green eyes widened in amazement, her lip curled. "How many balls do you think a man has?"

Louise took a sip of beer, trying to hide her face in the mug. She felt sure that whatever answer she gave would be wrong. She drank, swallowed, looked nonchalantly at the wall, and said, "Three."

The look on Drew's face made her wilt. "Louise," she said in a strained voice, clumsily tapping a cigarette out of her pack, "listen to me. A man has two balls, one, two. Two, OK?"

Louise shrugged, as if one more or less ball made no difference to her, but Drew knew better. "Jesus," she said softly. "What am I going to do with you?"

When Louise got home that evening, Florida was sitting at the kitchen table with a plastic bag on her head, looking at a photograph of the burnt-out farmhouse in Red Cavern, Kentucky. "I'm hennaing my hair," she said. "Your father is downstairs asleep in his chair. I'm going to be a redhead whether he likes it or not. Like you were when you went to Ferdinando's in Atlanta. You might want to think about going back to him. You're looking a little sloppy. I refuse to be old and gray. How was your movie?"

Leaning against the wall to balance herself, Louise shut one eye and said, "Fine." God had taken Florida's sense of smell away when her first child was born, so she never knew when anyone had been drinking, until that person was unable to walk or talk.

"Your father won't go to the movies with me," Florida said.

"Mom, don't start."

"He just sits in that chair every night. Doesn't communicate. Doesn't have anything to talk about but work, work, work. That plant. That's his life. He's married to Southern Board, not to me. I don't know why he even comes home." She looked at her hands spread over the photograph, then lightly touched her neck, fingering the loose skin. "I'm old," she said. "Wrinkled. Dried up."

Louise braced herself against the wall as she silently repeated the mantra, "You will not throw up. The room is still. You will not throw up."

"You're young," Florida said in a flat, cold voice. "Attractive to men. Your father used to be attracted to me."

"I'm seventeen," Louise said cautiously. She began to edge away from the wall, taking delicate steps, as though the kitchen floor were laid with mines.

When she was safely out of eyesight, she heard her mother's first sob of the night. The sound followed her down the hall, into her room, and under the covers where it played on and on in her dreams, long after Florida was silent.

The next day, as Louise slumped over her ham on rye, T. C. Curtis meandered into the break room, tossed his black lunch box on the table and, to the astonishment of first shift, sat down next to her. When someone popped the tab off a Fanta grape can, it sounded like a gunshot.

"T. C., don't mess with the boss's daughter," said Smiley. "You'll get fired."

T. C. bit into a pecan twirl. Louise sat stiffly, careful not to brush her arm against his shoulder, afraid to eat lest she offend him. When he had finished, he wiped his mouth with the back of his hand and pushed the wrapper to her. "How do you say that?" he asked, pointing at the label. She was suddenly terrified that he might be illiterate. Could she be in love with someone who couldn't read and write? Drew would be aghast. Drew would say, "This isn't even funny, Louise. You're sick. You need to be rehabilitated or shot or something."

"Pecan twirl," Louise said quietly. Even though she hadn't moved an inch, their shoulders were touching.

"What was that?" He grinned. "I'm a little hard of hearing." Leaning his face close into hers, he asked, "Did you say 'pe-con' or 'pee-can'?"

"Theodore Curtis, you better get back over here on your side of the tracks," someone called out. He laughed and offered Louise half of his sandwich. The sandwich was nearly lost in his big hand, and seeing the shallow indention of his fingers in the soft white bread, she couldn't help but imagine how he would hold her breast.

"Thank you," she said. He leaned even closer. He put one hand around his ear.

"Is that a yes or a no?" His arm was as big around as her leg, and as he turned closer to her, the span of his chest hid her face from the other men. He took jagged, heavy breaths, like an old man with a bad heart.

"Yes," said Louise, trying to keep her hand steady as she removed a cigarette from her pack. When he lit it for her, first taking it out of her mouth and turning it around, several men hooted. "I mean no," she said. Her voice sank into a whisper, the way it did when she showed her fake ID to a bartender. "I don't want a sandwich." She had no idea she was going to do what she did next. In plain view of every hand at Southern Board, in a loud voice, Louise asked T. C. for a date.

No one was as surprised as Theodore himself, who became suddenly shy. "Sure," he said, "I'll have a beer with you after work." He turned away from her to concentrate on his sandwich. She studied the back of his head, watched the white T-shirt stretching over the muscles in his back, the two damp curls swirling around his ear, and with a leap of faith, she allowed T. C. Curtis to become the man who loved the woman in every country song she had ever heard.

"He sounds like a real fixer-upper," said Drew, when Louise described T. C. to her over the phone.

"It's like negative capability," explained Louise. "You know. John Keats, the poet? He said that negative capability is required to read poetry or write it or something. I don't remember. It's the willing suspension of disbelief."

"Education is wasted on you," said Drew. "Does he have a big wang?"

"I don't know!" screamed Louise. More calmly, she said, "We've only gone to second base. I want him to fall in love with me."

"Next time you hold his hand," said Drew, "measure the distance between the bottom of his palm and the tip of his middle finger."

"What if he knows what I'm doing?"

"Louise, it's not supposed to be this hard for a girl to lose her virginity. Just focus."

• • •

The men at the plant knew the exact hour that Louise began meeting T. C. Curtis at the Golden Gallon on Highway 1 after work, but they didn't mention it to her. They continued to observe her and discuss her out loud, as if they were a team of scientists in white coats.

"What's that thing sticking out Experiment's cap?" asked Polecat. "She don't have enough hair to make a ponytail. Smiley, don't you think she ought to cut that thing off?"

"Polecat," he said, stepping around her with a load of board. "Are you cold?"

"Hell, it ain't but ninety degrees in here."

"Well, Experiment's wearing gloves."

"Experiment, how much do you weigh?"

"Hey, Experiment, how much does your daddy pay for you to go that private school?"

They all tested her to see if she had enough smarts to go to college, and she came up short. "Now listen, Experiment," Polecat would say, climbing down his ladder. "Say you got a litter of six black pigs, and a litter of seven white pigs, and two of them black pigs gets the cough, but only one dies, and the dog eats four of them white pigs, but somebody trades you three black pigs for a lawnmower, how many pigs you got?"

They wanted to know what she learned at Bridgewater Academy, which cost ten thousand dollars a year. She sputtered out replies, but none of them convinced the men that Henry had made a sound investment with his money.

"Latin? Who talks that?"

"Now what's the point in paying to study religion? Church is free."

"Hell, anybody can cut up a rabbit. The trick is to catch one."

Jeremiah was the only one who asked serious questions about Bridgewater; he wanted one of his sons to attend. "I've been saving for eight years now," he said. "He's going to have an education." Dutifully, Louise answered his questions about entrance exams, course requirements, and dress codes, but she hoped the boy wouldn't go. Out of the five hundred students at the upper school, only two were African Americans. One had an ulcer, and the other one, who always ate lunch by himself, had developed insomnia and a stutter.

"Why do blacks work at the back of the plant?" Louise asked Henry one afternoon when he was driving them home from church. He nosed the Buick LeSabre around a hairpin curve, slowing down at the guardrail to see if there were any new dents from the Saturday night rabble-rousers who raced up and down Mount Zion for thrills.

"The county needs to get out and cut back the kudzu," Florida said.

"Look at that," said Henry, slowing down in front of a broken mailbox. "Those rednecks knocked that sucker right over. Now why on earth anybody would get a kick out of driving by with a stick and hitting mailboxes is beyond me."

"Henry," said Florida. "She asked you a question."

"I'm listening. Look, there's another one. The good ole boys had a real time up here last night."

"They make a dollar less an hour," said Louise. "All the machines at the back of the plant pay a dollar less."

"That's just circumstance, honey. There's no discrimination in it. Each machine requires a different level of skill, and the work pays accordingly."

"Your father is prejudiced," Florida explained.

"Dad, please don't!" cried Louise, as he pulled over to the side of the road, about five hundred yards from the bottom of their driveway.

"You can't stop him," said Florida.

Shaking his head angrily, he got out of the car, slammed the door, and began to pick up beer cans along the shoulder of the road. Louise sighed, took the garbage bag Florida handed her, and tripped along behind him in her high heels, holding the "Keep America Clean" sack open while he filled it with trash. When he was done, he wiped his hands with his handkerchief and got back in the car.

"Can you imagine the mentality of a person who just drives along and throws a beer can out the window?" he asked.

"Joyriding," said Florida grimly.

The next afternoon at the Golden Gallon, T. C. bought a six-pack of Miller for himself, a six-pack of Heineken for Louise, and a bag of popcorn. "Maybe I'll take you to a movie sometime," he said. "We'll go to the Red Lobster, and then to a late show. I treat women right."

Louise imagined him sitting at a plastic-covered table in the noisy, crowded room, with his arm around a frosted blond in shoulder pads, pancake makeup, and long magenta nails who sat stiffly, as if at church. She felt as though she had stepped inside that woman, and was delighted. He wore black sunglasses and looked slightly dangerous, wheeling the Monte Carlo along back roads. She popped Kenny Rogers tapes into his stereo, pushed her hair behind her ears, and drank with abandon. Each time she finished a beer, she hung out the window and sailed a bottle through the air.

Lately at work, Dopey had been singing "Good-Hearted Woman." As Louise threw boxes into the screaming blades of the bailer, she mouthed the words,

She's a good-hearted woman, in love with a good-timing man. She loves him in spite of his ways she don't understand.

In her mind, she lived out the seductive tragedy of her life with T. C. Curtis. It had all the appeal of a suicide, but it was better because she would be alive to see the looks of shock and regret.

"You ever seen a cat catch a rat?" Jeremiah asked her one day. Since Dopey was out sick that day, and hadn't dragged her up to the break room to eat with the white people, she was having her lunch in the sunshine, on the ramp that ran up to the warehouse doors. After a morning in the dim green light of the plant, the sunlight burned her eyes, and she had to shield her face with her hand to look up at Jeremiah. He wore polished black shoes, perfectly creased trousers, and a short-sleeve shirt with a tie. His thick, curly hair was graying at the temples, but he stood like a young man. "Old Jeremiah could have been a pro ball player," Henry had said. "Never seen a cat catch a rat!" he cried. "Where you been?"

"Here," she said. "Working."

"Uh-huh." He broke a stem from a tall weed growing up the wall and chewed on the tip. "Well," he said, "goes like this: the old cat smells him a rat and gets up real close, sniffing around, and then he starts playing with it. He don't eat it right off." Jeremiah shook his head slowly. "He plays with it, chasing it into this corner and that corner yonder. He runs that rat back and forth, teasing it, until the varmint don't remember where it came from. Then you know what happens?"

Louise shook her head.

"Then he eats it."

"The cat eats the rat."

"Yes, indeed." Jeremiah bit off the tip of the weed.

"But what if I'm the cat," Louise asked, nervously lighting a cigarette.

"Wouldn't that be something," he said, and walked away.

No one believed that Louise would actually bring T. C. Curtis to the house. The first time she invited him, he said, "Wear your bikini," and he stood her up.

She cried until her nose turned pink, and the next time her parents went out of town, she invited him over for dinner. "Steak and champagne suit you?" she asked as he lifted a thousand steaming Frigidaire boxes on his forklift. She thought, "I'm the cat!" But she had doubts.

That evening, hiding behind a Chinese vase in the living-room window, she watched the Monte Carlo curve around the long drive-

way as the red sun slid behind the pines. The shiny black car looked
wrong parked beneath Roderick's old basketball goal. The Peppers
never drove black cars; neither did their friends. Slowly, the door
opened, and T. C. stepped out, swigging a fifth of tequila. For a few
moments he stood spraddle-legged beside his car, holding the fifth
in one hand, and a flower in the other, eyeing the property. He
stared across the freshly mowed lawn, to the edge where the ground
dropped off into a slant of treetops, and the necklace of lights he
finally recognized as Counterpoint, Georgia. Then he looked back
up at the house and thought, *I'd at least paint the thing.*

Watching him from the window, Louise worried that he wouldn't
be able to find the door. The house had seven entrances, but only
one was the veritable front door, according to Henry, and thus the
only one through which he would admit Louise's suitors. This was
not a problem for anyone until a redheaded boy with skin so white
it was nearly blue, and who was stricken with shyness, asked Louise
to the Junior-Senior Prom.

Henry announced that the young roustabout would be sent
home if he came to the wrong door. Relieved that she might not
have to go, Louise grabbed the phone to tell Drew, but Florida
took up the boy's cause. "He reminds me of Roderick," she said
gently, "except that he's ugly." With a wood-burning tool, she
made a tasteful sign out of driftwood that said, FRONT DOOR,
drawing an arrow under it to point the way.

Louise let T. C. ring the front doorbell twice. As soon as she
opened it, he swooped down on her and stuck his tongue in her
mouth. He reeked of tequila and aftershave, but the biggest disappointment was his outfit. Instead of the faded Levi's and white
T-shirt he wore to the plant, with a pack of Marlboro Reds rolled
up in one sleeve, he had dressed up in a pair of jeans with an elas-
tic waistband, and a two-toned terry cloth shirt. Louise smiled and
took the rose he offered, which was wrapped in green tissue and
tied with a pink ribbon.

"I was going to get you a dozen," he said, "but I thought one
was more romantic." He bent down to kiss her again, but she

slipped under his arm and offered him a glass of champagne. Her mouth hurt from smiling.

"You're beautiful," he said, reaching for her again. She suggested that he have a seat in the living room, but he followed her into the kitchen, grabbing her from behind when she reached up to get the sorbet cups, the closest thing Florida kept to champagne glasses. When she turned around, he smashed her against his chest and said, "Let's dance." They staggered around the kitchen for a few minutes, stepping all over each other's feet, then he whispered in her ear, "You're sexy. I want to eat your pussy."

Louise punched him in the stomach. "Stop it," she said. "You're going too fast."

"Sorry." He held his hands up as if he were being arrested, then pushed them in his pockets. "I had a couple of beers before I came." He lit a cigarette for each of them. "I'm sorry I molested you. I guess I got carried away. You are sexy, though." He put his hand between her legs.

"Stop it!"

"I'm sorry. Excuse me. What do you want me to do?" For a moment, they looked at each other under the bright kitchen light like actors who had forgotten their lines. He shifted, staggered against the wall, and regained his balance.

She realized that she had made a mistake. T. C. Curtis in person was not the T. C. Curtis she went to bed with every night.

"Do you know how to grill steaks?" she asked him severely.

"Baby, I know how to do everything." He examined the bottle of Moët Chandon she had set in a plastic bucket of ice, fingering the steak tongs resting on a white linen napkin beside it. When she left the room, he filled the sorbet dishes with tequila.

Leaning against the deck railing, where Henry always said, "You will fall off backwards and bust your head wide open, I'm just telling you," Louise shook some salt onto the web of skin between her thumb and forefinger, licked it, took a sip of tequila, winced, and bit into a lime.

"Let me try that," T. C. said. He was across the deck before she could turn her head, licking her hand, and then her neck. "What's the matter?" he asked, pushing his hand between her legs. Without waiting for her to answer, he swept one arm behind her back and unfastened her bra. It took Bridgewater Academy boys at least four tries to work off a bra, but T. C. snapped it off like a piece of tape. The bra was called the Mary Jane, white with pink rosebuds in the lace; it looked ridiculous in his callused hand.

"Wait!" Louise said, pushing against his heavy chest, "You're going too fast." He pressed himself tighter against her, so that she felt his wang poking into her thigh; it felt like another hand, a baby's fist. She had the sickening feeling she'd had once when she saw a water moccasin swallow a duckling.

In her ear, he whispered, "I'm going to rape you."

The sun was about to go down, and the birds had shut up. A few katydids said, "Katie did," once or twice, like musicians tuning their guitars, but they never started up the band. Louise tried to go limp. She had read in *Glamour* magazine that a man can't rape a woman if she relaxes all of her muscles, but she couldn't relax a single one. He had her jeans unzipped, and was trying to fit his hand inside them, when she bit him.

"Shit!" he yelled. "What the hell—"

"You can't rape me," she said in a high, strained voice, backing away until the grill was between them. The smell of sizzling meat made her feel suddenly homesick, as if this house were no longer her home. She saw Florida's face staring into the photograph of blackened stone and ash, saying, "My home," as she touched her hand to her neck. "This place is wired all over with alarms," Louise said. "All I have to do is push a button, and the police will come."

He scratched his neck. Then he ambled over to the grill and flipped the steaks. "S7 security system," he said. "The main box is buried by the bird feeder. I installed it myself, two years ago."

"You're lying," she said, but she took another step away from him.

"You scared of me?" He put on a grill glove shaped like a cow and pointed the black and white face at her. "Moo," he said. Then he put the steaks on the platter and told her to open the door for him. She considered running past him, slamming the sliding door shut, and calling the police. Then she straightened her back, making herself as tall as she could, and in her most matronly voice said, "Come in. Have a seat."

She had set the dining-room table with Florida's wedding china, one place setting at each end, with tall red candles in the middle. "Why do we have to sit so far apart?" asked T. C., picking up his plate and putting it down next to hers. He sat so close to her that their knees touched and he put his hand between her thighs as soon as she began to cut her steak.

"Aren't you going to eat?" she asked him.

"I'm going to eat you," he said. She handed him the champagne, to distract him, and made a haughty face while he fumbled with the corkscrew.

"You *un*screw it," she said, with bravado, as if Drew were sitting next to her. "Think you can do that?"

He said, "Girl, you ain't grown into your mouth." They were more comfortable with each other then, and when the cork popped, and the champagne bubbled through his stained fingers, they laughed.

The champagne seemed to cancel out the tequila, and everything else in Louise's head. T. C. began to look the way he was supposed to look at her dining-room table: his thick legs spread on the Queen Anne chair, his hair mussed and curly, one big paw around the sorbet glass, lips wet with wine.

"You can't rape me if I want to make love to you," Louise said. "It's my idea, too. I invited you over."

"Experiment, you're a trip," he said. When she leaned forward to kiss him, he touched her nipples through her T-shirt and said, "Let's go over to the couch for a minute." She saw the white curve of her breast surfacing like a fish into his hand. Her legs were spreading by themselves. Suddenly it did not seem so stupid to let the steaks grow cold, or even to leave some champagne in the bottle. She allowed him to carry her to the couch, and when he kissed her there, she put her hand on his knee, daring herself to touch his zipper.

On the count of ten she was going to touch his zipper, but on three he went crazy again and pulled her under him so fast she felt that she was being sucked down a current. He continued to say, "I'm going to eat your pussy," which she found offensive. She wanted him to say something like, "You have the most intriguing eyes," but he probably didn't know that word. He ought to at least tell her that she was beautiful. Her panties were white with pink rosebuds, part of the Mary Jane set, but he didn't even look at them before he jerked them down to her ankles.

"You'll like it," he argued, when she began to kick him in the chest. "All the ladies say I eat pussy good. I can make you come. I ain't lying. Now that's the truth. You'll go wild." He laughed all to himself.

"Gross," said Louise. Yanking her Mary Janes back on, she slid into the corner of the couch and wrapped her arms around her knees. They were both panting. She could still feel the wet spot his lips had left on her. "You can sit on the couch," she said. "Just don't lick me."

"All right, I ain't gonna bite ya." He sighed and lit a cigarette. "And I ain't gonna lick." Then he looked over at her face and laughed. "I swear you'd like it. Women love that. You never had a man go down on you before?"

"I haven't had regular sex yet."

"Shit." Drawing on the cigarette, he looked through the wall of glass to the lights of the town below and said, "What am I doing here?" He rubbed his head for a moment, and suddenly Louise was afraid that she had lost his interest. Florida had coached her to encourage men to talk about themselves on dates, explaining that in some mysterious way this would make them find her interesting, so she focused her attention on T. C. and said, "So tell me, what's it like to be married?"

"We're separated," he said. She jumped up to get them each a cold Moosehead and then settled back into the couch for a story.

"It's hard work," he said. He had his hands flat on his thighs now and didn't move them except to pick up his beer.

"When you were married, did you live in a trailer?"

"Naw. I built her a real nice house. Washer, dryer, dishwasher, satellite TV; she had everything."

"What's it like to have sex when you're married?"

"With your wife? Well, it's good. I mean, I like sex. Every morning you wake up, and she's right there beside you. What is this, an interview?"

"I just want to know. Is being married like having a roommate?"

"Yeah, when she puts you on the couch."

"Didn't you ever want to sleep by yourself?"

"No, like I said, when you're getting along with a woman, having sex with her is nice. Do you want to turn on the TV or something?"

"I don't watch TV. What's it like when you get along?"

"Well, let me think." He took the cigarette out of his mouth with his thumb and forefinger and stubbed it out in the ashtray. "Say I get off work at four-thirty and get home around five. She's waiting for me in her housecoat, lying on the bed like."

"Why is she wearing a housecoat at five o'clock in the afternoon?"

"I'm just saying, OK? Say she's wearing her bathrobe. So I take a shower and come lie down with her."

"What kind of bathrobe is it? Is it terry cloth?" Louise hoped it wasn't terry cloth. When T. C. was married to her, they'd live in a real trailer, and she'd wear Victoria's Secret gowns that she'd wash by hand and hang out on a line to dry.

"It's a short one or something," he said impatiently. "Anyway, I reach inside it, feeling her titties and all, and say, 'Hey, honey.' Then we make love and all."

For a while, T. C. was so quiet that she was afraid he had fallen asleep. She was miffed that he didn't have his arm around her and hoped he wasn't sorry that he was here with her instead of with his wife. She promised herself to touch his zipper on the count of one hundred, and asked casually, "So have you ever slept with a whore?"

"That depends on what you call a whore."

"Do you think I'm a whore?"

She hoped he would say yes. Then she would slap him and forget all about this zipper dare she had made to herself.

"No," he said, with an irritated shake of his head that reminded her of Henry.

"I bet you wish I was a whore," she said. She was on seventy-two.

He rubbed his temples and sighed. "Well, we've both got to go to work tomorrow, so I guess I better be going."

"Stay."

"I'd like to, but I think I better be going." He stood up and began to look around for his shirt.

"We could sleep together without having sex."

"You think I am going to sleep beside a naked woman and not have sex with her?"

"We could wear clothes."

"You ain't doing too good at being a whore. Anyway, I sleep in the raw. Are you sitting on my socks over there?" As he stood before her, frowning, she reached up and stretched her hand across his zipper. They both froze. Finally, he said, "I don't mean to be crude or nothing, Louise, but if I go to bed with you, I'm going to fuck your brains out."

She looked into his face. In the Monte Carlo, he wore a pair of black sunglasses, and in the plant, he kept his head down most of the time, but now she could see him clearly: the lines around his eyes, the faint shadow on his jaw. He was a man, nothing like the boys at Bridgewater, boys with soft cheeks, damp hands, and voices that squeaked. Those boys would never be a man like T. C. Henry said, "Poor old Joe Redneck doesn't have a chance. He goes to public school, goes into debt to get a sports car he can't afford so he can get a girlfriend, gets her pregnant and marries her, then he has to quit school and go to work at a factory for the rest of his life—by the time that car is paid off it's sitting up on cinder blocks in the front yard, good for nothing but parts."

When T. C. brushed his rough finger along her cheek, she wanted to say, "I can see your soul in your eyes." Instead, she went to bed with him.

Even though Florida gave her a wake-up call from her hotel at six A.M., Louise was twenty minutes late to work. At lunch, she sat alone at her table, eating a steak sandwich while the men discussed her tardiness.

"Her daddy wasn't home to tie that string on her," Polecat said. "Every morning, he's got to tie that string on her so she can find her way out of that big house."

"Florida must have gone on with him because nobody wrote 'Louise Peppers' on her lunch bag today. What's she eating anyway?"

"She looks a little peaked to me. Experiment, did you go out drinking last night?"

T. C. sat in the corner with Smiley and didn't even look at her.

"Wink at me," she whispered to him at the water fountain.

"I can't."

"Do you think everybody knows?"

"You might as well wear a sign."

"Really?" She grinned. "Do I look different?"

"You look like trouble." He shuffled away with his head down, and just when she began to hate him, he turned around and winked.

Half an hour before quitting time, T. C. cut doors and windows into a Frigidaire box, drew a license plate on the back, a Mercedes symbol on the front, fitted the box over the forklift, and drove to the back of the plant to offer Louise a ride. Jeremiah stepped out of his office just as T. C. was honking the horn. After a moment's reflection, he strode to the forklift, lifted the Frigidaire box over T. C.'s head, and tossed it in the bailer. T. C. drove away muttering, "Nigger."

Jeremiah turned to Louise. Then, turning the wedding ring on his finger, he looked away and said gently, "Get on back to work, girl. The day's not over yet." If there was a warning in his voice, she missed it. She felt simply that Jeremiah loved her, as the whole world loved her, and as she loved the world. When she threw her next bundle into the bailer she thought of the Keats letter Mr. Rutherford had read to them in English Honors at Bridgewater, and under the roar of gnashing blades, she said aloud, "O for a life of sensations rather than of thoughts."

"You know what I like about you?" asked T. C. that afternoon at the Golden Gallon. "I like it when you bite your lip, like you did last night in bed. That was real cute."

"How did I do it?" Louise bit her lip and looked in the rearview mirror to study the effect. Suddenly, she screamed.

"What the hell," T. C. began, but then he saw the LeSabre pulling up silently beside the Monte Carlo. A hard July sun flashed off glass, mirror, and silver flank, throwing a glare over Henry as he stepped out of the car. He was wearing kelly-green golf pants and a white polo shirt with "Palm Beach" embroidered on the pocket, and he had a sunburn. After opening T. C.'s door, with one hand clenched around the door frame, he leaned so far into the car that Louise could smell the aloe lotion Florida had put on his red nose. Tendons stood out in his neck.

He said, "I will kill you."

There was a long silence in which the three of them soaked in their own sweat. In the past two days Louise had entertained only a vague recollection of Henry and Florida. It was as though ten or fifteen years had gone by, and now, suddenly, here was Henry, with a bright red face and a strangled voice, as though someone were tightening a rope around his neck. He was saying, "If you ever, ever touch my daughter again, if you speak to her, or look at her, you are fired. Do you understand?"

T. C. said, "Yes, sir."

Henry said, "Louise, get out of the car."

• • •

Louise climbed into the LeSabre, staying as close to the door as possible while Henry drove them over to the pay phone at the edge of the parking lot and cut the engine. The cashier inside the Golden Gallon chain-smoked and watched them through the window, with the receiver of a telephone resting on her shoulder. There was no shade. Already, the vinyl seat was sticking to the back of Louise's arms. Sweat soaked her T-shirt, and the new smell of the car's interior began to make her feel that she had eaten vinyl for lunch. Henry gripped the steering wheel, staring straight ahead, as if he were driving. He wasn't supposed to be home until tomorrow.

Finally, he said, "I should fire you. I knew it was a mistake to hire you in the first place, but I didn't listen to my better judgment. I trusted you."

Louise considered praying, in case there was a God, but she stuck to her principles and simply sat, with her arms crossed, mouth shut tight. Finally, because he wasn't going to say another word until she did, and he could sit there in the hot car for a week, without anything to eat or drink or ever going to the bathroom— that was his will, forged from the molten ores at the center of the earth—she said, "I'm sorry."

At once, Henry unleashed his rage. He shouted, "Do you realize that it's between baseball and football season and those men have nothing to talk about but you! Every single minute of every single day they have watched every little move you made. Everything! Did you know that? Do you know what those men were thinking when you . . . when you . . ." Suddenly he slammed his fist on the steering wheel. He began to shake it, rocking back and forth until his knuckles were white. "Answer me!" he yelled.

"No, sir," she said. "I never thought about it."

He looked at her for the first time since he had entered the parking lot of the Golden Gallon. His face was misshapen, with the mouth all stretched out, eyes bulging.

"You never thought about it," he repeated in a soft, stunned voice. "It has taken me twenty-eight years to earn the respect of those men, and in two months, you threw it all away. Twenty-eight years of my life, and you never thought about it. Not once." His eyes became wide and clear, like the eyes of a child. He said, "He isn't even handsome."

Louise looked through the window at the cashier: smoke blew through her nostrils as she laughed into the phone. She thought, *I would trade my life with yours right now.*

"What goes on in your head?" Henry asked. "You don't have good sense, do you?" He sighed. "Or maybe I just don't know you."

A tear ran down his cheek, and then he began to sob. He had not cried in fifteen or twenty years, and the tears came hard, breaking over the creases in his face, falling into his open mouth as he made a dry, choking sound. He kept his hands gripped firmly on the steering wheel while his entire body shook.

Louise said, "Please turn on the air conditioner. I love you."

"You sure don't act like you love me."

"I do!" she yelled. "I do love you!" When she began to cry, he removed the folded white handkerchief from his back pocket and handed it to her.

"Your mother is torn up," he said. Thinking of Florida's pain gave him strength. Slowly, he regained his composure. He let go of the steering wheel, wiped his eyes, blew his nose, and sat up straight in his seat. "She's just sick about this." He shook his head back and forth.

Then, in a calm, distant voice, he began to talk about God. God, Henry said, had given her certain gifts and talents, which she should use to His glory and not in the wrong way, not in a cheap way. Maybe God had made her a little different than he made most people, being creative and all like her mother, but that wasn't necessarily a bad thing. She had free will. She could still make the right choices. "I don't want you to be some man's tool," he said.

"Everyone is a tool," she said, but he wasn't listening to nonsense.

"You have a good heart. You're a good . . .," he hesitated, searching for the word, "woman."

"I don't want to work at the plant anymore," she said. "Can we go home?"

"Now wait a minute. You're a Peppers. We don't quit our jobs. You're going back into that plant on Monday morning with your head up. Now if you speak to that man again, he'll lose his job."

Louise put her hand on the door.

"There's one more thing."

"Dad, please."

"Listen to me."

"What."

"I forgive you." He leaned over and kissed her on the head. All the way home, he kept the bumper of the LeSabre right on the fender of the Bonneville, even running yellow lights to stay with her, in case she took a wrong turn.

At Owl Aerie, Florida was sitting in a straight-backed chair by the kitchen door. The henna had turned her hair bright red, but her face was gray and drawn up in wrinkles. When Louise and Henry came in, she said, "You found her." She looked at Louise as if she had a repulsive growth on her body— an extra arm or leg, or even an extra person, like the man growing out of the chest of a larger man in a book she had pored over as a child, *Very Special People.*

"Where was she?" asked Florida, still staring.

"She's home now."

"She was there, wasn't she, at the Golden Gallon? With him." Then she spat out his name to Louise, "T. C."

"That's enough," said Henry. "I talked to her."

"I showed your diary to your father," said Florida. In the stark kitchen light, her hands looked like Grandmother Deleuth's hands, like gnarled trees. The fingers with their swollen knuckles and broken nails, the single bright gold band now embedded in the spotted flesh, spread out like roots over the blue cover of Louise's spiral-bound notebook.

Between her mother's fingers she read her own handwriting: PRIVATE PROPERTY. "Repulsive," said Florida.

Louise hoped she would go mad that instant. Silently, she willed herself to get on her hands and knees and bark like a dog, but sanity held her in place like a chain. She stared down at her mother's gold spandex house shoes.

"I pray for you," said Florida. "I pray that you will let Jesus back into your heart. That's what God wants you to do."

Louise laughed nervously. She remembered an hour when she sat on Dr. Frommlecker's brown couch, asking about insane asylums. He said, 'The entrance is always easier to find than the exit.'"

"Hush," said Henry. "Go on to your room now."

"How do you know what God wants, Mother? Does God talk to you?"

"Yes, He certainly does."

"Well, maybe God talks to me, too."

"Did God tell you to fornicate with T. C. Curtis?"

"Stop it, both of you," said Henry. "This discussion is closed." The buzzer on the dryer went off, and Florida stood up. "I'm washing the sheets," she said.

In the kitchen, Louise fixed herself a half glass of orange juice and took it to her bedroom, where she filled it to the rim with vodka.

In the morning, Louise's hands shook as she tied her brogans. Desperately, she tried to think of another place to go: Drew's house, New York City, Swaziland. But she was a Peppers, so she went to work.

Raymond Patch assigned her to the slitter. She trudged over there with her hands in her pockets, ignoring Polecat when he called out, "Watch out, Experiment; don't trip over that long face," but when she reached the machine she stopped and smiled. There was T. C., in a clean white T-shirt with a fresh pack of Marlboros rolled up in his sleeve, waiting to catch slit boards. Never before had they been assigned to the same machine.

She felt a flutter of hope as she said, "Good morning."

He nodded curtly, looked away. She put on her gloves and picked up a short stack of boards.

"Ready?" she asked icily, and when he nodded, she shot the boards catty-cornered under the blades, so that they flew over his left shoulder. He caught them, threw them away, and resumed his stance, legs spread, palms open to catch the whizzing board. She bit her lip.

"Go," he said. There was nothing in his voice. He didn't know her, didn't want to know her. She was a tool, the slitter was a tool, and he was a tool.

She packed the boards against the edge of the table like a stack of cards, then slid off the top one, giving it a clean shove under the blades so the corners wouldn't turn. T. C. caught it. He caught the boards as fast as she sent them, never looking at her. In a gray suit, with his hands folded behind his back, Henry walked up and down the aisles, noting every squeaking wheel, every crooked board, every piece of string on the floor. As a hush fell over the men, the whirring blades, the slam of metal against metal, the crunch and grind of the bailer grew into a deafening roar. At the slitter, he stopped. For the next hour, he stood at that machine, watching the boards as they left Louise's hands and fell into T. C.'s hands.

For the rest of the summer, Louise was assigned to the slitter with T. C. At a different time each day, Henry approached the machine and stood with his hands folded behind his back, watching them. All around them in the hot green light, metal slammed against metal, fires burned, forks lifted bales, whistles blew, and, buzzing all over with the sad songs of men as small as ants, the plant grew. Every morning, the numbers on the calendar declared another day of safety.

Melanie Sumner has published *Polite Society* and
was a winner of the Whiting Award. Her work
has been published in *The New Yorker, Story,
Seventeen, DoubleTake, The New York Times, Conde
Nast Sports for Women,* and other journals and
anthologies. *Good-Hearted Woman,* a book of
fiction, is forthcoming. Sumner has been a fellow
at the Fine Arts Work center and Yaddo. She lives
in Taos, New Mexico, with her husband and
daughter.

JOHN ROSENTHAL

*I first attempted to write the story of "Good-Hearted Woman" in a college
writing class. My teacher, Max Steele, said, "Throw that one in the trash
can," so I did, and that was right. Ten years later, the story reemerged (the
soul has no trash can). By this time, I understood more of what goes on inside
of people. I was living in a cabin on Chappaquidick with the poet Faith
Shearin, a fellow Southern expatriate. Perhaps I told her the story as it
happened to me in my youth, or perhaps I read it to her as I wrote it.
What I do know is that I wrote it for her ears, and she has great ears. (I
was also writing for Max, as I always do.)*

Romulus Linney

THE WIDOW

(from *The Missouri Review*)

Rebecca Tull her name was when she moved here. She was the daughter of a preacher from the Shenandoah Valley, from a town and a church more refined than what she had to face on this back-of-beyond North Carolina mountain. I was about eleven or twelve. I was at the house-raising for the family, which was just Rebecca, her Virginia preacher father, and her mother.

I wasn't so slow I couldn't see her looking the men over while they scored off the logs, laid a rock foundation, and chinked the house dry with river-bottom clay. She never hid it neither, smiling, laughing, sashaying about while speculating on men's back muscles, front muscles, sweat and swearing, hands and fists, legs, tongues, lips, shoulders, tops and bottoms. And when, into the four rooms and a loft, we moved that family's Virginia furniture, silver goblets, oak chairs, the table for the family Bible, and hung two painted pictures of her momma's momma and her daddy's daddy on the wall, she even smiled at me. She was the most beautified young woman I had ever seen, and I had been mountain ready since nine or ten to start seeing one.

It wasn't long before men came courting. Well, three men. She expected more, sitting there in that room made for her, under the satisfied faces of her grandmother and grandfather. She was a widow reasonably young, with rosy cheeks, pouty smile, wet lips, bedtime eyes, and a pushed-up bosom she understood how to heave.

First came Clink Williams. He was young, good-looking and full as a flood of himself. He told her he had about as much use for a blue-blooded Virginia sweetheart as a pig for a Bible. But here she was in Dog Slaughter Creek, her husband died on her, she was hot as a horseshoe in a forge, and she'd marry again, since any woman looks at men the way she did at her house-raising had to marry or bust.

She told him that between what a muscle-headed man like him saw at that house-raising and what was truly going on was a great big two-piece sodbusted difference. She told him she had no need to marry a man whose preference was forever at the front of his pants. As he left, he told her she might be a high-born widow with Daddy in the church, but she was twenty years old, and men on this mountain commence low-rating a woman the day she hits fourteen. As the only young man in Dog Slaughter Creek not married, so long, he'd be back.

Next came Slade Foley. He was maybe sixty-five, most likely more. She said he should speak to her daddy. Slade Foley said he wasn't studying her daddy, he was studying her, just like she studied him at that house-raising. So walk outside with him a little ways and she could study him some more. She asked if he thought she was do dizzy all he had to say was lie down and she'd do it. He said, that has been known to happen. She said, to a bubble-headed milkmaid maybe, but not to her, and Slade Foley let her hear it. He told her men here didn't dance Virginia reels. No man here had time for such stuttering and stammering around. His first wife died of pneumonie, second of distemper. He was still feisty and might consider her. Outside, right now, or next week when they married—either, how about it?

She said she wasn't throwing her life away on a back-slope cow-path to a split-britches-hasty, shallow-headed fool forty years older than she was. If it was the ugliness of him or nothing, so be it. Before she'd give over her days on earth to a clod-faced, bark-faced, slit-eyed barnyard roughneck, she'd live alone every last day of her life. As he left, Slade Foley told her no, she wouldn't. Nights on these slopes are cold, and blood gets hot. Spit out all the stinging words she'd a mind to now, come three or four hard winters on Dog Slaughter Creek, she'd take the man who'd have her fast and gladly; there was worse than him. At her door, she said she didn't believe it.

He said he knew an old boy name of Ollin, took him a high-minded wife like her would could read and write and talk. She didn't come to care for him and told him so. Ollin put her through a school of his own, and she never talked to nobody after that. On the porch steps, when Rebecca Tull said she would die first, he said that could be. He told her about a man named Skeets who shot his wife. The next day her brothers come and shot him. And their six chilluns. And a granddaddy too, and that's the kind of real trouble flighty damn women like her got into around here. He said, you watch what you say to men, they live powerful lonely around Dog Slaughter Creek, fires bank up, meanness lies eternally smoldering. You don't know what you are fooling with in this country. What you need is a man hard but fair and old as he may be, will keep you safe. Who might never hit you at all, like most, might never have to, once the flirtation is over and you lay down and like it. At her gate, getting shown out of the yard, he told her to consider what he'd said, and he'd be back.

The third and last man in Dog Slaughter Creek to come to see her was Radley Nollins. He was about forty, plump and kindly faced. He told her he comprehended how she must feel. A finely tuned woman with sensitive complexion and dainty ways. Men here, like the bull goose, get ramptious, fractious. They have no reliable guide. They burn and marry, then marry and burn, but not him. He was protected from such misery. When she said, by what, he picked her family Bible off a table and held it up, saying, by this. He said a man of God he forever was. A virtuous woman is a crown to her husband. She that maketh him ashamed is a rotten-ness in his bones. Proverbs two and thirteen.

She said, you have been married before. He said he had. Satan called his wife, and she ran off with a scoundrel named Buzzmore. She that liveth in pleasure is dead while she liveth. First Timothy five and six.

Then Rebecca Tull said, and men shall be lovers of their own selves, from such turn away for they creep into houses and lead captive silly women. Second Timothy two and six. And he said, you have read the Bible. He said, favor is deceitful and beauty is vain, but a woman that feareth the Lord, she shall be praised. Proverbs thirty and thirty-one.

And she said, oh, Radley, you know what that is. That is last month's lard. Favor is good, Radley, and beauty is plain wonderful. The woman that goes about eternally afraid of God is scared of daddies and husbands, and I will not live thataway, so go home.

Radley Nollins got just as mad as the others did. He said he understood Clink Williams and Slade Foley had been there courting her. Along with him they were the only men she could expect to see in Dog Slaughter Creek. Any other men hereabouts were razorback hogs, don't be a fool, pick one of us and he'd be back to find out which.

Rebecca waited and waited, but no other man, not even a hog, came to court her. On the tenth day of waiting, she found herself on her knees. She prayed. She said, Lord Jesus Christ, I am in the wilderness here on this dreadful mountain. I know I am too willful for a decent widow like my momma and daddy say, but I can't abide these men. Must I live in ignorant meanness and hateful contention all my life? Help me, Lord. Deliver me from this female death. Or if you won't, give me some sign it is not crazy I will be in Dog Slaughter Creek. In your sacred name amen.

That's when me and my Aunt Lottie Stiles called out from her yard. Aunt Lottie went around in her cowhide skirt and jacket with her sack of roots and herbs, and hands tough as any man's. She never married. She enjoyed her life, a free woman. You became that in the Smoky Mountains one of two ways. Either you were a midwife or you killed a man, since men were as afraid of breech births and deadly sickness as they were of a woman who would hide behind a tree and when they came by on a mule, shoot them off it. Because Lottie Stiles was a powerful herb doctor, and because it was thought but not proved she had aimed a shotgun at a husband who beat her and blowed off his damned head, men paid her respect. She lived well, and I was her nephew.

I was sitting on the floor by the big oak rocker Rebecca sat Aunt Lottie in, staring at her like at nothing ever in my boy life, while Aunt Lottie was getting the feel of the situation by way of herbs and medicines.

My Aunt Lottie said she recollected very cure in these mountains, and did Rebecca comprehend walnuts. Rebecca said, well, she knew what they were. Aunt Lottie told her that the shell of a walnut is like your skull. The meat is like your brain. Eat it when you get woobles in the head.

Rebecca said, woobles in the head with some scorn, and Aunt Lottie told her if she commenced growing a goiter, but Rebecca said, ugh. Aunt Lottie told Rebecca, bathe that goiter in the blood of a grey rat. If you're burning with a high fever, take off your shoes and split a trout. Lift out the bones. Tie each half of that trout to the soles of your feet. Walk around. You think I got woobles in the head? Rebecca said, yes.

Aunt Lottie said, cure a blister, kiss a dog. Pick a husband, talk to me. Rebecca said, oh.

Aunt Lottie told her it was common knowledge she was being pestered by peckerwoods powerful horny, did she comprehend horny? Rebecca said, yes, she certainly did. My Aunt Lottie told her there was nothing wrong with that, long as it was pleasant. But she doubted Rebecca liked not just our nasty peckerwoods but any men at all, which is why she teased and played with all of them. The one who ain't horny here was her because she was night-owl scared. Did Lottie still have woobles in her head? Rebecca said, no, ma'am.

Aunt Lottie asked her to answer just yes or no. Was she married before? Yes. Was her husband a man content? No. A scoundrel? No. Just a man? Yes.

Aunt Lottie wondered it out loud. She said, to make what's already bad rock bottom, your momma and daddy want you breeding and right now. Rebecca said, oh, yes ma'am.

Aunt Lottie said, tell me this. You ever know a man you'd gladly have? No. You fancy ary man you ever met? No. Well, when you was the least little girl, as pleasant as the flowers are made, did you ever dream of that boy who was a-walking around that same minute, who'd grow up to take you, the man you'd gladly have? Yes. Do you fancy him still, a boy in your head you never met? Yes. Well, there is a way to make him appear, and them otherns disappear.

Rebecca said, how. Aunt Lottie said, it's a spell, a charm, and Rebecca said, woman, I am a Christian preacher's daughter, and Aunt Lottie told her yes, she knew that, but just you say something, to men, about their noses.

Say what about their noses, Rebecca asked her.

Aunt Lottie sat back and rocked in that chair, saying, once this is heard it can't get unheard, and Rebecca said, so tell me, and so Aunt Lottie did.

To find the man for you, in a bunch of God-awful puddle jumpers, you say this to them, a man's horn is times three the size of his nose.

Rebecca's eyes got as wide as mine, and she wanted to know now what was this. Aunt Lottie said, that's the charm, that's the spell, what it would do she couldn't tell. She turned to me on the floor, saying, Vester, what do you have to say about it.

I was just a loony little boy but somewhere down inside of me I knew what to say. I said, the cat looks big until the dog shows up, which that turned out to be the truth of it finally, but Rebecca looked at me like I was as crazy as my Aunt Lottie, who then asked Rebecca if she would let me work around her house and keep her company for a while after that. Rebecca said, yes.

Clink Williams showed up and said, well? Rebecca said, a man's horn is times three the size of his nose. Clink Williams studied her the longest time before jumping up saying he'd fancy a wife a mite more delicate, who didn't spend her time pondering horns, and he was gone.

Slade Foley showed up and said, well? Rebecca said, a man's horn is times three the size of his nose. Slade Foley said making fun of a man's horn was a damn deadly thing to do, he'd about made a mistake here, so long, and he was gone.

Radley Nollins showed up and said, well? Rebecca said, a man's horn is times three the size of his nose. Radley Nollins said, that ain't the Bible, and he was gone.

Then there was a long time when nobody came to see Rebecca Tull. She did have some things for me to do in the afternoons so I was there when the dog showed up.

His name was Sam Bean. He was a short, dark-faced little man, older than thirty but nimble and straight. His skin had a pleasant, leathery smoothness, and when he was set in the oak rocker, her in a slat chair, me on the floor, he wasn't afraid to look Rebecca dead in the eye because he told her right off he had asked her daddy if he could come calling, did she remember him at all. She said, yes, you helped to raise the house, she remembered him but he never said a word to her, why was that, and Bean said, I figured you flighty, genteel, and snakey. Rebecca said, well, what are you doing here now, and Bean asked her if she really said to Radley Nollins, Slade Foley, and Clink Williams, a man's horn is times three the size of his nose.

She said she did. Bean thought a minute and said, why?

She fired up red in the face, said it was none of his business why, if he didn't like the way she talked, go home, and Bean said, you been married before. She said, that's what widow generally means. Bean said, what happened to him. She said, God Amighty, Mr. Bean, he died. Widow, died, and Bean said, I mean how, and she said, oh I killed him off with deadly nightshade in his corn soup of course and I'll do it again if I have to marry Clink Williams or a Slade Foley or a Radley Nollins or a Sam God help us Bean.

Sam Bean said she didn't have to marry him, was she content with her husband? She fired up some more, what kind of judge and jury did he think he was, and he said he thought the woman who wasn't afraid to talk about the size of a man's horn might talk turkey to a man ready to talk squirrel.

That sobered her. She looked at him different then. Talk turkey, talk squirrel is it, she said, have you been married, Bean, and he said, onct, his wife died too. Rebecca said, you content with her, and he said, only when she died.

That sobered her up even more. What does that mean, she asked him, and Bean said, it means I am telling you the truth. Her stomach is what killed her. Milk sick, poorly deathly over a year. She didn't like it. We had a hell of a time but we always had that. We were hateful and contentious. My chilluns, I got two, boy four, girl three, lost one, they was scared to death. It was like she faulted me, like us being married got her sick ready to die. Then about three week afore she died, all that stopped. What had been meanness and spite went away. There was nothing left of it. There was nothing hateful betwixt us. We got so close, there wasn't nothing, not plumb line, not stob measure, not yardstick ruled, in our way. There was not one hard thing between us. Then she died.

There was a long time before Rebecca said anything, but when she did, she said, my husband got hisself gored by a bull.

And Sam Bean laughed.

What's so damn funny, I didn't laugh at your dead wife, Rebecca said, and Bean said, no, no, it's just that you can't say bull up here. You say cow brute instead, the good women can't abide bull. Can't say stallion, neither, say stable horse. A cock is a he chicken. What's wrong with women like that, are they modest, and Rebecca said, no, scared, and Bean said, of horns, and Rebecca said, of getting pleasure easy, then Bean said, that could be. Gored by a bull, was he?

Whole side tore open, she said, like his flesh was jelly and his bones paper. He was a preacher, like his daddy, and mine. He went eternally about with his Bible and a stopwatch, calculating hourly wages of sin, minutes in a day bodies had left to repent, and such weariness as that. But when he got sick, to face God hisself, he didn't fancy no stopwatch then, he didn't call for his Bible even.

No, what the man wanted then was me. I did my best to comfort him, but I didn't do no good at all. And he died, like your wife, and this is squirrel now and turkey both Sam Bean, I am glad he died and I am free of him, but I dread the way it had to come about, and what I just didn't have to give my husband.

Bean thought and asked, was his horn times three the size of his nose, and Rebecca said, on occasion.

Then Rebecca said, you'd expect me to raise your younguns, and he said, I would, and she said, where would we live, and he said, halfway up the mountain on seventy-five acres in a log house with rooms and a wood floor, and she said, what kind of bed, and he said, seven-foot-long rope-held feather-down mattress and a Cumberland quilt.

Then there was a sadness to it. I didn't understand that but I do now, and part of the way I do is what I heard them say to each other then.

How long, she said, do you calculate it will be, Mr. Bean, afore you get tired and familiar with me in your feather bed and do it just to ease yourself on cold nights, turning away from me and my comfort to your own?

Bean said, turkey now, and Rebecca said, and squirrel, Sam, and I was a little boy but I could see this was the powerful question what bothered the widow Rebecca Tull about all men. So I listened to Sam Bean answer her.

No man, Bean said, can prophesy how long he will treasure his wife. It ain't in his power to do so. Love grows old and waxes cold fast, so might mine for you. I might have to leave you one day, to set alone on the other side of the porch. But I would never disgrace you with that, nor would ary other living soul ever hear of it. Now then. How long would you pleasure yourself with me, with bold sayings about the size of horns, afore you'd commence like other women saying cow brute for bull and press them purty wet lips into parched-out thread stitches at the touch of my hand.

No woman, said Rebecca, can say how long she will pleasure at the hand of her husband. It ain't in her power to do so. It may be, in my fashion, I too will go to that other side of the porch. But if you do not disgrace me with your disdain, I will abide you with mine.

Bean said, hand me the Bible there.

Rebecca said, don't ruin everthing by mortifying me with scripture.

Bean said, find Genesis, chapter two. That's when man and woman God created. Rebecca said, I know that, Sam, I know what, and Bean said, on what day of the month was you born? Rebecca said, huh. Bean said, just tell a man before he dies, and Rebecca said, the twenty-fifth. Bean said, read it, Genesis chapter two, verse twenty-five.

Rebecca read it aloud. This is what it said. And they were both naked, the man and the woman, and they were not ashamed.

Sam Bean and Rebecca Tull both got excited then and about reached for each other, but there I was, a quiet boy sitting on the floor staring at them. They stood up. Bean asked her if he should come again to expound this further, and she said, do. I ran to Aunt Lottie and she said she thought as much, go back and ask her if she believed in spells now. I ran back to Rebecca.

Bean was gone, but she was now sitting in the oak rocker where he sat.

I was able to just watch her a while before she saw I was there. She was dreamy. She said, oh, Vester, what is it? I said, my Aunt Lottie asks if you believe in spells now. She said, you can tell her I used it. Your dog did show up to cure my blisters, tell her that.

I said I would and I said, I know a riddle, you want to hear it, and she said, yes, and I said, why is a tongue like an unhappy woman, and she said, why, and I said, both are down in the mouth. I said, I know two more, what colors would you paint the sun and the wind, and she said, what colors, Vester, and I said, the sun rose and the wind blew. Then I couldn't say it, the third one, because I was so full of my enchantment by her, but she saw that and she really looked right at me and gave me the smile I see still on that face, all these years later, and she said, number three, Vester. I said, how can I tell you what you are in six letters, and she said, how, and I said, U R A B U T, I would marry you if I could. And I ran home.

She became Mrs. Bean. They had four chilluns to go with his two. And at eighty years old, she buried him. At his funeral, over his body, when her preacher grandson said horn and nose in the same sentence, Rebecca and Vester, in spite of anything Dog Slaughter Creek would think or imagine, we laughed out loud.

That's what I told my wife, and she said, maybe.

———————

Romulus Linney is the author of three novels and more than thirty plays, produced throughout the United States and abroad. His stories have appeared in *The Missouri Review, Fiction, Shenandoah, Image,* and *Pushcart Prize,* among others. Awards include two Obies, one for Sustained Excellence in Playwriting, and both the Award in Literature and the Award of Merit Medal for Drama from the American Academy of Arts and Letters. He is a member of the American Academy of Arts and Sciences.

LAURA CALLANAN

I spent my childhood in the western North Carolina Appalachian mountains. I have returned there often throughout my life, and have never lost my respect and relish for that way of life. The bawdy folk saying upon which this story is based seemed to me to contain, as so many of them do, a hidden wisdom. Using the ways of a spirited young lady like one I knew at the time, I set out to find out what it was.

Allan Gurganus

HE'S AT THE OFFICE

(from *The New Yorker*)

Till the Japanese bombed Pearl Harbor, most American men wore hats to work. What happened? Did our guys— suddenly scouting overhead for worse Sunday raids—come to fear their hatbrims' interference? My unsuspecting father wore his till yesterday. He owned three. A gray, a brown, and a summer straw one, whose maroon-striped rayon band could only have been woven in America in the nineteen-forties.

Last month, I lured him from his self-imposed office hours for a walk around our block. My father insisted on bringing his briefcase. "You never know," he said. We soon passed a huge young hipster, creaking in black leather. The kid's pierced face flashed more silver than most bait shops sell. His jeans, half down, exposed hatracks of white hipbone; the haircut arched high over jug ears. He was scouting Father's shoes. Long before fashion joined him, Dad favored an under-evolved antique form of orthopedic Doc Martens. These impressed a punk now scanning the Sherman tank of a cowhide briefcase with chromium corner braces. The camel-hair overcoat was cut to resemble some boxy-backed 1947 Packard. And, of course, up top sat "the gray."

Pointing to it, the boy smiled. "Way bad look on you, guy."

My father, seeking interpretation, stared at me. I simply shook my head no. I could not explain Dad to himself in terms of tidal fashion trends. All I said was "I think he likes you."

Dad's face folded. "Uh-oh."

By the end, my father, the fifty-two-year veteran of Integrity Office Supplier, Unlimited, had become quite cool again, way.

We couldn't vacation for more than three full days. He'd veer our Plymouth toward some way-station pay phone. We soon laughed as Dad, in the glass booth, commenced to wave his arms, shake his head, shift his weight from foot to foot. We knew Miss Green must be telling him of botched orders, delivery mistakes. We were nearly to Gettysburg. I'd been studying battle maps. Now I knew we'd never make it.

My father bounded back to the car and smiled in. "Terrible mix-up with the Wilmington school system's carbon paper for next year. Major goof, but typical. Guy's got to do it all himself. Young Green didn't insist I come back, but she sure hinted."

We U-turned southward, and my father briefly became the most charming man on earth. He now seemed to be selling something we needed, whatever we needed. Travelling north into a holiday—the very curse of leisure—he had kept as silent as some fellow with toothaches. Now he was our tour guide, interviewing us, telling and retelling his joke. Passing a cemetery, he said (over his family's dry carbon-paper unison), "I hear they're dying to get in there!" "Look on the bright side," I told myself: "we'll arrive home and escape him as he runs—literally runs—to the office."

Dad was, like me, an early riser. Six days a week, Mom sealed his single-sandwich lunch into its Tupperware jacket; this fit accidentally yet exactly within the lid compartment of his durable briefcase. He would then pull on his overcoat—bulky, war-efficient, strong-seamed, four buttons big as silver dollars and carved from actual shell. He'd place the cake-sized hat in place, nod in our general direction, and set off hurrying. Dad faced each day as one more worthy enemy. If he had been Dwight Eisenhower saving the Western world, or Jonas Salk freeing kids our age from crutches, O.K. But yellow Eagle pencils? Utility paperweights in park-bench green?

Once a year, Mom told my brother and me how much the war had darkened her young husband; he'd enlisted with three other guys from Falls; he alone came back alive with all his limbs. "Before that," she smiled, "your father was funnier, funny. And smarter. Great dancer. You can't blame mustard gas, not this time. It's more what Dick saw. He came home and he was all business. Before that, he'd been mischievous and talkative and strange. He was always playing around with words. Very entertaining. Eyelashes out to here. For years, I figured that in time he'd come back to being whole. But since June of '45 it's been All Work and No Play Makes Jack."

Mom remembered their fourth anniversary. "I hired an overnight sitter for you two. We drove to an inn near Asheville. It had the state's best restaurant, candlelight, a real string quartet. I'd made myself a green velvet dress. I was twenty-eight and never in my whole life have I ever looked better. You just know it. Dick recognized some man who'd bought two adding machines. Dick invited him to join us. Then I saw how much his work was going to have to mean to him. Don't be too hard on him, please. He feeds us, he puts aside real savings for you boys' college. Dick pays our taxes. Dick has no secrets. He's not hurting anyone." Brother and I gave each other a look Mom recognized and understood but refused to return.

The office seemed to tap some part of him that was either off-limits to us or simply did not otherwise exist. My brother and I griped that he'd never attended our Little League games (not that we ever made the starting lineup). He missed our father-son Cub Scout banquet; it conflicted with a major envelope convention in Newport News. Mother neutrally said he loved us as much as he could. She was a funny, energetic person—all that wasted good will. And even as kids, we knew not to blame her.

Ignored, Mom created a small sewing room. Economizing needlessly, she stayed busy stitching all our school clothes, cowboy motifs galore. For a while, each shirtpocket bristled with Mom-designed embroidered cacti. But Simplicity patterns were never going to engage a mind as complex as hers. Soon Mom was spending most mornings playing vicious duplicate bridge. Our toothbrush glasses briefly broke out in rashes of red hearts, black clubs. Mom's new pals were society ladies respectful of her brainy speed, her impenitent wit; she never bothered introducing them to her husband. She laughed more now. She started wearing rouge.

We lived a short walk from both our school and his wholesale office. Dad sometimes left the Plymouth parked all night outside the workplace, his desk lamp the last one burning on the whole third floor. Integrity's president, passing headquarters late, always fell for it. "Dick, what do you do up there all night, son?" My father's shrug became his finest boast. The raises kept pace; Integrity Office Supplier was still considered quite a comer. And R. Richard Markham, Sr. — handsome as a collar ad, a hat ad, forever at the office — was the heir apparent.

Dad's was Integrity's flagship office: "Maker of World's Highest Quality Clerical Supplies." No other schoolboys had sturdier pastel subject dividers, more clip-in see-through three-ring pen caddies. The night before school started, Dad would be up late at our kitchen table, swilling coffee, "getting you boys set." Zippered leather cases, English slide rules, folders more suitable for treaties than for book reports (" 'Skipper, A Dog of the Pyrenees,' by Marjorie Hopgood Purling"). Our notebooks soon proved too heavy to carry far; we secretly stripped them, swapping gear for lunchbox treats more exotic than Mom's hard-boiled eggs and Sun-Maid raisin packs.

Twenty years ago, Dad's Integrity got bought out by a German firm. The business's vitality proved somewhat hobbled by computers' onslaught. "A fad," my father called computers in 1976. "Let others retool. We'll stand firm with our yellow legals, erasers, Parker ink, fountain pens. Don't worry, our regulars'll come back. True vision always lets you act kind in the end, boys. Remember."

Yeah, right.

My father postponed his retirement. Mom encouraged that and felt relieved; she could not imagine him at home all day. As Integrity's market share dwindled, Dad spent more time at the office, as if to compensate with his own body for the course of modern life.

His secretary, the admired Miss Green, had once been what Pop still called "something of a bombshell." (He stuck with a Second World War terminology that had, like the hat, served him too well to ever leave behind.)

Still favoring shoulder pads, dressed in unyielding woollen Joan Crawford solids, Green wore an auburn pageboy that looked burned by decades of ungrateful dyes. She kicked off her shoes beneath her desk, revealing feet that told the tale of high heels' worthless weekday brutality. She'd quit college to tend an ailing mother, who proved demanding, then immortal. Brother and I teased Mom: poor Green appeared to worship her longtime boss, a guy whose face was as smooth and wedged and classic as his hat. Into Dick Markham's blunted constancy, she read actual "moods."

He still viewed Green, now past sixty, as a promising virginal girl. In their small adjoining offices, these two thrived within a fond impersonality that permeated the ads of the period.

Integrity's flagship headquarters remained enamelled a flavorless mint green, unaltered for five decades. The dark Mission coatrack was made by Limbert—quite a good piece. One ashtray—upright, floor model, brushed chromium—proved the size and shape of some landlocked torpedo. Moored to walls, dented metal desks were gray as battleships. A series of forest-green filing cabinets seemed banished, patient as a family of trolls, to one shaming little closet all their own. Dad's office might've been decorated by a firm called Edward Hopper & Sam Spade, Unlimited.

For more than half a century, he walked in each day at seven-oh-nine sharp, as Miss Green forever said, "Morning, Mr. Markham. I left your appointments written on your desk pad, can I get you your coffee? Is now good, sir?" And Dad said, "Yes, why, thanks, Miss Green, how's your mother, don't mind if I do."

Four years ago, I received a panicked phone call: "You the junior to a guy about eighty, guy in a hat?"

"Probably." I was working at home. I pressed my computer's "Save" function. This, I sensed, might take a while. "Save."

"Exit? No? Yes?"

"Yes."

"Mister, your dad thinks we're camped out in his office and he's been banging against our door. He's convinced we've evicted his files and what he calls his Green. 'What have you done with young Green?' Get down here A.S.A.P. Get him out of our hair or it's 911 in three minutes, swear to God."

From my car, I phoned home. Mom must have been off somewhere playing bridge with the mayor's blond wife and his blond ex-wife; they'd sensibly become excellent friends. The best women are the best people on earth; and the worst men the very worst. Mother, overlooked by Dad for years, had continued finding what she called "certain outlets."

When I arrived, Dad was still heaving himself against an office door, deadbolt-locked from within. Since its upper panel was frosted glass, I could make out the colors of the clothes of three or four people pressing from their side. They'd used masking tape to crosshatch the glass, as if bracing for a hurricane. The old man held his briefcase, wore his gray hat, the tan boxy coat.

"Dad?" He stopped with a mechanical cartoon verve, jumped my way, and smiled so hard it warmed my heart and scared me witless. My father had never acted so glad to see me—not when I graduated summa cum laude, not at my wedding, not after the birth of my son—and I felt joy in the presence of such joy from him.

"Reinforcements. Good man. We've got quite a hostage situation here. Let's put our shoulders to it, shall we?"

"Dad?" I grabbed the padded shoulders of his overcoat. These crumpled to reveal a man far sketchier hiding in there somewhere—a guy only twenty years from a hundred, after all.

"Dad? Dad. We have a good-news, bad-news setup here today. It's this. You found the right building, Dad. Wrong floor."

I led him back to the clattering, oil-smelling elevator. I thought to return, tap on the barricaded door, explain. But, in time, hey, they'd peek, they'd figure out the coast was clear. That they hadn't recognized him, after his fifty-two years of long days in this very building, said something. New people, everywhere.

I saw at once that Miss Green had been crying. Her face was caked with so much powder it looked like calamine. "Little mix-up," I said.

"Mr. Markham? We got three calls about those gum erasers," she said, faking a frontal normality. "I think they're putting sawdust in them these days, sir. They leave skid marks, apparently. I put the information on your desk. With your day's appointments. Like your coffee? Like it now? Sir?"

I hung his hat on the hat tree; I slid his coat onto its one wooden Deco hanger that could, at any flea market today, bring thirty-five dollars easy, two tones of wood, inlaid.

I wanted to have a heart-to-heart. I was so disoriented as to feel half sane myself. But I overhead Father already returning his calls. He ignored me, and that seemed, within this radically altered gravitational field, a good sign. I sneaked back to Miss Green's desk and admitted, "I'll need to call his doctor. I want him seen today, Miss Green. He was up on four, trying to get into that new head-hunting service. He told them his name. Mom was out. So they, clever, looked him up in the book and found his junior and phoned me to come help."

She sat forward, strenuously feigning surprise. She looked rigid, chained to this metal desk by both gnarled feet. "How long?" I somehow knew to ask.

Green appeared ecstatic, then relieved, then, suddenly, happily weeping, tears pouring down—small tears, lopsided, mascaraed grit. She blinked up at me with a spaniel's gratitude. Suddenly, if slowly, I began to understand. In mere seconds, she had caved about Dad's years-long caving-in. It was my turn now.

Miss Green now whispered certain of his mistakes. There were forgotten parking tickets by the dozen. There was his attempt to purchase a lake house on land already flooded for a dam. Quietly, she admitted years of covering.

From her purse, she lifted a page covered in Dad's stern Germanic cursive, blue ink fighting to stay isometrically between red lines.

"I found this one last week." Green's voice seemed steadied by the joy of having told. "I fear this is about the worst, to date, we've been."

If they say "Hot enough for you?," it means recent weather. "Yes indeed" still a good comeback. Order forms pink. Requisition yellow. Miss green's birthday June 12. She work with you fifty-one years. Is still unmarried. Mother now dead, since '76, so stop asking about Mother, health of. Home address, 712 Marigold Street: Left at Oak, can always walk there. After last week, never go near car again. Unfair to others. Take second left at biggest tree. Your new Butcher's name is: Al. Wife: Betty. Sons: Matthew and Dick Junior. Grandson Richie (your name with a III added on it). List of credit cards, licnse etc. below in case you lose walet agn, you big dope. Put copies somewhere safe, 3 places, write down, hide many. You are 80, yes, eighty.

And yet, as we now eavesdropped, Dick Markham dealt with a complaining customer. He sounded practiced, jokey, conversant, exact.

"Dad, you have an unexpected doctor's appointment." I handed Dad his hat. I'd phoned our family physician from Miss Green's extension.

For once, they were ready for us. The nurses kept calling him by name, smiling, overinsistent, as if hinting at answers for a kid about to take his make-or-break college exam. I could see they'd always liked him. In a town this small, they'd maybe heard about his trouble earlier today.

As Dad got ushered in for tests, he glowered accusations back at me as if I had just dragged him to a Nazi medical experiment. He finally reemerged, scarily pale, pressing a bit of gauze into the crook of his bare arm, its long veins the exact blue of Parker's washable ink. They directed him toward the lobby bathroom. They gave him a cup for his urine specimen. He held it before him with two hands like some Magi's treasure.

His hat, briefcase, and overcoat remained behind, resting on an orange plastic chair all their own. Toward these I could display a permissible tenderness. I lightly set my hand on each item. Call it superstition. I now lifted the hat and sniffed it. It smelled like Dad. It smelled like rope. Physical intimacy has never been a possibility. My brother and I, half drunk, once tried to picture the improbable, the sexual conjunction of our parents. Brother said, "Well, he probably pretends he's at the office, unsealing her like a good manila envelope that requires a rubber stamp—legible, yes, keep it legible, *legible,* now speed-mail!"

I had flipped through four stale magazines before I saw the nurses peeking from their crudely cut window. "He has been quite a while, Mr. Markham. Going on thirty minutes."

"Shall I?" I rose and knocked. No answer. "Would you come stand behind me?" Cowardly, I signalled to an older nurse.

The door proved unlocked. I opened it. I saw one old man aimed the other way and trembling with hesitation. Before him, a white toilet, a white sink, and a white enamel trash can, the three aligned—each its own insistent invitation. In one hand, the old man held an empty specimen cup. In the other hand, his dick.

Turning my way, grateful, unashamed to be caught sobbing, he cried, "Which one, son? Fill which one?"

Forcibly retired, my father lived at home in his pajamas. Mom made him wear the slippers and robe to help with his morale. "Think *Thin Man.* Think William Powell." But the poor guy literally hung his head with shame. That phrase took on new meaning now that his routine and dignity proved so reduced. Dad's mopey presence clogged every outlet she'd perfected to avoid him. The two of them were driving each other crazy.

Lacking the cash for live-in help, she was forced to cut way back on her bridge game and female company. She lost ten pounds—it showed in her neck and face—and then she gave up rouge. You could see Mom missed her fancy friends. I soon pitied her nearly as much as I pitied him—no, more. At least he allowed himself to be distracted. She couldn't forget.

Mom kept urging him to get dressed. She said they needed to go to the zoo. She had to get out and "do" something. One morning, she was trying to force Dad into his dress pants when he struck her. She fell right over the back of an armchair. The whole left side of her head stayed a rubber-stamp pad's blue-black for one whole week. Odd, this made it easier for both of them to stay home. Now two people hung their heads in shame.

At a window overlooking the busy street, Dad would stand staring out, one way. On the window glass, his forehead left a persistent oval of human oil. His pajama knees pressed against the radiator. He silently second-guessed parallel parkers. He studied westerly-moving traffic. Sometimes he'd stand guard there for six uninterrupted hours. Did he await some detained patriotic parade? I pictured poor Green on a passing float—hoisting his coffee mug and the black phone receiver, waving him back down to street level, reality, use.

One December morning, Mom—library book in lap, trying to reinterest herself in Daphne du Maurier, in anything—smelled scorching. Like Campbell's mushroom soup left far too long on simmer. Twice she checked their stove and toaster oven. Finally, around his nap time, she pulled Dad away from the radiator: his shins had cooked. "Didn't it hurt you, Dick? Darling, didn't you ever feel anything?"

Next morning at six-thirty, I got her call. Mom's husky tone sounded too jolly for the hour. She described bandaging both legs.

"As you kids say, I don't think this is working for us. This might be beyond me. Integrity's fleabag insurance won't provide him with that good a home. We have just enough to go on living here as usual. Now, I'll maybe shock you and you might find me weak or, worse, disloyal. But would you consider someday checking out some nice retreats or facilities in driving distance? Even if it uses up the savings. Your father is the love of my life—one per customer. I just hate to get any more afraid of him!"

I said I'd phone all good local places, adding, giddy, "I hear they're dying to get in there."

This drew a silence as cold as his. "Your dad's been home from the office—what, seven months? Most men lean toward their leisure years, but who ever hated leisure more than Dick? When I think of everything he gave Integrity and how little he's getting back . . . I'm not strong enough to *keep* him, but I can't bear to *put* him anywhere. Still, at this rate, all I'll want for Christmas is a nice white padded cell for two."

I wished my mother belonged to our generation, where the women work. She could've done anything. And now to be saddled with a man who'd known nothing but enslavement to one so-so office. The workaholic, tabled. He still refused to dress; she focussed on the sight of his pajamas. My folks now argued with the energy of newlyweds; then she felt ashamed of herself and he forgot to do whatever he'd just promised.

On Christmas Eve, she was determined to put up a tree for him. But Dad, somehow frightened by the ladder and all the unfamiliar boxes everywhere, got her into such a lethal headlock she had to scream for help. Now the neighbors were involved. People I barely knew interrupted my work hours, saying, "Something's got to be done. It took three of us to pull him off of her. He's still strong as a horse. It's getting dangerous over there. He could escape."

Sometimes, at two in the morning, she'd find him standing in their closet, wearing his p.j.s and the season's correct hat. He'd be looking at his business suits. The right hand would be filing,

"walking," back and forth across creased pant legs, as if seeking the
. . . exact . . . right . . . pair . . . for . . . the office . . . today.

I tried to keep Miss Green informed. She'd sold her duplex and
moved into our town's most stylish old-age home. When she
swept downstairs to greet me, I didn't recognize her. "God, you
look fifteen years younger." I checked her smile for hints of a possible lift.

She just laughed, giving her torso one mild shimmy. "Look, Ma.
No shoulder pads."

Her forties hairdo, with its banked, rolled edges, had softened
into pretty little curls around her face. She'd let its color go her nat-
ural silvery blond. Green gave me a slow look. If I didn't know her
better, I'd have sworn she was flirting.

She appeared shorter in flats. I now understood: her toes had
been so mangled by wearing those forties quonsethuts of high
heels, ones she'd probably owned since age eighteen. Her feet had
grown, but she'd stayed true to the old shoes, part of some illusion
she felt my dad required.

Others in the lobby perked up at her fond greeting; I saw she'd
already become the belle of this place. She let me admire her
updated charms.

"No," she smiled simply, "it's that I tried to keep it all somewhat
familiar for him. How I looked and all. We got to where Mr.
Markham found any change a kind of danger, so . . . I mean, it
wasn't as if a dozen other suitors were beating down my door.
What with Mother being moody and sick that long. And so, day
to day, well . . ." She shrugged.

Now, in my life I've had very few inspired ideas. Much of me,
like Pop, is helplessly a company man. So forgive my boasting of this.

Leaving Miss Green's, I stopped by a huge Salvation Army
store. It was a good one. Over the years, I've found a few fine Federal side chairs here and many a great tweed jacket. Browsing
through the used-furniture room, I wandered beneath a cardboard

placard hand-lettered THE WORLD OF EARLY AMERICAN. Ladder-back deacon's chairs and plaid upholstered things rested knee to knee, like sad and separate families.

I chanced to notice a homeless man, asleep, a toothless white fellow. His overcoat looked filthy. His belongings were bunched around him in six rubber-banded shoeboxes. His feet, in paint-stained shoes, rested on an ordinary school administrator's putty-colored desk. THE WONDERFUL WORLD OF WORK hung over hand-me-down waiting rooms still waiting. Business furniture sat parlored—forlorn as any gray-green Irish wake. There was something about the sight of this old guy's midday snoring in so safe a fluorescent make-work cubicle.

Mom now used her sewing room only for those few overnight third cousins willing to endure its lumpy foldout couch. The room'd become a catchall, cold storage, since about 1970. We waited for Dad's longest nap of the day. Then, in a crazed burst of energy, we cleared her lair, purging it of boxes, photo albums, four unused exercise machines. I paint-rolled its walls in record time, the ugliest latex junior-high-school green that Sherwin-Williams sells (there's still quite a range). The Salvation Army delivers: within two days, I had arranged this new-used-junk to resemble Integrity's workspace, familiarly anonymous. A gray desk nuzzled one wall—the window wasted behind. Three green file cabinets made a glum herd. One swivel wooden chair rode squeaky casters. The hat rack antlered upright over a dented tin wastebasket. The ashtray looked big enough to serve an entire cancer ward. Wire shelves predicted a neutral "in," a far more optimistic "out." I stuffed desk drawers with Parker ink, cheap fountain pens, yellow legal pads, four dozen paper clips. I'd bought a big black rotary phone, and Mom got him his own line.

Against her wishes, I'd saved most of Dad's old account ledgers. Yellowed already, they could've come from a barrister's desk in a Dickens novel. I scattered "1959–62." In one corner I piled all Dad's boxed records, back taxes, old Christmas cards from customers. The man saved everything.

The evening before we planned introducing him to his new quarters, I disarranged the place a bit. I tossed a dozen pages on the floor near his chair. I left the desk lamp lit all night. It gave this small room a strange hot smell, overworked. The lamp was made of nubbly brown cast metal (recast war surplus?), its red button indicating "on." Black meant "off."

That morning I was there to help him dress. Mom made us a hearty oatmeal breakfast, packed his lunch, and snapped the Tupperware insert into his briefcase.

"And where am *I* going?" he asked us in a dead voice.

"To the office," I said. "Where else do you go this time of day?"

He appeared sour, puffy, skeptical. Soon as I could, I glanced at Mom. This was not going to be as easy as we'd hoped.

I got Dad's coat and hat. He looked gray and dubious. He would never believe in this new space if I simply squired him down the hall to it. So, after handing him his briefcase, I led Dad back along our corridor and out onto the street.

Some of the old-timers, recognizing him, called, "Looking good, Mr. Markham," or "Cold enough for you?" Arm in arm, we nodded past them.

My grammar school had been one block from his office. Forty years back, we'd set out on foot like this together. The nearer Dad drew to Integrity, the livelier he became; the closer I got to school, the more withdrawn I acted. But today I kept up a mindless overplentiful patter. My tone neither cheered nor deflected him. One block before his office building, I swerved back down an alley toward the house. As we approached, I saw that Mom had been imaginative enough to leave our front door wide open. She'd removed a bird print that had hung in our foyer hall unloved forever. A mere shape, it still always marked this as our hall, our home.

"*Here* we are!" I threw open his office door. I took his hat and placed it on its hook. I helped him free of his coat. Just as his face had grown bored, then irked, and finally enraged at our deception, the phone rang. From where I stood—half in the office, half in the hall—I could see Mom holding the white phone in the kitchen.

My father paused—since when did he answer the phone?—and, finally, flushed, reached for it himself. "Dick?" Mom said, "You'll hate me, I'm getting so absent-minded. But you did take your lunch along today, right? I mean, go check. Be patient with me, O.K.?" Phone cradled between his head and shoulder, he lifted his briefcase and snapped it open—his efficiency still water-clear, and scary. Dad then said to the receiver, "Lunch is definitely here, per usual. But, honey, haven't I told you about these personal calls at the office?"

Then I saw him bend to pick up scattered pages. I saw him touch one yellow legal pad and start to square all desk-top pens at sharp right angles. As he pulled the chair two inches forward I slowly shut his door behind me. Then Mother and I, hidden in the kitchen, held each other and, not expecting it, cried, if very, very silently.

When we peeked in two hours later, he was filing.

Every morning, Sundays included, Dad walked to the office. Even our ruse of walking him around the block was relaxed. Mom simply set a straw hat atop him (after Labor Day, she knew to switch to his gray). With his packed lunch, he would stride nine paces from the kitchen table, step in, and pull the door shut, muttering complaints of overwork, no rest ever.

Dad spent a lot of time on the phone. Long-distance directory-assistance charges constituted a large part of his monthly bill. But he "came home" for supper with the weary sense of blurred accomplishment we recalled from olden times.

Once, having dinner with them, I asked Dad how he was. He sighed. "Well, July is peak for getting their school supplies ordered. So the pressure is on. My heart's not what it was, heart's not completely in it lately, I admit. They downsized Green. Terrible loss to me. With its being crunch season, I get a certain shortness of breath. Suppliers aren't what they were, the gear is often second-rate, little of it any longer American-made. But you keep going, because it's what you know and because your clients count on you. I may be beat, but, hey—it's still a job."

"Aha," I said.

Mom received a call on her own line. It was from some kindergarten owner. Dad—plundering his old red address book—had somehow made himself a go-between, arranging sales, but working freelance now. He appeared to be doing it unsalaried, not for whole school systems but for small local outfits like day-care centers. This teacher had to let Mom know that he'd sent too much of the paste. No invoice with it, a pallet of free jarred white school paste waiting out under the swing sets. Whom to thank?

Once, I tiptoed in and saw a long list of figures he kept meaning to add up. I noticed that, in his desperate daily fight to keep his desktop clear, he'd placed seven separate five-inch piles of papers at evened intervals along the far wall. I found such ankle-level filing sad till slowly I recognized a pattern—oh, yeah, "The Pile System." It was my own technique for maintaining provisional emergency order, and one which I now rejudged to be quite sane.

Inked directly into the wooden bottom of his top desk drawer was this:

> Check Green's sick leave ridic. long. Nazis still soundly defeated. Double enter all new receipts, nincompoop. Yes, you . . . eighty-one. Old Woman roommate is: "Betty."

Mom felt safe holding bridge parties at the house again, telling friends that Dad was in there writing letters and doing paperwork, and who could say he wasn't? Days Mom could now shop or attend master-point tournaments at good-driving-distance hotels. In her own little kitchen-corner office, she entered bridge chat rooms, E-mailing game-theory arcana to well-known French and Russian players. She'd regained some weight and her face was fuller, and prettier for that. She bought herself a bottle-green velvet suit. "It's just a cheap Chanel knockoff, but these ol' legs still ain't that bad, hmm?" She looked more rested than I'd seen her in a year or two.

I cut a mail slot in Dad's office door, and around eleven Mom would slip in his today's *Wall Street Journal.* You'd hear him fall upon it like a zoo animal, fed.

Since Dad had tried to break down the headhunters' door, I hadn't dared go on vacation myself. But Mother encouraged me to take my family to Hawaii. She laughed. "Go ahead, enjoy yourself, for Pete's sake. Everything under control. I'm playing what friends swear is my best bridge ever, and Dick's sure working good long hours again. By now I should know the drill, hunh?"

I was just getting into my bathing suit when the hotel phone rang. I could see my wife and son down there on the white beach.

"Honey? Me. There's news about your father."

Mom's voice sounded vexed but contained. Her businesslike tone seemed assigned. It let me understand.

"When?"

"This afternoon around six-thirty our time. Maybe it happened earlier, I don't know. I found him. First I convinced myself he was just asleep. But I guess, even earlier, I knew."

I stood here against glass, on holiday. I pictured my father face-down at his desk. The tie still perfectly knotted, his hat yet safe on its hook. I imagined Dad's head at rest atop those forty pages of figures he kept meaning to add up.

I told Mom I was sorry; I said we'd fly right back.

"No, please," she said. "I've put everything off till next week. It's just us now. Why hurry? And, son? Along with the bad news, I think there's something good. He died at the office."

Allan Gurganus was born in Rocky Mount,
North Carolina, in 1947. After teaching at
Stanford, the Iowa Writers' Workshop, and Sarah
Lawrence College, he returned seven years ago to
live in his native state. Gurganus's novels include
Oldest Living Confederate Tells All and *Plays Well
with Others.* His story collection, *White People,*
will be followed this year by a group of novellas,
The Practical Heart.

MARION ETTLINGER

*N*abokov, banished by the Russian Revolution from his vast inherited
holdings, wrote, "Memory is the only real estate." By age fifty, we are
all potential exiles. If we lose our car keys one day, might we not forget our
grandparents' names the next? Total recall matters to everyone mortal, but
for writers, it means life or death. Though my own parents expired with their
senses blessedly intact, forgetting has remained my own worst fear. "He's at
the Office" is a windsock riding the North wind of my greatest terror.
A concert pianist I know writes his weekly letters while seated at his concert
grand. He claims, "Proximity to your instrument is itself a form of practice."

I imagine myself at ninety; even if cursed with Alzheimer's, I bet I will
still daily trundle to my desk. I'll probably sit there, meditative, striking the
letter J all morning, the letter R all afternoon. I just hope for a kindly care-
taker who'll whisper to visitors, "Shhh. He thinks he's rewriting War and
Peace. Or at least, Oldest Living Confederate."

I designed this tale from its last line forward. I constructed an altar—
one cleverly intractable as a steel-trap, one plain looking as some green filing
cabinet. It is a little altar dedicated to that most inward, tender, and
ennobling of human privileges: Remembering.

John Holman

WAVE

(from *Image*)

Sometimes because of traffic Ray cut through a neighbor-hood that emptied out behind the hotel where he worked. He operated a wait-staff service that was contracted to a small hotel in Research Triangle Park. It was a quiet street, twenty miles per hour, though fairly busy just before school in the mornings and in the afternoons when school got out. At one house about halfway in, there was a man who sat on his porch and waved. The man waved no matter who was passing by. He waved every time, at every car, at everybody. He was always on the porch, unless the weather was bad, and then he sat on a tall stool inside the glass storm door and waved.

Ray had recently discovered this alternate route, finally found a way around the clogged stretch of expressway. Lately the usual wrecks and congestion were caused by sandbags in the lanes, and chickens, lumber, or wet paint. The oddities seemed to compete, to Ray's amusement and frustration. There had been roofing shingles, cats, loaves of bread, golf balls, and a washing machine blocking the way. The hazards of the thriving economy. So Ray needed the shortcut. After the first two greetings from the man, when Ray realized the man was not simply friendly but somehow stunned into a compulsion to wave, his dilemma was whether or not to wave back. If he was in a rush, Ray sometimes noticed too late and threw up his hand at the neighbor's porch, as if his wave might trail backward like a ribbon and flutter at the man before snapping forward to catch up. He felt silly waving to a possible idiot. It made Ray feel like an idiot, making an empty gesture at an empty-headed old white man who waved because he couldn't help it. It was like talking to a doll. He couldn't fully pretend it was meaningful. Yet, if he did not wave, he felt guilty. Sometimes, traffic or no, he stayed on the main road to the front of the hotel, only to chastise himself for preferring the stress of traffic to the stress of simply waving.

Occasionally, policemen pulled over cars for exceeding the street's speed limit, drivers late for school or work, or maybe rushing because of fear of the waving man. The man's house was small and blue, with a neat little yard. Azalea bushes trimmed the border along the porch. A clean concrete walkway led to three porch steps. The porch was fenced by a painted wooden rail, and the man sat on a rocking chair and waved. He was a big man, as chubby as an infant, with an infant's bald head and an infant's dimpled smile. He had gleaming small teeth and silver-rimmed glasses. In cool weather he wore a dove gray cardigan, and when the temperature was warm he wore pressed, pale-colored sport shirts. He was neat, clean, with plump soft-looking hands. Sometimes he leaned forward from his chair and waved. When he was behind the glass door, as he was this morning, and Ray had to make an effort to find him, the man would also be ducking and leaning in an effort to be seen.

Desperate optimism, Ray thought. This on a bleak, wet, early March morning when, the rainy night before, Ray had discovered someone lying drunk and crying in his backyard, trapped in the narrow space between his back hedges and rusting chain-link fence. Hearing the cry, Ray had gone out in the downpour and aimed a flashlight on him, a ruddy-looking man with soaked dark hair streaking his face — some kind of Indian maybe, in sopping denim shirt and pants and wearing the weight of wet black cowboy boots. Ray asked if he was all right, what's wrong, tried and failed to pull him up by his limp heavy arm. Shivering, Ray held the umbrella over the man for a while. This man was inordinately sad, eyes closed, speaking no language but despair. Sobbing and moaning. Rhythm and lilt.

So Ray covered him with a blanket and a bunched sheet of blue plastic tarpaulin. Ray's friend Alma was visiting, standing at the opened back door and looking out. She wanted to call the police, or an ambulance. "He'll freeze, catch pneumonia and die," she pleaded when Ray came inside.

"Catch pneumonia, maybe. He can't freeze out there tonight." He talked Alma into waiting. The police would be more trouble for the man, and an ambulance didn't seem warranted; he was just depressed, breathing well, not hemorrhaging. But they watched the Weather Channel to check the forecast for the night. The temperature would stay in the forties and rain would persist. Then they turned off the kitchen light and stared out the back window, but they couldn't see the man where he lay. He still sobbed loudly now and then, and his intermittent wails reassured them.

Standing there in the dark, sharing a bottle of red wine, was awkward. Alma was not exactly Ray's girlfriend although he had thought she was, or could be. When she first moved to town, months ago, he was all for some romance, and she had a flirty way of being friendly that sustained anticipation. And that night he still hoped for her affection, except the presence of the sad man was an impediment. No way to talk of love, and no sign from her other than her being there. She had come with a betting sheet for the NCAA basketball tournament, wanting Ray's help choosing winners for her office pool. The paper with the names of the hopeful teams in their starting brackets was held by a magnet to his refrigerator, where it semi-glowed in the weak tree-filtered light from a neighbor's back porch. Ray went over and pretended to study it in the near-dark.

"Maybe we should take him something to eat, or some coffee," Alma said.

So Ray opened the refrigerator and realized the uselessness of taking food out there. "He's not going to eat anything. He's too

. . . disconsolate." He pulled out lunch meat anyway. And mustard and mayo and lettuce. "Are you hungry?" he asked Alma.

The man outside moaned. "A sandwich would disintegrate in this rain," Ray said.

"Oh I can't bear this," Alma said. "Either that guy goes, or I do. I mean, get him inside or something, which is not really what I want while I'm here."

"Well, you're not going anywhere just yet."

"But he's out there like a wounded dog, or deer, or bear. What moans like that? There's nothing human about any of this."

Ray turned to look at her. She was making gestures of frustration and impatience, flexing her fingers and pivoting in her hiking boots, performing in the fan of refrigerator light, her short braids lifting slightly, like tentacles.

"I can't put him out of his misery. Besides, a wounded animal is the most dangerous kind, they say."

She stopped pivoting. "You're not making jokes about this, are you? You're using that poor person to make fun of me?"

Ray closed the refrigerator. But Alma was still dimly visible in front of him. "Sorry. It's just a way of being patient, of passing time here. No offense to you or him. I mean, if I were heartbroken and lost, drunk on the ground in the dark rain of somebody's raggedy backyard, I'd want to be left alone. I wouldn't want anybody to know I was even there. I'd want to suffer until I was through without some do-gooder guy and his happy young friend meddling with delusions of rescue."

"Then you ought to shut the hell up instead of moaning and crying to high heaven. And who the hell you calling happy?"

Ray laughed at that. "All right. Damn. Sorry about that, too. I thought you were happy. Why aren't you happy?"

"None of your business." She turned away, and when she turned back, in the semi-darkness, he thought she held her wineglass. There was a glint of light at the position of her heart.

"Aw, you're happy. You're just ashamed to say it."

"If I were happy, you'd know it."

"How?"

She didn't say anything. She raised her glint of light and drank from it. She'd had some troubles he knew about, the job for one—struggling a little bit when she first came to town to be Assistant Director of Special Programs at the college library; she was young, just out of grad school. And housing for another—such as having to move suddenly when her apartment building caught fire, and then moving in with a co-worker and another roommate who was either on crack or struggling with some other alternate reality. That roommate had taken to wearing Alma's clothes and claiming they were hers, that she and Alma had clothes just alike. But all Alma needed to solve the problem was to move again. In with him, would be nice. She could wear *his* clothes. And they could be amused together at what the roommate's disturbance would cause next.

"What would make you happy?"

"I don't have a clue," she said, cheerlessly. "Maybe the end of all wars, and all people experiencing personal adoration with humility." She looked down at her wine.

"Of course. Well, that's a clue." Ray stepped over beside her and poured more wine into his glass, and then hers, wishing she would ask him that question. Then he could say that she would make him happy, that he was happy with her just being there, but that holding her would work the magic, having her hold him back. Something real rather than pretend or cursory like their cheek-to-cheek kisses when they said hello or goodbye.

The man outside was quiet now. Ray flicked on the flashlight and shined it through the window but it was hard to see through the yellow glare on the glass to the spot of ground the light shined on. He raised the window a little, to the splatter of rain on the soggy earth.

"Well, it's not good for him to spend the night out there," he said finally, because he imagined water rising up and around the man, head in a pool, nostrils filling with puddle and silt.

"Maybe he'll just leave," Alma said. She put her glass down and left the kitchen, went to the bathroom Ray thought.

"There's pretty good drainage out there," he called to her. There had never been any real flooding that he knew about.

Ray took the tournament diagram into the living room where he sat on the blue sofa and lay the sheet of paper on the glass-topped coffee table. There was light from a chrome floor lamp and the TV was still on, *Animal Planet*—leopards lounging in tall dry grass. He watched that a few seconds, the image of the man out back swelling onto it. Dry leopard, wet man; if it was meaningful he didn't know how.

For the first round, he picked the teams he knew about but soon understood that filling all the brackets would take some time, some very considered guesses. Everybody picked Duke to win the whole thing, be the team of the decade—the nineties—but the teams Duke would beat were harder to choose. Among them, some-where, was the team of the 'oos. The zeros. Was anybody even hopeful for that distinction, Ray wondered.

Alma came and sat beside him. She turned up the volume and changed the channel to ESPN in case they were analyzing the teams. But it was hockey night, so she muted the sound.

Ray watched her as she went into the kitchen to bring the wine bottle. He said, "Are you hopeful, then?"

"About what?"

"Hopeful. If not happy?"

"Sure." She slid the betting sheet in front of her and took the pencil from Ray's hand.

While she scanned his guesses, Ray thought to tell her about the man who waved, but his mind skipped over to the subject of his boss, the hotel manager who seemed hopeful *and* happy, but was also mean. He was burly, with a British accent and tight suits. He treated Ray like a servant. Ordered him recently in a room full of his staff to raise their wages (necessitating some struggle not to offend either his staff or the manager, while trying to disguise his anger and humiliation), threatened to hire another serving group within earshot of customers and staff alike, but then pretended to be friendly, as if he'd been only teasing—such an arrogant, meaty thug, in Ray's opinion. So that was a problem, since Ray's contract was up for renewal. His regular staff depended on him, he thought, and he kept a pool of extras active. This contract kept him steady at the one hotel with pretty good money. He was developing a hate for the manager, but he didn't want to quit.

He wasn't ambitious, he chided himself. At thirty-one, he should have already accomplished more than becoming a glorified waiter. This week he was to meet with the manager to discuss contract renewal, terms thereof. Still, he wasn't sure he wanted it— another year of that bull. Except the manager might be leaving, he'd heard from Jamal, the assistant manager, who might take over— a better man altogether. So maybe stick it out— maybe something good could happen— a nice long-term contract eventually, and an employer who treated him like an equal, like another boss.

He knew better than to get into all that with Alma. Those thoughts colliding in his head sounded like complaint, like whining, even more so with a brokenhearted man watering the backyard with tears.

So, "Did I tell you about this guy on my way to work who waves at everybody?" he asked. The way it came out, like mockery, even that sounded like complaint.

"No. Something wrong with that?"

"I don't know."

"People wave, don't they? It's a common, person-like gesture." She tucked her braids behind her ears. She had funny ears. They stuck out, even more with the braids pushing behind them. She didn't seem self-conscious in the least. He found that utterly charming, such a pretty, comical face.

"People don't do it like he does. Not like that," Ray said of the waving. "He's automatic, compelled, troubling."

"You don't like him?"

"Yeah, I like him all right. He makes me feel funny, though. It's like he went crazy and his mind stuck on friendly, which is better than taking the serial killer turn. Still, while you want to feel good about chronic cheerfulness, it doesn't look any more sane than chronic moping, hatred, and murder."

"Ray," she said, leaning to stare facetiously into his eyes. "What's wrong with you?" She held up her hand and wiggled her fingers in his face.

"What's wrong with *you?*"

"Nothing." She leaned away.

"I want it normal. I want that waving son-of-a-bitch to be sane. He's got somebody inside the house to put a sweater on him when it's cold and to sit him inside when it's freezing and wet, to buy his shirts and shave him, maybe."

"The Luckiest Man, you mean."

"You got it. One time I was going by and he was helping some lady bring a couple of small suitcases from a car in his driveway— the first time I'd seen him on his feet— and you should have seen the panic on his smiling face. He couldn't wave 'cause of the suitcases, so he just stood there looking at me passing as if I was an ice cream truck coming to flatten him. You know, something both welcome and troubling. So I waved, and felt perfectly evil, then. It was like he was drowning and those suitcases were concrete blocks tied to his wrists."

"Not waving but drowning."

"Well, I guess."

"It's a poem."

"What is?"

"That line. It's from a poem about somebody seeming to wave when actually he's drowning, and somebody else misreading the gesture. I think that's the reading."

"Oh. Maybe I remember that poem, then. But this guy is just waving. It was like drowning when he couldn't wave."

"You're not evil, Ray," she said, patting his knee. She handed him his wine glass and clinked hers to his. "But speaking of drowning, do you think your boy out back is dead yet?"

"Aw, that guy." Ray glanced back at the dark kitchen window.

"What's the matter with him, anyway? How come he gets to do that?"

"He's a drunk man. Desperate. Down on his luck and on the margins of society, lying up against your fence."

"Now you get to make the joke," he said.

He took the flashlight back outside. The rain had eased to a hard drizzle. In the beam light, rain flashed. The grass was spongy, and Ray stepped over illuminated bare spots of glistening mud. The sound of rain in the trees was enthralling and Ray didn't want to go over to the man. Didn't care to see him lying there passed out or dead, or to hear the sobbing, and the thick splat of blunted rain hitting the slick face and wet clothes.

When Ray walked to the hedges by the fence, the man was gone. The light revealed matted grass, flattened tufts of daffodil stems. He pointed the light through the fence in case the man had climbed over and collapsed there. Nothing. Not even a liquor bottle left behind. Alien abduction, perhaps. Alma, he thought, would be relieved.

She left soon after, the betting sheet thoroughly guessed at. Ray put away the sandwich makings, finished the bottle of wine, and fell asleep on the sofa to the hockey game. The next morning going to work he was waving at the man sitting on the stool in the doorway.

It wasn't until after work that he felt bad about the man in his yard again. He had two lunch meetings to serve and one of his waiters got sick during the shift while another just didn't show up, and still another came in late during the serving with hair limp from rain, her white shirt wet and sticking to her shoulders, which showed pink through the thin fabric. Meanwhile, Ray tried to fill in, going from room to room to keep plates moving, but the hotel manager kept popping in, stupidly commenting on contract points while Ray was hoisting trays of *cordon-bleu,* hustling with pots of coffee and pitchers of tea. Then, still shorthanded, he had to break down both rooms and set up a larger one for a breakfast meeting tomorrow, check with the kitchen to synchronize the head count because the manager told him late that the number had been increased, and often the kitchen never learned of such changes. While he was there, he had a talk with the dishwasher staff about sending out racks of glasses and cutlery covered with spots that his crew was obliged to wipe away. Then he got on the phone to some of his staff, to leave messages, persuade others to come in very early tomorrow morning to cover the crowd.

Raining all day, a steady, sharp drizzle. Ray had sneaked a couple of moments to stand on the kitchen's loading platform and sip a glass of tea. Then at 5:30, before leaving for the day, he stood there again and looked out on the lushly wet cedar trees that buffered the hotel from the expressway, and at the stretch of green yard through which the jogging trail coursed. He was tired; yet he imagined the insistent rain excited the earth. Flowers were already springing up, opening. Azalea buds dotted the bushes. Daffodils were already everywhere. He was thinking of Alma of course, thinking of how romantic the rain could be—the way it encouraged huddling under umbrellas, as it had when he walked her to her car the night before, and the way it sent people indoors with the options of what to do there; he often imagined the intimacy of the hotel guests in their rented rooms, and envied them. And then the rain became sad again, gray and relentless, falling all night and all day and probably all night again. He and Alma had done nothing much indoors last night. And the image of the man in his backyard returned. "Forlorn," he said aloud, tasting the sour age of the word. Another little something from a poem. Keats. Alma wasn't the only one with an education.

It was time to go home, the deflated mood of low expectation upon him. Alma wouldn't come by again tonight, two nights in a row, and there was no excuse to go see her, and her strange roommate. Surely Alma knew he longed for her, and obviously it didn't matter.

He sat in his car awhile and listened for the traffic report. Incredibly, cattle were loose on the expressway, their transport-

ing truck overturned. The rain slowed a little. Ray circled out of
the parking lot and steered onto his alternate route. At a traffic
light, he noticed a line of cars behind him, and much of it followed as he turned onto the street through the neighborhood
where the waving man lived. He wanted to be alone, not leading
a procession through his secret. But maybe it was everybody's
secret, and he wondered whether the others imagined a relationship with the waving man, too.

It was then, thinking of the waving man, and the sad man still
on his mind, that he felt himself held in a balance, sustained
between his own hope and despair, caught between the waving
man and the wailing man. He realized that he was afraid to move,
to risk sinking under the weight of his pessimism, or rising up too
happy and untethered by solemnity, of being lost in space like the
waving man. It was why he wouldn't drive over to Alma's and
climb through her window and wait for her in her bed—that and
her roommate—and why he wouldn't simply leave her alone. To
contemplate either one wobbled him, because for her to accept
him would mean his giving up his hold on his reality, his suffering, and for her to reject him would send him crashing. It was not
a stasis that cheered him.

Maybe, he thought, a similar stasis, a similar fear, kept Alma
from being happy. Maybe all it would take was for him to upset
the balance, push her off her anchor. And maybe they could soar
into a new life, a new decade and new century together. And
maybe not.

At the blue house, the man was on his stool behind the storm
door and waving. Ray waved back. He looked in his rearview mirror and saw that driver also wave. The driver was wearing a suit
and tie, in a soft-gold Lincoln with green tinted windows. A
wealthy man, it seemed, the car old and well-kept, water beading
on the polished gold surface like wet jewels. Behind the Lincoln,
the wet headlights of the other cars filtered through those green
windows, creating a gliding capsule of soft-green glimmer, the
color of water in an ocean. Ray slowed and kept glancing back to

hold the slow float of green headlights, the glimmering green rain on the Lincoln's windows, to ride it around the curves and out beyond the neighborhood to the unobstructed expressway, the wealthy man's car creating a green lens of comfort in the gray day.

On the expressway, the Lincoln pulled around to pass, and Ray waved, thankful for that sustained moment. The man waved back and sped by. Other cars sped by, too, spraying thick rain onto Ray's windshield. Ray quickened his wipers and soon could see well enough to drive safely home.

John Holman is a native of North Carolina. He lives in Atlanta, where he teaches in the creative writing program at Georgia State University. He is the author of *Luminous Mysteries* and *Squabble and Other Stories*.

*O*ne rainy evening when my wife and I were *newly married, we found a man sprawled and crying in a hard-to-get-to path beside our house. We were afraid of and for him. Months later I saw him walking by the house during the day. He didn't seem to recognize me and I never saw him again. Years later, along the route I drove my son to school, we passed a man who waved at everybody from his porch. He seemed desperate somehow. For "Wave," I tried to use something of both of those guys to discover a few things about Ray.*

Clyde Edgerton

DEBRA'S FLAP AND SNAP

(from *Image*)

Lying here now, I can look back.

I was always overweight, though not a whole lot, and was never popular with the boys in high school because of my weight. But L. Ray Flowers liked me enough to, you know, do something ugly in front of me in his car one night, the night of the eighth grade dance — after the dance — and I want to go ahead and tell about that night.

It was the only time I went to a school dance. I never was invited to the prom. There were lots of dances after the high school football games and I went a few times with other girls but didn't dance.

L. Ray was in special education, but he went on to be an evangelist, and had a radio show and for a while, a television show out in the Midwest somewhere. He got to be pretty famous — got a big hair hairdo, the works.

He killed a woman trying to heal her one time. It was a freak accident. You can look it up. It happened out there in the Midwest and the local papers here carried the story. What happened is that they were up on a pretty high stage and she walked backwards in ecstasy off the edge of the stage, hit her head on the base of a flag stand and died on the spot. Honest. Her husband sued L. Ray and lost. Think about the places they put American flags. At restaurants they fly them in the rain and at night. My daddy was always concerned about the flag. He fought in World War II.

L. Ray was seventeen when I was in the eighth grade and he was in shop. They didn't have special ed back then. They just called it shop. I was fourteen. And I don't think the fact that I was overweight made one bit of difference to him. It was not something that mattered to him it seemed like. He didn't feel like he had to be like everybody else in this respect and shun the overweight, or ugly in the face, or anything else. In fact one of the ugliest girls in our school, in the face, had a body I would have killed for and nobody would date her except L. Ray and L. Ray ended up marrying her. That's the truth. But it didn't last. Another story.

See, I have always hated L. Ray for doing that—masturbating is the word—in front of me the way he did. But the more I've thought about it, and the way he's ended up—his radio show failing and him losing everything to the IRS—there is a way in which I feel sorry for him, too. Although that is not exactly what I mean. I can't quite say it right. He didn't have to take me out is one of the things. He chose me over everybody else. I also can tell about it now because it was long before what all you see on television and especially the movies nowadays.

This happened in 1956 and that's all it was—what he did. Think about what people do in cars and everywhere else nowadays. But even back then my dancing and his dancing was on the same wavelength. Even though I'm feeling a little contradictory I can also say that the experience at the time left me feeling filthy, and thus mad at L. Ray. And I'm sure he forgot me. See how complicated it gets. And he never asked me out again after that night, which I regretted only after I got married. You can see something about my husband from that. My first husband.

As to L. Ray these days, I've seen him up here twice visiting his aunt. She's just been here a few days. I asked Traci, because I thought it was L. Ray. He stood outside my door talking to somebody—looked in here but didn't recognize me. I guess he's over sixty now. Let's see . . . he should be sixty-one. He looks a lot the same, except for his white hair. He's about six feet two, narrow shoulders, little pot belly, fairly long white hair he combs forward and then sweeps around. He's got a kind of redhead complexion, and those black snake eyes, set back in his head and sometimes looking almost crossed. And real narrow lips. His eyes are quick, quick, quick. I saw him one time maybe a year ago, when I was in the checkout line at Food Lion before I got sick. He was two people in front of me, had done bought his food and had come back to the checkout girl with his long receipt. Wanted to see a coupon he'd just used—or something about a coupon. The coupon was for fifty cents and he hadn't got credit he said. He showed the receipt to her and she told him the coupon was for something different, slightly different, than what he'd got—like a wrong kind of cereal or something. Would he like to change them, she said, and he said yes and looking kind of intent, headed back into the store up the checkout line, right by me. Just then he caught the eye of the man standing behind me, somebody who might have been a little perturbed about him holding things up, and he gave him that big, gentle, little boy smile and said, "How do you do?"

It was the eighth grade end of the year dance. And in assemblies and parties and trips and all that, shop was considered eighth grade. Whenever all of us in eighth grade went roller-skating, shop went along.

I was a very friendly overweight person, not the depressed, withdrawn type. I was like Miss Piggy in a way, if you can get a picture of Miss Piggy in your head—her sort of like a cheerleader jumping in the air, tossing flowers out behind her. I was this kind of person, always very happy, with lots of girlfriends, always talking, always giggling about the boys and things and always full of curiosity about who liked who and who was going steady with who. And for the entire eighth grade, L. Ray kind of liked me. I could tell it but at the same time I wouldn't admit it to anybody because L. Ray was in shop, and they all met with Mrs. Waltrip down in the shop—where they had electric saws and everything. They didn't do shop—they just met down there. People who went down there for shop would just more or less put up with them. On second thought, some of them did do shop.

So, anyway, I had bunches of girlfriends and then too I was a go-between between girlfriends and boyfriends. You know what I mean. I was somebody overweight who would take messages from a girl to a guy and back, giggling when I needed to and looking forward to gossip in general. I made all As, too, and teachers liked me. I was not bad looking at all. I never had the first pimple if you can believe that. And I was class secretary my sophomore and junior year in high school. Not much other than that, though. Not much to write home about.

L. Ray was really dressed up that night. My mama and daddy were okay with him picking me up. Most anything was okay with them. I had five brothers and sisters and a lot going on, and I lied to Mama and told her that L. Ray was in the tenth grade, which of course he would have been if he hadn't been in shop. No, he would have been a junior or senior.

He was intense looking like he is now, but of course he had red hair then, a kind of dark red, and his eyes had that quickness and he had that thin-lipped mouth that would always break into a big smile at nothing, right when he was looking so hard through those eyes. That gives you a picture.

He brought along a present when he came to pick me up, and I knew enough to know that that wasn't required. It was a brown leather billfold—with the flap and snap and a change purse and zip-up paper money holder. It was in a box, wrapped nicely, with a big white bow. It was green paper. When the doorbell rang and I opened the door, there he stood with that green present.

As you might can tell, L. Ray was not unpopular, nor was he like other people in shop. It was like he, and therefore everybody else, knew in some kind of way that he didn't belong there. He actually seemed pretty smart, and back then in times when boys combed their hair, he combed his very nicely. Dark red hair.

L. Ray was always talking to people, patting them on the back, laughing out loud at his own jokes, making fun of people in nice, very acceptable ways, and all this. He actually had a kind of adult presence about him. I do admit that I'd always felt something a little bit strange about him, but because he liked me, I overlooked this feeling, and now looking back on everything, I'm convinced that the strangeness which caused him to do that in front of me is the strangeness that I felt.

He was standing there in a light grey suit, white shirt, bow tie, and black shoes—holding that green present with the white ribbon and he gave a little bow with his hands under his chin like a Japanese. Which is something I forgot—that Japanese bow. He stuck the present under his arm just before he made the bow. Just about anytime L. Ray came up to you and spoke, he'd do that— give a little head bow with his hands in prayer-fashion below his chin. But this was before he really got religion and went on the road as an evangelist. That happened mainly when he left the Baptist Church and joined the Pentecostals.

It was to be a big night for me. It was my first date. (And, it turns out, the last to any kind of dance. I only had six real dates as a teenager.) I didn't imagine at the time anything could go wrong. I of course was wondering if he'd try to kiss me goodnight, but in the main I was seeing this as the beginning of a high school career of dates and fun times. I hadn't for some reason connected being slightly overweight to being unpopular with the boys. All that didn't dawn on me until later. After all, L. Ray was a boy and had been interested in me for a whole school year.

Daddy was a housepainter and Mama worked at the Laundromat and they both worked unpredictable hours which is why they weren't home. This was not long before they broke up, which was when I was in the tenth grade.

I was wearing my sister Teresa's blue crepe-like dress with the silk top and frilly bottom and fake pearls and earbobs and lots of lipstick and eye makeup. Teresa was seven years older than me and married. She had always been normal sized until after her first child and then during the next year or so she got to be about the size I was at fourteen.

I remember me and L. Ray walking down the walk to his car. We had a rock walkway, flat slate rocks lined up, but they were too close to each other so that if you took regular steps you'd hit in between every other one or two unless you took short steps. I took short steps to hit every one and so did L. Ray—I guess, coming behind me. He let me go first. It had rained and the wet grass hadn't been cut. L. Ray's black shoes were patent leather. He was always saying something funny, always making a joke. When we got to the end of the walkway he showed me the beaded water drops on his shoes and got real serious and said something like, "Looks like little water worlds resting on the hard dark universe, don't it." See. He'd surprise you. He was not a bad evangelist—even that early.

He opened the passenger car door for me. It was his daddy's Oldsmobile or Pontiac, one of those big ones with a lot of chrome, but it was very old and worn-out looking also. L. Ray's daddy sold eggs.

"I think I'll stop and get us a pack of cigarettes," said L. Ray. He pulled the car into the Blue Light, which was a main nightspot back then. "And then how about we stop back in here after the dance for a couple of tall Busches."

Me and Belinda McGregor had drunk beer twice. I was ready to bop. There were lights in my eyes. Blue lights from the Blue Light. Red lights from the cigarette I was about to smoke. White lights from the dance. Green lights from the dashboard of the car when we drove off somewhere later, maybe out to lake Blanca. I knew a lot about life. I had gone to the movies with Diane Coble more than once—us sitting in the back row when Duane Teal would come in and I would sit quietly and watch them out of the corner of my eye. They would kiss for an hour while his hands wandered ever so gently all over her, all approved, accepted, wanted and needed by her. And by me. Not to speak of what I'd seen my sister and her boyfriends do when they stayed over sometimes and all that when Mama and Daddy were gone.

So we arrived, after smoking a cigarette on the way.

The dance was in the library. We parked by the tennis courts and walked around to the front of the school and up the high outside brick steps and in through the doors, and then down that long, long wooden hall. If floors were still made of wood in America then there would be less horror. Wooden halls meant safety, and God knows plastic and cable TV helped bring a horror to America that in my day and my teenage years was peaked out only by this retarded boy doing something in front of me in his daddy's old Oldsmobile or Pontiac. I know what's going on these days. People are killing each other in schools, but so what—people have always killed each other. But not in schools. The problem is that we used to each have a separate nervous system and now people who are alive all have the same nervous system and everybody feels everything on the surface and there's so much to deal with on the surface nothing ever seeps down to your heart.

I regret I never sat on the ground and stared at a tree for a long time just thinking about all the stuff that was going on inside it— I mean a big tree. You sit there, look at it and think about the water going up inside it, just inside the bark and on out a limb to visit the leaves and then getting in the leaves and doing what all it does. Photosynthesis and all that. It is something I never had time for of course. But then you have something like a helicopter sitting on the ground not cranked up, and absolutely nothing is going on inside a helicopter unless somebody cranks it up, and then you've got all that expense of fuel, and little fires going off in the engine. It is so different from a tree. We couldn't be satisfied with a tree, we had to go manufacture a helicopter.

Mr. Albright, my teacher, was standing at the library door greeting students. We got in line behind a few couples. We had to show our tickets that had been handed out in school that day. "Debra, L. Ray," he said. "And how are you all tonight?"

"Just fine, Mr. Albright," said L. Ray, in his very adult way. Did his little Japanese bow.

"Have a good time," said Mr. Albright. "No smoking or profanity."

"I'm here to boogie," said L. Ray.

We made our way in through the door, L. Ray stepping back to let me go first, because one of the double doors was closed.

The library had a book smell that held on above the punch and cookie and balloon and crepe paper smell. There was a record player operated the whole time by Paul Douglass who was also in shop, but Paul was certified retarded. He was a favorite of Mrs. Latta, another chaperone, who got him to participate in all sorts of things, for some reason nobody every knew. He was just her pet, and not even in her class. She taught sixth grade.

Anyway, I could dance like a fool—Teresa, my older sister, had taught me and Melanie, my younger sister—and so could L. Ray, so that's exactly what we did. We danced just about every dance. We were be-bopping. People would stop dancing to watch me and L. Ray dance and I will tell you this: it turned me on. It really turned me on like nothing else. When I did it real hard, I could pick up a leg and twist and turn and bend in a way that it felt like little lightning bolts of gold. It was delightful, and the way L. Ray moved when he was dancing made me hungry for love even at my age or maybe especially at my age. If L. Ray had just had sense enough he could have worked wonders. If any boy over a period of four years of high school had had sense they could have worked wonders.

You get the idea of how it was—people dancing, and us dancing like fools, sweating our heads off, and me having one of the best times of my life. We danced and drank punch and danced and drank punch and ate cookies and potato chips, and more than once people stood and watched me and L. Ray dance all over the place, and all that gold lightning through me, and I was thinking to myself, this is what my life in high school is going to be like. Boys will watch me dance and are going to be asking me to football games and dances all the way through high school, and I'll be a cheerleader and popular and very happy. And three or four times I went to the bathroom with my girlfriends and we freshened our lipstick and makeup and giggled and talked about each other's date and what we were wearing. There seemed to be no jealousy, no bickering. It was a dream night.

Mostly parents came to pick up their children, sticking their heads in the library for their son or daughter, or stepping inside for a minute or two.

L. Ray and I were among the last to leave. We walked down that long wooden hall, and out the door. I remember that door, the clanky handles, and how heavy it was, though on this night L. Ray held it open for me. Then down the steps and around to his car.

"Boy, that was fun, fun, fun," said L. Ray. "Want to go out to the Club Oasis for a little while?"

"Sure." I was game for just about anything.

The Club Oasis advertised on the radio and had live bands and all that. We stopped at the Blue Light and L. Ray went in and got two tall Busches in a paper bag.

"Reach in that glove compartment and get me that church key," he said. He got out the beers and opened them, making the swush sound, and then punched a little hole at the other side of the beer can top.

"Drink up, Debra," he said. "Here's to a long and happy life," and we clunked our beer cans together and I took a swallow. It was cold and it helped me move right on toward the top of the world where I knew I was headed. Then he pushed in the lighter, and, since he was driving, I lit us both a cigarette. I was in the boat of my life heading down the River of Heightened-and-Met-Desires.

Inside the Club Oasis I didn't know too many of the girls, because for one thing they were all older than me. But we danced and danced and danced and sweated and sweated and sweated and went outside and smoked a cigarette and I thought L. Ray might try to kiss me, but he didn't, and then we showed the stamps on our hands and went back inside.

The eighth grade dance had been from seven to nine, and I had to be home I figured no later than about midnight. We left the Club Oasis at about eleven. When I got in the front seat with L. Ray this time, I moved a little ways away from the passenger door toward him. He didn't say anything at all as we left, which seemed a little odd, and he hadn't driven more than I'd say a mile when he simply turned onto a side road, drove maybe a half mile and then pulled over on the shoulder and cut off the ignition. I thought to myself, this is where we neck. I was nervous and I wondered about cars that might drive by.

No sooner was his hand off the car keys, he said of all things, "Debra, have you ever seen a man's pecker?"

I was surprised to death. I thought about my brothers and daddy when they went swimming in the pond. I wasn't afraid or anything—this was just L. Ray Flowers up to something strange. "Yes," I said.

"Well, let me tell you what I'm going to have to do," he said. "I'm going to have to take mine out and give it a beating. It's been a naughty boy, and what you can do for me is sit right there and I think you'll like what you see."

What could I do? I felt like I was locked in a casket.

He sat right there under the steering wheel, unzipped his pants and pulled out his thing. I slipped over against the passenger door and looked out the window but it was like looking in a mirror— the window reflected everything that was in the green light from the dashboard. "Oh, blessed Jesus," he said, and he started masturbating and I just looked out the window at the night and my mind was blank, everything suspended-like, and suddenly there were headlights coming from behind us, and a car whizzed by, and he kept at it, "Oh, blessed Jesus, would you look at me, Debra? Would you look at me?" I couldn't help but see his reflection. He threw his head back and started his hand going faster and . . . well, I don't need to go into all that here. I just want to somehow explain two things.

The first is the collapse of my insides, of my heart and my

hopes. Everything about this was sad and filthy. But at the same time it was clear to me that I wasn't going to get hurt. I did not feel threatened in a physical way, but what had happened might as well have been physical for the hurt and dirty and completely useless and invisible way it made me feel. I tried to look out the window and he said, "Look, look, look," and I said, "I can see you in the reflection, L. Ray. I don't want to look if you don't mind." And he said, "Arrrrrrrrr. Hallelujah! Praise the Lord. Praise the Lord!" Then he opened his door and the inside light came on and he slung his hand toward the ground. I don't mean to gross you out or anything. I'm trying to describe what happened. Then he says, "This is what God gave me, Debra. I can get it going again right away, if only you'll do it with me, if only you do it while I do it and we watch each other. It can make really fun things happen."

I didn't ask him what he meant or anything. I said. "L. Ray, you have to take me home now, or I'm going to tell Mr. Albright."

"Okay," he said. "Let me clean up a little here." He got out his handkerchief. And in no time we were driving home. Total silence. I could feel my face and neck red as a beet.

He walked me to the door, said goodnight, did his little Japanese bow and was gone. I would not look at him in the face.

On the table beside the couch was the box and green paper and white bow. I had the billfold he'd given me in my pocketbook. I sat down on the couch and realized my legs were shaky. And then I started crying.

Mama and Daddy weren't home yet, nor my older brothers and sisters, but my little sister, Melanie, came in and said, "Where have you been?" She was in her pajamas. She was seven then. They were soft pajamas, flannel, white with yellow ducks—they had been mine when I was little. She was wearing her thick glasses and her eyes were looking in different directions.

"Where's Mama and Daddy?" I asked her.

"They went to the drive-in."

"Why didn't they take you?"

"They said it was a dirty movie and I couldn't go. Where have you been?" She was standing there. She was the sister I ended up being closest to.

"To a dance."

"Who did you go with?"

"A boy I know."

"Who?"

"Just a boy."

"Was it fun?"

"Yes. I even went to two dances."

"Then why are you crying?" She jumped up on the couch beside me, crossed her legs, and grabbed her toes.

"I'm crying because I'm happy," I said.

"You can't do that."

"Yes, you can. Sometimes you laugh so hard and so long and you have such a good time that there's nothing left inside except crying. You can be so happy you cry and you can be so sad you laugh. The good thing is that I'm not laughing after all I've been through tonight."

"What have you been through?"

"I told you. A dance. Two dances."

"What did you get for a present?"

"I'll show you." I got my pocketbook from the floor at my feet and pulled out the leather billfold.

"Can I have that bow?"

"Yes."

I still have the billfold. I kept it in my pocketbook all the way through the ninth grade, saying to myself that the next time I had a dance date, I would throw it away and buy myself a new one, and somewhere in there I put the billfold, worn-out, in my top dresser drawer, and then along came this disease with me holding on to that billfold, still. In my life it was L. Ray, my husbands, my children, my grandchildren, then my life with illness.

So is it possible for you to understand that that night was supposed to be the first big dance night of my life? Can you understand if you lived this long without ever having much of a night-life, when dancing was what you were born for, a gift?

————————

Clyde Edgerton was born and raised in Bethesda, North Carolina. He served as a United States Air Force pilot from 1966 to 1971. He has taught English and creative writing at the undergraduate and graduate levels and English at the high school level. His first novel, *Raney,* was published in 1985 and his seventh, *Where Trouble Sleeps,* in 1997. He's the recipient of a Guggenheim Fellowship, the Lyndhurst Prize, and the North Carolina Prize for Literature, and his stories have been anthologized in *Best American Short Stories* and *New Stories from the South.* Currently, he teaches in the MFA Program at the University of North Carolina at Wilmington.

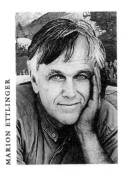

MARION ETTLINGER

This story came about when I remembered an image from my adolescence and decided to write a story around it. The image was of me sitting in the passenger seat of an automobile one night looking out the window but unable to avoid the reflection of the driver masturbating. This happened after the driver, an older male, had taken a girl who was my age home from a dance, and was then taking me home. He just pulled over, stopped, and I guess relieved himself. No words were spoken, and the incident was never mentioned. As Francois Mauriac once said, "We had to live united with a wild beast whom it was important not to know." I decided, when I wrote the story, to take the point of view of the girl as if it happened to her. Being a former (in some ways, forever) Southern Baptist, I find it troubling to write about sex, and so I'm working my way up toward intercourse—through masturbation. I may not live long enough to get there. The ending of this story came to me only when I got there on the first draft and seems to me to be the most important part of the story.

Cathy Day

THE CIRCUS HOUSE

(from *Story*)

The Colonel and Mrs. Ford
Fall in Love and War; Duty Calls

Why did they fall in love? This is what she thought: It was The War Between the States. It was nothing but boys and old men to look at for months at a time. It was his uniform. It was his orders to report back to the front and the subtle way her people encouraged quick marriages to keep up morale. It was being fifteen.

This is how she told the story: She was only fifteen the first time she saw the Colonel—at a cotillion to raise money for the cause. He was only a captain then, dashing in his gray uniform and mutton-chop whiskers, galloping up the shaded drive. All the other girls wanted to dance with him, but he followed her with his eyes the whole night. He knew when her cup of punch was empty, and new ones appeared in her hand like magic. When he finally asked her to dance, she refused, but he persisted. And so she danced with him, and he whirled her away. After a weeklong courtship, they married.

And there you have it. The good part anyway.

P. T. Barnum Loses His General Agent;
Mrs. Colonel Gains a House

In 1901, Wallace Porter, proprietor of the Great Porter Circus & Sideshow Menagerie, hired a new general agent. The renowned

Colonel Ford had been the former assistant of P.T. Barnum him-self, and he took the job with Porter on one condition—that his wife, Mrs. Colonel, would have a decent roof over her head. For twenty years, she'd accompanied her husband on the road, spend-ing her days cooped up in hotel rooms and her nights trying to sleep in Pullman cars. "I'm tired of traipsing around like a gypsy," she complained. A week later, a telegram arrived from Wallace Porter that read, MADAM, YOU WILL HAVE YOUR HOUSE. STOP.

The Great Porter Circus spent summers crossing the country by rail, but come late fall, it headed for Peru, Indiana. The show rested, trained, and repaired itself in a complex of barns, paddocks, and bunkhouses on the outskirts of town. On a hill overlooking the winter quarters was Wallace Porter's mansion, two-storied and three-pillared. Once, he'd lived at the bottom of the hill in a clap-board farmhouse, back when he owned the biggest livery stable in northern Indiana, before he bought the ailing Hollenbach Menagerie for a song, built himself the mansion, and abandoned the farmhouse to the wind and rain. It had stood empty for sixteen years. Sparrows nested under the eaves; at dusk, they rose from the trees like a wave against the sky and descended on the house for the night.

Porter ordered a group of roustabouts to fix the house and drive the birds away. The men knocked down the nests under the eaves with long-handled brooms. Inside, they cleared away the cobwebs draping the doorways and the piles of mouse droppings. The milky light filtering through the clouded windows lit up a universe of float-ing dust motes. For days, the roustabouts wore bandannas like masks, lifting them to their eyes to rub away dirty tears. While Colonel Ford tended to his business in the barns or in Porter's man-sion, Mrs. Colonel flitted through the house in her black lace dresses, shaking her black parasol at the roustabouts like an angry señorita.

SOCIAL CALLS; A MAID IS SECURED; THE RUBY BRACELET

Once the house was restored to order, Mrs. Colonel spent her days strolling through the winter quarters, paying visits on the circus people. All those years alone, she'd dreamed of a home to furnish, a porch where she could sit on hot summer nights, a landscape that changed only with the seasons, and most of all, a circle of intimates to entertain and amuse. This was the life Mrs. Colonel had been raised to lead. She decided, *My husband mostly runs this circus, and that makes me First Lady, of sorts.* She knew the duties this role required: entertaining, taking up causes, providing a woman's influence, softening the circus's rougher edges by genteel example.

Each day on her stroll through the winter quarters, she brought with her a loaf of bread, a cake, a plate of cookies, and one by one, Mrs. Colonel visited the bunkhouses of the performers. "Now that we're to be neighbors," she'd say, "we'll want to get acquainted." Startled by her cordiality, the circus people scrambled to serve her tea in chipped cups. The Hobzini Sisters, Bareback Riders and Equestrienne Beauties, were still lounging around in their night-gowns well after noon. They took turns escaping to dress, put up their hair, and dot their cheeks with rouge. The Fukino Imperial Japanese Acrobatic Troupe smiled and nodded their heads in appreciation when Mrs. Colonel spoke, although they understood no English, a fact Mrs. Colonel chose not to notice.

Not long after Mrs. Colonel began her social visits, the ele-phant trainer, Hans Hofstadter, was killed by one of his bull ele-phants along the banks of the Mississinewa. Mrs. Colonel asked her husband what was to become of his widow. "I suppose we should keep her on in some way," he said, "after what happened." A few days later, Mrs. Colonel paid a condolence call. She found Nettie Hofstadter half-dressed, nursing her newborn son, Ollie. Mrs. Colonel asked, "Would you like to work for me? I could use the help." Nettie looked up then, her eyes blank. Mrs. Colonel leaned in closer. "It'll be better than working in the cookhouse or sewing. The Colonel and I weren't so blessed, so it will be nice to have a child around." Mrs. Colonel touched the down on the child's head. Nettie said without enthusiasm, "Yah, I work for you." Mrs. Colonel hugged her. "We have to take care of one another, don't we?"

The next day Mrs. Colonel visited Jennie Dixianna. The acrobat answered the door in a red satin robe, hair snarled, eyes puffy and bruised. Mrs. Colonel was going to apologize for disturbing her until she smelled the sour whiskey on the acrobat's breath. A ruby bracelet hung around Jennie's wrist, and Mrs. Colonel bent slightly to get a better look, but found that it wasn't a bracelet at all, but an open wound with jewels of blood. "I wanted to pay you a call, but I see you're indisposed at the moment. I'll be on my way then."

That night in bed, she asked the Colonel about Jennie's wrist. He described her aerial act, the Spin of Death: She placed a loop around her tiny wrist and dangled from a rope, winding it between her legs, holding it at arm's length like a snake charmer. "She spins herself around in a blur of red, white, and blue for the finale. Chronic rope burn on the wrist, and I can't get her to wear a glove. Doctor says she'll die of gangrene eventually, but I don't believe it myself." He rolled over, his back to his wife, and a few minutes later began to snore. Mrs. Colonel considered sending over a salve, but decided against it, remembering the loud slam of Jennie's bunkhouse door.

The Sleeping Prince; An Idea Strikes Mrs. Colonel

Within two weeks, Mrs. Colonel had visited every bunkhouse but one, a small cabin on the far side of the winter quarters, half-hidden by trees. She heard no sound within and was turning to leave when she noticed a blanket draped over ropes strung from the eaves. Behind the curtain, Mrs. Colonel found a young man sleeping in his suit, collar unbuttoned, an open book on his chest. Mrs. Colonel studied him carefully, noting his smooth, pink cheeks, aristocratic nose, curly, brown hair, and long fingers. He reminded her of a prince from fairy-tale books, perfectly formed and beautiful. Most circus men, Mrs. Colonel had found, were either hulking brutes or skeletons with bad coughs. *Oh, but this one*, she thought, *this one is a gift from God.*

He awoke then with eyes wide. Mrs. Colonel said, "I beg your pardon. How rude of me."

The man jumped up and straightened his coat. He closed a small suitcase sitting on the chair next to his bed. Before the lid snapped shut, Mrs. Colonel caught a glimpse of starched white shirts and long underwear. "Please excuse me," he said. "I wasn't expecting company."

"I'm Mrs. Colonel Ford. The Colonel is my husband," she said, drawing out the last word, *huzzz-band*. She offered her limp, black-gloved hand.

"Jeremy Trainor. Painter." He bowed ever so slightly.

Mrs. Colonel noted how gently he'd taken her hand, as if it were a flower he didn't wish to bruise. She thought a firm handshake very common. "I brought these," she said, pulling out a bundle from her drawstring bag. "Peanut butter cookies. I'm trying to acquaint myself with everyone."

Jeremy Trainor asked, "Won't you have a seat?" but Mrs. Colonel blushed, since the only place to sit was on his bed. He offered her his arm. "On second thought, please join me, my lady, on the veranda." She laughed. They spent the better part of the afternoon sitting on the bunkhouse stoop, eating the cookies and talking. He'd been with Porter's circus for over a year, painting the advance posters and touching up the calliopes and wagons with gilt daubings. He shared the bunkhouse with six other men, carpenters and blacksmiths, coarse and crude. They found him sissified, so he'd strung up the partition to keep himself separate.

Mrs. Colonel sighed. "I did the same all those years traveling on trains, but I suppose I've resigned myself to the fact that these are my people now." She told him how she'd ended up the wife of a circus man—the Waltz at the Cotillion Story—and he told her how he'd ended up a circus painter. He had been raised to farm his family's patch of stony soil. As a child, he'd drawn pictures in dirt and ashes, the only medium available. But when his father and brothers saw his work, he was whipped and sent to his room without supper. "I ran away two years ago to be an artist, and look how far I've gotten."

Mrs. Colonel remembered then that first ladies performed another important function. She said, "I have a whole house in need of an expert's hands. I think I have just the thing that can get your career off the ground." Their relationship began that day, that old and regal association called patronage.

A Theme Is Decided Upon; Mrs. Colonel Gets Her Way

Instead of wallpaper, Mrs. Colonel Ford wanted to cover the walls of her house with murals by Jeremy Trainor. *Imagine. Floor to ceiling. Every wall. It will be magnificent.* She sent a note to Jeremy, telling him he could start right away. The next morning, she waited for him on the porch. A fog had risen from the Mississinewa, and she saw him walking through that low-hanging cloud, dressed in overalls. It was late fall, the trees bare. Winter wouldn't be long in coming, and Mrs. Colonel imagined all those days, standing at the foot of his ladder, sending up words of praise. She imagined for a moment that the young man walking through the mist was actually her lover. It had been years, even decades, since she'd felt that old ache, and it surprised her that her body was still capable of producing such a want.

Inside the parlor of ghost furniture, they drank coffee and discussed what Jeremy would paint. "I thought a nice lawn scene would work well in the dining room," Mrs. Colonel said. "Lords and ladies. Croquet. I visited a plantation in South Carolina as a girl that had a foxhunt." Her expression turned dreamy, faraway.

Jeremy shifted in his chair. "I was thinking of something more local, like the circus."

Mrs. Colonel laughed. "You already paint the circus."

"I want to do portraits, paint the landscape." Jeremy Trainor swept his hand wide across the room.

"I thought you weren't fond of land?"

Jeremy took a sip of coffee. "I'm not fond of *farming* the land." He sat forward in his chair, elbows on his knees, staring earnest into the eyes of Mrs. Colonel. "I have a vision."

She patted his leg. "Well, of course you do."

He took Mrs. Colonel's hand and squeezed it softly. "I paint posters. Do you understand?" She did not, and Jeremy explained that when the circus paraded through towns, he saw people along the sidewalks sitting on his posters. "They even fold them like accordions and fan themselves." Later, he said, the posters littered the streets and fluttered on fence posts. The wagons he painted chipped in the wind and rain and had to be restored with the same colors year after year. "But your house will last. It's very important to me."

Mrs. Colonel swallowed hard. "What would you start with?"

"Hofstadter and the elephant."

She knew that at least one room of her house would be dedicated to the memory of the elephant keeper and the awful circumstances of his death. *Oh dear,* she thought. *What will the Colonel think?*

The Colonel was not amused. He bellowed and roared. "This idea of yours has gone far enough. I'll not have my house turned into a maudlin museum by some two-bit artist." Mrs. Colonel tried everything. She stroked his hands, played their favorite waltz on the Victrola, held the match as he lit his pipe, and brought him brandy sours, his favorite drink, on a silver tray. All the while she spoke in soft tones about increasing the value of the house, about posterity, but the Colonel would hear none of it.

Mrs. Colonel nurtured her longing in private. She took naps every afternoon with the door closed, and before sleep, imagined the Colonel had relented. Jeremy came to the house each day to paint and to see her. She acted the story out in her head, complete with dialogue, long afternoon teas, shy looks, and passionate embraces. Often when she awoke, she found that her hips moved of their own accord.

Finally, she resorted to what usually got her her own way; she locked herself in the bedroom and refused to open the door, even for meals. She sobbed and choked on tears. The Colonel couldn't understand what was so important. "Why are you doing this, dear?" he asked, standing at the door on the third day. Neither of them had ever held out for so long.

"You said I could decorate the house however I wanted. You've never let me cultivate myself. Never."

The Colonel finally relented. "It will look god-awful hideous, but have your way."

He was right. The house would be hideous, but that was no matter. Mrs. Colonel knew her body was doughy and shapeless, her hair grayed. She could never hope to seduce Jeremy. *He will never love me, but if I let him paint,* she thought, *he will at least have to appreciate me.*

Nettie Refuses to Clean the Study; Payday; Winter Walls

Jeremy began, as he'd said he would, with the death of Hans Hofstadter. Mrs. Colonel brought an easy chair into the study and sat amid the tarps and ladders. She allowed herself only momentary touches — a pat on the arm to call him to lunch, a stroke of his face to wipe off flecks of paint. He painted the brown Mississinewa, the trees, the gray sky, the elephant that held a small man in its trunk and lifted him like a prize. The keeper's red shirt was the only bit of color on the entire wall. When Nettie finally realized what the mural depicted, she yelled something in German that Mrs. Colonel couldn't understand. She refused to enter the room again and forbade Ollie to enter as well. But over the years, Mrs. Colonel would sometimes catch him in there, staring at the death of his father.

Each time Jeremy finished a room, Mrs. Colonel stuffed a roll of bills into the chest pocket of his overalls and turned her cool, powdered cheek to him for his thank-you. From the window, she watched him trudge home through the evening snow. She imagined him lying awake in his cot, hands folded over his chest, waiting for the snores of his bunkhouse mates to begin so that he could steal into the night to bury her money, their money, in a secret place for safekeeping.

It took him two winters to finish the first floor. In these rooms, Jeremy painted exactly what lay on the other side of each wall. The side of the house that faced the winter quarters was a mural of the barns, zebras and elephants ambling in their paddocks, camels grazing in a stubbled field, horses going through their paces in practice rings, and enormous cats jumping through fiery hoops. On the side of the house that faced the countryside was an Indiana winter—clods of earth powdered with snow, the sky gloomy and oversized. So accurate was Jeremy's work that during the winter, if Mrs. Colonel squinted her eyes almost shut, the effect was as if there were no walls on the first floor at all. But in the summer, she was left in the lonely house of winter walls broken by window squares of green.

This Is Why They Call It the Heartland

A long time ago—before French fur traders came to cheat the Miami Indians, before it belonged to anyone or even had a name— Indiana was a vast forest, but the land was scraped bare, first by ancient glaciers, and then by pioneers with axes and mouths to feed. There are hills in southern Indiana, but everything north of Indianapolis is so flat that sometimes, especially in winter, it is difficult to tell the difference between the earth and the sky.

In the summer, the fields around the winter quarters came brilliantly alive, waving like the tide under the dome of the sky. Sometimes, Mrs. Colonel felt her heart swelling up as big as the horizon. Only then could she say that Indiana was almost as beautiful as her Virginia. During these lonely months, Mrs. Colonel fancied herself shipwrecked and stranded. Outside her windows was a green ocean dotted by islands of trees, and on each island stood a farmhouse, sheltered from the sun and the prairie winds by those blessedly spared shade trees. Each island looked remarkably the same, and sometimes she thought about walking out her door, diving into this ocean, and swimming to the next stand of trees. Maybe there, she'd find another woman waiting for her men to return, a woman as heartsick as herself.

The Boela Tribe of African Pinheads and the Negro Question

The third winter, Jeremy started on the upstairs and decided to devote each room to a different performing act—The Fukino Impe-

rial Japanese Acrobatic Troupe, The Great Highwire-Walking Wor-
thingtons, even The Boela Tribe of African Pinheads, whom he
brought to Mrs. Colonel's house, "for sketches," he said. Colonel
Ford came home one afternoon to find the Boela Tribe sitting on
his sofas, drinking from his china. Bascomb Bowles, the elder of
the family, was stooped over the Pianola, plunking out "Amazing
Grace." "For God's sake," he told his wife later, "did he have to bring
them here?" Mrs. Colonel secretly agreed, but Jeremy was insistent.
For a week, she kept watch for the Colonel while Jeremy studied the
Boelas in an upstairs bedroom, which he locked at the end of the day.
"A surprise for you," Jeremy said. "My masterpiece." When he
finished, he covered her eyes and led her into the room. "Voilà!"
The room was a jungle of vines and trees, glowing eyes peering out
of the night, and around a fire danced the Boela Tribe in loincloths
and bone necklaces, shaking spears. Mrs. Colonel almost fainted.
When the Colonel saw the room, he screamed, "Holy Mary, Mother
of God!" and stayed up all night whitewashing the walls. To spare
Jeremy's feelings, she kept the room locked from that day on. "The
Colonel is quite progressive on the Negro question," she explained,
"but this might be too much for him, I'm afraid."

PAINTING A SOMERSAULT; THE COLONEL AND MRS. FORD STOP SLEEPING IN THE SAME BED

After the Boela Tribe incident, the Colonel almost put an end to
the painting, but Mrs. Colonel assured him their bedroom would
be to his liking. She invited Jeremy to dinner so they could discuss
the matter. "Why are you asking me my opinion all of a sudden?"
the Colonel asked, pushing back his plate and lighting his pipe.

"I assume," Jeremy said, "you'll want something you don't mind
looking at a lot."

Mrs. Colonel said, "Yes, what would you like, dear?"

The Colonel took two thoughtful puffs off his pipe. "The prettiest thing in this whole goddamn place is Jennie Dixianna. If I'm
going to have to look at something every morning, I'll look at her."
Then he stood and left the room.

Mrs. Colonel felt her face pinching and tears welling up, but she kept her composure in front of Jeremy. "I believe that I'd like you to put Alberto Coronado on the other wall of the room. His triple somersault is just lovely. Yes. That will do nicely." She walked to her bedroom, slamming the door behind her.

The east wall of the Fords' bedroom captured the somersault in all its stages: Coronado posed before takeoff with the trapeze bar in hand; Coronado in midflight, tucked and spinning; Coronado triumphant, hanging in the strong arms of the catcher. "See how lifelike it is," Mrs. Colonel said to her husband, pointing out the raven hair and mustache, bronzed skin, and tight leotard. The Colonel only nodded his head.

That night, the Colonel walked into his newly painted bedroom and sniffed. "I can't sleep in here. The smell makes my head hurt." For a week, he tested the room every night and still found the smell too strong. Then, he did away with the formality of testing the room altogether and continued sleeping in the Fukino room. By the time the circus left that spring, Mrs. Colonel had grown accustomed to the spacious bed in her half-painted room.

CORRESPONDENCE

Dear,

Hope all is well with the show. It's been most quiet around here, with notable exceptions. Nettie's boy, Ollie, is getting to be a handful. Yesterday, he broke the antique vase. Nettie gave him a good lashing. Caught him drawing on the walls in the study, but didn't tell her. You know how Nettie is about the study. Weather humid, but not bad for this time of year. Hope you've been enjoying good weather on the road. I will write more next week.

Fondly,
Your loving wife

May 21. Radford, Virginia. Population 4,000. Found an empty lot on top of hill, one-half mile from town. Rain and thunderstorms all day. Miss Stella Hobzini lost her balance in the tandem horse race over obstacles and fell from her saddle. She hurt herself severely and had to be carried to her dressing room. Parade at twelve o'clock. One bandwagon, mounted people and elephants only. One show. Attendance good. Traveled forty-three miles on N&W. Overall, show going well. Will write more later.

[unsigned]

Please note:

1. The above personal letter is a copy of the May 21 entry in the Great Porter Circus route book, a daily record kept by the Colonel for business purposes.
2. A comparison of the Colonel's letters to his wife and his route-book entries reveals this method of correspondence had been his practice for more than ten years.
3. Mrs. Colonel had always suspected as much, but the diligence it took him to copy his entry twice had always satisfied her as a kind of romance.
4. Despite their mutual promise to send more letters, during the 1904 circus season, this brief exchange between the Colonel and Mrs. Ford constituted the sum total of their communication.
5. Neither one noticed.

THE TROUPE RETURNS; THE SPIN OF DEATH

When fall came, Jeremy returned with a sketchpad full of Jennie Dixianna. "I watched her a great deal this season," he explained to Mrs. Colonel. "I wanted to capture her act and her passion." Mrs. Colonel tried to smile when she saw the cream-colored pages full of the blur of Jennie's act, but covered her mouth when she saw Jennie Dixianna's bare back as she soaked in a washtub. Jeremy's voice was level. "Miss Dixianna was kind enough to sit for me a few times. I found it very helpful. I think the Colonel will be pleased with the results."

The next week, he worked on the west wall almost constantly, and for the first time, the Colonel took an interest in Jeremy's work, offering suggestions and praise. Like the painting of Alberto Coronado, Jennie Dixianna was represented more than once. Climbing the rope to do the Spin of Death. The Spin of Death itself. Standing in the sawdust, her ruby bracelet thrust in the air, receiving applause after her Spin of Death. "I'd like to bring her here," Jeremy said one day, "for a final touch-up."

On the appointed afternoon, Colonel Ford burst into the house a half hour before Jennie arrived to change his shirt. When Mrs. Colonel walked into the living room with the tea tray, she found Jennie seated between Jeremy and the Colonel, laughing with her head thrown back, one hand on the Colonel's knee and the other on Jeremy's. Mrs. Colonel plunked the tray down on the table and sat in a nearby armchair. After listening to the three of them chatter about the last season on the road, Mrs. Colonel rose from her seat. "Gentlemen, I think Miss Dixianna has business to attend to?"

"Yes, of course," Jeremy said, taking the hand of Jennie Dixianna, helping her rise from the couch. Colonel Ford reached for her other hand, but when he caught Mrs. Colonel's stare, he touched his pipe instead. Jeremy and Jennie mounted the stairs that led to the bedroom.

The Colonel and Mrs. Ford munched cookies and sipped tea in the darkening room. Neither rose to light a lamp nor spoke a word. For the next half hour, the house was completely still until they heard the steady thrump and squeak of the bed above their heads. They lifted their eyes and studied the ceiling together. Mrs. Colonel sobbed into her cupped hands, but the Colonel did not rise from the sofa to comfort her, nor did he charge up the stairs and stop what was going on. He clenched his pipe between his teeth and spat out the word "whore," which only made Mrs. Colonel cry harder.

The Same Old Story

No woman sets out to make a fool of herself, but it still happens. All the time. A girl marries but forgets why. She wants to remember, but her husband has forgotten as well. They grow apart. A man appears. Suddenly, she remembers love; it is a bird inside her heart that flies out the top of her head. Then, she remembers lust; it is a bird inside her womb that flies out between her legs. Her need for this new man makes her do foolish things, and the man knows this. He isn't worthy of her loyalty, her love. He is weak, lured away by money and a scheming temptress. For the first time in her life, the woman understands why someone might commit suicide, because there are days when her humiliation is so total it seems only death can take her far enough away from it.

Sometimes the woman dies. If she lives, sometimes she leaves her husband, but not always. Sometimes he leaves her. It's an old, old story, but as often as it's been told, only one version ends with walls like those in the house of Mrs. Colonel Ford.

The Colonel and Mrs. Ford Dance; The End

Despite her pleading, the Colonel refused to let her paint over the murals. "We spent a small fortune on these walls," he told her. "You get what you pay for in this life."

A few weeks after Jeremy Trainor disappeared from the winter quarters, Mrs. Colonel snuck into her bedroom and caught the Colonel dancing in front of Jennie's wall, his arms outstretched, eyes closed. Despite his wide girth, the Colonel still waltzed as smoothly as he had the night of the cotillion, when she'd refused to dance with him until she could no longer bear his ardor. *You are the prettiest little thing here,* he'd whispered in her ear.

Mrs. Colonel knew the form he envisioned before him was Jennie's and not her own, but she moved softly into her husband's outstretched arms and matched his step. In that brightly painted bedroom in Indiana, many miles and years away from that night in Virginia, the Colonel and Mrs. Ford swayed to a lost song, weeping together at how little difference time made.

Cathy Day received her MFA from the University
of Alabama and teaches creative writing at the
College of New Jersey. Her work has appeared in
*American Fiction, Vol. 10: The Best Unpublished
Short Stories by Emerging Writers, The Cream City
Review, The Distillery: Artistic Spirits of the South,
The Gettysburg Review,* and *Quarterly West.* The
Bush Foundation awarded her an artist fellow-
ship in 1999 to complete *Circus People,* a
collection of linked short stories. She was born in
Peru, Indiana, the winter home of many traveling
circuses.

MARK DREW

*W*hen I was young, my grandma took me to a local house that had
lawn scenes and fox hunts painted on the walls. She said the murals
were done by an itinerant artist who painted in exchange for meals and a
bed. My great-grandmother said the murals were the work of a circus painter
who spent the long, cold months practicing his craft. When I started this story,
my head was crowded with characters I'd seen in those murals. When I
showed an early version of "The Circus House" to my teacher, Thomas
Rabbit, he said, "This story is like a Victorian dollhouse. You've got the
period details, but your characters aren't people. They're little dolls you pose
and move from room to room." Briefly, I considered jumping off the balcony
of Manly Hall, but then I realized he was right. Essentially, I'd written a
story about walls.

I sent the story out anyway, was rejected many times (even by the
magazine that eventually accepted it), and then put the story away for three
years. By that time, I was back home in the Midwest but, like Mrs. Colonel,
missing the South terribly. For months, a line kept repeating in my head:
"No woman sets out to make a fool of herself, but it still happens. All the
time." I realized that voice belonged to this story, and finally, I found myself
inside Mrs. Colonel's house, her marriage, and her lonely heart.

Tony Earley

JUST MARRIED

(from *Esquire*)

Late one night, the summer my wife and I lived on the mountain, we saw a deer standing on the traffic island at the end of our street. We saw the headlights of a car coming up the highway. We saw the deer fidget and leap into the light.

By the time we made it to the wreck, the old woman had called 911 on the car phone. The old man held on to the wheel with both hands and stared straight ahead through the webbed glass of the windshield. On the old woman's knee was a large drop of blood shaped like an apostrophe.

"Well," said the old man.

"Well," said the old woman.

"I guess I wrecked your car."

"But it was just a car," she said. She patted his hand.

"We just got married," he said.

"Tonight," she said. "Six hours ago. In Huntsville. We stayed too long at the reception."

"Everybody was there."

"All the grandkids. His and mine. We didn't want to leave."

The old man almost smiled. "Well," he said. "We did and we didn't."

"That's true enough, she said. "But we had a grand time."

"We've been married for a hundred years," he said.

"Just not to each other."

"I was married forty-nine years. She was married fifty-one."

"That makes a hundred. Isn't that something?"

"We were high school sweethearts."

"We just didn't get married."

"Not until tonight, anyway."

"Because of the war."

"I was on a destroyer in the Pacific."

"That's why we didn't get married."

"I had to leave before we figured things out."

"We didn't get anything decided."

"And when I came back, she was married."

"Oh, you make me sound so bad. It wasn't like that. We just never decided anything."

"I didn't mean it like that. I knew Frank. We played ball together. Frank was a good man."

"And Nell was a good woman. I always liked Nell."

"I was always faithful to Nell."

"Of course you were. Of course you were faithful to Nell."

"We were married forty-nine years and I was always faithful."

"Nell and Frank died last year," she said.

"Within a week of each other."

"Isn't that odd?"

"Then one day I just up and wrote to her. And she wrote me back and said she had been thinking about writing to me."

"And I was. Isn't it funny the way things work out? Sometimes you can almost see the plan."

"I still have her letter. It's in my suitcase. In the trunk."

"I put his letter in my safety-deposit box."

"Oh, it's just a letter."

"Not to me."

The old man tapped the steering wheel once with his forefingers. "Let me tell you something," he said. "I always knew she was the one. I was married forty-nine years, and I loved my wife, but I always knew she was the one."

"And I felt the same way about him. I always knew that he was the man for me."

I saw my wife glance up at me. I could tell she was wondering if I was the right man, or if there was a better man, a different life, waiting out there somewhere. And I could tell she knew I was thinking the same thing.

"You just can't say those things," the old woman said.

When the ambulance came, we walked up the highway and looked at the deer. It had slid on its side maybe fifty yards up on the road. A sharp piece of bone stuck out of one of its legs. The eye staring up at us seemed made of dark stone. We stared at the deer, and we sneaked looks at each other. We didn't talk. In the woods beside the highway, we could hear small living things moving beneath the leaves. We could hear the cicadas and the crickets and the tree frogs and the night birds calling out, all the breathing creatures looking for something in the dark.

Tony Earley is the author of the short story collection *Here We Are in Paradise,* the novel *Jim the Boy,* and *Somehow Form a Family,* a forthcoming collection of personal essays. His fiction and nonfiction have appeared in *The New Yorker, Harper's, Esquire,* and *The Oxford American,* where he is a contributing writer. A native of western North Carolina, he lives with his wife in Nashville, Tennessee, where he is an assistant professor of English at Vanderbilt University.

VANDERBILT UNIVERSITY

Okay, suppose there was this writer, who, while living one summer on top of a mountain in Tennessee, was stricken in the middle of the night by a craving for a frozen burrito and a Diet Coke. And suppose this writer, as he approached the highway near his home, happened to see a car traveling at a high rate of speed strike a deer. What if inside the wrecked car the writer found a man and a woman, both in their seventies, who had been married earlier that evening and were on their way to their honeymoon? And what if these hypothetical newlyweds told this hypothetical writer a story much like the one in this anthology? If you found out that the writer appropriated the story of these strangers, added a fourth character to provide symmetry and dramatic tension, and sold it to a magazine as fiction, would you think less of him than if he had told you that the whole thing was a product of his imagination? What if the writer told you that he drove to the motel where the couple had reservations and made arrangements to pay for their breakfast? If such a writer existed—and I'm not saying he does—your opinion might determine whether or not he told you the truth.

Christopher Miner

RHONDA AND HER CHILDREN

(from *Confrontation*)

Walter asked me to pray for him and Rhonda, his new girl-friend. Someone from the office called her an idiot and his stomach turned and he knew he cared for her. He told Lynda, his wife, that he had met someone else but that he had not had sex with her. They were eating dinner when he told her. He said he'd call her later but that he couldn't stay.

It was a busy morning. He met an atheist at work that same day and couldn't believe it. "This guy admitted that he didn't believe in God at all. I know I've got problems but at least I'm going to heaven." Walter needed a place to spend the night and I let him. I gave him a pillow and an old toothbrush and cleared off the couch.

Walter and Lynda will make the eighth couple of their Sunday school class to split up this year. Their Sunday school teacher called and suggested that Walter should've gone ahead and had an affair with the woman before he told Lynda so he'd have know whether it was worth getting a divorce over. Walter agreed that it made sense but nodded and smiled at me across the room and answered into the phone, "Gene, there are some things I don't have to ask God about and that's one of 'em. Lynda's upset but I assured her

I was faithful." He hung up the phone and stretched out on the couch and told me I should stay away from women.

Rhonda could cook. He assured me of that the second night. He had his first meal with her a few hours earlier. The office has a makeshift kitchen with a hot eye and a refrigerator full of ketchup packets and Diet Cokes. Walter said it was like being on a date for the first time since college. She brought her two sons, a four-year-old and an eleven-year-old. Walter said they had fun playing in the coffee creamer.

"That's the thing about Lynda. I know it's not her fault that she couldn't have a baby, hell I don't think a kid would've wanted to live in a house as God awful boring as ours, but it'd be nice to take a kid to a movie or something, but I don't even know what you do with two boys."

The next morning Rhonda's husband apologized for saying he was going to kill whoever she was seeing but he did call her a bitch for not saying anything sooner. Walter assured me that her husband never physically beat her. He just verbally abused her, which Walter would never do, I could ask Lynda if I didn't believe him.

Walter wanted to figure out exactly what God wanted him to do and how he wanted him to go about the divorce. He asked God the best way to love his wife through the whole thing. Maybe the legal stuff should wait until she got over the initial blow. He was willing to do whatever God wanted, get the divorce now and get it over with or take it easy and just move in with Rhonda and the boys.

He saw Lynda that morning at the house while he was getting a change of clothes. He didn't try to speak to her. She was sitting at the table staring at the leftover dinner plates. She had to have heard him come in, though he walked in through the living room to keep from passing her. On his way out the door the phone rang and he stopped with his hand on the doorknob. Lynda didn't move. He knew he couldn't control what she heard from other people. He knew God didn't want him to play mediator. That would wear him out and he had bigger things to deal with.

At work people were talking and someone asked Rhonda what was going on between her and Walter. "That's the thing about Rhonda," he told me. "She's an honest person. She doesn't care about what other people think about her. Only a real Christian with their security in something other than this world could be so honest. She's a good mother too and she knows that God wants her to do what's best for her kids. We've even prayed about it together. We prayed that God would show us what to do about her children. Should we move to a neighborhood where they can be close to their fathers? If so, I'm willing to sacrifice. The Christian life is about sacrifice, I know that. Lynda and I couldn't even do that. We never prayed together other than at church. Rhonda and I can pray anywhere. We pray in the car, in the office, and even over the phone."

People started calling the house the next morning asking if what they heard was true. Walter asked them all to pray for him and Rhonda that God's will would be done. One of Lynda's close friends from church called and told Walter that everyone knew what he was doing and that he couldn't hide forever at my house. He laughed and told her he wasn't hiding but just doing what was best for Lynda. He asked her friend on the phone if she knew of anything he could do for Lynda. She said she hadn't talked to Lynda yet but that she would call Walter back if she thought of anything.

While Walter was still on the phone someone knocked at the door. I walked into the foyer as Lynda was closing the door behind herself. She turned and clasped both hands together and rested them on top of her oversized purse. I asked her if she would like to come in and sit down but she turned her head and stared at the clock in the hallway until I stopped talking.

"Is Walter here?" she asked plainly. I heard Walter in the room behind me still on the phone. He looked up and stopped talking, still holding the phone to his head.

"Honey, are you all right?"

She looked away from the clock to my feet and then down at her hands still resting on her purse. The sound from the phone that needed to be hung up repeated itself quietly from Walter's hand. I asked him if he wanted me to hang it up and he handed it to me without saying anything.

"Lynda, I know it's hard but I'm willing to wait upon the Lord till he tells me the best way to go about this. You're gonna have to trust me and trust Him. You know that, don't you?" A few moments passed and Walter walked back into the kitchen.

"Where's the phone?" he asked.

"Margot, I'm sorry we got cut off, Lynda just came over here. Yes, here, she was just here in the house. I don't know what she wanted she just walked in and I tried to talk to her and she left. If she's not willing to work things out then all this is going to be messier than it has to be. You've got to talk to her. You know she's never been good at expressing herself, but that's no excuse for acting like a child, you know that. I don't know if she's called anybody or not. I was there this morning for a few minutes and she didn't even answer the phone. I'm serious Margot, you know I'm committed to what God wants, I didn't even know I had feelings for Rhonda until three days ago. She works in the office, Margot you would love her so much. She's such a fine woman and a Christian mother to her two boys. I spent time with them last night, we made dinner up at the office and she is so good with them. You ought to see her, it's like she was made to be a mother. Who, Lynda? No. She's never met her. She's only been working with us for four months. Who, me and Lynda? Twenty-seven years this month actually. I know the timing is bad, but there is nothing I can do about it."

Rhonda's husband decided again that he might kill whoever she was seeing "if the son of a bitch ever showed his face at this house." Walter asked if I could believe someone would use such language in front of an eleven-year-old boy, much less his own son. Walter assured me he would never talk like that in front of the boys.

"I'm gonna raise them up in a God-fearing home the way that only two good people are capable of doing, not some city worker. I'm not dumb enough to go to his house," Walter said, "but when Rhonda divorces him he won't have any legal right to tell me I can't come over there to help her move. He's good for nothing but drinking beer every night. As long as I've been going to church I've never met anyone who drinks as much as he does in front of his own children."

Rhonda called again tonight from the office but asked for me. She wanted to make sure that everything was all right with me and if I needed anything. She would be glad to do something for me. Walter told her I was impressed with the fact that she could cook. Rhonda thanked me for letting him stay at my house until everything was final. She wanted to make sure I knew he appreciated it. In the background he was asking the boys if they wanted to go out to eat at McDonald's. Rhonda paused for a moment to listen to them and returned.

"He's so good with the boys too, I'm sure he told you that. My parents are both dead so I know it's good for them to have somebody interested in taking them places and just being fun with them. My husband was like that at first, I think all of them are. They want you to get out the camera every time the kid crawls up in his lap, but then after a while they won't do anything with them."

When Walter walked into my kitchen a few hours later he was followed by a woman carrying a child's backpack over one shoulder and a small pillow under her left arm. Two boys in matching grey sweat suits followed at her side. The woman, who I assumed to be Rhonda, extended her hand towards me dropping the pillow to the floor causing the older child to stumble.

"I'm Rhonda I'm so glad to finally meet you, I can't tell you how sweet it is of you to let Walter sleep over for a few days." She looked at Walter who was helping himself to a glass of water.

"You know . . ." He paused. He kept looking at the sink. "There aren't many people I know who would let me do what I'm about to ask you to let me do. . . . Their dad came home tonight and told them if they didn't want to eat dinner at his house then they could all find somewhere else to spend the night. Can you believe it? His own wife and children. I'm never gonna do that to 'em. We're gonna have a home and love each other like Jesus wants us."

Though I would not have put it past Rhonda to have told her husband where I lived and that they would be here tonight with his wife's boyfriend, I wasn't worried about him. When I told Walter to leave and to take Rhonda and her children with him, he put his glass of water on the counter and looked at me with confidence and asked if I was doing what I thought God wanted me to do. I didn't answer.

———————————

Christopher Miner grew up in Mississippi and recently received an MFA in Photography from Yale University.

I've always been amazed at people's attempts to figure out what God's will is for their lives.

KATIE MURREY

R. H. W. Dillard

FORGETTING THE END
OF THE WORLD

(from *The Virginia Quarterly Review*)

Often I find myself standing in a room, dazed, staring around with no idea why I've come there, what I've come for. I know that if I go back to where I came from and to doing what I was doing I will suddenly remember what I needed and why I came to this room. But try as I may, I cannot remember while I am in the room. When I tell my friends of these events they all, all of them, no matter how old or how young, say that they do this very thing, that they find themselves lost in a familiar space, dumbfounded by a failure of memory that has left them stranded as completely as a mutineer on a desert island. I do not find their stories reassuring.

I test my memory continually, run a sort of internal diagnostic check, asking myself to supply bits of data, small facts, names and dates, all of those trivial pursuits that make up our lives. And increasingly I find it easy to stump myself. I feel the requested information stir in the dim recesses of my brain, but when it attempts to come into expression it locks. My mind is as tongue-tied as I was as a tiny baby before the doctors clipped the webby membrane under my tongue and freed me to speak. And my friends and associates tell me that this, too, happens to them. At the lunch table at work, I will often ask a question only to see everyone around me seize up as tight as frozen gears, their faces twisted in hopeless concentration.

I do remember some things easily: moments of acute and perpetual embarrassment, social gaffes by a much younger self that still make me squirm and blush, moments of terrible and permanent loss, moments when the road was or was not taken to my permanent chagrin. These come easily. And I also remember easily other things that do not really matter, the number of pages in the book I'm currently reading, the phone number of my childhood home, or the pairings in the basketball tournament for the upcoming weekend. And I remember some things that do really matter.

I remember, for example, how the breeze on one bright spring afternoon ruffled the blond hair of Constance Everby. And how the light danced and shivered through her hair, and through the pale leaves on the trees and the blossoms on the plum tree under which we stood. And how her eyes caught the light and transformed it as she looked away from the wonders of the day and directly at me.

She had just gotten her new spring cut. Gone were the long curling tresses that had shielded the delicate nape of her neck from wintry gusts, and now she looked as young and fresh and new as spring itself. We were standing alone under the plum tree, the shadows of its blossoms a tremulous carpet spread around us, alone and together. Our friends had wandered down to the stream that wound its slow way through the pastureland below the summer cabin we were using for a weekend party, taking a break from the pressures of senior year and the stacks of note cards and annotated thesis pages that cluttered our desks and our lives.

I was, as you can probably tell, terribly in love with Constance Everby. And until that afternoon, that moment, she had been just a friend, perhaps even less than that, a friend of my friends. We were often together but very seldom alone together. She laughed at my jokes along with everyone else, or listened patiently as I explained yet again my theories about the latest assassination or disappearance. I am sure that I never even crossed her mind when we weren't together with the crowd. Until that afternoon.

She was wearing a short pale dress that fluttered in the spring breeze, and she walked toward me with extraordinary care across the grassy yard around the cabin, placing her bare feet carefully one before the other in the grass, but all the time looking directly at me with a look on her face that I had never seen there before. She moved with the dangerous grace of a cat easing across the grass toward an oblivious rabbit or chipmunk. And the power of her beauty, her trembling short hair, her legs moving under the lapping of her skirt like water, caught me and held me as I awaited the explosion of her pounce.

But it never came. We talked, quietly, intimately, and then, responding to the calls of our friends from the stream's bank, she placed her hand gently through the loop of my arm and urged me to escort her to them. Echoing the Van Halen song that had just been pounding out of the window of the cabin a few minutes before, my heart pounding as hard as its beat, I said to her, "Why can't this be love?" She looked closely at me for a moment, then rising on tiptoe kissed me, a long, lingering, delicate, powerful kiss that I have never forgotten, through all that has happened, to this day.

I remember almost nothing else of that afternoon. I do remember that Constance left school suddenly a few days later, stricken by an illness severe enough to force her withdrawal even in the last semester of her senior year, severe enough that she could not even (or so her parents said) respond to the long distance phone calls and letters that marked my desperate attempts to reach her. And then she simply disappeared from my life the way people sometimes do, even people with whom you are hopelessly in love.

I worried about her. I even mourned her for a time. I developed a wounded romantic air. I sulked and pitied myself, and then eventually, as we always do, I told myself that I had forgotten Constance Everby, and I went on about my life.

I have speculated long and hard about why that single afternoon remains so ready to recall in my memory while other far more important events in my life have faded away. I have, for example, only flickering memories of my wedding day, and, when I am required to supply the information for legal forms or other inquiries, I can never remember the year of our divorce. I do manage to remember the boys' birthdays almost every year, but the whole time of my marriage and their childhood is basically only a set of random snapshots of a day at the beach or an evening reading *Goodnight, Moon* to them or an afternoon soaking them in tomato juice and scrubbing them in the tub after an odorous encounter with a neighborhood skunk. My friends, too, report that large swatches of their lives have been blanked out of their memories, that they, too, are startled when they find an old letter or newspaper clipping that refers to something they did but which they no longer remember in any way. They all report how alien to and distant from themselves they feel when these discoveries occur, as though their own lives were just subject matter they had crammed for a test years ago and hadn't really thought of or used since.

I reached no conclusions about the possible meaning of these apparently universal vagaries of memory until the evening of our 20th college reunion a year ago. I was standing near one of the bars set up around the quadrangle with a group of my old classmates, who were comparing their thickening middles and thinning heads, when Constance Everby walked by, peering before her as though she were looking for someone or something in particular, honey-haired and as beautiful and graceful as I remembered her, apparently not having aged a day or a moment or even a second since I had seen her last. A wave of terror and desire swept over me, and I could not move, could not utter a sound. But one of my old roommates had no such compunction, and he called out in a loud voice, "Constance, Constance, over here, over here."

She turned, her face lit up with recognition and delight, and spreading her arms wide and shouting "Bobby!" she rushed into his eager, clumsy embrace. She then offered her hand to each of us in turn, speaking our names aloud, but just before she spoke mine I saw her eyes flick down just for a second to the name tag I wore glued to my lapel. Everything went by in a dizzying blur as I heard her receiving compliments and answering questions about her health—yes, she was fine as long as she kept on her medication, and no, there were no side effects, although she could never have children. And I heard her making knowledgeable comments about children and wives and promotions, just as though she had kept in close touch with everyone for the last two decades, everyone but me.

Finally my time did come, a chance to talk to her before we were all herded off to the formal dinner with its predictable menu and pleas for funds.

"Constance," I said, "do you remember that afternoon at the cabin a few days before you had to leave school when we talked under the pear tree?"

"The thesis break party?" she asked. "Oh, yes, I remember."

"You wore a short pink dress and your hair had just been cut," I said, trying to hold her attention, to lure her into shared recollection.

"No," she said, "no, I know that my hair was still long because when I went into the hospital, they cut it short there. And I was in jeans that day, too. Man, do I remember those ragged jeans; how did I ever stand wearing them every day?"

"No," I said, "that must be some other time you're thinking of. Don't you remember? We stood and talked under the peach tree. You were barefooted, and Van Halen's 'Why Can't This Be Love' was on the radio."

She laughed at me then and put her hand on my sleeve. "Dear," she said, "that song wasn't even released until 1986. And I know I wasn't in bare feet. I was always so afraid of pinworms at the cabin that I never took my shoes off, not even when we waded in the stream."

I must have looked so baffled and so worried that she added, giving my arm a couple of firm pats, "Don't be nervous. Memory's a funny thing, but I never forget a thing, not a single thing. Trust me, it wasn't the way you remember it. Not at all." She gave my arm a parting squeeze and turned eagerly back to Bob.

We went in to dinner, but I left soon after, left the whole reunion without saying good-bye to anyone, and drove home overnight. It was during that drive down the interstate that the truth came to me, a revelation as bitter as wormwood, as stunning and more terrifying, to my mind, than the one given to St. John the Divine on the island of Patmos. For I suddenly knew exactly how the world will end.

Mine was no millennial vision replete with multiwinged warriors and precise dates, but rather one of those sudden moments of insight when the answer to a problem comes completely clear, so clear in fact that you realize you knew everything about it all along but had just never put it together in the right way before. The world, I realized, will not end as the poets have suggested in fire or in ice, with a bang or a whimper. It will rather wear away like the honed edge of a knife or like a vivid memory that begins slowly to fade and erode from disuse until it finally disappears altogether. I do not know why this will happen, only that it will. Is the world getting just too hard to remember, or are we just getting too overburdened to care? I do not know, but that awful night I did see this simple truth: that when the last thing in the world is finally forgotten, when all memory is drained and empty, then the world might as well no longer exist, time will cease to matter, and the world will reach its end at last.

Memories leave us stranded now in the upstairs bedroom, but soon we will no longer even remember how to get there, much less why we came there. The world will become a confused hodgepodge of social blunders and tragic misunderstandings. He will insist that she whispered "I love you" in his ear, and she will only shake her head in mute denial. She will swear that he is the father of her child, and he will say that he's never seen her before in his life. Treaties will be unknowingly broken, and laws unwittingly ignored. Justice will become a mockery, and history will be a sad joke.

Minds will struggle to fill the growing void, will try to replace lost memories with imagined substitutes. She will tell of her life as a nun, while he knows that he picked her up once in a seedy bar. He will speak to her of a spring day, a pear tree, and a lingering kiss, and she will remember only pinworms and torn jeans and the moment illness struck her down. As imagined stories replace real ones, all of them will become unsatisfactory, and people will even cease trying to remember them. Even the greatest and truest stories will lose all detail like thumb-worn coins until only shiny, meaningless blanks remain.

Two boys will one day ask their father to tell them once again the best story he ever told them.

"A sailor," the father will say, "was mending a sail by the sea. A god was walking on the shore. The god beckoned, and the sailor left his chore and followed him. Then one day the sailor saw the god arrested, tried, convicted, and executed. The sailor wept."

"You forgot the chicken," one of his sons will say.

The father will feel a sudden emptiness in his mind that will show on his face.

"Yes," the other boy will say, "the rooster crowed three times."

"If you say so," the father will say, no longer entirely sure just who these strange boys are.

I do not know what will be the final things to be remembered. Perhaps some of the lines of a sonnet painfully learned by rote in school, or the words of a sacred chant, or perhaps just images stripped of all language: a sunset burning down into a salty gulf, three monkeys tightly holding their eyes and ears and mouth, light and shadow caressing freshly cut hair, a pink dress rippling over slowly moving bare legs. Or a sound, a bell's chime, the desperate cry of a tiny animal in the night, a song pulsing from a radio into sunny open air. Or perhaps it will be a touch, a mother's hand, a Brillo pad, expressive lips in a kiss that never ends. Or a silence.

Maybe the end of the world has been taking place for years, even for centuries, wiping away remembered details like tears. Or perhaps it has only just begun. Yet I am entirely sure of one thing: when my own memory has been almost completely erased and only a single thing remains, that one last thing will be the name of Constance Everby. And, trying not to forget, I will begin to scratch it in the dust with my finger: the crescent moon of desire, the full moon of satisfaction, the jagged letter with which nothing begins.

R.H.W. Dillard, a native Virginian, is the longtime director of the Creative Writing Program at Hollins University. He is the author of five collections of poetry as well as two novels, *The Book of Changes* and *The First Man on the Sun.* His collection of short fiction, *Omniphobia,* was published in 1995. He has recently completed a new collection of poems and is working on a second collection of short stories.

JULIA JOHNSON

I *do not remember having written this story.*

Margo Rabb

HOW TO TELL A STORY

(from *Zoetrope*)

There are three things I've learned, so far, in my graduate creative-writing program:

1. Deny, at all costs, that your fiction bears any resemblance to your real life (First Commandment of the MFA program: Autobiography Is Sin);
2. Sleeping with an attractive male classmate who is widely admired by fellow students will yield positive feedback on your stories (attractive male will comment enthusiastically, and admirers will echo his opinions);
3. Tequila shots in the women's bathroom before class enhance your ability to stomach painful criticism of your stories.

It's my third semester in the Master of Fine Arts program at Southwestern University, which is also known as the Master of Fucking Around, a term affectionately coined by one of our prominent male graduates, whose first book advance was larger than all of the faculty's salaries here, combined.

Today, my story's up in workshop. It's called "The Gift," and is about a nineteen-year-old girl whose mother and father die in a plane crash twenty miles off the coast of Maine. Coincidentally, my parents died in a British Airways crash off the coast of Maine five years ago, when I was nineteen. Half the workshop knows this about me; half doesn't, including Charles Chester, the professor. In our private, pre-workshop conference fifteen minutes earlier, he'd stared down his nose at me and asked, "Is this *autobiographical?*" His thin arms twitched under his camel-colored, elbow-patched cardigan, which he wears every day (do they give you a crate of those the moment you receive tenure?). Chester is rumored to be around fifty, though he looks ninety. He carries a doughnut-shaped hemorrhoid pillow around with him everywhere, to sit on during our three-hour class. Rumor has it he was once nominated for a National Book Award; I've search for his books in five bookstores, and all are out of print.

"No," I told him in the private conference. "It's not autobiographical."

If the pre-workshop conference is like being massacred slowly and having your inner organs scrupulously probed and dissected and analyzed, then the twelve-person workshop is like being a piece of raw steak fed to starving bears, all of them clawing you, chewing you up, and then spitting you out. And afterward, you're supposed to say "Thank you."

As the workshop of my story begins, everyone searches Chester's face for a verdict of what he thinks of the story. He's frowning; this, to my peers, is sufficient proof that my story sucks.

"It's just not believable. I mean—a plane crash?" Howard begins. Howard is the program prodigy. The faculty cream over him. They give him prizes. Awards. Nominations. Scholarships. His last story was about a pedophile who set fire to his own arm hairs. An allegory, the professor had called it.

"I think the plane's okay, the problem is there are too many characters. Why do you have *both* the parents die? How 'bout one?" Stacy asks. "One would be more real. Less dilution of tension. Also, you could probably begin the story on page ten." Stacy has four standard comments: Too many characters, Start on page [5, 10, 15, or 20], That's a red herring, and Show, don't tell. She offers these comments in different random combinations, like lottery numbers. She's learned them in classes at Southwestern and the University of

Iowa, where she received her previous MFA (several students in the program are working toward their second degrees, putting off the collective nightmare of having to get a regular job). "Also, you mention this gift thing and then you hardly discuss it directly again: total red herring," she goes on. "And I think you need to *show* the plane crash. Show the *suffering*, the *terror*. Make us cry."

"It did make me cry," Lily says, nearly whimpering, which is her usual tone of voice. "I think it's so sad. I mean, God . . . it's a gem. A real gem. Don't change a thing." I would hug Lily, except she's said the same thing about everyone's stories; we've all written gems.

"Anna, could you please read that page we talked about in our conference, aloud?" Chester asks.

"Okay," I say, trying not to let my voice waver. I'd rather uncap my pen and impale myself in the eye than read this story out loud. Reading a story I've written is like confessing, like being on *The Jerry Springer Show,* except the other guests punch you verbally instead of physically, and instead of breaking up the fight the professor nods encouragingly and takes notes.

"This is from, umm . . . page three?" I say, my voice sounding like a ten-year-old's.

My fifth day in Deer Bay, I received a letter, a plain white business envelope with no return address. For five days I'd been numb, walking around the streets of this town like a zombie, pacing aimlessly alongside all the other surviving relatives who'd been flown in, along with a bevy of grief counselors, by the airline. There were over a hundred of us "next of kin"; we gathered each morning by the shore to watch the divers try to find the remains of the plane. Every day I stared at the ocean, entranced, as if I expected my parents to miraculously emerge out of it, saying, "Oh hi, Amy, we're so glad you waited for us . . ." as if they'd survived the crash, the days in the ocean, safe in an underwater Atlantis, and were just waiting for the divers to rescue them and bring them ashore.

The days in Deer Bay had been so bizarre and surreal that I didn't even think it odd, at first, to get this unmarked envelope delivered to me there, in the middle of nowhere. The envelope was postmarked from Boston; I'd never even been to Boston. Standing outside the post office, I tore it open: it was a money order for $500, made out in my name.

It took several long minutes for it to sink in: that article in the paper. Someone must have read it, that piece in the *Globe*—I'd done an interview, they were profiling us, the surviving relatives; every day there was a new write-up on one of us. They'd run my picture two days before with the caption *Amy Appel, Orphan Girl*, like I was some kind of musical being advertised, or photo study, or curiosity, or freak. My fingers trembled on the envelope —to think of myself as the kind of person someone read about in the paper and felt so sorry for, they'd send money—it made me angry, to be the object of pity, and frightened, too. Against my will, I'd become a different person. I had no other family, no siblings or aunts or uncles; all my grandparents were dead. The world I'd always known had ended, now, and this week in Deer Bay was the knife that slowly carved my life in two.

"It's like a cheesy TV movie," Brian says to the class, avoiding eye contact with me. "If I saw it on channel nine, I'd turn it off."

"I agree—and the setting has to go. Why Maine? I could see this set in Germany, and maybe during another time period, like during the war," Calvin says.

"That first line—'My fifth day in Deer Bay'—it *rhymes*. My first thought was, What the hell is it, a sonnet?" Howard adds.

The comments go on. I half listen to Sam, the oldest student and a Vietnam vet, who agrees with everything that's been said and wants more *action, action, action;* Helen, Sam's twenty-two-year-old wife, who compares every story to Raymond Carver's; Leslie, bra-size DDD (she informed everyone at the first party of the year), who wants a sex scene. Then there are the silent students, such as Josh, who sit there, as always, in speechless disapproval, as if the story isn't even worth a disparaging comment. Josh drove me home from a party once, earlier this year, then invited himself in for a glass of water, read the spines of all the books on my shelves, gazed thoughtfully at the posters on my walls, kissed me on the cheek, and then practically flew out of my apartment, leaving me thinking, What the *hell* was that?

Despite the "autobiography is sin" clause, I know so much about these twelve people it's horrifying. It's too much, more than peers should know: that Lily was molested by her uncle (four stories); that Sam attempted suicide twice (three stream-of-consciousness pieces); that Leslie's father was an alcoholic (a novel). I know these things are true, because I'm the one who's asked, at parties and bars after class: Did that happen for *real?* And the answer is nearly always an embarrassed *yes.*

Chester interrupts my thoughts and says, "I think this selection Anna has read illustrates the difference between *sentiment* and *sentimentality*. Brian likened this story to a television movie. Why? Let's discuss this concept—*sentimentality.*"

Everyone stares at the ceiling.

Surprisingly, Josh speaks. "I disagree," he says, and shrugs. "I disagree with everything that's been said. I don't think it's sentimental, I think it's emotional, and the emotion works, considering the subject. The whole story works—I feel for this girl, this narrator, Amy. That her parents died is totally believable, and heartbreaking, too. The tension of receiving the money . . . it's a complex, moving story, and I don't think anyone's given it enough credit here."

Miraculous: I can't believe he just said that. Josh comments so rarely that whenever he speaks, everyone listens, and his approval of my work causes a ripple effect.

Stacy pauses, then says, "I do like the description of the town—there are some nice details there."

A few moments later, Calvin adds, "And yeah, the letter . . . the idea of the letter, that someone sends her this gift that she doesn't want . . . it's not a bad premise."

A few other people offer some semi-compliments about the

story's meager merits; they stare at me, surely thinking I've slept with Josh, viewing me with a new admiration.

Meanwhile, I can't believe that anyone, besides Lily, has actually said something positive about my story. The only time someone's ever said "I think this story works" was when Leslie wrote "Triple Irony," last spring—soon after she'd announced, to a group of us at a local bar, "I want to write a story about a ménage à trois but I've never had one, can anyone help?" During the workshop of that story, Brian and Calvin drew comparisons to Chekhov.

Chester ignores the positive commentary, and as the workshop winds down he embarks on a monologue about the horror of comma splices, then reminds us that there's a reading tonight by Bruce Ryan, who recently won the Pulitzer Prize. Everyone's going to this reading—we've been talking about it all semester. Ryan's book *The Lancet and the Plum,* a collection of short stories about being a military doctor in Vietnam, is taught in all the craft seminars; it's one of my favorite books. Rumor has it that his next novel, which isn't even completed yet, has already been sold for over $1 million. Everyone's so excited, nervous, and frenzied about meeting him, it's as if the messiah's coming to town.

"Don't forget the party after the reading, at my place," Stacy announces to the class, and passes out a map with directions. Stacy's convinced that she and Bruce Ryan are going to have an affair; she's been E-mailing him all year, since she met him at a reading he gave in Iowa City last summer. "He's really an amazing guy, he wants to spend time with me and may even mention me to his agent," she's told us.

Today's class ends just in time, as my pre-workshop shot of tequila is wearing off—Leslie and I had brought the flask, lime, and salt shaker to the girls' bathroom earlier, as we always do. Everyone adjourns to the Slaughtered Lamb, which serves free happy-hour food on Wednesdays. It's our Wednesday tradition: murder each other in class, then celebrate. As I pack my things up, Josh says, "I really did like it, Anna, I think it's an amazing story," and says he'll wait for me in the hall, to walk to the bar.

I'm emboldened by Josh's response, and surprised that I've survived yet another workshop in one piece. I'm also angry at Chester for making me feel horrible about the story for no reason, and I tell him, when it's just he and I left in the room, "Well, some people liked it. You know, I think I may submit this story for the Harden Prize."

The awarding of the Alice Harden Prize is the most significant event of the program: it's $2,000, and based on the story we submit for it, all forty-seven of us fiction writers are ranked from best to worst. From that ranking, it's decided who gets teaching fellowships and nominations for national awards and publications—and, more important, it represents wholehearted approval, and recognition that the winners have talent, and an actual chance of becoming *writers*.

Chester stares at me. "I don't know if it's such a good idea to submit this story for the prize." He sits on the corner of his desk. I wonder how his hemorrhoids are doing. "At least not without a lot more work," he says.

"I've worked on it so long, though. Really—this is like my hundredth draft. And some people, well, one person in workshop definitely liked it . . ."

"Anna, I have to tell you this. Whatever's happened in your own life"—he stares off at the blackboard, as if this is painful for him, talking to me—"does not necessarily make a satisfying story. Because a thing, an emotion, an event, is true in life, doesn't mean it will be true on the page. If you're going to be a *writer,* you should know what it takes—an ability to create an imaginary world, to separate your fiction from the facts of your own life."

He says the word *writer* almost mockingly, the way one might say *movie star.*

I gaze down at the floor. I sometimes wish that, instead of writing fiction, we were doing something hopelessly esoteric, like writing linguistic analyses of sixteenth-century pig Latin, because then there wouldn't be this tiny chance of making it. Because that's the hope we all have, buried in each of us, somewhere: we all want to make it. Past winners of the Harden Prize have gone on to publish stories in *The New Yorker* and *The Atlantic Monthly* and *Harper's;* they've won Guggenheim, Lannan, and NEA grants and PEN/Faulkner Awards; they've been to MacDowell and Yaddo and Bread Loaf; they've had their pictures in *Poets & Writers* and their books reviewed in the *New York Times,* and have even, now and then, appeared on the best-seller list. They've achieved my dream—not to be famous, or rich, or eternally remembered, but just to make a living as a writer, to keep telling stories for the rest of my life.

"I thought . . ." I say, "I'm just trying to tell a good story. I just want to . . . you know, keep doing this, writing stories, till I can make a living at it—that's all I really want."

He raises his eyebrows, as if I've just told him all I want is to fly to the moon.

"Anna, I'm going to tell you this, because no one else will. Before you make a mistake in planning your future. I don't know if you have what it takes to be a writer. I haven't seen one story of yours which has shown the potential to be published. Frankly, I haven't seen a sign of that ability in your work."

I flinch; it's almost as if he's slapped me, as if he's kicked me in the stomach. This is different from the disparaging comments on my stories: this is my whole goddamned life.

"I'm simply telling you this so that you can make appropriate decisions when planning how you will—as you said—'make a living,'" he says.

I don't know what to say. What can I say? "Well, huh." My face is hot; I look at my shoes and my watch and say, "Oh! Gotta go!" and bound out of the room and down the hall, past Josh and the lingering crowd, down the stairs and into the relentless southwestern sun, and I'm crying, weeping, because it's my heart that's just been trashed and trampled and critiqued, and because everything I've written is true, everything I've ever written is true.

It's not the Alice Harden Prize I've got any chance of getting, but the Weeping Prize, The Girl Who's Cried Most in the English Department. I walk the six long, sun-cooked blocks to my apartment, trying to gather myself back together.

I've attempted to write stories that aren't about losing my parents, about death. That aren't about orphans, or plane crashes, or lost love and feeling alone in the world—and I can't. The events, characters, and dialogue in my stories are only impressions of real life, but the emotions are completely, unmistakably mine.

And the thing is, it's not like I can just make myself stop. It's like a need, a compulsion, to *write*—a constant feeling, whenever I go into a bookstore, of wanting, more than anything, to read a story that will comfort me, a story about a girl who has no parents, who finds herself weeping, for no immediate reason, while standing on line at Safeway or Epic Café or while walking down the street. I want to read about a girl who feels she'll never get better, she'll never survive, and she's not quite an "orphan" like in *Great Expectations* and *Oliver Twist,* and she's too old for *The Secret Garden* and too jaded for *Anne of Green Gables,* and it seems there's no one else in the world like her, no one else who's felt this. And of course I can't find that story, that book I so want to read, because it doesn't exist, because it's in my head. And what else can you do, then, but write it down?

Ironically, it's not such a comfort once you do write it down —it's usually the opposite. One night in Maine, one of the grief counselors gave us notepads and said, "Write out your sorrow— it'll soothe you." Nancy, who was twenty-three and had just lost her husband and two-year-old daughter in the crash, shouted at the counselor, "Are you *fucked?*" And I think Nancy was right; it is kind of fucked, dredging up all the pain over and over, remembering how I identified my mother only by her watch, and my father, by his college ring. Sometimes, at night, I lie awake worrying that the Greek myths are true, that like the dead warriors in Hades, fated to live for eternity with their bloody war wounds and torn clothes, my parents are now left somewhere with their bodies destroyed beyond recognition, forever. Sometimes I even lie to people, and tell them my mother died of cancer and my father of a heart attack, because I'm too embarrassed that my life's a newspaper article, because I can't deal with the fact that I found out my parents had died not from a phone call from the airline (I had to call them, and it took hours to officially confirm) but because I saw the crash reported on a news break, interrupting a Sting video I was watching on MTV.

Why can't I stop writing? Because life can be so absurdly sickening that I have to rearrange it, alter it, turn it into fiction.

When I reach my apartment, my mail is waiting for me. There are the usual bills, a postcard from a friend in New York, and three envelopes addressed to me, in my own handwriting: SASEs. Rejections.

I send short stories out like a banshee. At the moment, I've got stories at eleven places, like little children at foster homes, trying to get themselves adopted. Right now "The Gift" is at three magazines, "The Flight" is at four, and "Deer Bay" and "Longing" are at two places each.

The first two rejections are printed notes, the usual "Thank you for your submission but we have no use for it, blah blah blah," one with a *Sorry!* scrawled next to it, to which I want to scrawl back *Fuck off!* on the little note and return it to them. I have a file of all the rejections I've received so far, a bit fat stack of notes and slips, some of which I've gotten back after a magazine has kept a story for two years. Once I received a note stapled to a soiled, crumpled copy of my manuscript, from the *Partisan Review,* explaining that their basement had flooded and my manuscript had been submerged under a foot of water; another favorite, from *The Paris Review,* apologized for the delay in my story's return, but it had been "misplaced" for six months under an intern's bed.

The last of today's notes, which I open now, is from *The Lion.* It's handwritten:

Dear Anna,

Thanks for your story, "The Flight." While a bunch of us here loved it, the final decision of the editors went against publication. We see too many stories about death, and are looking for something fresher. But please send more work. I enjoy reading your stories, and I hope to publish something of yours soon.
     Best Regards,

Tom Westlake

I hope to publish something of yours soon. Tom Westlake. Oh, Tom, what do you look like? Are you single? I'm in love with you, and I will marry you and have your children if you will please, please publish my story.

I take out "The Flight" and reread it, striking out entire pages and writing one more, and before I know it two hours have passed and there's a knock on the door. Leslie, Lily, and Josh are standing there.

"We were worried about you, when you left so quickly and didn't come to the bar," Lily says, and Leslie adds, "We thought maybe Chester tried to rape you, but then we realized he wouldn't have the equipment for that."

I smile and say I'm okay. I can't bring myself to tell them what Chester said to me, but I show them Tom Westlake's rejection slip, and everyone agrees it's certainly encouraging, there's no doubt, and Lily gives me the latest creative-writing-program news: "The word at the Lamb was that they're going to have Bruce Ryan judge the Harden Prize—it won't be decided by the faculty at all."

We walk to the reading together. "You should submit that story from class today," Josh says.

"Or just give Bruce Ryan a little extra attention tonight," Leslie says. "Wonderbra time."

I'll tell you something: there's a fashion problem plaguing writers. Bruce Ryan is wearing a Hawaiian shirt with four buttons undone, and his chest is covered in so much gray fluff it looks like a limp squirrel is napping between his pecs. He wears the kind of tinted eyeglasses serial killers wear, and a glittery bracelet that I think I saw on Puff Daddy at the Grammys. Someday, as a public service, I'm going to start my own company, Makeovers for Writers. Perhaps I could get NEA funding. Or at least a guest-speaking spot at Bread Loaf.

Ryan is reading a new story, which unfortunately bears no resemblance to his previous work; it's about a lecherous history professor with a predilection for groping female students. I wonder if *this* is autobiographical. The fact that our future in the program lies in his hands is not a comfort. I glance around the auditorium. In the back two rows sit the fiction faculty: there's the director of the program, Frank Ogden, who, according to program legend, punched out the former director in a fistfight; his wife, Karen Warren, who looks like she's perpetually sucking a lemon; Charles Chester, who towers over everyone because he's perched on his hemorrhoid pillow; Christopher Mann and Joseph Wilson, whose stomachs protrude so far past their shoes it appears they've eaten all their remaindered books.

I know I'm harsh. You must, dear reader, be thinking: She's judgmental, our storyteller. She's an unreliable narrator.

There are too many characters.

Too many red herrings.

She should've started on page 10.

The reading finally ends, Ryan climbs down from the stage, and Stacy kisses him on the cheek. She scrambles off to prepare for the party, and a tanned, hefty man with a face like a baked ham slaps Ryan on the back, fraternity-brother style. Eventually the two men make their way to the back of the auditorium, where Leslie, Lily, and I are standing. Baked-Ham Man sticks his arm out at me. "Carlos," he says, and shakes my hand too tightly. "And I guess y'all know Bruce Ryan."

We introduce ourselves. "You probably know Carlos already too, though you don't realize it," Ryan says. "The character Costas in *Lancet and Plum*? You're talking to him."

I remember Costas from the book—daring, emotional, sympathetic. I hadn't pictured him looking like something from the meat case.

"Hey—you girls like a ride to the party with me and Ryan?" Carlos says, and before we know it, we're all piling into Carlos's red sports car.

Ryan opens the door to the front seat for me. "You," he says, poking my arm. "*You're* a good writer."

"But you haven't read any of my work," I say.

He clutches my arm firmly. "I can *tell*."

Up close, Ryan's face looks like it's made of leather. He's lizardy. Worn. Thin. He spits when he talks. As we drive to the party, he lets loose a litany of non sequiturs: he used to be macrobiotic, but now he eats only green vegetables and steak; he will work only with female editors who are under thirty-five; his ex-girlfriend tried to kill him by poisoning his gin and tonic; girls in one-piece bathing suits should be arrested for prudishness. The man needs a verbal editor, and then he needs to be knocked in the head. How's it possible that he wrote such a beautiful book?

Carlos drives at about eighty miles an hour. "So you girls are writers, huh?" he says. He seems to get a kick out of this idea, as if we're a circus act.

"We are," Leslie says, giggling. When any powerful man is present, Leslie's entire frontal lobe has a meltdown. "What do *you* do?" she whispers to Carlos.

"An editor at Harvard Press," Ryan answers for him. "I got him the damn job." Ryan flicks Carlos's hair three times from the backseat, like a Boy Scout secret signal. "He's looking for new writers, girls, you know."

I'm in the front seat, next to Carlos, and as if on cue, Carlos pinches my knee. I gape at him, and in the backseat I see Ryan, who's sandwiched between Leslie and Lily, squeeze them both simultaneously. I can't believe this is happening. It's *The Benny Hill Show*, set in academia. All three of us women sit in their car, motionless, stunned, disgusted.

As we cruise through a stop sign, Carlos squeezes my knee again, and leaves his hand there. "What the hell are you doing?" I say.

"What do you mean?" Carlos asks, offended.

"Get your hand off my knee."

He looks at Ryan in the rearview mirror and rolls his eyes. "Jee-zus," he mutters, and ignores me until we reach Stacy's house.

When we get there, I think of leaving immediately, but I'm strangely drawn to this scene. I'm perplexed by how this man whom I once idolized for writing this amazing book—a book I read three times, which I slept with under my pillow—could be . . . a creep.

Everyone's here at the party—all the students, and the faculty. The faculty seem impressed but intimidated by Ryan; they gaze at him, surrounded by his harem of aspiring-writer girls, like the wallflowers staring at the popular kids at a school dance. I find Josh and tell him about the knee-pinching. He's too shy to go beat Carlos up, which would be the proper male thing to do, so we amble around the yard, observing. An MFA party is like a chemical experiment; you never know what new material might form. It's only been going on five minutes, but already almost everyone seems drunk. Leslie strips down to her bikini and swims through the pool. Calvin and Helen wrestle by the palm trees.

Around midnight, the faculty leaves; the students get in and out of the hot tub to talk to Ryan and his sidekick Carlos. The hot tub has become Ryan's office, his own version of Fonzie's bathroom. Ryan's wearing skin-tight Speedo bathing trunks, which reveal far more than any of us want to see; his chest is puffed out, his legs spread as if this is a *Playgirl* shoot. I haven't exchanged a word with Carlos or Ryan since we were in the car. Josh takes his shirt off awkwardly; he's built like a Calvin Klein model but seems nervous about baring his body. He voices what I'm thinking: "This man is judging us. Let's go in."

"I love that one story, of your wife, when she first becomes ill . . ." Lily is saying to Ryan as the water gurgles around her skirted bathing suit.

"I don't have a wife," he smirks. "I've never been married. It's bullshit! All of it. You *kids.* It's a fucking story. Have you ever heard of *make-believe?*"

Howard, perpetually sober, is perched on the edge of the tub, fully clothed, with just his feet dipped in. His hands shift clumsily, as if he wishes he could be taking notes. "What is it that made you become a writer?" he asks Ryan in earnest.

"To get laid!"

Even Howard seems depressed by what Ryan's turned out to be; he soon leaves, looking mournful and dejected, and Lily goes with him. Not long after, there's a commotion in the house; Stacy investigates, and reports that Calvin, Leslie, and Brian have wound up in her bed; she has to get them out. Josh gets up to make himself another drink. This leaves me alone with Ryan and Carlos. I'm quiet, not wanting to say anything to them, sitting far away from them at the opposite end of the tub. I repeat to myself that my status in the program is in this man's gnarly hands.

The two men are quiet, too. Carlos stares at me for an uncomfortably long time.

"Hey, I know who she is," Carlos says, suddenly. "I know who you are. Stacy mentioned what you write about—I *knew* I recognized you. That girl from the *Globe.* The plane-crash girl. God! I can't believe I remember that. Your parents were blown up," he says matter-of-factly.

Blood rushes to my head. Ryan's gazing at me, sickly amused. I'm nauseous and dizzy; I want to throw up. I'm sure that tomorrow I'll wake up and know exactly what to say at this moment, but right now I can't think of anything. I stand up and silently leave. I walk slowly toward the house, dazed, not knowing where to go.

Josh sees me. "Are you okay?" he asks. He sets down his drink. "Do you want me to take you home?"

I nod. We're quiet for most of the drive, until Josh says, "You know, I think Ryan lied to us—I read in a magazine once that he was married, and his wife did die, just as she does in his book, but he doesn't like to talk about it. It can't be easy to have thousands of strangers knowing the most intimate details of your life and thoughts. It almost justifies him being an asshole."

"Almost." We reach my house; he turns off the ignition.

"It's all true in your story, isn't it?" he asks.

"Some things." I don't feel like talking about it now. Josh is one of the few people in the program whose stories aren't exactly tragic—he's written about losing a bike race, and his parents missing his soccer games, and having ex-girlfriends from families less wealthy than his. And now that he's driven me home on two occasions, the entire program will be convinced we're having a full-fledged affair. I'm not even sure I want to kiss him. He's almost too good-looking, too pretty—teeth so white they're distracting.

"Do you know what Leslie said about you once?" he says. "'I envy her,' she said. 'I envy her being free.'"

"What does that mean?"

"Not having parents. No one yelling at you to get a normal job, no one sending those not-so-subtle hints that you're not good enough, 'Why can't you get an MBA or go to law school or med school or at *least* go for a Ph.D.? How will you ever make money? What are you going to do with your life? When are you going to grow up?' My parents say it all the time."

I want to say: Do you know what it's like, whenever someone mentions *parents, family?* How often it comes up in casual conversation, at parties, on trains, whenever someone asks why I don't fly; even on my computer, when I begin a letter with "Dear," Microsoft Word automatically suggests "Dear Mom and Dad" to save extra typing. How every time I go out with a new guy I ask him, What do your mom and dad do?, secretly hoping he'll say at least one of his parents is dead (or both—maybe both—then I'd really fall in love).

There's a huge gulf between the words I think and the words I want to say. So I sit there, unsure of what to say or do, until he

clasps my hands and kisses me, pulling me toward him in the front
seat of his Ford pickup.

I know I've become a writer when I think, while we're kissing,
Well, whatever comes of this, I can always put it in a story.

The Harden Prize is announced, and Howard's won it again, so
all of us, except Howard, are commiserating at the Slaughtered
Lamb on a Sunday night, staring into our beers.

"Sometimes I wonder why I'm doing this," Calvin says. "Sometimes I don't know why I'm in the program."

"I hate how we all call it 'the program,'" Helen says. "It sounds
like AA or something. I was at the food co-op the other day and
this guy said, 'You're in the program, right?' People around me
looked at me like I was nuts, like he'd just asked if I was in a cult
or something, like the Scientologists or the Moonies."

Josh offers to drive me home again, but I live nearby, and I
tell him I'll walk. I feel like being alone. I keep thinking about
what he said, that night in his truck, about people envying me;
I can't stop thinking about it. An answer to it has been welling
up in my head, and I have to get it out, I have to write it down.
It's almost 2 A.M. when I get back to my house, but I can't sleep.
I take out "The Gift," cross out the ending of the latest draft,
and write:

> The summer after the crash, I spent two weeks with my
> boyfriend Colin, my first boyfriend after my parents died—he
> invited me to join his family on their vacation to the South Car-
> olina shore—and his mother looked at me so queerly when she
> met me, cocking her head to one side and squinting, almost sus-
> piciously, and asking for "facts" about my family history, as if I
> was a foundling her son had adopted, a charity case. During that
> week there was a hurricane warning, and she was disturbed that no
> one called to ensure that I was fine. She couldn't fathom that I
> had no relatives; she came from a Southern clan with four gen-
> erations still living. "Nobody's phoned you the whole time
> you've been with us!" she said one night, tactlessly, distrustfully,

warily. At nineteen, legally an adult but still a teenager, I had no grownups checking on me, no one for her to okay things with, to get approval from. At the end of the week, I overheard her talking about "my son's girlfriend" to her cousin on the phone. "Colin has such a big heart!" she said, as if it required a particularly large heart for me to be loved.

After that summer I returned to school, and life went on, and eventually I got used to explaining to new friends and boyfriends and teachers and employers that my parents were dead. And through those years I never cashed that money order; I kept it stashed in the pages of my journal, waiting for the time when I could look at it and not double over in pain. It's stashed in my journal still.

I don't know where these paragraphs have just come from—I've barely thought of this old boyfriend, or his mother, or those weeks in South Carolina, for five years—I never even knew why I'd kept that money order all these years until I saw the reason before me on the page.

I think now that my writing is as dear to me as a family would be, and crazy as that sounds, I think writing requires the same kind of attention, of commitment, of love, that people do. To be faithful to a story even when it fails me, to come back to it again and again when I worry that I may never make it work, that it may always disappointment me, that everything I've put into it could be lost—to know this, yet still keep writing—what could that be, if not love?

And I think, maybe, that none of us really knows—not Ryan or the faculty or any of the students—how to tell a story. Because when I sit down, like this, in the middle of the night, pen in hand, something outside of myself tells me to keep going, for hours, to never, never stop . . . until it's not me writing the story anymore, but the story writing *me*.

Margo Rabb's stories have been published in *The Atlantic Monthly, Zoetrope: All Story, Seventeen, Glimmer Train,* and elsewhere, and read on National Public Radio. She lives in New York City.

I wrote "How to Tell A Story" while I was deep in the throes of grieving the deaths of my parents, and simultaneously recovering from three years in an MFA program. The story brought together a lot of questions I'd been asking myself about the importance of writing and storytelling—why I was compelled to write stories, what was the point of it, etc., as well as how I could make sense of all the bizarre drama inherent in the process of twelve people workshopping and criticizing each other's often intimate work.

For the record, I did enjoy and learn from my MFA program—although the tequila shots helped, too.

APPENDIX

A list of the magazines currently consulted for *New Stories from the South: The Year's Best, 2000,* with addresses, subscription rates, and editors.

Agni
Boston University Writing Program
236 Bay State Road
Boston, MA 02215
Semiannually, $18
Askold Melnyczuk

The American Voice
Kentucky Foundation for Women,
    Inc.
332 W. Broadway, Suite 1215
Louisville, KY 40202
Triannually, $15
Frederick Smock, Editor
Sallie Bingham, Publisher
(Has suspended publication as of
    2000)

Antietam Review
41 S. Potomac St.
Hagerstown, MD 21740-5512
Annually, $5.25
Susanne Kass

The Antioch Review
P.O. Box 148
Yellow Springs, OH 45387-0148
Quarterly, $35
Robert S. Fogarty

Apalachee Quarterly
P.O. Box 10469
Tallahassee, FL 32302

Triannually, $15
Barbara Hamby

Arts & Letters
Box 44
Georgia College & State University
Milledgeville, GA 31061-0490
Semiannually, $15
Gail Galloway Adams

The Atlantic Monthly
745 Boylston Street
Boston, MA 02116
Monthly, $17.94
C. Michael Curtis

Black Warrior Review
University of Alabama
P.O. Box 862936
Tuscaloosa, AL 35486-0027
Semiannually, $14
Christopher Chambers

Boulevard
4579 Laclede Ave., Suite 332
St. Louis, MO 63108-2103
Triannually, $15
Richard Burgin

The Carolina Quarterly
Greenlaw Hall CB# 3520
University of North Carolina
Chapel Hill, NC 27599-3520

Trianually, $12
Fiction Editor

The Chariton Review
Truman State University
Kirksville, MO 63501
Semiannually, $9
Jim Barnes

The Chattahoochee Review
Georgia Perimeter College
2101 Womack Road
Dunwoody, GA 30338-4497
Quarterly, $16
Lawrence Hetrick, Editor

Cimarron Review
205 Morrill Hall
Oklahoma State University
Stillwater, OK 74078-0135
Quarterly, $12
Fiction Editor

Columbia
415 Dodge Hall
Columbia University
New York, NY 10027
Semiannually, $15
Lori Soderlind

Confrontation
English Department
C.W. Post of L.I.U.
Brookville, NY 11548
Semiannually, $20
Martin Tucker, Editor

Conjunctions
Bard College
Annandale-on-Hudson, NY 12504
Semiannually, $18
Bradford Morrow

Crazyhorse
Department of English
University of Arkansas at Little
 Rock
2801 South University
Little Rock, AR 72204
Semiannually, $10
Judy Troy, Fiction Editor

The Crescent Review
P.O. Box 15069
Chevy Chase, MD 20825-5069
Triannually, $21
J. Timothy Holland

Denver Quarterly
University of Denver
Denver, CO 80208
Quarterly, $20
Bin Ramke

The Distillery
Division of Liberal Arts
Motlow State Community
 College
P.O. Box 88100
Tullahoma, TN 37388-8100
Semiannually, $15
Niles Reddick

DoubleTake
55 Davis Square
Somerville, MA 02144
Quarterly, $32
Robert Coles

Epoch
251 Goldwin Smith Hall
Cornell University
Ithaca, NY 14853-3201
Triannually, $11
Michael Koch

Esquire
250 West 55th Street
New York, NY 10019
Monthly, $15.94
Adrienne Miller

Fiction
c/o English Department
City College of New York
New York, NY 10031
Triannually, $20
Mark J. Mirsky

Five Points
GSU
University Plaza
Department of English
Atlanta, GA 30303-3083
Triannually, $15
Pam Durban

The Florida Review
Department of English
University of Central Florida
Orlando, FL 32816
Semiannually, $7
Russ Kesler

The Georgia Review
University of Georgia
Athens, GA 30602-9009
Quarterly, $18
Stanley W. Lindberg

The Gettysburg Review
Gettysburg College
Gettysburg, PA 17325-1491
Quarterly, $24
Peter Stitt

Glimmer Train
710 SW Madison St., #504

Portland, OR 97205
Quarterly, $32
Susan Burmeister-Brown
    and Linda Davies

GQ
Condé Nast Publications, Inc.
350 Madison Avenue
New York, NY 10017
Monthly, $20
Ilena Silverman

Granta
250 W. 57th Street
Suite 1316
New York, NY 10017
Quarterly, $34
Ian Jack

The Greensboro Review
Department of English
University of North Carolina
Greensboro, NC 27412
Semiannually, $8
Jim Clark

Harper's Magazine
666 Broadway
New York, NY 10012
Monthly, $18
Lewis H. Lapham

Habersham Review
Piedmont College
P.O. Box 10
Demorest, GA 30535-0010
Semiannually, $12
Frank Gannon

High Plains Literary Review
180 Adams Street, Suite 250
Denver, CO 80206

Triannually, $20
Robert O. Greer, Jr.

Image
P.O. Box 674
Kennett Square, PA 19348
Quarterly, $30
Gregory Wolfe

Indiana Review
465 Ballantine Ave.
Indiana University
Bloomington, IN 47405
Semiannually, $12
Laura McCoid

Inkwell
Manhattanville College
Purchase, NY 10577
Semiannually, $14
Karen Sirabian

The Iowa Review
308 EPB
University of Iowa
Iowa City, IA 52242-1492
Triannually, $18
David Hamilton

The Journal
Ohio State University
Department of English
164 W. 17th Avenue
Columbus, OH 43210
Semiannually, $8
Kathy Fagan and Michelle Herman

Kalliope
Florida Community College
3939 Roosevelt Blvd.
Jacksonville, FL 32205
Triannually, $14.95
Mary Sue Koeppel

The Kenyon Review
Kenyon College
Gambier, OH 43022
Triannually, $25
David H. Lynn

The Literary Review
Fairleigh Dickinson University
285 Madison Avenue
Madison, NJ 07940
Quarterly, $18
Walter Cummins

The Long Story
18 Eaton Street
Lawrence, MA 01843
Annually, $6
R. P. Burnham

Lonzie's Fried Chicken
P.O. Box 189
Lynn, NC 28750
Semiannually, $14.95
E. H. Goree

Louisiana Literature
SLV
Southeastern Louisiana
    University
Hammond, LA 70402
Semiannually, $12
David Hanson

Lynx Eye
c/o Scribblefest Literary Group
1880 Hill Drive
Los Angeles, CA 90041
Quarterly, $25
Pam McCully, Kathryn Morrison

Meridian
P.O. Box 5103
Charlottesville, VA 22905-5103

Semiannually, $10
Elizabeth Styron

Mid-American Review
106 Hanna Hall
Department of English
Bowling Green State University
Bowling Green, OH 43403
Semiannually, $12
George Looney

Mississippi Review
University of Southern
    Mississippi
Box 5144
Hattiesburg, MS 39406-5144
Semiannually, $15
Frederick Barthelme

The Missouri Review
1507 Hillcrest Hall
University of Missouri
Columbia, MO 65211
Triannually, $19
Speer Morgan

The Nebraska Review
Writers Workshop
Fine Arts Building 212
University of Nebraska at Omaha
Omaha, NE 68182-0324
Semiannually, $11.00
James Reed

New Delta Review
English Department
Louisiana State University
Baton Rouge, LA 70802-5001
Semiannually, $8.50
Andrew Spear

New England Review
Middlebury College

Middlebury, VT 05753
Quarterly, $23
Stephen Donadio

The New Yorker
20 W. 43rd Street
New York, NY 10036
Weekly, $44.95
Bill Buford, Fiction Editor

Nimrod International Journal
The University of Tulsa
600 South College
Tulsa, OK 74104-3189
Semiannually, $17.50
Francine Ringold

The North American Review
University of Northern Iowa
Cedar Falls, IA 50614-0516
Six times a year, $22
Robley Wilson

North Carolina Literary Review
English Department
East Carolina University
Greenville, NC 27858-4353
Semiannually, $17
Margaret Bauer

Northwest Review
369 PLC
University of Oregon
Eugene, OR 97403
Triannually, $20
John Witte

The Ohio Review
344 Scott Quad
Ohio University
Athens, OH 45701-2979
Semiannually, $16
Wayne Dodd

Ontario Review
9 Honey Brook Drive
Princeton, NJ 08540
Semiannually, $14
Raymond J. Smith

Other Voices
University of Illinois at Chicago
Department of English (M/C 162)
601 S. Morgan Street
Chicago, IL 60607-7120
Semiannually, $20
Lois Hauselman

The Oxford American
P.O. Box 1156
Oxford, MS 38655
Bimonthly, $29
Marc Smirnoff

The Paris Review
541 E. 72nd Street
New York, NY 10021
Quarterly, $34
George Plimpton

Parting Gifts
March Street Press
3413 Wilshire Drive
Greensboro, NC 27408
Semiannually, $12
Robert Bixby

Pembroke Magazine
UNCP, Box 1510
Pembroke, NC 28372-1510
Annually, $5
Shelby Stephenson

Ploughshares
Emerson College
100 Beacon Street
Boston, MA 02116-1596
Triannually, $21
Don Lee

Prairie Schooner
201 Andrews Hall
University of Nebraska
Lincoln, NE 68588-0334
Quarterly, $22
Hilda Raz

ProCreation
6300-138 Creedmoor Rd., 260
Raleigh, NC 27612
Semiannually, $12
Stephen West

Puerto del Sol
Box 30001, Department 3E
New Mexico State University
Las Cruces, NM 88003-9984
Semiannually, $10
Kevin McIlvoy

Quarterly West
317 Olpin Union Hall
University of Utah
Salt Lake City, UT 84112
Semiannually, $12
Margot Schilpp

River Styx
3207 Washington
St. Louis, MO 63103-1218
Triannually, $20
Richard Newman

Roanoke Review
English Department
Roanoke College
Salem, VA 29153
Semiannually, $9.50
Robert R. Walter

Salmagundi
Skidmore College
Saratoga Springs, NY 12866
Quarterly, $18
Robert Boyers

Santa Monica Review
1900 Pico Boulevard
Santa Monica, CA 90405
Semiannually, $12
Lee Montgomery

Shenandoah
Washington and Lee University
Troubadour Theater
2nd Floor
Lexington, VA 24450-0303
Quarterly, $15
R. T. Smith

The South Carolina Review
Department of English
Clemson University
Clemson, SC 29634-1503
Semiannually, $10
Frank Day

South Dakota Review
Box 111
University Exchange
Vermillion, SD 57069
Quarterly, $18
Brian Bedard

Southern Exposure
P.O. Box 531
Durham, NC 27702
Quarterly, $24
Pat Arnow, Editor

Southern Humanities Review
9088 Haley Center
Auburn University
Auburn, AL 36849
Quarterly, $15
Dan R. Latimer

The Southern Review
43 Allen Hall
Louisiana State University
Baton Rouge, LA 70803-5005

Quarterly, $25
James Olney

Southwest Review
307 Fondren Library West
Box 750374
Southern Methodist University
Dallas, TX 75275
Quarterly, $25
Willard Spiegelman

Sou'wester
Department of English
Box 1431
Southern Illinois University at
  Edwardsville
Edwardsville, IL 62026-1438
Triannually, $10
Fred W. Robbins

Story
1507 Dana Avenue
Cincinnati, OH 45207
Quarterly, $22.00
Lois Rosenthal

StoryQuarterly
P.O. Box 1416
Northbrook, IL 60065
Quarterly, $12
Anne Brashler, M.M.M. Hayes

Tampa Review
The University of Tampa
401 W. Kennedy Boulevard
Tampa, FL 33606-1490
Semiannually, $10
Richard Mathews, Editor

Texas Review
English Department
Sam Houston State University
Huntsville, TX 77341
Semiannually, $10
Paul Ruffin

The Threepenny Review
P.O. Box 9131
Berkeley, CA 94709
Quarterly, $20
Wendy Lesser

TriQuarterly
Northwestern University
2020 Ridge Avenue
Evanston, IL 60208-4302
Triannually, $24
Susan Hahn

The Virginia Quarterly Review
One West Range
Charlottesville, VA 22903
Quarterly, $18
Staige D. Blackford

West Branch
Bucknell Hall
Bucknell University
Lewisburg, PA 17837
Semiannually, $7
Robert Love Taylor

William and Mary Review
College of William and Mary
P.O. Box 8795
Williamsburg, VA 23187
Annually, $5.50
Brian Hatelberg

Wind Magazine
P.O. Box 24548

Lexington, KY 40524
Semiannually, $10
Charlie G. Hughes

Words
School of Visual Arts
209 East 23rd St.
New York, NY 10010-3994

The Yalobusha Review
P.O. Box 186
University, MS 38677-0186
Annually, $8
Fiction Editor

Yemassee
Department of English
University of South Carolina
Columbia, SC 29208
Semiannually, $15
Melissa Johnson

Zoetrope
126 Fifth Avenue, Suite 300
New York, NY 10011
Triannually, $15
Adrienne Brodeur

ZYZZYVA
41 Sutter Street
Suite 1400
San Francisco, CA 94104-4903
Triannually, $28
Howard Junker

Previous Volumes

Copies of previous volumes of *New Stories from the South* can be ordered through your local bookstore or by calling the Sales Department at Algonquin Books of Chapel Hill. Multiple copies for classroom adoptions are available at a special discount. For information, please call 919-967-0108.

NEW STORIES FROM THE SOUTH: THE YEAR'S BEST, 1986

NEW STORIES FROM THE SOUTH: THE YEAR'S BEST, 1987

James Gordon Bennett, DEPENDENTS

Robert Boswell, EDWARD AND JILL

Rosanne Caggeshall, PETER THE ROCK

John William Corrington, HEORIC MEASURES/VITAL SIGNS

Vicki Covington, MAGNOLIA

Andre Dubus, DRESSED LIKE SUMMER LEAVES

Mary Hood, AFTER MOORE

Trudy Lewis, VINCRISTINE

Lewis Nordan, SUGAR, THE EUNUCHS, AND BIG G. B.

Peggy Payne, THE PURE IN HEART

Bob Shacochis, WHERE PELHAM FELL

Lee Smith, LIFE ON THE MOON

Marly Swick, HEART

Robert Love Taylor, LADY OF SPAIN

Luke Whisnant, ACROSS FROM THE MOTOHEADS

NEW STORIES FROM THE SOUTH: THE YEAR'S BEST, 1988

Ellen Akins, GEORGE BAILEY FISHING

Rick Bass, THE WATCH

Richard Bausch, THE MAN WHO KNEW BELLE STAR

Larry Brown, FACING THE MUSIC

Pam Durban, BELONGING

John Rolfe Gardiner, GAME FARM

Jim Hall, GAS

Charlotte Holmes, METROPOLITAN

Nanci Kincaid, LIKE THE OLD WOLF IN ALL THOSE WOLF STORIES

Barbara Kingsolver, ROSE-JOHNNY

Trudy Lewis, HALF MEASURES

Jill McCorkle, FIRST UNION BLUES

Mark Richard, HAPPINESS OF THE GARDEN VARIETY

Sunny Rogers, THE CRUMB

Annette Sanford, LIMITED ACCESS

Eve Shelnutt, VOICE

NEW STORIES FROM THE SOUTH: THE YEAR'S BEST, 1989

Rick Bass, WILD HORSES

Madison Smartt Bell, CUSTOMS OF THE COUNTRY

James Gordon Bennett, PACIFIC THEATER

Larry Brown, SAMARITANS

Mary Ward Brown, IT WASN'T ALL DANCING

Kelly Cherry, WHERE SHE WAS

David Huddle, PLAYING

Sandy Huss, COUPON FOR BLOOD

Frank Manley, THE RAIN OF TERROR

Bobbie Ann Mason, WISH

Lewis Nordan, A HANK OF HAIR, A PIECE OF BONE

Kurt Rheinheimer, HOMES

Mark Richard, STRAYS

Annette Sanford, SIX WHITE HORSES

Paula Sharp, HOT SPRINGS

New Stories from the South: The Year's Best, 1990

Tom Bailey, CROW MAN

Rick Bass, THE HISTORY OF RODNEY

Richard Bausch, LETTER TO THE LADY OF THE HOUSE

Larry Brown, SLEEP

Moira Crone, JUST OUTSIDE THE B.T.

Clyde Edgerton, CHANGING NAMES

Greg Johnson, THE BOARDER

Nanci Kincaid, SPITTIN' IMAGE OF A BAPTIST BOY

Reginald McKnight, THE KIND OF LIGHT THAT SHINES ON TEXAS

Lewis Nordan, THE CELLAR OF RUNT CONROY

Lance Olsen, FAMILY

Mark Richard, FEAST OF THE EARTH, RANSOM OF THE CLAY

Ron Robinson, WHERE WE LAND

Bob Shacochis, LES FEMMES CREOLES

Molly Best Tinsley, ZOE

Donna Trussell, FISHBONE

New Stories from the South: The Year's Best, 1991

Rick Bass, IN THE LOYAL MOUNTAINS

Thomas Phillips Brewer, BLACK CAT BONE

Larry Brown, BIG BAD LOVE

Robert Olen Butler, RELIC

Barbara Hudson, THE ARABESQUE

Elizabeth Hunnewell, A LIFE OR DEATH MATTER

Hilding Johnson, SOUTH OF KITTATINNY

NEW STORIES FROM THE SOUTH: THE YEAR'S BEST, 1992

Peter Taylor, THE WITCH OF OWL MOUNTAIN SPRINGS

Abraham Verghese, LILACS

NEW STORIES FROM THE SOUTH: THE YEAR'S BEST, 1993

Richard Bausch, EVENING

Pinckney Benedict, BOUNTY

Wendell Berry, A JONQUIL FOR MARY PENN

Robert Olen Butler, PREPARATION

Lee Merrill Byrd, MAJOR SIX POCKETS

Kevin Calder, NAME ME THIS RIVER

Tony Earley, CHARLOTTE

Paula K. Gover, WHITE BOYS AND RIVER GIRLS

David Huddle, TROUBLE AT THE HOME OFFICE

Barbara Hudson, SELLING WHISKERS

Elizabeth Hunnewell, FAMILY PLANNING

Dennis Loy Johnson, RESCUING ED

Edward P. Jones, MARIE

Wayne Karlin, PRISONERS

Dan Leone, SPINACH

Jill McCorkle, MAN WATCHER

Annette Sanford, HELENS AND ROSES

Peter Taylor, THE WAITING ROOM

NEW STORIES FROM THE SOUTH: THE YEAR'S BEST, 1994

Frederick Barthelme, RETREAT

Richard Bausch, AREN'T YOU HAPPY FOR ME?

Ethan Canin, THE PALACE THIEF

NEW STORIES FROM THE SOUTH: THE YEAR'S BEST, 1995

Caroline A. Langston, IN THE DISTANCE

Lynn Marie, TEAMS

Susan Perabo, GRAVITY

Dale Ray Phillips, EVERYTHING QUIET LIKE CHURCH

Elizabeth Spencer, THE RUNAWAYS

NEW STORIES FROM THE SOUTH: THE YEAR'S BEST, 1996

Robert Olen Butler, JEALOUS HUSBAND RETURNS IN FORM OF PARROT

Moira Crone, GAUGUIN

J. D. Dolan, MOOD MUSIC

Ellen Douglas, GRANT

William Faulkner, ROSE OF LEBANON

Kathy Flann, A HAPPY, SAFE THING

Tim Gautreaux, DIED AND GONE TO VEGAS

David Gilbert, COOL MOSS

Marcia Guthridge, THE HOST

Jill McCorkle, PARADISE

Robert Morgan, THE BALM OF GILEAD TREE

Tom Paine, GENERAL MARKMAN'S LAST STAND

Susan Perabo, SOME SAY THE WORLD

Annette Sanford, GOOSE GIRL

Lee Smith, THE HAPPY MEMORIES CLUB

NEW STORIES FROM THE SOUTH: THE YEAR'S BEST, 1997

PREFACE *by Robert Olen Butler*

Gene Able, MARRYING AUNT SADIE

Dwight Allen, THE GREEN SUIT

NEW STORIES FROM THE SOUTH: THE YEAR'S BEST, 1998

NEW STORIES FROM THE SOUTH: THE YEAR'S BEST, 1999

Tom Franklin, POACHERS

William Gay, THOSE DEEP ELM BROWN'S FERRY BLUES

Mary Gordon, STORYTELLING

Ingrid Hill, PAGAN BABIES

Michael Knight, BIRDLAND

Kurt Rheinheimer, NEIGHBORHOOD

Richard Schmitt, LEAVING VENICE, FLORIDA

Heather Sellers, FLA. BOYS

George Singleton, CAULK

THE BEST

Shannon Ravenel read over 10,000 stories in her first 10 years as editor of the annual anthology, **New Stories from the South.** She chose only 163 stories for inclusion in the series, which each year offers the year's best contemporary Southern short fiction.

THE BEST OF THE BEST

Bestselling fiction writer and short story fan Anne Tyler went one step further. From Ravenel's 163 selections she chose her 20 favorites for the celebratory anniversary anthology, **Best of the South.**

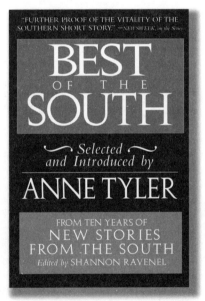

"FURTHER PROOF OF THE VITALITY OF THE SOUTHERN SHORT STORY." —*NEWSWEEK, on the Series*

BEST
OF THE
SOUTH

~ Selected ~
and Introduced by

ANNE TYLER

FROM TEN YEARS OF
NEW STORIES
FROM THE SOUTH
Edited by SHANNON RAVENEL

A delectable treasury of contemporary Southern literature.

Available in bookstores everywhere.
$15.95 paper
ISBN 1-56512-128-7

RICK BASS

RICHARD BAUSCH

MADISON SMARTT BELL

JAMES LEE BURKE

LEON V. DRISKELL

TONY EARLEY

BARRY HANNAH

MARY HOOD

EDWARD P. JONES

NANCI KINCAID

PATRICIA LEAR

FRANK MANLEY

REGINALD MCKNIGHT

LEWIS NORDAN

PADGETT POWELL

MARK RICHARD

BOB SHACOCHIS

LEE SMITH

MELANIE SUMNER

MARLY SWICK